While We're Apart

While We're Apart is Ellie Dean's eighth novel. She lives in a tiny hamlet set deep in the heart of the South Downs in Sussex, which has been her home for many years and where she raised her three children. To find out more visit www.ellie-dean.co.uk

Also by Ellie Dean

There'll be Blue Skies
Far From Home
Keep Smiling Through
Where the Heart Lies
Always in My Heart
All My Tomorrows
Some Lucky Day

Ellie Dean
While We're Apart

arrow books

Published by Arrow Books 2015

2 4 6 8 10 9 7 5 3

First published in Great Britain in 2015 by
Arrow Books
Random House, 20 Vauxhall Bridge Road,
London SW1V 2SA

www.randomhouse.co.uk

Addresses for companies within The Random House Group Limited
can be found at: www.randomhouse.co.uk/offices.htm

The Random House Group Limited Reg. No. 954009

A CIP catalogue record for this book
is available from the British Library

ISBN 9780099585329 (Paperback)
ISBN 9781448165278 (eBook)

Typeset in Palatino by Palimpsest Book Production Ltd, Falkirk, Stirlingshire
Printed and bound in Great Britain by CPI Group (UK) Ltd, Croydon, CR0 4YY

MIX
Paper from
responsible sources
FSC
www.fsc.org   FSC® C018179

Penguin Random House is committed to a
sustainable future for our business, our readers
and our planet. This book is made from
Forest Stewardship Council® certified paper.

While We're Apart

Chapter One

East Sussex, October 1942

It was Mary Jones's eighteenth birthday but, as usual, it was a day like any other. She had received a hastily scrawled card and an absent-minded hug from her father, but there had been no acknowledgement of the occasion by her mother.

Mary flicked her long dark hair back from her face, determinedly suppressed her disappointment and walked quickly down the narrow country lane, the weight of her laden shopping basket dragging on her arm. It wasn't the lack of gifts that upset her, for at the rectory they were exchanged only at Christmas – it was her mother's cool disinterest towards her. She should be inured to it by now, and yet, no matter how hard she tried, she couldn't quite manage not to be hurt by it, and that neediness for Emmaline's love and approval made her fretful.

She plodded along the rough lane in her wellingtons as fast as she could for it was a bitterly cold morning, the wind scything across the empty patchwork of fields and the South Downs. She could feel the cut of it on her face and in her unshed tears, and she paused for a moment to dry her eyes, tuck her hair into her coat collar and wrap the knitted scarf more firmly round her neck and over her mouth. She'd been queuing for almost half an hour outside the village grocery shop, and now her hands and feet were numb with the cold despite her gloves, thick coat and woollen socks.

As she picked up the basket again and headed for home, she gazed out beyond the hedgerows to the iron-hard ploughed fields and the distant South Downs which undulated beneath a leaden sky. She had lived here all her life, and although she had no real wish to leave these familiar surroundings, there had been moments recently when she'd begun to yearn for something more – something different, perhaps even exciting, that would take her to new horizons. And now she was eighteen there was a distinct possibility that this might happen, for she was no longer a student, and if she didn't decide quickly on what she wanted to do for the war effort, she would be assigned a job by the recruitment people.

Her thoughts were in a whirl as she tramped along, for there were several possibilities, even for someone as unsophisticated and inexperienced as she was. She could become a land girl and stay in the village to work with Jack Boniface on his father's farm, which would mean they could see more of each other. However, even the allure of being with her darling Jack every day didn't make the job any more appealing, for she knew how tough it was to be up before dawn and out in all weathers until after dark. The Land Army needed a special breed of worker, and very few of the city girls, who'd had no idea of what they'd let themselves in for, had lasted more than a few weeks – and neither would she.

As for office work – she didn't know one end of a typewriter from the other, and shorthand was a complete mystery. The idea of working in a factory didn't really appeal either, although according to her best friend, Pat Logan, who caught the factory bus every morning with a group of other village girls, it was great fun and paid very well. It was also, she'd told Mary, a good way to make friends and see a bit of life at the parties and dances that were frequently held in the town for the allied servicemen. But Pat had few responsibilities at home, was confident enough to meet new people and experience new things, and her mother didn't seem to mind her going to dances and staying out late.

Mary paused again, gave a deep sigh and shifted the basket to her other hand. The only real talent she had was for singing and playing the piano – which wasn't exactly of much use to the war effort – and her parents disapproved of her doing either unless it was in the schoolroom or the church. With a frown of anxiety, she continued walking and tried to dispel this sense of uselessness by concentrating on her surroundings.

The village of Harebridge Green sprawled between the farms and woodlands of East Sussex. The narrow lane running through it like a frayed grey ribbon led to the nearby market town of Hillney in the east, and the hamlet of Gorse Green to the west. Yet its isolation hadn't protected it, for it lay beneath the flight path of the enemy bombers on their way to London and the Midlands, and there were numerous reminders of that in the craters in the fields, the bullet holes scarring the walls of the Saxon church, and the shattered remains of a farmhouse and barn that had taken a direct hit.

Mary again heaved the basket from one hand to the other, wishing fervently that she'd mended the puncture on her bike so this journey would have been easier, but what with one thing and another, there just hadn't been time. She trudged along past the village green, the shuttered and locked pub, the cottages, the abandoned village school and empty playground. The village didn't feel the same without the sound of children playing, but after the first two serious tip-and-runs, it had been decided to evacuate them to somewhere safer.

Mary's low spirits ebbed further, for she'd always wanted to be a teacher and she'd enjoyed helping the local schoolmistress with the little ones, and getting them to sing along while she played the rather tinny upright piano. Now it was rarely used and badly out of tune, and she suspected it would remain as silent as the church bells until this war was over.

She had just begun her teacher training in September, when the college in Hillney took a direct hit one night during an enemy raid. With the children gone, and her teaching course brought to an abrupt end, she was feeling adrift, and although she had thought of applying for another assistant teaching post elsewhere, she suspected her youth and lack of qualifications would count against her.

Of course she could continue her interrupted studies and get her teaching certificate, but it would mean a very long bus or train journey each day to the nearest big town, which she simply couldn't afford. The thought of trying again to persuade her elderly father to help pay for accommodation in college digs was just too discouraging. He was now almost seventy and very stuck in his ways, and although her mother, for once, had supported her plea, he'd refused even to contemplate the idea when she'd approached him before, deeming it dangerous and not at all respectable for a young woman to live so far from home. Mary knew all too well that once he'd made up his mind about something, nothing could change it.

She paused again to put down the heavy basket. It was all very well trying to plan ahead, or dream of new horizons, but the reality of her situation meant that she'd probably be stuck here for the foreseeable future. Her father had three parishes under his care since the old vicar of Gorse Green had died, and he relied on her to help him with his pastoral duties now that Emmaline's health had deteriorated. And then there was the rambling great rectory to manage – a task beyond both her ageing parents, and one that even she found daunting.

'Penny for them.'

Mary's heart missed a beat and she turned with a smile to face the tall brown-haired, dark-eyed young man who strode towards her in his shabby working clothes and mud-encrusted boots. 'Jack! Where did you spring from? I didn't hear you.'

His eyes twinkled as he pulled off his worn cap and stuffed it into the pocket of his rather grubby corduroy trousers. 'You were miles away,' he replied in his soft Sussex burr. He took a step closer and looked with affection into her uplifted face before he reached for the basket. 'Let me take that,' he said quietly. 'It looks heavy.'

Mary quickly glanced over her shoulder to make sure they weren't in sight of the rectory or the local gossip. 'Just for a bit then,' she replied. 'If Mother sees us there'll be trouble, and she's in a bad enough mood with me already this morning.'

His expression darkened as it always did when Mary mentioned her mother, but he made no comment, for they both knew nothing would change Emmaline Jones's puzzling, almost dismissive attitude towards her daughter. He gently took her arm. 'Come on. Let's get out of this wind and spend a few minutes together.'

She hesitated before letting him lead her across

the ice-encrusted mud puddles to the five-bar gate that opened into a field and the shelter of the thick hedgerow. Her mother disapproved of Jack and would be furious if she heard they'd been seen alone together, but Mary had loved him ever since they'd shared a desk at the village infant school, and she was willing to risk Emmaline's wrath for the pleasure of being alone with him for a few precious minutes.

They found a dry hummock of grass within the shelter of the hedge and sat down, the basket at their feet. He took her gloved hand in his and looked deeply into her cornflower-blue eyes before he softly kissed her cold lips. 'Happy birthday, Mary.'

Mary savoured his sweet kiss, for it warmed her on this bitter day. 'It is happy now I can be with you for a while,' she murmured shyly as they drew apart. 'But I daren't stay too long. I'm already later than I said I'd be.'

He wrapped his strong arm round her shoulders and held her close as he kissed the top of her head. 'A few minutes more won't do any harm, and I have something for you,' he said as he fished in his jacket pocket and handed over a small brown paper package.

Her eyes widened. 'A present? For me?'

His boyish grin made him look younger than nineteen. 'Well, you're the only one who's got a birthday today, aren't you? Go on, open it.'

She was all fingers and thumbs as she undid the knotted string and drew back the paper to reveal a small box. With eager anticipation she opened it and gasped with delight, for nestled within the velvet lining was a gold locket and chain.

'Oh, Jack, it's beautiful.' She held it up and let the long chain dangle from her fingers. 'But it must have cost an awful lot, and you really shouldn't have.'

'Why not?' he said as he took it from her and, after finding a way through the scarf, long hair and coat collar, fastened it round her neck so it hung almost to her waist. 'You're my special girl, and only the very best will do on her birthday.'

Tears welled as she caressed the gold heart. It was the first birthday present she'd ever received, and because it had come from him, it was extra special. She leaned across and brushed her lips against his. 'Thank you, Jack. I'll treasure it always.'

He reddened with pleasure. 'I'm glad you like it,' he said. 'It took me ages to decide what to buy you, but the lady in the shop said it was a good choice.'

Mary took off her glove and held the locket, feeling it warming in her palm. 'Oh, there's a little clasp.' She fumbled to open it. 'And you've put your picture inside.'

'I cut it out of the rugby club photo we had taken at the end of last season,' he replied. 'It's a bit blurred, cos Billy Watkins poked me in the ribs and made me move.'

She regarded the tiny black and white photograph

and then snapped the locket shut, loving the feel of it nestling in her hand. 'It's perfect,' she said on a sigh.

'I thought you might like something to remember me by.' He shifted awkwardly beside her, his gaze fixed on something in the distance.

She looked at him a little sharply. 'That's an odd thing to say,' she said. 'I'm hardly likely to forget you when we see each other most days.'

'Things change, Mary,' he said quietly as he shifted on the grass again. He fumbled into his pocket and brought out a rather squashed packet of cigarettes. As Mary didn't smoke, he lit one for himself and then continued to gaze out over his father's frozen fields, his thoughts unreadable.

Mary experienced a sharp pang of alarm as he remained silent, but knew better than to badger him into telling her what he meant by that remark for, like his father, Jack measured his words carefully before he spoke. She waited, her tension increasing as he smoked his cigarette.

'Mary, there's something I've got to tell you,' he said hesitantly, his gaze now fixed on his muddy boots.

Mary's heart thudded against her ribs. 'You sound very serious all of a sudden,' she replied, making light of the awful fear that gripped her.

'Well, it is something I've thought about for a while now,' he said through the smoke he had exhaled. He dipped his chin and studied the cigarette between his fingers. 'And I'm so sorry I've got to spoil your special day, but I've left this too long already, and now I have no choice.'

Her pulse was racing as she watched him struggle to voice his thoughts. Was he about to tell her he didn't love her any more? Was the locket his parting gift? She desperately tried to stem the rising panic, but her voice betrayed her as she brokenly asked, 'What is it, Jack? What are you trying to tell me?'

He crushed the cigarette beneath his boot and grasped her hands. 'I've joined up, and I have to catch the troop train tonight at half past eight,' he said all in a rush.

She stared at him in horrified disbelief. 'No,' she said sharply. 'You can't do that, Jack.'

He squeezed her hands. 'But I have to, you see, Mary. I'm young and fit and strong, and I need to do my bit with the other lads. I can't be sitting about here while they're fighting on the front line. I'd never be able to face them again.'

She tore her hands away. 'Of course you would,' she stormed. 'You're in a reserved occupation, fighting a battle here to feed us all now the convoys are finding it so hard to get through. And you're part of the Home Guard, as well as doing your bit with fire-watching and warden duties.'

His lip curled. 'Dad's Army's fit only for old men and boys. As for the farm, there are land girls to do my work and Dad will keep them on their toes, never you fear. The rest of it is easily covered.' He reached for her hands again. 'England needs every able-bodied man she can get, Mary. And I need to stand up and be counted.'

'But I need you here,' she said through her tears. 'Please, Jack, don't . . .'

He silenced her with a soft kiss. 'I must,' he murmured. 'Don't you see?'

She shook her head, her hair tumbling about her shoulders as hot tears ran down her cold face. 'No,' she stuttered. 'I don't see at all. You have responsibilities here, and they are just as important as being on the front line.'

'Oh, Mary,' he sighed as he pulled her to him and held her close. 'I'm so sorry I've upset you – and especially today. But I've been dreading this moment, which is why I've put it off until the very last minute.' He tipped back her chin and kissed away her tears, his eyes begging her to forgive him. 'I love you, Mary,' he whispered, 'and I will think of you every moment while we're apart. But this is something I have to do. Please give me your blessing.'

Mary saw the determination in his expression and realised then that he couldn't be persuaded to stay, no matter how much he loved her. She held him tightly, fearing the awful loneliness his absence would bring – and the dreadful possibility that he might not come home. Yet most of all she feared that the sights and sounds of battle – the company of hardened, more worldly men and the excitement of war – would change him, and that despite all his promises, he would stop loving her.

Jack seemed to sense some of her thoughts, for he held her even closer and stroked her long hair, winding it round his fingers and letting it slip over the palm of his hand. 'I know we're both still young,' he said softly, 'and that this war will change us. But I love you, Mary, and nothing will alter that. When I come back we'll get married, I promise.'

She nodded against his broad chest, unable to speak. This was the first time he'd mentioned marriage; it had simply been tacitly understood between them that they would make a life together one day. But now he was leaving, and the longer the war went on the wider the distance between them would grow. She curled her arms round him, her tears dampening the rough fabric of his old tweed jacket and the thick sweater he wore beneath it.

He hugged her close, rocking her in his arms, his voice gentle as he rested his cheek on her head. 'It won't be for ever, my love. And once it's all over I'll come home to you and we can be together as we've always hoped.'

Mary fought desperately to get her emotions under control as she nestled into his embrace. She loved the earthy scent of him, the strength of his arms about her, and the sound of the steady drum of his heart against her cheek. But in a matter of hours he would be gone, and treasured, secret moments like this would be at an end. He was the ray of light in her dowdy, drear world and she didn't know how she could bear him leaving. But bear it she must, and for his sake she had to be strong and keep her fears to herself.

'Yes,' she finally managed. 'We'll be together again. Of course we will.'

He eased away, his big work-roughened hands gently holding her arms as he looked into her face. 'I promise to write whenever I can, and you must tell me what's happening here and what you're doing, so I can picture you going about the village.'

Mary gazed back at him and because she had no doubt that he loved her and was finding it just as hard to face this awful parting, she discovered the strength to give him a tremulous smile. 'I'll write every day,' she replied. 'Though I don't know what I'll have to say,' she added with a lightness that belied the heaviness in her heart. 'I lead a very quiet life at the rectory now I'm not going to college.'

He regarded her for a moment, and then softly ran a finger down her cheek and over her lips. 'You're eighteen, Mary, and you have a lot more to offer than you think. You need to get away from here and experience a bit of life.'

'I'd like to, but I can't, Jack,' she replied. 'My parents couldn't manage without me.' She gave a wry smile. 'Although, having said that, Mother would probably be glad to see the back of me, but that huge house is too much for her to cope with on her own.'

'You might have no choice in the matter,' he warned. 'As a young single girl, you'll be expected to do some sort of war work.'

'I'll deal with that when I have to,' she said softly, 'but at this very moment all I can think about is you.' She held his hands and gazed into his face, committing to memory his thick brown hair that needed cutting, the arch of his brows over the dark eyes, the long, straight nose and generously drawn mouth. 'Where are they sending you?'

'Somewhere in the west to a training camp. The army don't tell us anything much,' he said with a slight shrug. 'But there was mention of home leave before we're assigned to our postings, so I could be back here in a matter of weeks.'

A thrill of hope shot through her. 'Then that's what we must look forward to,' she replied determinedly.

They kissed again, holding each other tightly against the bitter wind that had suddenly changed direction and found their hiding place. 'You're shivering,' he said as he drew her to her feet. 'Come on, let's get you home before you catch your death of cold.'

Mary didn't want these precious moments to end, but the church clock struck the hour and she knew they must. 'Can I come to the station to see you off?' she asked as he carried the heavy basket through the gate and carefully closed it behind him.

'I'd like that,' he admitted as they moved out of the cutting wind. 'But I think it's best if we say our goodbyes here in private,' he added softly.

They kissed and clung to one another in a silent desperation of words unsaid, and of overwhelming emotions. With a tender, lingering kiss he reluctantly stepped away, took her hand and walked beside her down the narrow lane towards the rectory. As they reached the final bend he crushed her to him, kissed her passionately and then turned to hurry away towards his family's farmhouse at the other end of the village.

Mary was blinded by tears as she watched him go, his shoulders hunched, hands in his pockets, head down – clearly fighting his own emotions and not daring to look back.

She stood there in the pitted lane until he was out of sight, then, like a small, wounded creature, crept back into the lee of the hedge where she huddled in a tight ball of heart-rending misery.

Mary had no idea how long she'd been crying, but eventually the well of tears had run dry and she realised she was aching, not only with loss and loneliness, but with the bitter cold that had now seeped into her bones. She drew her gloves back on and stamped her feet to try to get some feeling into them, but she was numb inside, her heart heavy.

She caressed the gold locket and kissed it before tucking it beneath her clothes so it lay warm against her skin, hidden from her mother's prying eyes. Adjusting her scarf and coat collar, she took a last, longing look up the lane, then picked up the basket and trudged home. She knew her mother's sharp eyes wouldn't miss her swollen, reddened eyelids and tear-streaked face, but Mary decided she could blame it on the wind.

She rounded the last bend just as the church clock struck two. She was very late and there would be trouble, but she realised that it didn't matter. Nothing mattered now that Jack was leaving.

Her footsteps slowed as she approached the large grey flint church which stood back rather grandly from the lane, sheltered by trees behind a low wall that was smothered in ivy. Despite the centuries of wars, civil unrest and the Reformation, it still retained some of its Saxon heritage in the vaulted roof beams and sturdy pillars that lined the broad flagstone aisle. The lovely old stained-glass windows had been carefully removed and stored in the crypt to protect them from bomb blasts, and the bells in the square Norman tower had been silenced for the duration.

Mary stood by the lychgate and noted that the deep shadows beneath the arched wooden porch didn't quite hide the leaves that had blown in from the surrounding trees and were now piled against the heavily bossed, solid oak door that creaked alarmingly when opened. The sprawling graveyard looked sadly neglected since the old gardener had passed away in the summer, for the grass had grown long, the weeds rampant amongst the leaning headstones, lichen-stained stone angels and Victorian table tombs. Dark yew trees swayed in the wind beneath the lowering sky, and the mournful caw of crows merely emphasised the bleakness of it all.

Her gaze fell on the three new gravestones that had been set close together in acknowledgement of their brotherhood in arms. Mary had known the boys from childhood, and had watched them proudly parade through the village on their way to the station, their boots gleaming, their khaki uniforms pressed, buttons polished. Yet they, like so many others, had made the ultimate sacrifice, and the whole village had come to honour their own, and to lay them to their final rest in the chalky soil of home. For them the war was over. But for Jack, it was just beginning.

Mary quickly turned away and hurried down the long driveway to the ugly great house that was the rectory. Churchill had talked about sacrifice, and the need to pull together and be courageous even in the darkest hours, and now she understood just how hard that would prove. Yet her own sacrifice was so much less than others had been forced to make, and she was determined to square up to whatever lay ahead and do her best to keep the home fires burning until this war was won and Jack and all the other boys came home.

Her boots crunched over the weed-strewn gravel drive and she eyed the house with little affection, for although she'd lived in it for as long as she could remember, it had never really felt homely. Standing squarely in an acre of land, the three-storey Victorian red-brick building looked over the churchyard and across to the South Downs. It had been built at a time when churchmen had huge families, and perhaps her parents had once planned on having more children, but as she was the only one, born late in their lives, they rattled about the place like peas on a drum.

The attic rooms had been closed up after the roof was damaged following a particularly fearsome air raid, for no one could be found to mend it. Dust sheets had been put over the good furniture in the two large reception rooms now it was too cold to stay in either of them for more than a few minutes, and the bedrooms were so bleak that they woke each winter morning to discover a thin crust of ice on the inside of the loose-fitting sash windows. With coal being rationed so severely the cast-iron radiators had been turned off, and although her father had a single-bar electric fire in his study, the only heating in the rest of the house came from the vast range in the kitchen – but even that was measly.

Mary bypassed the front door and headed round to the back of the house where her bicycle leant against the kitchen wall, the punctured tyre as flat and forlorn as her failed vegetable patch. Both needed attention, but the days were getting ever shorter, and there never seemed to be enough time to get through all the things she had to do.

As she stepped inside the kitchen she felt the frail warmth after the chill of outdoors, and gratefully dumped the basket of shopping on the scrubbed table. She stood in front of the range, her gloved hands slowly thawing as she held them out to the meagre flames in the grate.

The windows rattled from the buffeting wind as the sky darkened and the first needles of sleet hit the glass. At least the bad weather would mean no enemy raids, she thought as she warmed enough to remove her scarf and gloves and undo her overcoat. Glad to have these few moments of solitude to gather her wits and come to terms with Jack's imminent departure, she checked that the locket remained hidden beneath her knitted sweater, the chain masked by her hair, and then began to unpack the shopping.

There was a tin of spam, and another of bully beef, and two loaves of what the government were calling the National wheatmeal bread, which none of them enjoyed eating, but served to stave off hunger pangs; a parcel of liver and kidneys; potatoes, onions, parsnips and carrots; a tiny portion of cheese, another of margarine, a packet of dried egg, another of tea, and a bottle of Camp coffee. There had been no sugar or tins of syrup, neither had there been any flour or suet, but at least she'd got the majority of things on her list.

She placed the ration books on the old dresser along with her purse, then stowed the shopping away in the various rickety cupboards, her wellington boots clumping over the uneven flagstone floor. The kitchen was her favourite room, even though it was shabby and the floor chilled your feet if you dared to take off your shoes. The window above the stone sink had been nailed shut since the cord in the sashes had rotted away, the ceiling was high, the once-white paint now a tobacco yellow from years of cooking and the smoke from the range. The dark green tiles behind the sink and wooden draining board were chipped, the grouting crumbling and grey with age, but the pots and pans that hung above the freshly blackened range gleamed with her meticulous polishing.

Mary filled the tin kettle and placed it on the hob. She was reaching for the teapot when the sound of a brusque voice stilled her.

'Where have you been?'

Mary placed the teapot carefully on the draining board before she turned to face her mother, who was leaning heavily on her walking stick in the doorway.

Emmaline appeared to be the quintessential sweet little old lady, for she was short and plump, with a round, usually cheerful face, apple cheeks, blue eyes and curly white hair. Dressed in a pink cardigan, grey wool skirt and white blouse, and with a lavender-blue woollen shawl about her shoulders, she looked like everyone's favourite granny.

Mary knew her mother was well aware that this outward show of sweetness and care made her popular amongst the villagers, and admired by the charities she ran, and she used it to get her own way with everyone, especially with her husband Gideon. Yet there was a different side to her that showed only when they were alone, for her eyes would become cold, the soft voice scathing, and the smile would be replaced by a sneer.

'There was a long queue at the grocer's,' Mary replied.

'Liar.' Emmaline's voice was soft but with a flat note of accusation underlying it. Her expression was frosty, her lips thinly drawn as she held Mary's gaze.

'I'm not a liar,' Mary replied with studied calm.

'Yes you are,' Emmaline said almost dismissively, as she hobbled into the kitchen with the aid of her walking stick. 'Mrs Hobbs said you left the grocer's almost an hour ago. Where have you been?' As Mary hesitated, her mother's eyes narrowed. 'Or should I ask who you've been with?'

Mrs Hobbs was the local gossip and could always be relied upon to pick up her telephone and spread her vicious tales to Emmaline. Mary took a deep breath. 'I've been with Jack Boniface,' she said quietly as she took off her coat and hung it on the hook behind the door.

'You're nothing but a trollop,' hissed Emmaline. 'A cheap little tart.' Her arthritic fingers clutched the walking stick as her flinty gaze bored into Mary.

Mary tipped up her chin. 'I'm not a liar or a tart,' she retorted, 'and I don't think Dad would like to hear you calling me such names.'

Emmaline's lip curled. 'If he's too soft to see what you really are, then that's his lookout,' she muttered as she sat at the table. 'But you were born with the stain of sin on you – and it's still there in every wanton inch of you.' Her disdainful gaze swept over Mary's curvaceous figure. 'You're a liar, and no better than you should be, considering . . .'

'That's quite enough of that sort of talk, Emmaline,' interrupted Gideon Jones from the doorway. He came into the kitchen as if weary of life and sank into a chair, his long face drawn and pale from the cares that burdened him. At sixty-nine his dark hair was liberally sprinkled with grey and receding fast from his thin but strong-boned face. Dressed in his shabby black suit and shirt, with the starched white collar that denoted his calling, he looked old and haggard, and Mary's heart went out to him.

'Oh my dear Gideon,' Emmaline sighed, her expression suddenly contrite. 'I'm in such pain with my arthritis that I hardly know what I'm saying.' She placed her crippled hand over his, her eyes brimming with tears. 'But Mary was late home and she upset me by lying about where she'd been.'

His puzzled dark gaze rested on his wife for a moment, and then his expression softened as he turned to Mary. 'We are all born with sin, my dear,' he said in the melodious deep Welsh accent that held his parishioners in thrall every Sunday. 'But it is washed away in the love and forgiveness of Our Lord.' He eyed her with gentle reproach. 'Have you lied today, Mary? Is that why your poor mother is in such distress?'

Mary had always been amazed at how easily Emmaline could bring on the tears, but as she looked into her father's loving, trusting eyes, she had to confess. 'I was late home and didn't explain fully where I'd been, so yes, I lied to Mother by omission.'

As Gideon was about to speak, Emmaline placed her hand on his arm. 'She was with Jack Boniface again,' she said quietly, 'and I'm deeply worried about how she flaunts herself with that boy.' She gave Gideon a tremulous smile, and dabbed a handkerchief over her moist eyes.

Mary bunched her fists in an attempt to control the indignation and hurt caused by her mother's manipulation of the situation. 'Jack's enlisted,' she explained hurriedly to her father. 'He's leaving tonight and we just wanted some time together to say goodbye.' She took his hand, her eyes pleading with him to understand. 'We've done nothing wrong,' she added softly.

Gideon ignored Emmaline's tut of disbelief. 'I can understand you wanting to say goodbye, after all you've known each other since you were small children. But it's unseemly to be alone with Jack, or indeed any other man. A woman's virtue is beyond price, Mary, and you are of an age when temptation is at its strongest.'

Mary blushed as she remembered the stolen kisses and the way Jack had embraced her.

'You see that, Gideon?' crowed Emmaline. 'She's nothing but a hussy.'

'Be still, Emmaline,' said Gideon calmly. 'Let our daughter speak.'

Mary met her father's gaze squarely. 'Jack and I love each other,' she said, 'but we've done nothing shameful. I wish you and Mother would learn to trust me.'

Emmaline's lips curled in a sneer as she eyed her daughter, then smoothed into a soft, rueful smile for Gideon. 'How can we trust her when she meets that boy in secret and then lies about it? I'm worried, Gideon, not only for her reputation, but for the shame it might bring to you.'

Gideon hated scenes, and he fidgeted in the chair as his worried gaze drifted between his wife and his daughter. 'I think, Emmaline, that you should apologise to Mary for your harsh words,' he said eventually. 'I know you're concerned, but I don't wish to ever hear you speak to her like that again.'

Emmaline stiffened, and although her voice was taut with suppressed anger, her eyes brimmed. 'It's not me at fault here,' she said, blinking at the tears. 'The girl is wayward and needs to be disciplined before she shames us all with her wanton ways.'

'It is you who brings me shame,' he said sadly,

his eyes sorrowful. 'Couldn't you find it in your heart to love our daughter – to trust her and be as kind to her as you are to others?'

Emmaline's true character showed in her pursed lips and narrowed eyes as she glared at her husband with righteous indignation – but something in his expression silenced any reply she might have been tempted to make, and she looked away.

Mary hadn't missed that intense look in her father's eyes, or the way her mother had reacted to it, and she wondered what it meant. Her father's plea echoed her own feelings, and she wished she could have heard her mother's answer.

As the awkward silence lengthened, Mary regarded her mother and felt a profound sense of regret for the lack of warmth between them. Emmaline had never raised a hand to her, and she'd conducted her motherly duties with brisk, cool efficiency as Mary was growing up. Yet her spiteful tongue had wounded deeply, always finding fault, never missing a chance to denigrate and accuse her of being sinful when her father was out of earshot.

Despite her motherly figure and sweet facade, there had been no cuddles and bedtime stories, no kisses or interest in her progress at school, and Mary had had to rely on her gentle father to provide the affection she so sorely needed. Now she was on the cusp of womanhood, she could look back over the years and see that Emmaline had merely been performing a necessary and rather onerous duty, and was incapable of giving more.

As the sleet rattled against the window and Emmaline's dispassionate gaze came to rest on her, Mary had to accept that nothing would ever change between them. Heartsick, she turned away and took the boiling kettle off the hob. 'Let me make a cup of tea,' she said in an effort to dispel the awkward atmosphere. 'This cold wet weather is obviously making Mother's arthritis very painful, and I'm sure you must be thirsty by now, Dad.'

Gideon visibly relaxed as Mary set the teapot on the table and hunted out the cups and saucers. 'Thank you, Mary,' he replied quietly. 'I'm sure your mother appreciates your thoughtfulness.'

Mary doubted that very much, but she had other things on her mind. 'I'd like to go to the station tonight to see Jack off,' she said as she poured the tea.

'But you have said goodbye already,' he said with a puzzled frown.

'I know.' She sat down and reached for her father's pale hand. 'But he's going to war, Daddy, and I might never see him again.'

He regarded her thoughtfully. 'You say you love one another,' he said finally, 'and I have seen how one can get emotionally carried away in such circumstances. I think it's best if you don't go tonight. It wouldn't be seemly.'

'But—'

'You heard your father,' purred Emmaline. 'He has said you're not to go, and that is that.'

Mary saw the spiteful gleam in her eyes but didn't rise to it. Her father was exhausted and he hated it when there were ructions.

She began to make the spam sandwiches for lunch, her thoughts on Jack as the wind howled around the house, the rain hammered on the windowpane and the kitchen clock ticked away the minutes to his departure. Despite the trouble it would cause, she was determined to get to the station tonight.

Chapter Two

Cliffehaven

The kitchen at Beach View Boarding House was a haven of warmth and comfort as the rain pelted against the windows and the wind howled in from the sea. The blackout curtains had been drawn despite the early hour, a rabbit stew was slowly cooking in the range oven, and there was a soft glow from the fire and the single low-watt ceiling light.

Peggy Reilly finished ironing the last pillowcase and added it to the pile of crisp laundry on the table. She placed the iron to one side of the range hotplates, folded up the towel she'd been using on the table as an ironing board, and ran her fingers through her freshly washed, and still damp, curly dark hair. Her smile was tender as she watched her father-in-law, Ron, amusing baby Daisy with her toys. He was a scruffy old Irish rogue who went his own sweet way, and he and his lurcher, Harvey, were the cause of most of her troubles, but she loved him, and knew that this house of women relied upon him.

Despite the homeliness of this little scene Peggy was rather distracted, for her thoughts were scattered, and she was filled with a restless, nervous energy. Her husband Jim was coming home on leave tomorrow, and although her best dress had been carefully pressed, her shoes polished and Daisy's outfit was folded and ready, she was certain there had to be something she'd forgotten to do in preparing for it.

The house had been in chaos following Kitty Pargeter's wedding to Roger Makepeace, and she'd spent the last six days dashing about trying to clean and tidy and make everything perfect. Not that it was easy in a house this size, for it was getting shabbier by the day and needed a thorough renovation – which was neither affordable nor practical in these times of strict rationing and seemingly endless raids by the Luftwaffe. All the frenetic activity had kept her too busy to think how she might feel if Jim's leave was cancelled at the last moment again, but now she'd begun to dare to hope that he really would be coming home.

Peggy gathered up the pile of freshly ironed laundry and carried it upstairs to the linen cupboard before checking that Ron had cleaned the bath properly, and not left damp towels all over the floor, or whisker shavings in the basin. Satisfied that everything was tidy and clean, she inspected each of the bedrooms, and then paused a moment to look out of the top-floor front window which had the only view of the sea. It was as grey as the sky, the murky waves whipped into white, crashing foam as the rain came down like stair rods in the wind that howled across the Channel.

Beach View had been Peggy's home all her life, for it had belonged to her parents, and she and Jim had taken over the business once they'd retired to a bungalow further along the coast. They were gone now, and she still missed them, but at least they'd been spared yet another awful war, and had lived long enough to see most of their grandchildren come along.

As the threat of war had become reality, the once thriving boarding-house business had died, and with only the two nurses, Suzy and Fran, and the elderly widow, Cordelia Finch, as lodgers, Peggy had been at her wits' end to know how to keep the place going. But with every dark cloud comes a silver lining, and with the help of government grants to supplement the low rents, her empty rooms had been filled by the billeting office. The past three years had been interesting, to say the least, with all the comings and goings, and she still got the occasional letter or card from those who'd stayed for a while before moving on.

Beach View Boarding House stood three streets up the hill from the seafront in one of the many terraces of Victorian houses that were such a feature of Cliffehaven. Four storeys tall, it provided five bedrooms on the top two floors, another in the hall, and two more in the basement which Ron filled with all his clutter and shared with his dog, Harvey, and his two ferrets. Apart from the kitchen and basement scullery, there was a dining room which was rarely used now, and Peggy and Jim had scrimped and saved to have a bathroom put in upstairs. It was a luxury that had been worth every penny, even though strict rationing meant the days of soaking in deep hot water were gone.

In the long narrow back garden Ron's vegetable patch had taken over most of the space between the house and the ugly Anderson shelter. The outside lav had been rebuilt after the bomb blast from two streets up had flattened everything, and although the new lav and cistern were very posh, Peggy still felt guilty every time she saw it, for Ron had liberated it from the rubble of a bombed-out hotel. He'd assured her that it was all legal and above board, but Peggy knew him too well and still had her doubts.

There was also a shed which housed more of Ron's clutter and provided a hiding place for him when she needed things done about the house, and a chicken coop for the hens who managed regularly to lay enough eggs for everyone, despite the racket of air-raid sirens and squadrons of planes roaring overhead.

A large store of wood was piled next to the water butt and almost empty concrete coal bunker; a washing line was strung from a post nailed into the flint of the back-garden wall up to the house, and the two bicycles were sheltered from the elements by a sheet of tarpaulin that Ron had fixed beneath the kitchen window.

Peggy gave a wistful sigh as she thought about her lovely car which was now under wraps for the duration in a friend's garage, its tyreless wheels propped up on bricks. She did miss it, and now she had Daisy she couldn't even use her bike to get about.

She turned away from the dreary view and headed back downstairs. On reaching the kitchen she saw Ron was still entertaining Daisy with her wooden bricks, and Cordelia was engrossed in the afternoon wireless programme while she tried to make sense of her tangle of knitting. Harvey was sprawled in front of the range fire, snoring happily, his ears twitching only slightly every time Daisy knocked down the pile of bricks with a gurgle of delight.

With a sense of deep contentment, Peggy lit a Park Drive cigarette and sat down at the table, glad for a moment's respite before everyone came home for tea. She let her gaze drift to the mantelpiece over the range where she kept the framed photographs of her loved ones amidst the clutter of ration books, discarded lists and old bills.

There was Jim, so handsome in his REME uniform as he smiled back at her; and her two young sons, arm in arm in the back garden, mischief in their cheeky grins. Her spirits faltered somewhat as she looked at the photograph of her eldest daughter,

Anne, who stood beside her husband, Wing Commander Martin Black, with their little Rose Margaret in her arms. Jim had been stationed God knew where up north, and Anne, the baby and Peggy's two boys were down in Somerset for the duration. She felt their absence keenly, for Rose and the boys were growing up without her, Jim's many letters couldn't compensate for the loss of his warm and loving company, and she ached to have them all home and to be a proper family again.

Refusing to dwell on these thoughts, she smoked her cigarette and admired the lovely studio shot of little Daisy who was now just two months away from her first birthday, and then moved on to the one of her nephew Anthony and his fiancée, Suzy, who'd been her lodger since before the war. Their wedding would be next – and as Peggy loved weddings, the thought cheered her up no end.

She grinned at the snapshot of Cissy, her second daughter, who had just turned twenty-one and looked very trim and glamorous in her WRAF uniform. Peggy was still smiling as she looked at the photograph of her lodgers. It had been taken in the back garden with her rather battered Box Brownie early this summer when Kitty Pargeter was still living here, and it gladdened her heart to see Cordelia and the six girls so clearly happy to be together.

Kitty's bright smile told of her courageous determination to live life to the full after having lost part of her leg in a plane crash. Suzy was the quintessential English rose and her fellow nurse, Fran, the fiery-haired Irish imp. Rita was dark-haired and, as usual, wearing trousers and that moth-eaten WWI flying jacket, and the sisters, Jane and Sarah, were fair and pretty. They had escaped Malaya just before the fall of Singapore, and were Cordelia Finch's great-nieces.

Peggy fondly regarded Cordelia, who'd given up on her tangled knitting and was dozing before the fire. Cordelia was in her late seventies and this cold, wet weather played havoc with her arthritis, but she remained cheerful and bright and keenly interested in what all the girls got up to. She had lived at Beach View for many years now and had become very dear to all of them, but her increasing deafness and her rather cavalier attitude to using her hearing aid caused a great many moments of hilarity as well as frustration – and it sometimes meant that conversations took very strange turns indeed.

As for Harvey! She eyed the large brindled lurcher with affection, despite the fact he was a ruddy nuisance at times. His latest escapade had been to impregnate a pedigree whippet whose owner had dumped the resulting puppy at Beach View. The pup, Monty, was now happily ensconced at the Anchor pub with the landlady, Rosie Braithwaite, and although Peggy was relieved not to have him under her feet all day, she still rather missed him.

Peggy stubbed out her cigarette as Harvey opened

his eyes and yawned luxuriously. He was always blotting his copybook, but he was a faithful dog, and an intelligent one too: he'd become quite famous in the town for sniffing out people trapped in their bombed buildings. He and Ron were as scruffy and wayward as each other, but Peggy knew that the house simply wouldn't be the same without either of them.

Harvey pricked up his ears as a gust of cold wind blew in from the hall and the front door slammed.

Peggy headed for the kettle as Suzy and Fran shed their sodden nursing cloaks and shoes. 'You look soaked through,' she said fretfully. 'Go and dry off, or you'll catch your deaths.'

'To be sure, Aunt Peggy, 'tis filthy weather out there,' Fran told her, as she unpinned the soggy white cap and shook out her damp tumble of russet curls.

'The wind makes it worse,' said Suzy as she undid the button on her starched collar and stripped off her apron. 'It drives the rain right through you.'

'I'll make a pot of tea,' said Peggy. 'Go and change.'

As the girls ran up the stairs, Daisy decided she'd had enough of her bricks and began to clamber over the recumbent Harvey, who lay and suffered in silence. Peggy placed the kettle on the hob and, carefully stepping over the scattered bricks, rescued the dog from Daisy's clutching fingers. 'Can you tidy up these toys before someone breaks their neck tripping over them, Ron?'

Cordelia woke from her doze. 'What boys?' she asked in confusion. 'Are Bob and Charlie here?' She looked expectantly round the kitchen.

Peggy experienced a sudden pang of sadness. 'No, Cordelia,' she said clearly. 'Daisy's toys are in the way, that's all.'

Cordelia eyed her over her half-moon spectacles and frowned. 'I do wish you wouldn't shout, dear,' she said with a cluck of annoyance. 'I'm not deaf, you know.'

Ron dumped the bricks and toys into the playpen before turning to her with a mischievous smile that made his blue eyes sparkle beneath the wayward brows. 'To be sure, Cordelia, you have a fine way of ignoring the truth,' he said.

Cordelia tried to be cross with him and failed. She could never resist his smile. 'Get away with you, you old scallywag,' she retorted. 'You wouldn't know the truth if it bit you.'

Peggy listened to this exchange while she settled Daisy in her high chair and made the tea. They had both hit the nail on the head, for Cordelia wouldn't accept the level of her deafness and, when it suited him, Ron had only a distant and rather vague acquaintance with the truth. But they enjoyed their little spats, and there was no harm done.

Cordelia struggled out of the armchair and began to lay the table for tea. 'Is everyone home tonight?'

Peggy placed the teapot and cups on the table. 'Everyone but Rita,' she replied. 'She's going to the pictures with her nice young man, and they're planning to have a fish supper afterwards.'

Cordelia's face lit up with pleasure. 'I do like Matthew,' she said. 'And it's delightful to see our sweet little Rita start to blossom, don't you think?'

Peggy nodded. Rita had met Pilot Officer Matthew Champion at Kitty's wedding, and by the look of it, it had been love at first sight for the pair of them. He was a lovely lad, just into his twenties, and as dedicated to the RAF as her son-in-law Martin. But Matthew flew one of the large bombers that spent night after terrible night on raids over Europe, and she knew that Rita suffered dreadfully every time he went up.

Ron sank into a chair and lit his pipe. 'I know what you're thinking, Peg,' he said once he'd worked up a cloud of smoke, 'and it'll do no one any good. The heavy toll on the RAF is the same for our boys out there with the Atlantic convoys and those fighting in Egypt. We have to stay positive, or we'll never win this war.'

Peggy knew he was right, but it didn't make her fret any less, for Martin still flew his Spitfire on those raids into Europe. She determinedly pushed away the gloomy thoughts and put the potatoes and sprouts on to boil. Jim would be home tomorrow and she must concentrate on that, and be grateful that he was still in England, and would probably not be sent to fight anywhere. He was, after all, in his mid-forties and had done his bit in the last war.

As Ron and Cordelia carried on with their non-too-serious bickering, she checked the stew and ladled out a small portion for Daisy. Setting it to one side so it could cool, her skittering thoughts turned to the knotty problem of how to tell Jim about her close brush with death during the bombing raid earlier in the year, which had led to an early miscarriage and a hysterectomy. The telegram informing him of her operation had clearly not been delivered, for he hadn't mentioned it at all – and as the censors read everything she'd felt uncomfortable about revealing such intimate details in what should have been a very private letter.

She had almost decided on the best way to do it, but she was afraid he'd be upset that she hadn't told him earlier, and had battled through the ordeal without him by her side. She could only hope that her obvious good health and a meal of his favourite sausages, mashed potato and onion gravy would prove he really had nothing to worry about.

Suzy and Fran came back into the kitchen having changed into knitted sweaters, comfortable slacks and slippers. While Suzy made a fuss of Harvey and chatted to Cordelia, Fran carefully placed her vanity case and two towels on an empty chair. 'I'll set your hair after tea, Auntie Peg,' she offered. 'And then I'll do your nails and give you a face pack.'

'Oh, I'm not sure I want that green goo on my face again,' said Peggy.

'Well, we'll see about that,' said Fran, tossing her

curls back. 'But at least it will give you a chance to sit down and take a breather while I do your hair. To be sure,' she continued in her Irish lilt, 'you've fair worn us all out with your dashing around these past few days.'

'Aye, she's right about that,' said Ron as he puffed contentedly on his pipe. 'You haven't sat still since the wedding, and if you're not careful you'll be worn to a frazzle by the time that son of mine gets home.'

'A bit of hard work never killed anyone,' Peggy retorted, 'and I don't want him coming home and thinking I've let things go.'

'Ach, Peggy girl, he'll not be worrying his head about spit and polish,' said Ron. 'He'll have had enough of that in the army, so he will.' His greying brows lowered as he suddenly noticed Fran's vanity case and the towels. 'I hope you're not contemplating attacking me with your scissors again,' he rumbled.

Peggy, Suzy and Fran giggled, remembering the last time Fran had brought her hairdressing things into the kitchen, when she had forced him to sit still while she cut his hair and trimmed his flyaway brows.

Fran shot him an impish grin. 'Ach, Uncle Ron, you're quite safe. 'Tis Peggy's turn today.'

'I'm glad to hear it,' he muttered.

Jane came up the cellar steps, shivering with cold and thoroughly drenched. 'Is autumn always like this in England, Auntie Peg?' she asked wanly.

'I'm afraid it often is,' Peggy replied as she helped

her off with her far-from-adequate raincoat. 'But you'll soon get used to it.'

Jane smoothed her hands over her fair hair and flicked the long, thick, soggy plait over her shoulder. 'And to think I used to moan about the heat and humidity in Malaya,' she said with a wry smile. 'What I wouldn't do for a bit of sunshine now.'

Peggy watched her leave the kitchen to go and get changed. Jane worked at the dairy with the shire horses in the early mornings, and then did the books for the local uniform-factory owner each afternoon. She was a sweet, rather naïve girl and much less sophisticated than her older sister Sarah. Both girls were still homesick, even after all these months, and there was the added worry over their father and Sarah's fiancé, neither of whom had been heard of since the fall of Singapore.

Rita came clumping up the cellar steps, the rain slicking off her heavy-duty trousers and the old flying jacket that she wore over her fire-service uniform. 'Whew! It's filthy out there,' she said as she pulled off the sheepskin-lined jacket and plumped down on a chair to untie her bootlaces. 'At least this weather will keep the planes grounded, so there's no danger of a raid or any fires to tackle.' She ruffled her fingers through her mop of dark curls and grinned at everyone.

'I expect everyone at the fire station will be glad to have a night off,' Suzy remarked, as she put the dinner plates to warm in the smaller of the two ovens.

'Oh, we are,' Rita agreed cheerfully as she grabbed one of Fran's clean towels and roughly dried her hair. 'And I wouldn't mind betting the boys up at Cliffe aerodrome are feeling just the same.'

Fran snatched back the towel. 'This was for Peggy,' she said. 'Now you've got it all wet.'

'Keep your hair on, Fran,' replied Rita. 'I'll bring down another one after I've got changed.' She shot Fran an impish grin, gave Cordelia a kiss on the cheek and ran out of the kitchen and up the stairs.

'My goodness,' sighed Cordelia with a little shrug of pleasure. 'How that girl has changed since she met Matthew.'

'It just goes to show what love can do,' said Suzy happily.

Fran gave a dramatic groan. 'Honest to God, Suzy, I'll be glad when you're married. All this starry-eyed nonsense is getting me down.'

Suzy laughed. 'Jealousy will get you nowhere, Fran. You wait. It'll happen to you one day.'

'Hmph.' Fran folded her arms and tried hard to appear at ease with the fact she'd only recently fallen foul of a lying toerag of a married American whom she'd adored. 'With all the hours I have to do at the hospital, chance would be a fine thing – not that I'm at all bothered.'

'When you've all quite finished discussing your love lives,' grumbled Ron, 'perhaps we could have our tea. Me stomach's sticking to me backbone, so it is.'

'I'll dish up when Sarah gets in,' said Peggy. 'She'll need warming up after her long walk back from the Cliffe estate.'

Peggy sat down and spooned the cooled stew into Daisy's mouth. She was rather worried about Sarah, if the truth was told. It was a long, exposed walk across the hills from the estate where she worked in the office for the Women's Timber Corps – and it was pitch black out there.

Ten minutes later she realised she couldn't keep everyone waiting any longer and began to dish up. She had just sat down when she heard the front door slam and hurrying footsteps across the hall. Looking up as the girl entered the kitchen, she realised immediately that Sarah had not walked home, for her WTC uniform was only lightly speckled with rain. Curiosity sparked, but she made no mention of her appearance, for no doubt Sarah would explain sooner or later.

'You're very late,' Peggy said. 'I was getting worried about you.'

'I'm so sorry, Auntie Peg,' Sarah said rather breathlessly as she took off her heavy overcoat. 'We had an audit, and it went on much longer than we expected. I would have telephoned, but Captain Hammond insisted upon giving me a lift home, and promised I wouldn't be more than a few minutes later than usual.' She glanced at the clock on the mantel as if to confirm this.

At the mention of this mysterious Captain Hammond, Peggy's natural curiosity was on full alert. 'Well, it is only twenty minutes over your usual time,' she said as she served the stew. 'It was very kind of the Captain to bring you home,' she continued with studied care. 'You should have brought him in and introduced him.'

'He had to get back to his duties,' Sarah replied.

Fran giggled. 'Perhaps she's keeping him all to herself, Auntie Peg.'

Sarah reddened. 'It's not like that at all,' she said firmly. 'He just gave me a lift home when he realised how far I had to walk in this appalling weather.'

'I just bet he did,' retorted Fran sourly. 'The Yanks are nothing but charming and helpful when they're after something.'

Sarah carefully put down her knife and fork. 'Fran, don't be like that. You had a bad experience with that Chuck, I know, but not all Americans are out for what they can get. Captain Hammond is an ordinary, very nice man who kindly offered me a lift – so I'd appreciate it if you didn't make more of it than it really is.'

Fran was about to reply when Peggy cut in sharply. 'Sarah's right, Fran. You're trying to make something out of nothing. And you seem to forget that Sarah's engaged to Philip. She isn't interested in other men.'

Fran reddened at the mild rebuke. 'I was just teasing,' she muttered.

As the meal progressed and Harvey was surreptitiously fed morsels of the rabbits he'd helped to catch, the atmosphere lightened and conversation

43

flowed round the table. Rita rushed in looking very pretty in a pink sweater and black slacks, her dark eyes bright with anticipation of her evening out. Having kissed Peggy and Cordelia goodbye, she pulled on a raincoat and headscarf and rushed out again to meet Matthew in the Anchor for a drink before the pictures.

Once the dishes were cleared away and washed, Peggy bathed Daisy and settled her in her cot with her favourite teddy. She then made another pot of rather weak tea while Jane read the newspaper, Fran opened her vanity case, Sarah did some mending and Cordelia tackled her knitting with help and advice from Suzy.

Ron warily eyed the vanity case, scissors and brushes. 'Well, I'll be off to walk Harvey and then see Rosie,' he said as he dragged on the long waterproof poacher's coat over his second-best trousers, reasonably new shirt and knitted sweater. 'This is no place for man nor beast if you're about to turn it into a beauty parlour.'

Harvey eagerly wagged his tail and followed closely behind Ron's heels as he went down the concrete steps to the cellar and out into the teeming rain.

The women shared a knowing smile as the back door slammed, and then Fran became businesslike. 'I'll have to dampen your hair again, Auntie Peg,' she said as she held the brush under the tap. 'The setting lotion doesn't work if it's dry.'

Peggy sat still and finished her cigarette as Fran placed a towel over her shoulders, ran the wet brush through her hair and then combed in the lotion. This was all too reminiscent of the last time she'd expected Jim home, and she wasn't at all sure if she should be tempting fate again.

'I really don't think I'll have the face pack this time,' she said once Fran had finished pinning all the curlers in and started painting her nails a soft pink.

'Stuff and nonsense,' declared Cordelia as she looked up from her ruined knitting. 'It's time you let Fran spoil you.' She peered at Peggy over her glasses, her blue eyes stern. 'You do want to look your best for Jim, don't you?'

'Well, yes,' she admitted, 'but . . .'

'But nothing,' said Cordelia airily. 'You can't possibly welcome him home looking so frazzled. He'll think we aren't taking care of you.'

Peggy rather took objection to being described as frazzled, but let it pass. 'I felt a right fool sitting here with all that green goo on my face and cucumber stuck over my eyes. So, if you don't mind, Fran, I'd really rather leave it this time.'

'There's no cucumber today, Auntie Peg, but cotton wool soaked in cold water will do the same trick. Please reconsider,' Fran said softly. 'You've been running yourself ragged ever since the wedding, and the face pack will help to make your skin look and feel fresher and lighten the dark shadows under your eyes.'

Peggy was a bit miffed at all this criticism, even though it had been meant in the kindest way. Yet, as she hadn't had time to look in a mirror lately, she couldn't really defend herself, and it was easier to give in than to keep resisting. 'Oh, all right,' she sighed as Fran finished her nails.

She closed her eyes and was actually soothed by the cool paste Fran was slathering over her face. She could feel it begin to harden already, and if it was anything like the last time, it would take ages to wash off.

'Are you sure this will work, Fran?' she asked, managing not to move her lips too much.

'Absolutely,' she replied. 'Just don't talk or move a muscle or you'll spoil the effect. Now, I'm putting these soaked pads of cotton wool over your eyes, so just relax and think sweet thoughts.'

Peggy sat there feeling completely foolish as Fran bustled round her. Taking care not to ruin her nail polish, she lit a cigarette and tried to relax, but she could hear Cordelia tittering and the girls giggling. It was clear that everyone else thought the whole rigmarole was much funnier than she did.

Time dragged and she was getting restless. 'How long am I expected to sit like this?' she asked as Fran took the cigarette stub away from her.

'Ach, I'm thinking it won't be long,' giggled Fran.

Peggy was highly suspicious of what they were all up to while she was unable to see them. She could hear rustling and more giggles and the shuffle of footsteps around her. 'Don't you dare leave me like this,' she hissed through tight lips.

'Me darlin' girl, as if I would.'

'Jim!' Peggy was on her feet and across the deserted kitchen into his arms before she could take another breath. She clung to him as she kissed his mouth, his face and his neck. 'Oh, Jim,' she breathed against his cheek. 'I can't believe you're really here.'

He kept his arms round her as he leant back and burst out laughing. 'What the divil have you got on your face, Peggy girl?'

She stiffened with horror as she remembered the face pack, and then tried frantically to smear it away.

Jim was still laughing as he plucked the cotton wool from her cemented cheeks. 'Is this green stuff edible?' he teased. 'Am I supposed to kiss you, or eat you?'

Peggy was mortified, but his mirth was catching and she was soon laughing along with him. 'You weren't supposed to see me like this,' she finally spluttered. 'What must you think?'

He stilled her hands as she reached to remove the curlers, and pulled her to his heart, devotion in his eyes. 'I don't care about the curlers and the cement on your face. I'm just glad to be home with my beautiful girl again.'

She melted into his embrace as he kissed her thoroughly. She was in the arms of the man she loved, and at peace. It didn't matter that all her plans for his homecoming were in ruins – or that she looked a fright – for finally, finally, he was here.

Chapter Three

Gideon had retired to his study to prepare his Sunday sermon, but as Mary washed the dishes and put them away after their very late lunch, she was all too aware of Emmaline's continuing presence at the kitchen table. Her mother's very silence spoke of disapproval as she went through the accounts for the numerous charities she supported, but when she occasionally looked up and caught Mary's eye, it was as if she was looking straight through her.

Mary sighed with relief as Emmaline finally left the kitchen and went upstairs to her bedroom. The tension had built during that long silent interlude, and it had made Mary clumsy to the point where she'd almost broken a plate as she'd put it away.

Left alone to get on with things, Mary relaxed, finished the ironing, cleaned the bathroom and swept the hall floor. She would have liked to have gone into the drawing room to practise the Sunday hymns on the piano, but as Emmaline hated to have her afternoon rest disturbed, Mary knew she'd have to wait until morning.

It was late afternoon and quite dark by the time

she brought her soaking-wet bicycle into the kitchen so she could mend the puncture. The tyre was old and getting very threadbare, but as it was almost impossible to acquire a new one, she had to hope that this latest repair would hold long enough at least to get her to the station and back tonight.

She was slowly turning the tyre in a bowl of water to find the hole when she heard her father come out of his study and into the hall. The creak of the cupboard door opening beneath the stairs, and the rattle of a padlock being unfastened, told her that he was once again delving into the large trunk that had stood there amidst the cobwebs and dust for as long as she could remember.

What was in the trunk was a complete mystery, for he'd always kept it locked and replied when asked that it was just used as storage for his old parish records. However, Mary had always been intrigued by that trunk, especially when she'd been a small girl, and she'd made up stories of hidden treasures, or secret maps. As she grew she'd begun to wonder romantically if perhaps there were old photographs and letters hidden there. Private letters tied with ribbon that spoke of a lost love he couldn't quite forget.

Now, of course, she knew her father was not that sort of man at all, and that the trunk probably really did only contain fusty old ledgers and ancient correspondence that related to the church. Quite why he was so secretive about it was beyond her, but she supposed he liked to keep something to himself for a change.

She concentrated on mending the puncture as the rain continued to pelt against the window, the wind howled, and the day darkened into premature night. It was a five-mile round trip to the station and back, and in this weather it wouldn't be at all pleasant, even on a bicycle, and yet it would be worth it just to see Jack again before he was snatched away from her.

Mary was warmed by the thought as she repaired the puncture and fitted the tyre back on the front wheel. Jack would look very handsome in his uniform, she just knew it, and his surprise at her turning up would make the trip worthwhile. His parents might be there to see him off, but that didn't matter, for they knew how things were between Jack and Mary, and approved. And if they were there, then they'd surely offer to put her bike in the back of their farm truck and give her a lift home, which would be marvellous.

She glanced up at the clock. It was after four, but if she could have supper ready on the dot of six, then . . .

The telephone rang in the hall and she heard her father sigh before he tramped across the scarred parquet floor to answer it. Mary hoped it wasn't something that would take him out on such a filthy day. He was already tired after a late night with the grieving Mrs Burton, who had just learnt that her husband had been killed at El Alamein.

She wheeled the bike back outside. Covering it quickly with a sheet of old tarpaulin, she returned to the relative warmth of the kitchen. Her father was still on the telephone, and she fervently hoped it wasn't the Bishop, for he was a pedantic, hectoring man who expected far too much from his over-worked vicar, and made Gideon nervous and depressed.

Mary checked the large saucepan of vegetable soup she'd made the day before, and decided there was just enough left for three small helpings. She then began to peel the potatoes to go with the evening meal of liver and onions, glad to have the kitchen to herself for a while. Emmaline was still in bed with a hot-water bottle in an attempt to ease the awful pains in her joints, and although Mary felt genuinely sorry that she was so unwell, it didn't alter the fact that she felt far more comfortable without her.

'That was Dr Haywood,' said Gideon as he came into the kitchen some minutes later. 'Old Mrs Perry is failing fast and not expected to last the night.' He wearily scrubbed his face with his hands and gave her a wan smile. 'I must go to her, Mary, she's been asking for me.'

'Oh, Dad,' she sighed as she put a consoling hand on his arm. 'You're already exhausted after last night.'

'I know, my dear, but Mrs Perry has been a parish-ioner here for over eighty years, and needs the comfort of prayer before she goes to God. I cannot fail her now.' He cleared his throat. 'And neither can you,' he added regretfully. 'I'm sorry, Mary, but I will need you to come with me to look after Gladys.'

Mary glanced anxiously at the clock, and then was deeply ashamed of her selfishness. Gladys was almost fifty, but had the mind and manner of an eight-year-old. She would be confused and frightened about what was happening to her mother, and Mary was mortified that she'd been thinking only of herself, and not what Mrs Perry's death would mean to her daughter. 'Of course I'll come,' she said as she reached for their coats. 'Has anyone told Mrs Perry's sister?'

'The doctor said he'd drive over and tell her. I've never met her, but from what I've heard she's almost as elderly as Mrs Perry, so I doubt she'll want to turn out on such a night even though her sister's dying.' Gideon pulled on his coat and laced his brogues. 'I'll just go up and tell your mother where we're going,' he muttered.

Mary's hopes of seeing Jack were doomed, and she wondered if it was God's way of punishing her for plotting and planning behind her parents' back. Perhaps her mother had been right all along about her sinful nature, for she was guilty of being devious.

She yanked on her wellingtons and shrugged into her overcoat as she felt the prick of tears. Poor Gladys. Her mother was her only mainstay, and if her aunt refused to take her in, she would be sent to live in the special hospital that Mrs Perry had resisted so determinedly ever since Gladys had been born.

Mary tramped into the hall and grabbed the car keys just as Gideon came downstairs. 'Your mother is warm and comfortable,' he said as he reached for the black Gladstone bag on the hall table. It was always packed and ready for occasions such as these. 'She said not to worry about her, and that she'd heat up some soup for her supper.'

Mary wrapped a scarf round her father's neck and handed him his hat. 'Stay here in the dry while I fetch the car,' she murmured.

Before he could protest, she was out of the front door and running through the lashing downpour to the garage. Dragging back the wooden doors, she smeared the rain from her face, turned the starting handle, and climbed into the Austin 7. The luxury of having a car in these austere times was not abused, for her father needed it to get about his widespread parish, and he'd been granted extra petrol coupons for just this purpose.

Mary pressed the starter button and carefully reversed the car out of the garage and then drove it to the front steps, where her father was waiting anxiously beneath the porch. She smiled at his concerned expression as he climbed in, for his car was his pride and joy and he still didn't really approve of it being driven by anyone else – let alone his young daughter.

'Slow down,' he said fretfully as the speedometer

inched up to ten miles an hour. 'And mind the hedge. You're getting much too close to it.'

Mary smiled and said nothing as she peered through the windscreen where the wipers were laboriously clearing the rain. With no street lights or moon to show her the way, she had to rely on the heavily shielded headlights that barely pierced the blackness of the country road, but she loved driving this car and just wished she could do it more often.

Gladys looked surprisingly calm as she opened the cottage door to them in her best cotton frock, hand-knitted cardigan, pyjama trousers and wellington boots. Her round face and rather blank eyes showed little sign of tears and she happily showed them into her mother's stifling bedroom, where a nurse sat by the bed.

'Thank you for coming so promptly,' the nurse said as she stood to greet them. 'I have another patient to see, so I'll leave you in peace if that's all right. There's nothing else I can do here, but I'm sure your presence will give her comfort.'

As the nurse quietly left the cottage and drove off to her next patient, Gladys turned to Mary. 'Mummy says she's going to Heaven to be with Daddy,' she said, 'and that I've got to be a good girl and not cry.' She kissed her mother's pale, sunken cheek and then gave Mary and her father a beaming smile. 'Would you like some lemonade?'

Mary left her father with Mrs Perry and followed

the girl into the hopelessly untidy kitchen at the back of the cottage. Dirty crockery and cooking pots were heaped in the sink and on the draining board, and the tiny black range was encrusted with spilt food. Despite the mess, Gladys had clearly been doing her best since her mother had taken to her bed, and Mary's heart went out to her.

'Let's tidy up the kitchen and then we can have that lemonade.' She smiled into Gladys's trusting face. 'Do you prefer to wash or dry?'

Gladys clapped her hands delightedly. 'Oh, wash,' she replied. 'And can we have lots of suds? I love suds.'

They spent almost an hour getting everything clean and tidied away, and while Gladys enjoyed her home-made lemonade with a digestive biscuit, Mary made a pot of tea and took a cup in to her father.

It was clear that Mrs Perry was close to the end, for her breathing rattled in her chest and her skin had taken on the waxen tone that heralded death. 'Should I ask Gladys to come in so she can say goodbye?' Mary asked hesitantly.

'You'll do no such thing.' The booming voice came from the doorway and startled them both. 'The girl is quite incapable of understanding death, so why upset her?'

'Mrs Wheatley,' said Gideon as he hurriedly got to his feet to greet the robust elderly woman in the ill-fitting tweed suit that seemed to be covered in cat hair. 'I'm so glad you could come. It will be such a comfort to your sister to know you're here.'

The weathered face below the black hat glowered. 'I doubt that very much,' Violet Wheatley said as she came into the room, her sturdily shod feet thudding on the wooden floor. She stood at the foot of the bed and frowned at the figure lying there. 'Cora and I haven't spoken for years,' she muttered. 'Nothing to say to each other after she married that wastrel. But the doctor was kind enough to give me a lift, and I couldn't let her pass without saying goodbye.'

In the silence that followed this statement they all became aware of Mrs Perry's struggle to breathe, and Violet's expression softened as she rounded the bed and took her sister's hand. 'It's all right, Cora,' she said gruffly. 'I'll see to all the arrangements and make sure you have a decent send-off. And I'll take Gladys in so she comes to no harm.'

Cora Perry's eyelids fluttered momentarily as if she had heard and understood. Then she stopped struggling and her final breath came with a deep sigh.

As Gideon prayed for her, Mary noticed the sheen of tears in Violet's eyes and knew that despite the gruff and rather hectoring manner, there was a deep regret for the years the sisters had been estranged. Sensing a movement behind her, Mary turned to discover Gladys standing in the doorway, her gaze fixed in puzzlement on her lifeless mother.

Violet must have noticed her too, for she hurried over and eased her out of the room. 'Mummy's gone to Heaven now, Gladys,' she said not unkindly, 'and you're coming to live with me. I hope you like cats.'

Gladys's face lit up and she shuffled her feet in delight. 'I love cats. But I especially love kittens. Do you have any kittens?'

'I expect we'll have a few before the year is out. Come, Gladys, let me help you get dressed in something warmer and pack a bag. I can come and fetch the rest of your things another time.'

As Violet and Gladys climbed the narrow wooden stairs, Mary caught her father's eye. 'Will she be all right with Violet?'

Gideon nodded and respectfully drew the sheet over Cora's face. 'Violet is certainly rather fierce, but I suspect there's a good heart beating under all that tweed and cat hair,' he replied. 'Gladys will be well cared for.'

They stayed until Gladys's case was packed, and Violet had checked that all the windows and doors were locked and had pocketed the keys, then Gideon drove them to the tiny hamlet of Dane's Cross where Violet lived in a rambling house that stood behind a high hedge. Gladys chattered away for most of the journey and seemed quite happy to follow her aunt up the neat garden path. She turned and waved enthusiastically at them before she was distracted by a cat rubbing against her leg, and Violet closed the front door.

By the time Mary had parked the car in the garage and they'd stripped off their overcoats and outdoor footwear, it was almost seven o'clock. Gideon traipsed upstairs to check on Emmaline, and Mary quickly put the potatoes on to boil while she fried the liver and onions and heated up the last of the soup. Emmaline had eaten most of it, but there was enough for her father.

They ate supper almost in silence and then shared a pot of very weak tea before Gideon declared that he needed to go to bed. Mary kissed his drawn cheek and gave him a hug. 'Try not to stay up reading for too long, Daddy. You need your rest.'

'I have a sermon to think about, and a eulogy to plan for Cora's funeral.' He gave her a weary, loving smile and kissed her forehead. 'Good night, Mary. God bless you, my dear.'

Mary watched from the kitchen doorway as he trudged up the stairs and closed his dressing-room door behind him. He and Emmaline had not shared a bed for many years, mainly because she complained about his having the light on while he read, and Mary knew that, despite his exhaustion, he wouldn't be able to resist reading some Dylan Thomas before he went to sleep. Gideon often used the words of his favourite writer and poet to illustrate his sermons and keep his parishioners enthralled.

Mary took the receiver off the telephone. If there were any other emergencies tonight, it would not be her father who attended them. The house creaked and old pipes rattled as she returned to the kitchen and noticed that it had finally stopped raining. The wind had suddenly dropped too, and there was a frail moon peeking out from the clouds.

She glanced at the clock. There was still just time to get to the station – but did she dare to leave the house? Could she face her father in the morning, knowing how deceitful she'd been? But the thought of Jack waiting on the station platform for the train to take him away was just too much, and she vowed silently that tomorrow she would confess to her parents and endure the awful disappointment in her father's eyes as her just punishment.

Her pulse was racing as she quickly dressed for the outdoors again and checked she had the key to the front door so she could get back in. She went out into the cold, still night, retrieved her bicycle and wheeled it across the side lawn, through the gap in the churchyard wall and along the path through the lychgate.

Having cycled away from the church, she sped along the lane, past the silent, darkened cottages, the old schoolhouse and the line of shops, the brisk night air stinging her eyes and nipping at her face. She pedalled furiously, the feeble beam of her bicycle lamp barely strong enough to show her the way, but soon she'd left Harebridge Green behind her and was zipping along between the high hedgerows of the wider, bending road that led to Hillney.

Eventually she began to make out the silhouettes

of the roofs and church towers of Hillney against the horizon, which was now dimly lit by the frail moon. The railway station was at the other end of the market town, and as she passed the Town Hall she noticed with alarm that it was almost half past eight.

Speeding down the hill, she skidded round a sharp corner and almost lost control of the bicycle. With her heart racing, she managed to keep her balance and pedalled even faster as she heard the distinct sound of a steam train chugging along the line. She fairly flew over the humpbacked bridge and swerved into a skidding halt as she reached the stationmaster's little cottage. Careless of the damage it might do to her bicycle, she leapt off and let it fall with a clatter as she ran on to the platform.

The train was already pulling in, the wreaths of smoke and steam veiling the small knot of men who waited there. 'Jack,' she called desperately. 'Jack, where are you?'

He appeared through the smoke, tall and handsome and disturbingly unfamiliar in his khaki uniform, his face lit by his delight at seeing her. 'So you decided to come anyway,' he smiled as she threw herself into his arms.

'I couldn't let you go without saying a proper goodbye,' she told him after they'd kissed.

'Well, I don't know how you managed it, but I'm glad you did,' he replied softly. 'Mum and Dad couldn't face seeing me off again after the army trucks picked me up from the farm.'

Mary kissed him again, glad of his strong arms around her, but aware of the nervous tension that ran through him. 'I had to come,' she murmured against his freshly shaven jaw. 'I couldn't bear to think of you leaving without seeing you just one more time.'

'Right, you horrible lot,' shouted a sergeant from somewhere in the mist of smoke and steam. 'All aboard – and jump to it. Yer in the army now, and I don't like idlers.'

Mary clung to Jack as he kissed her for the last time. 'I'll send you my address,' he said as he picked up his bag and edged back towards the open carriage door. 'Take care of yourself, Mary, until I come home again.'

'And you take care,' she managed as the tears welled. 'I love you, Jack.'

He ducked his head and reddened as the other men cheered and encouraged him to kiss her again, but he clambered on to the train, and the sergeant slammed the door behind him before marching to the next carriage.

Mary stood on the platform desperately searching for sight of Jack. And there he was, lifting the blackout blind and opening the window, leaning out as the whistle blew and the train began to roll slowly forward with a hiss of steam. She reached out and their fingers touched before the train gathered speed. 'I'll write every day,' she shouted as she tried to keep pace with him.

'So will I, I promise,' he yelled back.

Mary came to the end of the short platform as the carriages trundled noisily past her with their blacked-out windows. She stood and watched until the train was lost in the darkness. 'God go with you, Jack, and bring you home safely,' she stuttered through the tears she could no longer hold back.

'There, there, lass,' said the elderly stationmaster. 'He'll be back afore you knows it. Now, you dry them tears and I'll get the missus to make us a nice cuppa. How about that?'

Mary pulled herself together and nodded. 'That would be lovely,' she replied with a tremulous smile. 'It's a long ride back home to Harebridge Green.'

She sat drinking the tea in the stationmaster's cosy cottage, feeling the warmth of the roaring fire slowly thawing out her fingers and toes. She tried to ignore the coldness that had settled in her heart as she dutifully admired his wife's large collection of lovingly polished copper pots and horse brasses, and listened attentively as she talked about her equally large family of whom she was inordinately proud. Yet her thoughts were with Jack, her heart frozen at the thought she might never see him again.

Having finished her tea, she thanked the couple for their kindness and regretfully left the snug little home. It was well past nine o'clock and her journey would take at least half an hour now she was so tired and downhearted. She was relieved to find that her bicycle had come to no harm after being thrown to the ground so carelessly, and as the clouds disappeared and the moon's glow brightened, it was much easier to see her way.

As she rode through the sleeping countryside to the accompaniment of the tyres singing on the tarmac, she thought about Jack. He was the same lovely Jack she'd always known, but the uniform had already changed him in some indefinable way, and she wasn't at all sure she was happy about that. Even the smallest of changes could be amplified by distance and time, and she could only pray that this enforced parting wouldn't prove to be the end of all they'd planned and dreamed about.

She was snapped from her thoughts by the distant wailing of sirens, and she stopped pedalling to look back at the sky above Hillney. Searchlights were already piercing the darkness as the pitch of the sirens rose, and then she became aware of the ominous drone of a squadron of enemy bombers approaching from the north-west.

Realising she was very exposed out here on this country road she quickly turned off the lamp and wheeled her bike over to the hedge, where she pressed herself into the deep shadows. Looking up, she could make out the silhouettes of Dorniers, Heinkels and Junkers, accompanied by their smaller, swifter fighters. Spitfires, Typhoons and Hurricanes were harassing the fighters, and some furious dogfights had broken out.

The enemy planes were heading south, which

meant they'd completed their raid and were dashing for home. But Mary knew that the danger wasn't over, for those returning bombers often dropped the last of their deadly cargo on the towns, villages and farmlands of Sussex so they could make a lighter, swifter departure.

She cried out as she saw a Spitfire take a hit and burst into flames. Searching desperately for sight of a parachute, Mary watched the plane go into a nose-dive and heard the resulting crump as it hit the unforgiving ground. There had been no parachute, and Mary could only pray that the brave man flying that Spitfire had quickly lost consciousness before the end.

Amid the rattle of gunfire and the boom of the Bofors guns there was a distant explosion that had come from somewhere to the east, and another two that were nearer Hillney. She huddled into the hedge, aware of the glow in the sky to the east and west as the dogfights continued, the distant search-lights swept back and forth, and the enemy bombers continued laboriously on their way to the Channel. Had Jack's train been one of their targets? Was he still safe? The railway lines were horribly exposed on that branch, with only a couple of tunnels to hide in and wait out any raid. She closed her eyes and prayed fervently that those terrible images going round in her head would not become reality.

As the drone of the enemy bombers faded and the Spitfires chased their counterparts across the

Channel, Mary retrieved her bike from the roadside ditch. She was shaking from cold and a terrible fear for Jack. Her first instinct was to return to the station and see if there was any news of his train – but then she realised it was much too soon for any reports to filter through. She would go home, she decided reluctantly, and telephone the stationmaster first thing in the morning.

Her legs were trembling as she slowly continued her journey. The silence of the night was distantly disturbed by the 'all-clear' siren and the clanging of fire-engine and ambulance bells, but all she could think of was Jack, trapped on that train as the bombers flew overhead.

It was some minutes before she realised the sound of a clanging bell was getting louder. She stopped pedalling to look over her shoulder, and saw the hooded lights of one of the Hillney fire engines coming towards her at speed. Moving to one side, she watched it pass, and then quickly cycled after it.

The fire engine was soon lost from sight, but it was swiftly followed by an ambulance, and Mary's fear for Jack was overshadowed by the very real possibility that something could have happened in her village or nearby. If that was the case, then she would be needed to help her father bring solace and cups of tea to those in distress.

She was praying fervently that the fire was beyond the village, harmlessly burning in a field and not jeopardising any lives. Yet as she drew nearer to

Harebridge Green she could now see the red glow in the sky, and the thick dark smoke that billowed across the pale moon.

Mary pedalled faster, and as she entered the village she heard shouts from those who were on the pavement, and saw a human tide of hurrying men armed with stirrup pumps, sacking and spades. She was deaf to their shouts, blind to everything but the terrible red glow at the other end of the village.

As she took the final bend, she realised she was hurtling towards randomly parked farm trucks and fire engines, and the large group of men who were preparing to tackle the fire as the women looked on. She skidded to a halt, and froze in horrified shock at the sight before her. The rectory was ablaze, the flames spearing through the roof and shooting from the windows, blackening the red bricks and devouring everything within reach.

Mary dropped the bicycle, fighting against restraining hands from the gathered crowd as she searched wildly for her mother and father. She couldn't see them anywhere, and wrestled her way through the trucks, Home Guard members and wardens, and past the fire engine down the drive towards the men who were battling the inferno. 'My parents,' she screamed above the noise of water pipes and the shouts of firefighters. 'Where are my parents?'

A fireman turned, his face blackened with soot and sweat, his expression saying more than any words as he shook his head.

'No! No, they can't be!' Heedless of the danger and mad with fear, she tried to rush past him. 'I have to get them out,' she screamed as she struggled to escape his iron grip on her arm.

And then two sturdy arms were wrapped around her, leading her determinedly back to the lane, as a familiar voice penetrated the fog of hysteria surrounding her. 'It's too late, Mary, love. They've gone.'

Mary looked up into the soot-smeared face and kind eyes of Jack's father. 'But they can't have,' she sobbed. 'They can't have.'

Joseph Boniface continued to hold her, his dark brown eyes, so like his son's, looking down at her with infinite understanding and gentleness. 'The rectory took a direct hit,' he said in his slow, deliberate manner. 'They wouldn't have suffered or known anything about it.'

She stared at him and tried to absorb his words, but all she could hear was her father's blessing as he'd kissed her goodnight – all she could feel was a crippling, numbing guilt that she'd disobeyed him and hadn't been there when he'd most needed her. 'It's all my fault,' she sobbed. 'I shouldn't have left them and now Daddy's . . . Daddy's . . .' She collapsed against Joseph in a great storm of bitter tears.

Joseph held her while she wept, and muttered soft words of consolation. 'It's not your fault,' he said quietly. 'Of course it's not, and you must never even think it.'

He awkwardly patted her back until the storm ebbed, and then drew away. 'I have to help put out the fire, but Barbara will take you home to ours,' he said. 'She'll look after you, and you can stay with us for as long as you want.'

Mary looked from him to his wife and then was hypnotised by the sight of those terrible flames. They rose higher and higher despite the jets of water pounding on them, hungrily clambering up the crumbling walls and consuming everything in their path. Glass shattered in the heat, curtains withered to blackened wisps that floated in the swirling smoke, the chimneys toppled – and she cried out as the great roof finally succumbed and caved in with a mighty crash that sent sparks and debris flying.

As the men rushed forward to kill the swiftly travelling flames that were now igniting the overhanging trees, Barbara gently took Mary's arm. 'Come away, love,' she said. 'The men have work to do, and we're getting in their way.'

It was as if she was sleepwalking, for she put up no resistance as Barbara led her through the choking smoke and back into the lane. This was her punishment – the burden she would have to carry for the rest of her life – but it was her parents who'd paid the awful price for her deceit, and she knew that she would never find redemption.

Chapter Four

The Anchor had stood in Camden Road for almost two centuries. It had once been a coaching inn and a refuge for the Cliffehaven smugglers, who'd used the large cellar to hide their booty and then transported it through a secret doorway into the tunnels that led to the church and the parsonage. Ron and his son, Jim, had made similar use of this hideaway before the war when they took the fishing boats across the Channel, but now Ron had converted this cellar into a shelter so the customers could stay and keep on drinking during the air raids.

The old inn stables had long since disappeared and their Victorian replacements now provided shops on the ground floor and spacious apartments above. The ancient tiled roof of the pub dipped in the middle like a weary sway-backed horse and overshadowed the tiny diamond-paned windows, and the whitewashed walls that leant rather tipsily towards the pavement were veined with dark wooden timbers.

The iron-studded oak door opened on to an uneven brick floor, an inglenook fireplace, and bench seating beneath the front and back windows. An upright piano stood in one corner, and in front of an ornate glass and mirrored fitment that acted as storage for bottles and glasses there was a highly polished wooden counter, two porcelain-handled beer pumps, and a heavy brass till. A collection of pewter tankards hung from hooks above the bar, and various leather straps holding horse brasses decorated the weathered, blackened beams on either side of the inglenook.

A few tables and chairs were scattered around, but most of the customers preferred to stand by the counter, one foot resting on the shining brass rod that ran round the base. Lit only by a few wall-lights and a single low-watt bulb over the bar, and with the blackout curtains tightly drawn, entering it was like walking into a cave smelling strongly of pipe and cigarette smoke and spilt beer. And yet, in winter, when there was a log fire blazing in the inglenook, it was the snuggest place in Cliffehaven.

Ron was standing in his preferred spot at the end of the bar by the brass till, enjoying a welcome pint after his long walk with Harvey, and gazing with love and pride at the landlady, Rosie Braithwaite. Rosie kept everyone in order as she served the drinks and made sure the other, older barmaids were managing to cope with the hectic pace. She didn't miss a trick, his Rosie, and he felt the familiar glow of pleasure as he watched her sashay back and forth in her high heels, for she was the prettiest sight with her laughing blue eyes, platinum hair and luscious figure.

She exchanged some mild banter with one of the

airmen, and then flashed Ron a naughty grin just to let him know that although she flirted with her male customers, her heart was his.

He winked back, saw the envy in the other men's eyes, and only just managed to resist puffing out his chest like a rooster. He might be over sixty, and considered by some to be past it, but there was still plenty of life in this old dog yet, and with a woman like Rosie on his arm, he was a king.

Rosie had arrived in Cliffehaven to take over the pub some years ago and had caused a great stir amongst the male population of a certain age, for she was not only as glamorous as a film star, but it appeared she was unencumbered by a husband or children. She was also a bit of a mystery, for it was most unusual to have a lone woman owning and running a pub, and she wasn't at all forthcoming about her personal history. Yet this merely enhanced her would-be suitors' interest, and made the competition to snare her more intense.

Ron had been immediately smitten, but Rosie had kept him and all the other men at arm's length, seemingly preferring her own company, all too aware that a woman in her position could very quickly become the target of gossip. It had taken several years of making himself generally useful about the place before he'd been invited upstairs to her living quarters to share a cup of tea or a quiet drink after the pub was closed, and finally, through charm and gentle humour, he'd won her over.

Rosie was in her early fifties, though she had the demeanour and figure of a much younger woman, and liked nothing better than the camaraderie of a busy bar. Once she'd felt able to trust him, Ron had learnt that behind that sweet smile and cheerful facade lay a tragic story. Rosie wasn't footloose and fancy-free at all: she had a husband who was locked away in a mental asylum and would probably never leave it.

This was a dark shadow that lay between them, for while her husband was alive there could be no divorce. There had been little intimacy between them either, Ron thought wistfully as he watched the sway of her hips in that tight skirt. Rosie was a good Catholic girl, and she'd told him straight that she didn't mind a bit of smooching, but she wouldn't take things any further until she was free. It was all most frustrating.

The other problem was her brother. Tommy Findlay was a rotter through and through, and Ron wouldn't have trusted him as far as he could throw him. The toerag dressed like a spiv and carried rolls of banknotes in his pocket, for he was a wheeler-dealer and always on the fiddle. Light-fingered and utterly unscrupulous, Tommy wasn't averse to cheating on his wife who lived with their children further down the coast, and he treated these dalliances with total disregard for the hurt he caused. There had been a particularly nasty do many years before with Eileen Harris who worked in the local council offices, and although Ron didn't know how, the consequences of this affair had caused profound hurt to Rosie, which she still harboured.

Ron stared gloomily into his pint glass. Rosie refused to tell him what it had all been about, and so did the usually forthcoming Peggy, who clearly was in possession of the full story through her close friendship with Rosie. All he knew was that Rosie and Eileen had become sworn enemies, that Tommy had been at the centre of it all, and that Rosie still found it very hard to forgive him.

Ron grinned before he swallowed the last of his beer. He'd got his own back on Tommy for hurting Rosie – although he hadn't told her about the part he'd played in getting her brother arrested for hiding his ill-gotten black-market gains in the pub cellar while he was looking after the place during Rosie's absence last year. With Tommy in prison, life was very much better, and Ron hoped he never saw him again.

He emerged from his thoughts and looked round the bar. It was busy now the all-clear had sounded. No damage had been done in the town as the enemy bombers had headed back across the Channel, so the servicemen and women were enjoying a respite from their duties, alongside the factory girls and a few stalwart locals who regarded the pub as their own and jealously guarded their favourite places to stand or sit.

After a sing-song had begun someone had attempted to accompany it on the piano, but was so bad he was ousted from the stool and everyone carried on singing without him. Cigarette smoke lay in a thick fug along the beamed ceiling as the noise rose. The mood was happy, and no fights had yet broken out between the Yanks and the British boys over the dewy-eyed girls who clustered round them.

Ron drank his beer and looked at Harvey who lay snoring in front of the fire in the inglenook, his pup, Monty, stretched alongside him. Monty had definitely fallen on his feet since Rosie had taken him in, he thought. He'd grown a lot too, and was as leggy and ungainly as a young colt, constantly galloping about getting in the way, and chewing everything. Rosie was doing her best to train him not to ruin her shoes or the furniture, but like his sire, Harvey, he went his own way.

Ron looked from the dogs to the nearby table where Cordelia sat with the girls. None of them had planned to be out tonight, but they'd left the house so that Peggy and Jim could bill and coo in private, and had arrived at the Anchor to commandeer the table by the fire. They'd been here for over two hours, and if Cordelia had any more sherry, Ron observed with amusement, he'd have to carry her home.

Cordelia caught his eye and he grinned as he raised his beer glass in salute. She then swallowed the last of her drink and joined in the singing, heedless of the fact she was tone-deaf and trilled like a budgie with laryngitis. God love her, he thought with great affection. She might get his goat at times by calling him a scoundrel and scallywag and taking him to task, but Beach View had certainly been blessed by her presence.

He was immediately distracted by a glimpse of Rosie's magnificent bosom through the frills on her blouse as she slammed the till's drawer shut and reached over the bar for his empty glass.

'Careful, Ron,' she teased. 'Your eyes will pop out of your head if you stare any harder.'

'Ach, to be sure, you're a fine-looking woman so y'are, Rosie darlin',' he purred.

'I'd be flattered if you were actually admiring something other than my cleavage.' She took any sting out of her words with a giggle. 'Another pint?'

'Aye, I'll have a half, Rosie. It looks as if I'll be needed to escort a certain little old lady home, and we can't have both of us unsteady on our feet.' He admired the way she poured his drink, her slender arm flexing, her breasts rising a little as she pulled on the beer pump. He felt definite stirrings, and hurriedly looked away.

'This one's on the house,' she murmured as she placed the glass in front of him. 'I hear your Jim's home on leave at last, so there's a pint waiting for him too.' She smiled. 'Peggy must be over the moon.'

Ron took a sip of the beer and then grinned. 'Aye, no doubt she is. At least now he's home she might sit still for five minutes and not keep finding me jobs to do about the house. She's been rushing around like a headless chicken these past days and we're all worn to a frazzle.'

'You don't look too frazzled to me,' she replied with a teasing light in her eyes. 'In fact you look like a man full of energy.'

Ron squared his shoulders and stuck out his chest. 'Fit as a butcher's dog, me,' he boasted.

'That's what I thought.' Her lips twitched. 'As you're so fit, perhaps you could change a barrel for me and bring up a few more crates?'

'Y'are a wee tease,' he rumbled, his blue eyes twinkling beneath his bushy brows. 'And here's me thinking you might need the use of this fine specimen of a man to help you out with something rather more interesting upstairs.'

Rosie's answering chuckle was throaty and sensual. 'Full marks for trying, Ron, but I don't give in that easily.' She glanced at the crush waiting to be served. 'I'd really appreciate those crates, Ron, and we're almost out of bitter, so if you wouldn't mind . . .'

He realised their short, sweet interlude was over as she turned back to serve her clamouring customers, so he cheerfully headed for the cellar to do her bidding.

Peggy had finally fended off Jim's amorous advances long enough to wash the green stuff off her face and take out her curlers while he went to see Daisy. Then they had decided to take full advantage of an empty house and were about to tumble into bed when the blasted sirens went off.

Quickly scooping Daisy out of her cot, they'd run laughing to the Anderson shelter where they snuggled together in blankets against the cold and damp, and Jim rocked Daisy in his arms until she fell back to sleep.

He'd been quite shocked at how much she'd grown during his absence, and a little put out that she didn't immediately appreciate him waking her up to hold and fuss over her. She'd eventually succumbed to his charms, though, and Jim had a contented smile on his face as he now watched her sleeping.

Despite the fact that Peggy hated the Anderson shelter, she was enjoying the intimacy of cuddling up to Jim while their baby slept in her special canvas cot at their feet. Cold and smelly it might be, but they were cocooned within its corrugated iron walls as the dogfights went on overhead and the enemy bombers ran for home, the light from the flickering oil lamp making it almost romantic.

Once the all-clear had sounded, Jim had carried Daisy back to the house and tucked her in her cot. Peggy had watched with tears in her eyes as he'd lovingly kissed her soft, sweet cheek and tenderly adjusted the blankets. It was so good to have him home again.

An hour later, Jim had bathed and changed out of his uniform into slacks and a sweater, with his feet encased in slippers. He'd eaten a huge plateful of sausages, mash and onion gravy and was now sitting in the armchair by the fire with Peggy on his knee.

'This is what I've dreamed of for months,' he murmured as he nuzzled her cheek and held her close. 'My billet was comfortable and cosy and, to be sure, the old ladies treated me very well before I had to go back to barracks and off on that training course. But there's definitely no place like home.'

Peggy ran her fingers through his severely cut black hair that had only a glimmer of silver showing through, and looked lovingly into his dark eyes. 'I've missed you so much,' she replied as she kissed his lips. 'And when your last leave was cancelled I was so disappointed and furious that, given the chance, I'd have stormed up to that camp of yours and given your commanding officer what-for.'

Jim chuckled and squeezed her closer. 'He wouldn't have stood a chance, knowing you. My fierce, wonderful little Peggy.'

They kissed, lost in their own world as the empty house sighed and creaked around them and the rain began to fall again. Then he stood with her still in his arms and carried her into the bedroom where Daisy's night light glowed on the bedside table. Setting her gently on to the bed, and aware of the sleeping baby nearby, Jim drew her close and softly kissed her face and neck until Peggy thought she might die from pleasure.

But as his hand slowly began to inch up her leg to her stocking-tops, Peggy's desire was quenched by the realisation that she had yet to explain the rather large scar below her belly. 'Jim,' she said breathlessly as she struggled out of his embrace. 'Jim, could we wait just a minute? Only I've got something to tell you.'

He rose on to an elbow and frowned down at her. 'What is it, Peg? You haven't gone off me, have you?'

'No, of course not, silly.' She paused as she tried to think of the best way to tell him.

Jim sat up then, his frown deepening. 'I know it's been a while,' he said, 'but you were keen enough earlier on. What's changed?'

Peggy could see how tense he was and hurried to reassure him. 'Jim, something happened a few months ago which I didn't tell you about because there wasn't anything you could have done, and I didn't want you worrying,' she said all in a rush. 'And then there seemed no point in mentioning it as everything is all right now.'

His handsome face paled. 'What the divil happened to you, Peg? You weren't attacked by someone, were you?'

Peggy was horrified that she was making such a mess of this. 'No, Jim, no. I was ill, and had to go into hospital for an operation, but as you can see I'm perfectly all right, so there's no need to fret.'

'An operation?' His expression was fearful and shocked in equal measure.

His concern twisted her heart, so she quickly went on to tell him about the ectopic pregnancy and the life-saving operation she'd had to have following the bomb blast that she'd been caught in. His very real anguish brought tears to her eyes as she told him there would never be any more children.

'Good God,' he breathed as he pulled her into his arms. 'You shouldn't have had to keep all this to yourself. Why on earth didn't you tell me at once?'

'Ron sent a telegram, but it must have got lost, or not passed on when you moved barracks.' She touched his face, feeling infinitely better now that everything was out in the open. 'Once I was on the mend, I decided to wait until you came home to tell you. You have enough to cope with without having to worry about me.'

'I worry about you every day we're apart,' he muttered. 'I should have been here. You should have told me and not struggled on all on your own.'

Peggy was about to tell him she hadn't been on her own at all, when his lips silenced her and his hands began to move over her body, making her feel all unnecessary.

'I don't want to hurt you, Peg,' he murmured against her mouth. 'Is it all right if we . . . ?'

'Yes, oh yes,' she whispered.

It was quite a long time later before they lay still and sated in each other's arms, the warm glow of the night light bringing an added sense of comfort and security as they listened to the rain spatter against the window and the sound of their sleeping daughter's soft snuffles.

They'd been too lost in their own private little world to take much notice of the sounds outside their bedroom door as the others came back from the pub, and Peggy was surprised to see that the bedside clock showed it was now almost midnight.

She tenderly traced Jim's face with her fingers as she looked into his eyes. Her heart was full now he was finally home, and she was determined to treasure every precious minute. 'I do love you, Jim,' she whispered, 'and I'm sorry I didn't tell you about the op earlier. But I didn't have to struggle on my own, really I didn't.'

His warm hand gently stroked her shoulder. 'I just wish I hadn't been so far away,' he murmured.

Peggy had wished that too, but there was a war on, Jim was in the army and as there had been absolutely nothing she could do about it, there was little point in turning it into a drama. She snuggled into his embrace. 'The girls and Cordelia were wonderful, and of course your father was an absolute brick – especially after Doris moved in and tried to take over.'

'Your sister moved in here?' He shifted his head on the pillow and looked at her in shock. 'Since when does the snooty Doris deign to put one of her dainty, expensively shod feet over my doorstep?'

Peggy giggled softly and told him how Doris had discovered that her husband, Ted, had been conducting a long affair with a rather blowsy woman who worked for him on the fish counter at the Home and Colonial. She went on to describe the run-ins Doris had had with the girls, Cordelia and Ron as they'd tried to get her to leave – and how Harvey had done his bit for the cause by constantly sticking his nose up her sister's skirt.

Jim looked astonished. 'You never wrote to me about any of this.'

'I couldn't really,' she admitted. 'Not without telling you about my op and everything.'

'So what happened?' His eyes suddenly widened in alarm. 'She's not still living here, is she?'

Peggy smiled and shook her head. 'It got to the stage where we thought she'd never leave. But Anthony rescued us by persuading her to return home where he could look after her. Ted ditched the floozy and moved into a flat above the shop, and has almost been forgiven. Doris now lets him visit for his tea three times a week.'

'Who'd have thought it,' said Jim in awe. 'I never suspected Ted had it in him to have an affair – let alone have the guts to admit it to the fearsome Doris. He's a brave man, so he is, and if I see him while I'm home, I'll buy him a drink.'

'Mind how you go, Jim,' Peggy warned. 'Doris is still prickly about the scandal it caused, and if she hears you're siding with Ted, it could upset the apple-cart and spoil things for Anthony. He and Suzy are keeping their fingers crossed that things will have settled down by Christmas so they don't disrupt the wedding.'

They held each other while they collapsed into stifled giggles, aware of the sleeping baby, but comfortable and snug with each other in this cocoon of soft light and downy blankets.

'I still can't believe you went through all that without telling me,' Jim murmured eventually. 'But I'm relieved that you're all right.' Laughter bubbled up again as he kissed the top of her head. 'Mind you, we can have some fun and not worry about you falling for another bairn. Five is quite enough to be going on with, and I don't think my army pay will stretch much further.'

Peggy said nothing as she curled into him, for he could never understand how sad she was that her child-bearing years were over. The signs that she was already going through the change were not something to discuss with a man, even if he was her husband, but they meant she was no longer young, and at times she found that rather depressing.

He seemed to sense her sadness. 'You are all right about it, aren't you, Peg?' he asked.

'Of course I am,' she replied with a spark of false brightness. 'I've got five children to worry about already, and with Daisy still in nappies, I simply couldn't cope with any more.'

'Well, you do have a houseful of people to look after – and that's enough even for you. It's probably for the best.'

Peggy knew he was right, but she still mourned the passing of her youth. Not wanting to dwell on such things at this happy time, she nestled her face into the lovely warm spot on his neck. 'That's enough talk for now,' she murmured as she playfully ran her fingers over the dark hairs on his chest and hooked a leg over his thigh. 'I'm feeling frisky again.'

Jim didn't respond to this in the way she'd expected. He went still, and then instead of returning her overtures, he moved back from her. 'Peggy,' he began hesitantly. 'Seeing how this is the time for confessions, there's something I need to tell you.'

Peggy's sensual mood disappeared and she was suddenly tense with fear. Jim was a handsome man, liked the company of pretty women, and enjoyed more than his fair share of flirting. Being so far from home, and in the company of men who might lead him astray, he was open to all sorts of temptations. She'd determinedly cast off any doubts as to his fidelity, but these were different, dangerous times and flattery could go to a man's head. Yet now all those doubts and fears returned with a vengeance.

'Go on,' she managed through a tight throat.

'I've been given eight days' leave, two of which will be spent travelling unfortunately, which was why I was able to wangle a lift on an army transport plane and get down here a bit early.'

He paused, clearly searching for the right words, and Peggy's tension grew as she wondered where on earth this was leading.

'It's a special leave, Peggy, because once it's over the army is sending me overseas.'

Peggy shot out of his embrace and stared at him in horrified disbelief. 'No, they can't,' she whispered fiercely. 'You did your bit in the last war, and you're too old to go off fighting.'

He shot her a wry grin. 'Thanks for reminding me of that, Peg – not that I need it. I feel my age every time we're sent over that torturous obstacle course.'

Icy fingers seemed to be crawling up her spine. 'Where are they sending you, Jim?'

'I'm not supposed to say,' he replied with a teasing smile.

Peggy jabbed him hard in the ribs. 'You'd better, or I'll beat it out of you,' she retorted.

Jim took a deep breath. 'I'm going to somewhere in the Far East,' he said.

'But that's where the Japs are!' She was chilled to the soul and fighting to keep back her tears as she thought of the terrible battles being fought on the other side of the world. 'Where, exactly, in the Far East?'

'India,' he replied as he reached for her hand.

'India?' she breathed. 'But the Japs are crawling all over India. It isn't safe.'

His fingers gripped hers as his expression became solemn. 'I won't be fighting, Peg. I'll be in charge of a motor pool for our combined services, repairing and servicing the trucks, jeeps, ambulances, and so on.'

As she stared at him through her unshed tears he drew her towards him and kissed her trembling lips. 'I'll be miles away from any action, I promise.'

'But you don't know that for sure, Jim. The army could send you anywhere.' She had a terrifying vision of jungles and sweltering heat, and her imagination took flight. 'There'll be snakes and spiders and horrible diseases you could catch – and that's without the danger of the Japs coming at you out of the jungle.'

He gave a soft chuckle. 'We'll be miles from any front line, and the army has an excellent medical service. We've already been put on special medicines to ward off malaria and suchlike.'

Peggy could only stare at him in horror, for she was still in shock and remained unconvinced.

Sensing this, Jim continued to reassure her. 'You know me, Peg. I'll find a cushy number like I always do, and stay well away from any trouble. Colonel Grafton is coming with us, and I'm well in enough with him after driving him about and servicing his car to wangle something.'

Peggy couldn't bear it any longer. She threw herself into his arms and burst into tears.

Chapter Five

Mary simply couldn't blot out the awful images that haunted her, and although Dr Haywood had given her something to help her to sleep, and she was snug and warm beneath the soft blankets and eiderdown in one of Barbara's voluminous winceyette nightdresses, she lay awake in the darkness of the unfamiliar bedroom for many hours after she'd heard Joseph returning from fighting the fire.

Mary had seen enough of the inferno to know that it had destroyed everything she'd deemed precious – and even though she'd recently longed to escape the strictures of her domestic life and her mother's cruel tongue, she'd cried bitter tears for the loss of both parents and the only home she'd ever known. The knowledge that she would never again talk to her kind and gentle father, and had lost any hope of hearing the words of love she'd so longed for from her mother, was unbearable, for she hadn't even had the chance to say goodbye.

As her tears finally dried and the initial shock and horror of what she'd witnessed slowly ebbed, reason took over, and she realised that even if she had been there, she couldn't have saved them, for she too would have perished. Yet the guilt remained, for she'd deceived them during the final hours of their lives, and it was too late to ask for forgiveness.

She must have finally fallen asleep, for when she next opened her eyes it was to the sound of a ringing telephone, clattering milk pails and the tramp of booted feet on cobbles beneath her window. Disorientated momentarily by the unusual noises, she sat up in bed and tried to figure out where she was. And then, with blinding clarity, she remembered.

Mary felt the loss weighing heavy on her heart as the tears ran hotly down her face and she sank back into the pillows. Pulling the covers over her, she muffled her sobs, curling into her grief, unable to contemplate a new day without her parents or her home – or anything that she'd once considered to be set in stone.

The door creaked and light footsteps entered. 'Oh, Mary,' sighed Barbara as she perched on the side of the bed, drew back the covers and stroked her hair. 'Come on, love, you don't have to grieve alone.'

Mary flung herself into Barbara's motherly embrace and held on to her tightly as sorrow overwhelmed her. 'I never had time to tell them I loved them,' she sobbed. 'I didn't even go up to see Mother after we got home from Mrs Perry's, and the last words we had were angry and bitter, and I resented her for not loving me – for calling me names and . . .'

Barbara held her until the storm of tears was over,

rocking her as if she was a small, injured child, murmuring soft words of comfort. 'There, there, Mary, it's all right, really it is. Your father knew you loved him as he loved you, and your mother . . . Well, she had her own way about her, but I'm sure that deep down she did love you – she just found it hard to show it, that's all.'

'But I sneaked out to meet Jack at the station,' Mary gulped, 'and Daddy forbade me to go and thought I was safe in bed. I was going to tell him today and hoped he'd forgive me. Now it's too late.'

'Mary, you mustn't punish yourself thinking like that. You're a young girl, and in love. Of course you wanted to see our Jack off, and I'm sure your father would have come to understand why you disobeyed him.' Barbara gently extricated herself from Mary's arms, turned on the bedside light and gave her a handkerchief. 'Dry your eyes, love,' she said as she tenderly smoothed back the dark hair from the hot, tear-streaked face.

Mary did so, and then leant her cheek into that caressing hand, taking strength and courage from the knowledge that someone understood and cared. 'I'm sorry to be such a cry-baby,' she managed through the lump in her throat.

'You have absolutely nothing to apologise for,' said Barbara firmly. 'Tears are necessary and healing at a time like this.' Her broad, homely face wrinkled into a sweet smile. 'Goodness me, Mary, I've known you since you were a little girl. And with you and Jack being so close, you're as dear to me as a daughter, so you must never feel you're any kind of nuisance.'

The lovely sentiment comforted Mary, making her feel suddenly safe – but then she remembered the troop train and the enemy bombers. She was about to ask if there'd been news, yet quickly held back. Barbara might not have realised the danger Jack had been in last night, and she didn't want to upset her. 'I expect Jack will ring when he gets to the training camp,' she said instead.

'Oh, he already has,' Barbara replied brightly as she adjusted her apron over her well-upholstered bosom. 'That was him just a while back, from some telephone box in the middle of the moors. He arrived safely, but he said the journey was a bit hairy, because shortly after they'd left Hillney they were dive-bombed by Stukas. There was no damage done, and after a lot of stopping and starting they made camp at three this morning.'

The relief was immense, and Mary sagged back against the pillows. 'I was so afraid for him – for all those boys,' she said. 'I saw the bombers following the tracks as I was on my way home and thought . . .'

'Now don't go fretting over Jack,' soothed Barbara. 'He's absolutely fine, and told me to tell you he loves you and wishes he could be with you. And that he'll write the first chance he gets.'

'Does he know about . . . ?'

Barbara nodded and quickly handed Mary a cup

of tea from the tray she had brought in with her, before the tears started again. 'Drink your tea and eat the toast, then have a bath. I know it's still dark outside, but we start our days very early here.'

Mary nodded, and found that the tea did restore her spirits a little. 'Where are my clothes?' she asked, for there were only her shoes by the chair.

'Your coat is in the boot room, and I've washed everything else,' said Barbara. 'But I've dug out some bits and pieces which I think will fit you. I put them in the bathroom, which you'll find down the landing on your left.' She gave a wry smile as she ran her work-roughened hands over her plump hips. 'They certainly don't fit me any more, but at least they'll serve a purpose until your other things are dry and we can sort you out something better.'

'You're very kind, Auntie Barbara. Thank you so much.'

Barbara kissed her cheek. 'We're just glad to give you a home, Mary, and to provide some love and comfort at this very sad time.' She got up from the bed and smiled down at her. 'Now you sort yourself out, then come and find me in the kitchen.'

Once Barbara had left, Mary drank her tea and tried very hard to contain the overwhelming emotions she was experiencing after the night's events. Nibbling on the delicious buttery toast, she marvelled at the love she'd been shown by Jack's parents, and knew she could never hope to repay such kindness.

Determinedly blinking back the tears, she took in her surroundings. She had been coming to Jack's home since she was a small girl, for Emmaline had often been too busy with her charity work to mind her all day, and Barbara had gladly taken her in. She could remember having delicious teas in the large warm kitchen, and sitting with Jack on one of the sagging couches in the snug sitting room while Barbara cuddled them and read them stories, or let them listen to *Children's Hour* on the wireless. She could also remember hectic games of hide and seek amongst the barns and sheds, and how they'd dressed up from the large collection of coats, caps and boots that were scattered about in the chaotic and cluttered boot room. And yet she'd never been upstairs before.

The bedroom had the same warm, homely feel about it as the rest of the house, for it was snug beneath a sloping beamed ceiling, with blackout-lined sprigged curtains pulled over the small diamond-paned window, and a home-made patchwork quilt covering the sturdy iron bedstead that was made up with crisp white linen and downy blankets. The walls were whitewashed between the beams, the wooden floor dipping towards the window where a small dressing table stood in the narrow alcove. A heavy wardrobe took up most of one wall, and beside the bed were an upholstered nursing chair and a small chest of drawers.

Mary finished her breakfast in bed – a luxury she'd

never had before – and, refusing to let her emotions get the better of her again, hitched up the long night-dress and padded barefoot across the creaking floor to the window. Drawing back the curtain she saw that the sky was lightening into a grey dawn, and she could make out the cobbled yard below, and the collection of sheds and barns that stood on the edge of the field. Beyond that, stands of trees and lines of hedgerows led to the rolling hills of the South Downs. It must have rained again, for the corrugated iron roofs of the outbuildings gleamed wetly and there were puddles in the cobbles which the land girls were splashing through in their heavy boots.

She turned from the window and hesitantly made her way out of the bedroom and along the corridor in search of the bathroom. The bath proved to be a vast cast-iron tub with brass taps that took up most of the small room. There were towels on a rail, warming by the broad brick chimney breast that rose from the large kitchen range through the centre of the house, and a soft mat to stand on by the bath. A bar of soap, a sponge and a small bottle of shampoo sat on the wooden chair beside a neat pile of clothes, and there was a new toothbrush and tube of paste waiting for her on the basin. Mary was quite overcome by it all, for it was far removed from the arctic wastelands of the bathroom in the rectory.

Not wanting to dwell on such things, she quickly bathed, mindful of the small amount of water allocated for such purposes, and then got dressed. The knickers were as big as barrage balloons and the brassiere was so large it was of no use at all. Barbara's old worn dungarees swamped her and she had to hitch them up at the waist and use the belt to keep them – and the knickers – up; the knitted vest hung almost to her knees, but was an added layer against the cold, as were the blouse and bulky sweater. Pulling on the thick socks, she tied the laces on her shoes and then, pushing back the stark realisation that she owned only the clothes she'd been wearing the night before, and a battered bicycle, she cleaned her teeth.

Returning to the bedroom, where Barbara had laid out a brush, comb, hairpins and face powder on the dressing table, Mary avoided looking in the mirror, standing at the window to brush out her hair. The cows were moaning as they were herded out of the milking sheds by the land girls and harried back into the field by the dogs. The sky was pearly grey now, the distant hills clearer. The new day had begun, and she knew she must face it with the courage and strength that her father would have expected of her.

Mary made the bed and carried the stone hot-water bottle down the narrow winding wooden stairs to the kitchen. A large scrubbed pine table and a dozen chairs took up a good deal of the central space, the grey flagstone floor had also been scrubbed, and a huge pine dresser laden with crockery took up an entire wall. Pots and pans hung from hooks above the gleaming black range in the chimney hearth, and a stone sink and wooden draining board stood beneath the iron-framed window that looked over the yard. Black Briar Farm hadn't changed since she'd come here as a toddler, and as always it seemed to wrap itself around her like a lovely comforting blanket.

Barbara smiled in greeting as she continued to stir something in a large black pot on the range. 'You look better,' she said comfortably. 'Nice bath?'

Mary smiled back. 'It was lovely,' she replied rather shyly. 'Thank you for the toothpaste and soap and everything. And for the clothes.'

Barbara's smile broadened as she regarded her get-up. 'It looks like we'll have to kit you out from the WVS,' she said. 'I can't possibly let you go about looking like that, and as I'm on duty this afternoon, we can go together and find something that actually fits you.'

Mary didn't really care what she looked like, for it didn't matter, but she nodded and went to empty the hot-water bottle into the sink. Barbara was being so kind, but the realisation that she would have to rely on charity until she found her feet again made Mary fret. If only she was qualified to do something, she thought in despair, she wouldn't have to be so reliant on people such as the good-hearted Joseph and Barbara.

Barbara must have read her thoughts, for she left the range and came to stand beside her. 'Mary, I don't want you worrying about things,' she said softly. 'I realise you feel lost and terribly adrift at the moment, but you aren't alone, my dear. Joseph and I will look after you.'

Mary could only nod, for tears were threatening again.

Barbara took the stone bottle from her and placed it on the drainer. 'Now, I know things are going to be difficult for a while, but Joseph and I will see to all the arrangements and deal with the authorities. We'll sort out a new ration book and identity card for you, and deal with any legal or insurance matters. Joseph is very good at that sort of thing, and will make sure you get what you're entitled to.'

Mary hadn't given a thought to such things, so deep was her grief, and she looked at Barbara in confusion. 'The rectory belongs to the church, and I doubt Father had the money to pay any life insurance,' she said. 'But I'll do my best to find some work so I can at least give you some rent.'

Barbara put a comforting arm about her shoulders. 'Bless you, love. You don't have to think about things like work – not for a while yet. It's best to settle and come to terms with the situation first, then we can all sit down and discuss what you might do.'

'That's the problem,' Mary replied, her voice rasping with frustration. 'I'm no good at anything, and without my teaching certificate I won't be allowed to take any classes.'

'As I said,' Barbara spoke with infinite patience,

'we'll sort all that out another time. It's far too soon to be making those sorts of decisions.'

Mary nodded, for she knew she was right, but the thought of being a burden, of stretching the housekeeping and rationing even further, worried her. 'Then I'll do the housework and cooking for you,' she said. 'I know how to do that, and I can do the shopping, which will save you from having to queue for hours.'

'We'll see,' murmured Barbara.

Mary wanted so badly to help, to be useful. 'I'll go to the rectory later and see if I can salvage anything. You never know, there might be furniture or crockery, or . . .' She tailed off as she saw Barbara shake her head.

'I'm sorry, Mary, but everything has gone, including most of the church. Joseph went down there at first light, and all he could find was an old tin trunk.'

Mary stared at her, unable to absorb the fact that both the rectory and the church had been destroyed. 'Daddy's trunk?' she breathed finally. 'But how? He kept it under the stairs, so it must have been right in the heart of the fire.'

Barbara shrugged. 'I don't know. It's a bit buckled, bent and scorched, but it seems to have come through. Joseph put it in the small barn out of the way until you're ready to look through it.'

Mary took a steadying breath. 'I don't know if I can face it just yet, but I doubt there's anything of interest in it,' she said sadly. 'Daddy only used it to store old parish records.'

'Well, you know where it is,' Barbara murmured.

A silence fell between them, and Mary knew it was time to ask the question that had been troubling her all night. 'Where have they taken my parents?'

'The ambulance people took them to the hospital morgue in Hillney. They will remain there until we've made the arrangements with Mr Clough the undertaker.'

'I see.' Mary remembered her vow to be strong and blinked back the tears. 'I'd like the service to be held in Daddy's church,' she said. 'It's what he and Mother would have wanted. Is it really in ruins?'

Barbara's expression was solemn. 'I'm sorry, love, but the church won't be used again. But I'm sure we can arrange for them to be laid to rest in the churchyard.' She gave Mary a gentle hug. 'We'll see to that, never you worry.'

Mary nodded, unable to speak for the knot of tears in her throat.

'Come on,' coaxed Barbara, 'let's get our coats on and scrub out the dairy. There's nothing like a bit of hard work to keep our minds off things, and I don't trust those city girls to clean it properly. If it isn't up to scratch, I'll have the milk inspector round here complaining, and he's a horrid little man with a Hitler moustache and a total lack of humour.'

Mary dredged up a wan smile and trudged after her into the cluttered boot room. Being brave and stoic was much harder than she could ever have imagined, but she was determined to do her very best.

Peggy had lain awake for what seemed like hours after Jim had fallen asleep. She revelled in the lovely warmth of his long, strong body lying beside her and the soft snores she'd missed for such ages. But her mind was racing, despite his many assurances that he'd be far from harm's way, and her dread for him had deepened as the night wore on.

India was on the other side of the world, and even the journey there was fraught with danger, for the seas were the hunting grounds of the enemy U-boats which had caused such devastation to the supply convoys. It would take weeks to get there, and home leaves would be a thing of the past – for perhaps months, or even years. The thought of being apart from Jim for so long, and the realisation that Daisy was so young she might not remember him when he finally came home, tore at her heart.

And what of her other children? Bob and Charlie were miles away in Somerset with Anne and baby Rose Margaret, and none of them would get a chance to see him before he left. This war was tearing her family apart, scattering them to the four winds, and although she could take a little comfort from the fact that Cissy was a WAAF at the nearby aerodrome and could visit during his leave, she knew the girl would be heartbroken to learn of her father's overseas posting.

She must have fallen asleep at one point, for she woke to the sounds of Daisy grizzling and Jim's heavy snoring. Sliding quietly out of bed so as not to disturb him, she rammed her feet into her slippers, pulled on her dressing gown, and went to the cot. Lifting Daisy out, she bundled her in a blanket against the howling draught which came under the bedroom door and around the loose-fitting sash windows, and carried her into the warm kitchen.

Having stripped off her sodden nappy, Peggy bathed her in the sink and quickly dressed her in her prettiest knitted outfit – not that it would stay clean for long, she thought wearily, for Daisy was crawling now and getting into everything. She drew back the blackout curtains to find that it was barely past dawn and there were already dark clouds scudding across the sky – not a good omen for the day ahead.

Having heated up some milk, she gave Daisy a cuddle while she drank from her bottle, and was soothed by the weight of her in her arms, and her lovely baby smell. The house was quiet but for the usual creak of old timbers and the rattle of ancient pipes, and Peggy was glad to have these few moments alone with her baby so she could gather her wits, prepare for the day, and put on a brave face for everyone.

The back door slammed and Harvey came racing up the cellar stairs, tail wagging as he greeted Daisy by licking her cheek, at which she gurgled in delight and batted him with her tiny fist.

'Good morning, Peggy girl,' said Ron as he stomped into the kitchen. 'Get down ye eejit dog,' he rasped. 'Daisy doesn't need you washing her face.'

'Morning, Ron,' Peggy replied as she wiped Daisy's face clean of slobber. 'I haven't had time to put the kettle on, or start on the porridge. This one was up and grizzling, so I needed to keep her quiet in case she woke Jim.'

Ron stumped across the kitchen in his dirty wellingtons and put the kettle on the hob. Then he rattled the fire into life and added some more wood. 'So, how is the boy?' he said as he reached for the teapot.

'He's fine,' she replied.

Ron paused and looked at her from beneath his wayward brows, his blue eyes penetrating in their intensity. 'What's the matter, Peggy?'

'Nothing,' she retorted as she lifted her chin.

He sat down beside her at the kitchen table. 'You don't fool me, Peggy Reilly,' he said softly. 'Come on, out with it. What's wrong?'

Peggy tried desperately to be calm and accepting, but her voice betrayed her inner turmoil. 'He's on embarkation leave,' she told him tremulously. 'They're sending him to India.'

Ron paled and sat back in his chair. 'India? To be sure that's a far place to be going.'

'Aye, it is,' said Jim as he strolled into the kitchen in his rather splendid dressing gown. 'And I don't want any long faces or tears spoiling this leave. I'm thinking it will be an adventure to go travelling and visit all those exotic places I've only seen on a map.' His handsome face was quite youthful as he broke into a smile. 'At least I won't have to put up with English winters like poor old Frank stuck up there in the wilds of Yorkshire.'

Harvey was ecstatic to have Jim home again and he danced round his legs, jumping up to lick his face as Ron shoved back from the table and opened his arms to his son. With the dog whining and twisting at their knees, the two men embraced.

'Ach, Da, it's good to see you again,' said Jim. He grinned down at his father, who was a couple of inches shorter. 'I see you've had a haircut, Da. But d'ye not possess a single decent stitch of clothing to wear?'

Ron cuffed him on the arm. 'Aye, I do that,' he replied, 'but 'tis not for you that I wear me best.'

Jim laughed. 'It's about time you made an honest woman of Rosie,' he teased. 'How many years have you two been courting?'

'Enough,' said Ron with a sniff. 'Not that it's any of your business.' He went to make the tea while Jim made a fuss of a delighted and overexcited Harvey, who was trying to climb into his arms.

Peggy smiled fondly at the two men. Jim and his dad were as bad as each other – a couple of rogues who made great use of their blarney and the lilting, peaty Irish brogue to charm them out of trouble. As the pair of them settled down at the table to drink tea and yarn, she put Daisy in the playpen that was jammed in the corner so she could organise the porridge and set the table. If she kept busy she wouldn't think – and no matter how hard she might find it, she was determined to treasure every single moment of Jim's leave and not spoil it by being gloomy and frightened.

'I expect Frank's looking forward to getting his discharge papers,' Ron muttered after he'd listened to Jim's amusing tales of devilish obstacle courses and how he'd constantly had to dodge the sergeant major's beady eyes. 'What are his plans for when he comes home?'

'He's going back to fishing,' said Jim. 'With the convoys running the gauntlet of the U-boats, and fish not being rationed, he thinks he can still make a living out of it.'

'Aye, but it's a dangerous pursuit, what with all the mines in the Channel,' Ron remarked. He heaved a sigh and lit his pipe. 'Still, it's what he knows best, and it's a waste to leave a good fishing boat idle on the beach.'

Their conversation was interrupted by Jane who came bouncing into the kitchen, her long fair plait bobbing on her back as she gave Jim a swift hug of welcome and helped herself to a bowl of porridge and cup of tea. As she chattered away to him about the lovely shire horses she looked after at the dairy, and the customers who liked to gossip as she delivered their milk, the mood lightened considerably.

Minutes after she'd left on Peggy's old bike, Rita, Suzy, Sarah and Fran came in and with cries of welcome, hugged and kissed Jim, then settled down to breakfast before they started their shifts.

As the girls quickly cleared their dishes and pulled on thick coats against the wind which was buffeting the house, they all agreed that a bit of a party had to be organised for that evening. They left the house chattering and giggling, stopping at the back gate to say goodbye to Sarah before they headed for Camden Road, the hospital and fire station.

'Well, nothing's changed, I can see,' said Jim as he sipped his cup of tea and ruffled a swooning Harvey's ears. 'Those girls are like a flock of starlings with all their chatter. But it livens up the house and must make good company for you, Peggy.'

Peggy shot him a wry smile. 'They keep me on my toes, that's for certain,' she replied.

'Aye, you said in your letters,' he grinned. 'Fran seems to be over her broken heart, Suzy's radiant, Jane and Sarah obviously feel very at home – and little Rita is positively blooming, despite the motorcycle boots and that awful moth-eaten flying jacket she insists upon wearing. You're doing all right with those girls, Peggy.'

'Well, it's about time you showed your face,' said Cordelia as she came into the kitchen. 'Never mind those girls. How about a welcome hug for me?'

'Mrs Finch! Top of the morning to you, darlin'.' Jim gave her a beaming smile. 'How's my favourite girl, then? Have you missed me?'

'I've missed your blarney,' she retorted, with a twinkle of mischief in her blue eyes. 'I'd have thought the army would have knocked that out of you by now.'

He roared with laughter. 'Ach, it would take more than the army to do that,' he said. 'The sight of your pretty blue eyes is poetry so it is, and I can't help meself.' He carefully wrapped his arms around her and gently lifted her off her feet so he could plant a smacking kiss on both her cheeks.

Cordelia went scarlet and twittered like a flustered sparrow as she dangled in his arms. 'Put me down, you big lummox,' she ordered as she playfully beat against his chest and failed completely to hide her delight.

'Ach, Cordelia Finch, you're a sight for sore eyes,' Jim teased as he kept her several inches from the floor and slowly danced about the kitchen. 'But I hear you've been walking out with someone else, and me heart is broken, so it is.'

'That's quite enough of that,' she said, attempting to look stern. 'Bertram and I merely play bridge now and again, and go for little rides in his car,' she went on primly. 'I'm far too old for any other nonsense.'

Jim chuckled as he carefully set her back on her feet and made sure she was steady before he let her go. 'To be sure you're a spring chicken, and if Da can go courting then I don't see why you can't be going tiptoe through the tulips with Bertram.'

'Bertram does not tiptoe anywhere,' Cordelia giggled. 'In fact he spends most of his time stomping around a golf course.'

'I'll be thanking you to remember that Cordelia is at least a decade older than me,' grumbled Ron good-naturedly. 'And as deaf as a post.'

'Do you see what I have to put up with?' Cordelia asked Jim with a twinkle in her eyes, as she adjusted her half-moon spectacles and tried to look disapproving. 'Is it any wonder I have to find some decent male company outside this house?' She looked Ron up and down and gave an exasperated sigh. 'What Rosie Braithwaite finds to admire in him is beyond me.'

Ron stuck out his broad chest like a pouter pigeon. 'She can see a fine figure of a man who has all his teeth and hair and can hear what she's saying,' he retorted.

'I always knew you had an inflated idea of yourself,' Cordelia muttered without rancour as she plumped down at the table. 'Rosie's eyesight must be failing.' She shot Ron a naughty grin to take the sting out of her words.

'When you've all quite finished bickering,' put in a very amused Peggy, 'it's time to finish your breakfast and make plans for this party.'

Cordelia perked up instantly. 'We're having a

party?' She clapped her hands. 'Oh, how lovely. Will there be sherry and dancing?'

'I don't know about the sherry,' said Peggy.

'She had enough to sink a battleship last night, and I had to virtually carry her home,' muttered Ron.

'I was merely a little unsteady on my feet after sitting for so long on that nasty hard chair,' protested Cordelia.

'Well, as long as you had a good time, it doesn't matter,' said Peggy. 'But Jim and Ron will have to clear the dining room if you want dancing. It's become a bit of a glory hole over the past few months.'

'I might have known you'd find things for us to do,' muttered Ron. 'No doubt you've a long list hidden somewhere.' He winced dramatically and clasped his lower spine. 'To be sure 'tis a burden, Jim, to be bullied when this weather is playing havoc with me shrapnel.'

'That excuse is wearing very thin,' Cordelia declared disapprovingly. 'If you ask me, there never was any in the first place.'

'To be sure I never asked you,' he rumbled. 'But if you're after seeing me scar, then I'm happy to oblige.' He pulled up his shirt to reveal a taut abdomen and made to unfasten the bit of string that served as a belt to hold up his disreputable trousers.

Cordelia went scarlet once more and covered her face with her hands. 'You'll do no such thing,' she spluttered. 'I haven't had my breakfast yet.'

'Ron, really,' protested Peggy, who'd swallowed her tea the wrong way and was trying to laugh and cough at the same time.

'Well, she's questioning me war wound,' he replied with wide-eyed innocence that fooled no one. 'It comes to something when an old soldier is mocked,' he added gloomily.

'You're always coming the old soldier, Da,' laughed Jim, 'and I'm thinkin' you'll not be fooling anyone in this house today.' He finished his porridge and pushed back from the table. 'I'll be having a bath and getting dressed. Then Da and me will sort out the dining room for you, Peg.'

'Aye, and then we'll be off to the Anchor to organise the drinks,' said Ron cheerfully.

'I thought it wouldn't be long before you decided that,' Peggy said drily. She wagged a finger at the pair of them. 'Just don't take all day. I know what you two are like once you start drinking.'

'Ach, Peggy darlin',' as if we'd spend all day at the Anchor when there are things to do here about the house,' Jim murmured as he kissed her cheek and shot her an impish wink.

'Ach, Jim darlin',' she replied with a giggle, 'as if I'm fool enough to believe I'll see either of you for the rest of the day.'

Chapter Six

Mary had come to know the eight land girls from her previous visits to Black Briar Farm, and was genuinely touched by their sincere condolences – especially when Judy, a quiet little girl from Essex, handed her a scruffy brown paper parcel. 'We've had a whip-round,' she said shyly before scurrying off to catch up with the others.

Mary knew that none of the girls had very much in the way of luxuries, but as she'd opened the parcel, she'd been quite overcome by their generosity. There was a pretty tortoiseshell comb to put in her hair, the end of a lovely pink lipstick, a bag of boiled sweets, a couple of rather tattered books, two headscarves and a pair of woollen gloves.

However, the girls weren't the only ones who wanted to show their sympathy in a practical and loving way, for by lunchtime there had been a stream of visitors from the village and its surrounds, who brought gifts of clothing, writing materials, books and prayer cards – and even shoes and a pair of wellingtons.

'I feel so blessed by everyone's kindness,' she said to Barbara as they sat at the kitchen table later that morning. 'They have little enough as it is, and yet they've given me so much.'

Barbara nodded as she regarded the pile of things on the table. 'It's always been a close community,' she replied. 'We like to take care of our own in times of trouble.'

Mary pulled a pretty blue sweater from the tangle. 'But this has hardly been worn,' she breathed, 'and neither has this skirt – or these shoes.' She blinked back the ready tears. 'Everything is lovely,' she murmured, 'and far nicer than anything I had before.'

'Your parents were much loved, and so are you,' said Barbara as she scooped up the nightdresses, petticoats and a somewhat worn and faded dressing gown. 'I'll give these a bit of a wash, while you polish up those shoes and put the rest away.' She shot Mary a wry smile. 'The stuff you're wearing can come with us to the WVS centre this afternoon. They're bound to fit someone.'

Mary took the wellingtons and two pairs of lace-up shoes into the boot room, hunted out the brushes and tins of polish and buffed up the scuffed leather shoes until they shone. Then she returned to the kitchen to gather up her wonderfully generous gifts and carry them upstairs. The kindness that everyone had shown amazed her, and as she tried on skirts, trousers, sweaters and blouses she felt warmed by the spirit in which they'd been given.

By miraculous chance everything fitted but for

the beautiful black velvet evening gown which had been donated by the doughty wife of the district councillor, who lived in a huge house just outside the village. But even that could be taken to pieces and made into something she could wear, for the velvet was soft, and still in remarkably good condition.

Mary carefully hung it in the wardrobe, folded up Barbara's clothes and then changed into a pair of grey worsted slacks, white blouse and the gorgeous blue sweater which had come from the grocer's wife. The only thing she needed now was some proper underwear – but even cheap Utility knickers, vests and bras would require clothing coupons, and as she didn't have any she'd have to ask Barbara if she could borrow some.

Brushing her hair back from her face, she twisted it into a knot and tethered it with pins before sliding in the pretty comb on one side. She briefly regarded her reflection in the dressing-table mirror and although she looked very smart in her new clothes, she could see how pale and drawn she was, with dull, almost bruised eyes that stared back at her with profound sadness. Turning away with a deep sigh, she looked out of the window and saw that the sky was leaden, with black clouds scudding over the Downs and promising rain. The bleakness of the scene echoed the grief in her heart.

As her gaze drifted from the girls who were working in the ploughed fields to the smallest of the three barns, she thought about her father's trunk. It was all she had left of him, but the thought of opening it and prying into something he'd always kept private didn't sit well with her. She knew her reluctance was all part of her grief, and accepted that she wasn't yet ready to face whatever he'd hidden in there – however impersonal.

Mary turned from the window, picked up the bundle of Barbara's clothes and was carrying it downstairs when she heard the voice of the rural dean coming from the kitchen. She paused on the stairs, tempted to return to her room until he'd gone, for although her mother had thought he was wonderful, Mary had never liked him, and neither had her father.

The dean should have retired at least eight years ago, but he'd held on to the position with the tenacity of a leech, and once war was declared he'd simply stayed on. He wasn't a big man, but he made up for his size by being pompous and overbearing, and his poor little wife, Marjorie, ran about endlessly trying to placate and please him. His hands were delicate and soft like a woman's and his hair was a little too dark for a man his age, but it was the fish-eyed stare and pious sneer that made him unlike-able.

Mary dithered, then came to the conclusion that it was unfair to leave Barbara to deal with him alone. She took a deep breath and prepared herself for a long speech of condolence, which would, no doubt, completely gloss over the antagonism which had lain between him and her father for so many years. Clutching the folded clothes, she reluctantly went down the stairs.

The dean got to his feet, his expression suitably forlorn as she entered the kitchen and dumped the clothes on a nearby chair. 'Mary, my dear child,' he said as he grasped both her hands. 'Please allow me to offer my deepest condolences at this very sad time. My sorrow at your parents' passing has brought me to despair, for I feel as if I have lost my very best friends. But I have found comfort in the knowledge that they are now with God – and I hope that this too will be of some consolation to you.'

Mary eased her hands from his clammy grip and edged away. 'Thank you, Dean,' she replied. 'It's very kind of you to come all this way when I know how busy you are.'

He puffed out his chest and his face took on a sanctimonious expression as he placed a delicate white hand over his heart. 'But my dear child, how could I not? You have suffered – as we all have suffered – from your tragic loss. What is a twenty-mile journey on a very busy day when one of my flock is in need of succour?'

Mary had no reply to this, so she sat down and nodded her thanks to Barbara as she handed her a cup of tea.

The dean settled back comfortably in the wooden carver and adjusted his tailored suit jacket to cover his paunch. 'Mrs Boniface tells me that you've refused to have the service in my church at Hillney.'

'That's right,' said Mary, determined not to be intimidated by his stern gaze.

'That is a great shame,' he sighed. He plucked at a button on his jacket. 'Mrs Boniface also tells me she has already spoken to the undertaker, and that the funeral will be next week.'

Mary nodded. 'Eleven o'clock next Monday,' she managed as her throat tightened.

'I will, of course, be officiating at the service,' he said as he reached for the plate of biscuits. 'Your father was not only a close friend, but a stalwart member of my church. And Mrs Boniface has assured me that in the absence of your usual grave-digger, who has sadly passed away, her husband will prepare the ground in the churchyard for the interment. One can only thank God that it is still possible after His church has been so cruelly destroyed.'

Mary suddenly had an awful vision of two coffins being lowered into the cold, damp ground beside the ruined church. She gave a shiver and grasped Barbara's hand as she looked back at the dean. 'That's very kind of you and Joseph,' she said tremulously. 'Everyone is being so very thoughtful.'

'I don't think we need to discuss such things,' said Barbara rather flatly. 'Mary is upset enough already.'

'Of course, of course,' he said coolly, 'but these

practicalities must be faced.' He lifted his chin, his protuberant eyes glassy, his expression pious. 'Death, after all, is only the beginning of eternal life. Our earthly bodies are mere husks to be returned to the soil – and as we go to God, our souls are freed from this mortal world to take up their rightful place in Paradise.'

Barbara's lips thinned. 'I'm sure Mary finds great comfort in your words, but I think it would be best if we concentrated on the sort of service she would like.'

Mary was soothed by Barbara's understanding, for the dean's pontificating had begun to irritate her. As for his conducting the service, she knew she must speak out now before it was too late. The dean was known to give tediously long speeches at gravesides.

'I'd really appreciate it if the service wasn't too long,' she said with as much tact as she could. 'Most of the congregation is elderly, and with this bitter weather I wouldn't like them to be standing about and catching a chill.'

The dean looked rather shocked by this. 'But my dear child,' he protested. 'Your father and mother must have all due honour paid to their sterling service to the church – and as you refuse to allow me to conduct a full service in my church, then . . .'

'I do see your point,' she interrupted swiftly. 'But that doesn't have to mean a long, drawn-out cere-mony with lots of speeches.' He was about to protest, so she carried on quickly, 'If he agrees, I'd like Dr

Haywood to say a few words. He and Father have been friends for years, and Mother thought very highly of him.'

After an initial tightening of his lips at the idea of the doctor playing any part in the proceedings, he nodded solemnly. 'I too would like to say a few words,' he said as he chewed on a second biscuit. 'And although the Bishop will not be able to attend due to his heavy responsibilities, I'm sure he will gladly prepare a short, fitting eulogy which I can read out.'

Mary dipped her chin and gave a deep sigh. She was dreading the whole thing, and knew now that no matter what she said, the dean would have his way, and the ceremony would be dragged out to fulfil his need for grandstanding.

Reaching for a third biscuit, he contemplated it for a moment before he spoke. 'The Church will of course provide pastoral care, and find you cheap accommodation until you have the means to support yourself,' he said before dunking the biscuit into his tea.

'There's no need for that,' said Barbara as she moved the plate of biscuits out of his reach. 'Mary will be living here.'

He eyed her coolly. 'That is very charitable of you, Mrs Boniface.'

'It's not charity,' she replied briskly. 'We've taken her in because she's one of us and we love her.'

'Very commendable, I'm sure.' He finished the

biscuit, swallowed the last of his tea and brushed crumbs from his jacket. 'Church funds will pay for the service and the funeral expenses – as long as they are not too high – but I'm afraid that is all the financial help we can offer. We are not a rich organisation, and in these troubled times our fiscal responsibilities are stretched to the limit.'

Mary saw the disgust on Barbara's face, and knew her dislike for the dean could barely be contained, and that it was only through an innate sense of courtesy that she didn't speak out.

Mary felt the same way, for the Church had always pleaded poverty when it came to mending the organ, dealing with the woodworm in the rafters and repairing the rectory roof – and paying their vicars a decent stipend. Yet it was common knowledge that the Church of England was one of the richest landowners in the country, and that the extravagantly robed Bishops and Archbishops lived in palaces while the ancient churches crumbled.

'Don't you worry, Mary,' soothed Barbara. 'There'll be government compensation of some sort even if the Church won't put its hand in its pocket.'

The dean clearly realised his presence was not having the effect he'd desired, so he rose from his chair and shook Barbara's hand 'I must take my leave.' He turned to Mary. 'Goodbye, my dear. I will pray for you in your hour of need.'

Mary only just managed not to flinch from his touch as she shook his hand and thanked him for his visit. As Barbara showed him to the door and finally shut it behind him, Mary breathed a sigh of relief.

'Pompous old hypocrite,' muttered Barbara. 'Men like him are the reason I rarely set foot inside a church these days.' She reached for Mary's hand across the table and smiled. 'That's not to say I didn't enjoy your father's sermons. He had such a lovely deep, tuneful voice that I could have listened to him reading from a laundry list.'

For all her determination not to cry, the tears welled as Mary remembered his wonderful sermons. 'Do you think Dr Haywood would read "And death shall have no dominion" by Dylan Thomas? It was one of Daddy's favourites.'

'I'm sure he would, if he has a copy of it. If he doesn't, I expect we can find it in the library at Hillney.'

Mary's sorrow deepened as she thought of those precious books at home being so utterly destroyed. 'Perhaps the bookshop will have a copy,' she said as she determinedly dried her eyes. 'I'd like to have one for myself.'

Barbara nodded, glanced at the kitchen clock and became businesslike. 'Everyone will be wondering where their lunch has got to,' she said as she took the baked potatoes out of the range oven, and ladled a good portion of stew into a smaller pot.

'That's for us,' she explained. 'The girls eat in their accommodation hut, so if you take the spuds and the bread, I'll carry this big pot of stew. Joseph is right out in the back fields all day, so he took his lunch in a Thermos.'

Mary realised Barbara was trying to keep her busy and out of the doldrums, so she swallowed her grief and helped to ferry the food across the cobbled yard to the barn which had been converted into living quarters for the land girls.

The accommodation consisted of a series of bunk beds at one end of the barn, a large scrubbed table and benches at the other, with two sagging couches, a stone sink and wooden drainer in the middle. The cooking and washing facilities were basic, with an outside lav, the sink, hot and cold water, and a two-ring gas burner. Heating and hot water were provided by a pot-bellied stove, and the girls' clothes were kept in a couple of wardrobes and chests of drawers that had definitely seen better days.

The concrete floor had been covered with a collection of moth-eaten rugs, and someone had gone to the trouble of making thick curtains to cover the two windows in an attempt to keep out the draughts. The eiderdowns were colourful, the floor had been swept and the washing-up was drying on the drainer. With bedclothes, books, make-up and magazines strewn about, and photographs of loved ones and favourite film stars pinned to the walls, it was clear the girls had made it as comfortable and homely as possible.

They were nowhere in sight, so Barbara turned on a gas ring to keep the stew warm while Mary quickly set the table. 'I let the girls come in for a bath twice a week, and most evenings they're either down at the pub or huddled round the stove,' Barbara said. 'Poor things have it rather tough out here, especially in the winter. But there simply isn't room to have them all in the house.'

'I certainly don't envy them,' said Mary as she looked around. 'It can't be easy to be so far from family and home comforts, camping out here and working such long hours.'

Barbara nodded. 'It's surprising how quickly some get used to it. I can usually tell within minutes if they're stayers or not.' She smiled brightly. 'Let's get back and have our lunch, then we can go into Hillney and sort out your ration book and so on before I have to be on duty at the WVS. I expect they'll give you emergency coupons, so you'll be able to go shopping for some decent underwear.'

Mary smiled back, warmed by her love and the security of knowing she didn't have to struggle through these dark days on her own.

The day had flown past, and now it was almost five o'clock, with still no sign of Ron or Jim. Peggy was tired and hot and beginning to get annoyed. 'You'd think that as this party is for Jim, he'd at least bother to come and do something to help,' she said in exasperation.

Cordelia wrapped the spam sandwiches in dampened tea towels to keep them fresh. 'Men can't be expected to be useful in a kitchen,' she said cheerfully as she bobbed her head in time with the music on the wireless. 'They'd only get in the way, and eat everything the minute it came out of the oven.'

'You're probably right,' Peggy conceded, for she remembered only too well how Ron had snaffled more than his fair share of buns and cake the last time she'd had a good cooking session.

She regarded the plates of food on the table with the sense of satisfaction for a job well done. Jane had brought some butter, cheese and cream from the dairy before she went on to her afternoon work in the clothing-factory accounts office, and Rita had been to see Alf the butcher and brought home sausages, suet and two tins of spam during her lunch break. Fred the fish had dropped in with a parcel of sprats, and his wife had very generously donated a jar of sugar and three eggs.

With all this bounty, including their own eggs and the white flour Ron had somehow managed to get from a mate who dealt in such things under the counter, Peggy and Cordelia had worked miracles. There were sausage rolls, Scotch eggs, sandwiches, cheese straws and an onion flan. The sprats would be dipped in flour and egg and fried nearer the time, and the crowning glory was the Victoria sponge, filled with Peggy's home-made raspberry jam and thick cream. She fetched a clean tablecloth and laid it almost reverently over everything so it would keep off any dust.

'I got a gaaaaal in Kalamazoo, zoo, zoo,' trilled Cordelia, out of tune, as her favourite song came on the wireless. 'Ooh, I am looking forward to the party,' she said as she washed her hands in the sink.

'I take it that means Bertram has accepted your invitation.' Peggy smiled at her.

'He certainly has,' she replied, 'and he's promised to teach me how to butterjug.'

'You mean jitterbug,' laughed Peggy as she rounded up a crawling Daisy who was intent on inspecting the coal scuttle, which Ron had left on the wrong side of the fireguard. 'I think that's a bit ambitious, and best left to the young ones,' she added.

Cordelia pulled a face. 'Bertram and I can cut a rug as well as any youngster,' she retorted. 'You wait and see.'

'Lord help us,' muttered Peggy, who had visions of an overexcited Cordelia doing herself serious damage.

She carried the squirming, protesting Daisy to the sink and washed her hands and face clean of jam, flour and coal dust. There wasn't much to be done about her filthy clothes, but as it would soon be time for her bath and then bed, it didn't really matter.

The back door slammed and Harvey raced into the kitchen, shot his nose up Cordelia's skirt, licked Daisy who was now sitting on the floor, and then put his great paws on the table to sniff at the covered food.

'Get down,' shouted Peggy as she quickly hauled

on his collar. 'Don't you dare touch a thing, you great lump, or I'll have your guts for garters.'

Harvey slunk off and showed how hurt he was by this unreasonable threat with a grunt of despair and a deep sigh of martyrdom as he collapsed before the fire.

'To be sure that's a fine welcome after a long hard day,' said Jim in mock protest as he staggered up the concrete steps and into the kitchen, laden with beer crates. He dumped them on the floor so they were in everyone's way, then swooped to pluck up Daisy before he gathered Peggy into his arms. 'Have my girls missed me?' he asked as he gave them both sloppy kisses.

'Oof,' protested Peggy as she wafted away beer fumes. 'You've clearly been having the time of your lives while Cordelia and I have been slaving away here.'

'Ach, Peggy girl, it was a great craic, so it was. Fred and Alf popped in, then Stan arrived during the lull between trains, and . . .'

'All right, I get the picture,' she said with a giggle. Then she caught sight of Ron, who was surreptitiously looking beneath the cloth on the table. 'Don't you *dare*,' she snapped.

Ron snatched his hand away, his eyes wide with innocent hurt. 'I was only looking,' he complained. 'To be sure that is a fine spread there, Peggy, and it seems to me there's enough to feed an army. Surely one little sandwich wouldn't be missed?'

'It would,' she replied sternly as she tucked the cloth firmly round the plates. 'And if you and Jim had come back at lunchtime, you wouldn't be hungry now.'

'I told you that men were no use in a kitchen,' piped up Cordelia.

Peggy pointed at the beer crates. 'The pair of you can take those into the dining room while I make a pot of tea to sober you up.'

''Tis a terrible burden living in a house of women,' grumbled Ron as he staggered a bit and almost fell over the crates he was attempting to lift.

'Aye,' nodded Jim as he placed Daisy carefully in her high chair. He straightened up and swayed on his feet. 'But 'tis far worse in the army, Da. Our sergeant major can outboss my Peg any day of the week – and that's saying something.' He shot her a soppy smile and hiccuped.

Cordelia giggled and Peggy failed miserably to look cross. 'Get away, the pair of you,' she said in exasperation. 'And after you've drunk your tea, you can wash and change and have a shave before our guests arrive.'

'Are ye sure that sergeant major's worse than Peg?' muttered Ron as he and Jim weaved their way out of the kitchen and across the hall to the dining room. 'Cos it strikes me she could give old Hitler a run for his money and no mistake.'

Father and son thought this was hilarious and were chortling like schoolboys as they tottered into the dining room and out of sight. Peggy turned from the kitchen doorway and was smiling too, for it was as if Jim had never been away.

Two hours later, and after a bit of a struggle to get into her corset, Peggy was sitting in her dining room in her best frock, thinking how lucky she was. The table was positively groaning with the weight of food, for everyone had brought something. Now there were plates of biscuits, a trifle, two jellies, a box of crystallised fruit Alf's wife, Lil, had unearthed from the back of a cupboard, and a bread and butter pudding.

The level of noise was rising as the men huddled in the corner by the beer and told tall tales, while the women chattered like starlings and Harvey lay close to the table waiting for anything that might drop to the floor. Everyone was here but for Cissy and Peggy's son-in-law Martin, and she could only hope there wasn't a flap on at Cliffe airfield which would put a damper on things and stop them from coming.

Peggy noted that Cordelia's colour was quite high as she sipped sherry and excitedly watched everything going on around her. She was chatting to Enid the fishmonger's wife, who was splendidly arrayed in a deep purple two-piece. Cordelia looked lovely in a white blouse with a cameo brooch at the neck, and a smart navy skirt – no doubt in order to impress Bertram, who'd arrived looking very dapper in a beautifully cut suit with a sprig of heather in the buttonhole, and a large bottle of gin under his arm.

Peggy's gaze travelled to Jane, Sarah and Fran, who were youthfully pretty in colourful frocks and cardigans, their hair freshly washed for the occasion. Suzy, glamorous in her little black dress and pearls, was radiant as she looked up into Anthony's face. Anthony was wearing his usual tweed jacket with the leather elbow patches, and corduroy trousers, his hair flopping over his eyes as his horn-rimmed spectacles repeatedly slipped down his nose.

Rita, Peggy noticed with approval, had changed out of her usual tomboyish clothes into the very fetching blue dress she'd borrowed from Sarah, and a pair of low-heeled pumps. With her dark hair and eyes, olive skin and just a touch of make-up, she was turning into a real beauty. She was in animated conversation with Pilot Officer Matthew Champion who appeared to Peggy to be far too young to be doing what he did, but was extremely dashing in his RAF uniform. They were clearly besotted with one another, and Peggy could only pray that nothing spoilt their happiness.

'They make ever such a lovely couple, don't they?' said Ruby as she sat down next to Peggy and lit a cigarette.

Ruby came from the East End and had been Peggy's lodger earlier in the year. Now she lived with her mother, Ethel, in a rented bungalow on the northern borders of Cliffehaven, close to the tool factory where she worked.

Peggy nodded, aware that Ruby's young Canadian was still recovering from the life-changing injuries he'd sustained in the Dieppe raid. 'How's Mike? Are things a bit better between you now?'

'Yeah,' she replied happily. 'He's over all that nonsense of not wanting me about the place, and although he's still got to come to terms with losing his sight in one eye, he's put in a request to stay here in England and take up an army desk job.'

'Oh, Ruby, I am pleased.'

'Well it ain't all sorted yet, but his commanding officer is hopeful. We'll know tomorrow after the powers that be have their conflab.'

Peggy patted her hand in consolation, for she knew that if Mike was refused the posting here, it would mean him being sent back to Canada – and it simply wouldn't be possible for Ruby to go with him. 'I'll keep my fingers crossed that everything turns out all right,' she murmured. 'Speaking of which,' she added with a smile, 'Ethel and Stan seem to be getting on like a house on fire. I bet she's glad she got out of Bow.'

'Not 'alf.' Ruby grinned as she watched the portly stationmaster and her mother laughing together. 'She's 'aving the time of her life, what with bungalow and Stan and a decent wage at the factory.'

'She certainly looks well on it – and so does Stan by the width of his girth,' Peggy commented wryly.

'Yeah,' Ruby agreed. 'Some might say he's a bit old for 'er, him being in his sixties an' all, but he's a lovely bloke, and what does it matter anyhow? Live while you can, that's what I say.'

Peggy was about to reply when Cissy came running into the room and threw herself into her father's embrace. 'Da, I'm sorry I'm late, but we got a puncture,' she explained after she'd kissed him and been swung round in his arms.

'Ach, to be sure wee girl, you're looking quite magnificently grown up, so y'are,' he told her as he put her back on her feet and admired the dark blue uniform that enhanced her shapely figure and emphasised the colour of her eyes.

Then he saw Martin coming in and went to shake him vigorously by the hand. 'Good to see you, son,' he said. 'Glad you could make it.'

Peggy laughed in delight as Cissy rushed over to hug her. 'It's so lovely to see you, darling,' she breathed. 'It feels like ages since your last visit.'

'I hope you don't mind, Mum, but I've brought a friend with me.' Cissy blushed to the roots of her blonde hair as she turned to draw forward a tall, dark-haired pilot who'd been left standing rather awkwardly in the doorway. 'This is Flight Lieutenant Randolph Stevens. He's with the USAF on secondment at Cliffe,' she said breathlessly.

Peggy's hand was engulfed in a firm clasp, and as she looked into his face she saw brown, serious eyes, a long straight nose, clear skin, a well-defined mouth – and of course wonderful teeth. 'Pleased to meet you, I'm sure,' she stammered.

'Thank you, ma'am. It's a great honour to be invited to your party, and I hope you will accept these little gifts by way of appreciation.'

Peggy gasped as he opened the large bag he'd been carrying and drew out a bottle of whisky, four pairs of nylons, a box of chocolates, several packets of chewing gum and a whole carton of cigarettes. 'Goodness me,' she smiled. 'How very generous, but there was no need, really. We're just delighted you could come.'

'Don't be daft, Mum,' muttered Cissy as Randolph and his whisky bottle were carted off by the other men. 'Randy has found it hard to settle here, and this is the first time he's ever been invited to someone's house. He just wants to show how grateful he is that at last an English family wants to befriend him.'

Peggy was startled by this. 'Really? But I thought everyone was only too delighted to have them over here and on our side – especially all you girls.'

'That's half the trouble,' Cissy replied as she sat down and took a sip of her mother's gin. 'Our boys get jealous of all the attention the Yanks get from the girls, and because they seem to have an endless supply of luxuries which they distribute like confetti, some see it as showing off, or trying to buy people's affections.'

'Oh dear, is it really as bad as that?' Peggy looked

across at the young American. 'And he seems to be a very nice boy, too,' she sighed.

'You've heard the phrase, overpaid, oversexed and over here? Well, that's just jealousy,' Cissy continued. 'The Americans are very polite and clean-cut, and frankly rather bemused by the adverse reaction to them being here.'

Peggy thought of how upset Fran had been when her American had turned out to be married, and the father of several children. With men like that in their ranks, no wonder their reputations were sullied.

Cissy must have read her thoughts. 'I know what happened to Fran was simply ghastly, but they're not all rats, Mum,' she said softly. 'Randy's as honest as the day is long, and the sweetest man I could ever hope to meet. I feel as if I've known him for years, and I would trust him with my life.'

Peggy looked into her starry eyes, saw the glow of happiness in her face, and realised that Cissy had at last found someone she really did love. 'I'm sure he's lovely,' she said, 'and if he makes you happy, then I'm happy.'

'Oh, he does, Mum. Really he does.' Cissy kissed her cheek and hurried off to rescue Randy from her father, who was regaling him with yet another tall tale of his life in the British army.

Peggy saw the boy smile down at her daughter, and watched him fetch her a drink and make sure she was comfortably seated. He had eyes only for her and was charming and attentive, and Cissy was clearly head over heels, but Peggy feared for her daughter. Cissy had fallen in and out of love since she was sixteen, and the heightened pressure and excitement of wartime fed her lust for life. She could only hope it didn't all end in tears, as it had done before.

Her anxious thoughts were broken by the sound of the music coming from the gramophone, and Jim's warm hand drawing her to her feet.

'Dance with me, darlin',' he murmured as the hypnotic Latin rhythm of 'Begin the Beguine' filled the room.

Peggy moved into his embrace and rested her cheek against his chest as Ella Fitzgerald's smoky, enticing voice eased them into a slow tango. She was where she belonged, and she had no need to worry about anything or anyone while she was held so lovingly in her husband's arms.

Chapter Seven

That Monday morning dawned cold and bleak, the night's rain dripping from the trees and lying in puddles in the rutted lanes and fields – but at least it had finally dispelled the stench of smoke that had hung in the air for days.

Mary had dreaded this dawn, and after a disturbed night's sleep she'd finally dragged herself out of bed and begun to prepare for the ordeal ahead. She'd managed, so far, to avoid going to the other end of the village, unable to face the devastation of her home and church, and the stark reminder of all that had happened there. But today there was to be no escape.

The past week had been emotional, but she'd managed to put on a brave face for everyone – especially Barbara – and had set to with a will to help cook, clean and do the shopping. Mary had soon discovered that after their initial show of genuine goodwill and generosity, people found it difficult to talk about her loss, either glossing over it or stumbling through awkward, embarrassed condolences before hurrying away. She came to the conclusion that death divided the living not only from the dead, but from those who were left behind, and she'd made an effort to smile so people felt more at ease with her.

And yet she felt strangely distanced from everything, as if she was sleepwalking through the days, adrift from reality as she carried out her chores and tried to get through each long hour. Even the visits from her friend Pat couldn't cheer her as they usually did, for she was cold inside, her spirit withered, and she was still unable to comprehend the enormity of her loss and the consequences of it on her future.

Mary returned to her room after she'd helped Barbara to prepare and clear breakfast, and to put the finishing touches to the food for the wake. They'd been cooking all the previous day, and the villagers had kindly raided their larders and donated what they could, for it was expected that Gideon's parishioners would come from all three parishes to mourn the passing of their much loved vicar and his wife. Pat and the other village girls had wanted to support her, but their boss at the factory had refused to let them have the day off, and so they'd each written lovely cards which Pat had brought over the night before.

She plumped down on the side of the bed, regarded the thoughtful, handmade cards displayed on the dressing table, and then reached for the precious letters that she kept under her pillows.

Jack had been as good as his word and written every day, and although she now knew each letter by heart, she needed to read them again to garner strength for what was to come. His frustration at being so far away, and not being allowed to return home to be with her, was clear in every word, but his love for her shone through, and she was warmed and comforted by his endearments. When she'd read them all, she held them to her heart for a moment, soothed by the knowledge that although he couldn't be with her, he'd be by her side in his thoughts.

Returning the letters to their hiding place, she realised it was almost time to leave. Once she'd washed her face and hands, and stripped off her Utility trousers and thick sweater, she brushed out her hair and then twisted it into a tight bun at her nape. She carefully rolled up the neatly darned thick black stockings that Barbara had lent her, fastened them to her suspender belt, and then stepped into the simple black dress she and Barbara had fashioned from the donated ballgown. With cap sleeves and a square neckline, it skimmed over her narrow hips to her knees, the silky lining cool and smooth against her skin.

As she tethered Barbara's black felt hat with a hatpin, she caught sight of her reflection in the mirror and quickly looked away. Without make-up or jewellery to lighten the sombre outfit, she looked ashen, the shadows of her sleepless nights bruising the skin beneath her dull blue eyes, her almost bloodless lips drawn down with sadness. Not wanting to linger, she stepped into her low-heeled pumps, picked up the Bible she'd found amongst the books at the WVS, and went downstairs.

They were all waiting for her in the kitchen: Joseph in his Sunday suit, Barbara in her best tweed suit, polished brogues, dark brown hat and fox-fur wrap. The eight land girls were neat and solemn in clean trousers, polished boots and thick overcoats, and even the two elderly farmhands had made an effort with their best tweed jackets and caps, and freshly pressed trousers.

Mary gave them all a wan smile of greeting as she pulled on her dark grey overcoat that, despite having been sponged down, still held the faint reminder of smoke from the fire. Tying the belt firmly round her waist, she pulled up the collar against the chill outside and drew on her woollen gloves. She was as ready as she ever would be.

With a nod to Barbara, she slipped her hand into the crook of her arm and followed everyone as they trooped out of the kitchen into the hall.

As she stepped out of the front door beneath the shelter of Joseph's large umbrella, Mary was gratified to see the crowd of people waiting in the street, and could recognise not only those from her village, but from the outlying hamlets, and even Hillney. Yet all she could really focus on was the big shiny black car and the two coffins which lay side by side in the back.

There were no flowers, for it was the wrong time of year and all the growers had turned to planting vegetable crops, but Barbara had helped her to make a wreath of holly and ivy. They'd threaded this with a white ribbon which was tied in a bow over the small card Mary had written in loving memory of them both.

Mr Clough, the undertaker, wore black tails, pinstripe trousers, a pristine white shirt and black tie. He took off his top hat and bowed to her, his long pale face solemn. Holding the hat in the crook of one arm, he went to stand in front of the hearse, then raised his ebony-handled umbrella to signal to the driver and led the way down the lane and past the shuttered shops.

Men and boys took off their hats and caps as a sign of respect, and women dipped their heads before they joined the cortège. Mary soon became aware of a low murmur, and the tramp of many feet behind her, yet her gaze barely lifted from those coffins as she walked behind them, for this was the last time she could accompany her parents down the village street.

As they walked past the pub which wouldn't open today until after the service, and then past the deserted school and playground to the last house and the final bend, Mary's footsteps faltered, and she had to hold tightly on to Barbara's arm as she steeled herself to face what she'd been avoiding all week.

She stood trembling in shock as her horrified gaze took in the piles of rubble, the remains of a window-less wall, the charred beams and the single blackened chimney breast that stood like a sentinel above the ruins of her home. The lawns had been trampled into mud, the garage was merely a heap of ash and the nearby trees and shrubs had been scorched and withered by the heat.

She looked from the rectory to the skeleton of the lovely old church. The high, damaged walls were windowless, the altar and nave open to the skies beneath the few surviving blackened ribs of the once-soaring roof. The square tower was still standing, but looked forlorn without the flagpole and clock. The large stone font seemed much smaller than before as it stood stripped of its wooden cover, abandoned between the remaining pillars, the rubble surrounding it containing the detritus of sodden hymnals, burnt pews and charred vestments. Even the grass in the graveyard had been seared, and the new white headstones had been stained by the oily grime of smoke.

'Come, Mary,' Barbara said softly as Joseph turned away to do his duty as a pall-bearer. 'Everyone has congregated, and it's time for us to follow them.'

Mary made herself concentrate, for the undertaker was now organising Joseph and the men of the Home Guard who would help carry the coffins. Yet, as they were slowly brought from the back of the hearse and lifted on to the pall-bearers' shoulders, she was overwhelmed with grief and had to force down the lump in her throat, struggling to remain calm.

Determined not to cry or make a show, she kept

her head erect and her back straight as she followed the coffins into the rain-soaked churchyard. Quiet dignity was what her parents would have asked of her, and she silently prayed that she would find the strength and courage to fulfil their expectations.

The dean was waiting at the graveside, sheltered from the elements by the umbrella his wife held over him, resplendent in his white surplice, the deep purple sash hanging around his neck. He began to intone the first words of the service once the coffins were reverently laid on the ground before him, and the gathering drew nearer.

Mary stood between Barbara and Joseph, aware of the lingering smell of burnt stone and wood, and the chill of the wet grass beneath her feet as the rain pattered on their umbrella, and the wind blew shrivelled leaves to scurry and swirl through the silent headstones and among the church ruins. She was numb with grief, barely able to concentrate on the dean's seemingly endless speech, and his dreary reading of the Bishop's equally long eulogy.

Then her spirits lightened as Dr Haywood stepped forward. He gave her a smile of understanding and encouragement, and began to talk about Gideon and Emmaline with great affection. He told them how he and Gideon would sit long into the night playing chess or discussing books and poetry – and how Emmaline had worked so tirelessly for her charities and been such a wonderful comfort to him when his wife was dying.

'And now,' he said in his warm, deep voice that carried even to those furthest away, 'I will recite something that Gideon was passionate about. I doubt I'll do it justice, for I cannot hope to emulate his wonderful speaking voice, but I hope he will approve of my poor effort.'

As Mary listened to him, she suddenly felt at peace. The words of Dylan Thomas's poem were a comfort, and it was as if her father was speaking to her in his beautiful, musical Welsh lilt that had never faded despite his years of living in England.

The actual interment was an ordeal, but thankfully the dean kept it short, perhaps at last aware of the bitterly cold wind endangering not only his own health, but that of the many elderly mourners who were sheltering from the driving sleet beneath umbrellas.

As the dean solemnly intoned the final few words, there was a general shifting of feet and then a decorous but swift departure from the churchyard towards the promise of warmth and a strong cup of tea.

Mary turned to Barbara. 'I'd like to stay for a few minutes,' she said. 'Just to say my own goodbyes.'

'Will you be all right?'

Mary nodded, and as Barbara and Joseph turned to leave, having insisted she take the umbrella, she closed her eyes in prayer. Her parents were together as they had been in life, and were now at rest. She hoped that her father still watched over her, for his guiding hand had always been steady – and she would need it in the days and weeks to come.

Turning away finally, she realised it had stopped raining. Furling the umbrella, she slowly picked her way through the grass and around the headstones to the stone archway that still soared above the entrance to the church. There was nothing left of the oak door and wooden porch, and she carefully made her way down the worn stone steps that worshippers had trodden for centuries, into the heart of the devastation.

The majesty of this ancient building had not been diminished, she realised, even though the roof was gone, and the Gothic windows were empty. Her footsteps echoed as she walked amid the ruins, but she could feel an all-pervading sense of peace wash over her. This was where her father had felt most at home, and the knowledge that this lovely ancient place still held the power and presence of God gave her comfort.

Mary managed to get through the rest of the day by keeping busy. She passed round sandwiches and cups of tea, made sure she'd thanked everyone for coming, and listened to the stories of her parents' good works in the three parishes.

They had been loved and admired by everyone, it seemed, and Mary had found it difficult to reconcile this view of Emmaline with the woman who'd been her mother. But today was not the time to hold grudges and remember past hurts – it was a day to give thanks for all the good she'd done in the parish and for her unfailing years of loyalty to Gideon.

The dean had shaken hands and pontificated at length to anyone he could trap in a corner, as his wife Marjorie scuttled about with cups of tea and tried to fade into the background. The elderly women soon got into a group by the fire to try and outdo each other with tales of other funerals they'd attended, while the men ate voraciously, watched the clock, and wondered how soon they could decently leave. Joseph and the farmhands went back to work, while the land girls continued to make tea, cut sandwiches and wash the piles of crockery that soon mounted up.

Conversation ebbed and flowed, and by mid-afternoon the sense of solemnity and gloom had been replaced with chatter and laughter as people forgot why they were there and simply enjoyed the chance to gossip in the warmth of the farmhouse sitting room.

Barbara finally closed the door on the last of them and leant against it with a long, drawn-out sigh. 'I thought they'd never leave,' she said.

Mary gave her a hug. 'Thank you, Auntie Barbara. You've worked so hard all day, and I couldn't possibly have got through it without you and Uncle Joseph.'

Barbara's smile was warm as she regarded the clean kitchen. 'None of us would have got through it if it hadn't been for those girls. They've done sterling work today, and, as if that wasn't enough, they're now out with Joseph and doing the milking.' She cupped Mary's cheek in her hand. 'And what about you, love? The day must have been a terrible ordeal.'

'It was to begin with, but after Dr Haywood recited that poem, I found I could cope much better with everything.'

Barbara nodded and lit a rare cigarette as she kicked off her shoes and settled into a kitchen chair to relax for the first time that day. 'He's a lovely man,' she murmured. 'And he recited that poem so beautifully it was as if I could hear your father again.'

Mary took a deep quivering breath. 'Yes,' she replied softly. 'I felt that too.'

Barbara got up from the table, checked on the stew that had been slowly cooking throughout the day in the range oven, and fetched a bottle from the dresser in the corner. 'Why don't you sit down with me and have a glass of my parsnip wine? Supper's still two hours away, and I think we've earned a pick-me-up.'

Mary smiled. 'No thanks. The last time I tried that it went straight to my head.' She watched as Barbara filled a small glass and took a sip. 'If you don't mind, I'd rather like to be alone for a little while,' she said hesitantly.

Barbara was instantly alert. 'Oh, my dear. I knew

today would be too much for you. Aren't you feeling well?'

'I'm feeling fine,' she replied hastily. 'It's just that I've been avoiding Daddy's trunk all week, but now I feel ready to open it.'

Barbara knocked back the glass of wine in a single gulp, and got to her feet. 'Mary, there's something we didn't tell you,' she said hurriedly. 'The trunk wasn't the only thing salvaged from the fire.'

Mary frowned. 'But I thought you said . . . ?'

'Yes, I know I did,' she replied as she reddened. 'But Joseph and I thought it would be best not to mention it until you were ready, you see. You were already so deeply grieving, and we didn't want to make things worse.'

Mary shivered with apprehension. 'What did he find, Auntie Barbara?'

'Oh, darling, it's nothing to be frightened of, I promise,' she replied before breaking into a beaming smile. 'Let me put my shoes back on and I'll show you.'

Mary grabbed their coats as Barbara shod her feet and hunted out the heavy-duty torch. She followed her out into the dark of the early evening and hurried across the cobbles to the small barn, having to wait impatiently as Barbara fiddled in the darkness to get the padlock undone. And then the doors were open and they were stepping inside to be greeted by the sweet aroma of hay – and an underlying hint of petrol or oil.

'Are you ready?' asked Barbara as she closed the door firmly behind them and they were plunged into profound blackness.

Mary didn't know if she was or not, but Barbara was clearly excited, so the surprise couldn't be anything horrid. 'I'm on tenterhooks,' she said. 'Just for goodness' sake turn that torch on and put me out of my misery.'

She gasped in delight as the strong beam travelled across the stone floor and lit up the lovely old car that had been her father's pride and joy. 'But why didn't you tell me before?'

'We thought it was a rather too poignant reminder of your father, and didn't want to upset you any further,' Barbara replied, looking bashful.

'But how on earth did it get here?' Mary breathed as she ran her fingers along the glossy coachwork and peered inside at the leather seats. 'And there's not a mark on it.'

'Dr Haywood brought it here.'

Mary was utterly confused. 'Dr Haywood?'

'He'd been out to see a patient in Gorse Green the night of the tip-and-run, and was driving back when the sirens started going,' explained Barbara quickly. 'Deciding to risk continuing his journey home, he saw the bomb explode, knew it had to be somewhere at that end of the village, and that his services might be urgently needed. Realising the rectory had taken the full brunt of the explosion, and that it was too late to help either of your parents, he knew there was only one thing he could do to prevent an even worse disaster.'

Mary listened in silent awe as Barbara continued.

'Regardless of his own safety, he kicked in the garage door, loaded the car with the petrol cans and drove it back down the lane out of harm's way.'

'But he never said anything.' Mary was astounded. 'How brave he was to risk his life like that.'

Barbara nodded. 'The fire crews and Home Guard had already arrived by the time he'd walked back after parking the car. If it hadn't been for his quick thinking, those cans of fuel would have exploded and there would have been many more deaths that night.'

Mary blinked back her tears as she stroked the shining bonnet and traced the outline of the large headlamps. 'He deserves a medal,' she said quietly, 'not only for his bravery, but for saving so many lives.'

'Joseph has already had a word with the Mayor of Hillney, and it's under discussion at the highest county level.' Barbara smiled. 'Raymond Haywood has served this community well, and he deserves to be recognised, not only for that night's work, but for everything else he's done for us all over the years.'

Mary looked round the barn to the bales of hay that had been piled up in one corner, and to the scorched and buckled trunk which had been placed on the stone floor behind the car. 'I hope you haven't stored those cans in here,' she said. 'It's very near the house.'

Barbara shook her head. 'Joseph drained off the petrol and oil from the car, and stored the cans well away from anything important,' she assured her. 'Now, do you want me to stay while you open that trunk? Or will you be all right on your own?'

Mary smiled. 'I'll be fine now. Having the car here makes me feel nearer to Daddy, and I'm sure the contents of that old trunk will turn out to be very uninteresting and not at all upsetting. You go in and enjoy your glass of wine, and I'll join you once I've had a rummage.'

Barbara handed her the torch. 'Don't stay out too long,' she warned as she dug her hands into her pockets. 'It's cold enough in here to freeze a polar bear, and I don't want you going down with pneumonia.'

Mary waited until she'd shut the doors behind her before she turned the torch on again. She walked round the Austin 7, opened the door and slid in behind the steering wheel. Closing her eyes she breathed in the tang of leather from the seats, and the beeswax her father had lovingly polished into them every Saturday afternoon so they would stay supple and not crack. She could also clearly retrace every moment of that last journey she'd made with him, hearing the echo of his voice telling her to slow down, to take care, and not clash the gears.

She sat there for endless minutes in the silent

barn then blinked back her tears, climbed out of the car and almost reverently closed the door before approaching the trunk. It looked rather sad, sitting here, the metal dented in places, the leather straps scorched and frayed, the buckles and padlock blackened. She noticed that the padlock had been fused by the heat to the trunk's metal ring, so she went to the tools that had been neatly lined up on the side wall and took down a sturdy jemmy.

It didn't take much effort to break the link, for the thin metal had been further weakened by the heat, and after two attempts, the padlock fell to the floor. Pushing back the lid she was greeted by the smell of mothballs and leather, and she felt a momentary sharp pang of doubt about the wisdom of looking at what her father had hidden away. But, as she aimed the torch beam down on to the contents, she realised she had nothing to fear. Everything was exactly as he had said.

The heat of the fire had shrivelled and dried out the covers of the leather-covered tomes which contained the history of those who'd lived in the parish during the past century; and the documents which listed the many repairs to the church, the gifts bequeathed and the money donated for memorial plaques, stained-glass windows and a new cover for the font were browned, and slightly crisp at the edges. There were invoices for the purchase of communion wine, candles, vestments for the choir and new hymnals; and long letters from the Bishop, the Dean and the Church synod.

Mary drew each thing out and carefully placed it on the open lid to keep it away from the floor. She delved deeper and, with a soft sigh of pleasure, found the army chaplain's uniform Gideon had worn during the First World War, and the small silver brandy flask that had been dented by the bullet that should have killed him. Lying on top of the neatly folded jacket, an army-issue satchel enclosed a dirt-stained Bible alongside a packet of letters which, going by the dates on them, had been written during that terrible conflict.

Mary wondered at first if they were from her mother, but the writing was unfamiliar and seemed to be different on every envelope. Curious, she opened one and discovered it was from the mother of a boy who'd died at the Somme. It had clearly been in answer to her father's letter of condolence, and she'd thanked him fervently for being with her boy during his last hours. Mary skimmed another two and then put them back with the Bible. They made difficult reading, and she was still too emotionally raw to deal with such pain.

She carefully lifted out the khaki jacket and trousers, the black shirt and white collar, and the small bag in which he'd kept the sacraments needed for the last rites. Holding the jacket to her face, she found that there was no reminder of her father, only the smell of camphor and old cloth.

As she placed the jacket to one side she stilled, and her heart began to thud as she was transfixed by what lay in the very bottom of the trunk. Beside the battered leather briefcase were numerous books, a different year tooled in faded gold on each. She'd had no idea that her father had kept a diary, and as she lifted them out one by one and placed them in order, she realised he'd been doing so since 1912. He'd been thirty years old then, and celebrating his first year of married life with Emmaline in his new seaside parish of Carmine Bay.

Mary stared at the books in the torchlight, her thoughts and emotions in a whirl. Despite her initial excitement at finding them, and her growing curiosity about what they might contain, she was reluctant to pry into what were essentially her father's very private writings.

She finally decided she would take them indoors for now so they wouldn't deteriorate further in the cold and damp of the barn. She needed to think about the diaries, and whether or not it was right for her to read them. Taking out the briefcase to put them in, she returned everything else to the trunk and closed the lid. As she unfastened the catch on the scratched leather and opened the case, she saw there were documents inside, and her fingers were clumsy as she nervously drew them out to examine them.

There were three insurance policies dating back many years that looked as if they were still valid, for there was also a little notebook listing the dates of Gideon's yearly one-shilling payments – the last being only this February. More intriguing was the large brown envelope that contained both parents' certificates for their births, confirmations and marriage – and the sad and very poignant death certificates for four stillborn babies.

Mary dug about in the case looking for her own birth certificate, and although she found her confirmation and christening cards, there was no sign of it. Thinking that perhaps Gideon had forgotten to stow it with the others for some reason or another – he could be absent-minded at times – she examined those of the lost babies.

There were tears in her eyes as she looked at the heart-wrenching details of the brother and sisters she'd never known. Neither of her parents had ever mentioned them, and she could only imagine how deeply they must have suffered at their loss. Fate had been cruel to deny them the large family they'd clearly longed for. Yet, even as she ached for their undoubted pain, she was deeply puzzled. Why hadn't her mother rejoiced in her birth after losing her other babies – and been possessed with a powerful love for the one child she'd been blessed with?

Mary sniffed back her tears. Perhaps she had been too embittered by her previous losses – perhaps she'd never recovered her health before she'd had her, and simply couldn't find the courage to give her love fully again in case Mary didn't survive? But she had, and surely, surely Emmaline could have found a modicum of love to cherish her only daughter?

As the fading batteries in the torch began to make the light flicker, Mary's thoughts went round and round, but still she couldn't resolve the puzzle. She looked at the collection of diaries and wondered if the answers to her many questions lay within those pages. Although sorely tempted to ignore all her misgivings and open the one marked 1924, the year of her birth, she decided to wait until the morning. It was late now, and she was too wrung out from the rigours of the day to concentrate properly on anything.

She quickly and carefully put the papers back into the briefcase and fitted in as many of the diaries as she could. Carrying the rest, she took one last loving look at the car, then closed the barn doors firmly behind her and hurried through the sleet to the warmth and comfort of the farmhouse.

Chapter Eight

Ron tramped across the hills beside Jim, who was carrying a well-wrapped-up Daisy against his chest in the adapted army-issue satchel Ron had kept since the First World War. This would be the last time Ron could walk these hills with his son, for Jim was leaving tonight and wouldn't return until this awful war was over. Yet, despite his deep concern for Jim's safety, and the knowledge that it might be a very long time before they could do this again, Ron was feeling in robust good health and quite cheerful.

The bitter wind and lashing rain of the previous days had disappeared and now, in this crisp bright autumnal morning, the grass smelled sweet and the sky was a pale, cloudless blue. The sun glinted on the calm sea, and the clean, cold breeze invigorated the two men. Ron loved this time of day, and this season, for he usually had the hills to himself then, and this was where he felt most at home.

He strode out beside his son as he watched Harvey dashing back and forth ahead of them, nose to the ground, tail windmilling as he sniffed the scents of rabbit, fox and badger. The ferrets, Flora and Dora, were tucked into one of the deep pockets in his poacher's coat, their catch of four rabbits in two others.

'This isn't a race, son,' he panted as they began to climb a steep hill and he found, to his dismay and disgust, that he couldn't keep up the pace and was lagging further and further behind.

Jim paused to turn and grin at him. 'What's the matter, Da?' he called. 'Old age catching up with you at last, is it?'

'I'll give you age,' Ron grumbled as he reached him and tried not to show how out of breath he was. 'I remember the last time you came up here you were gasping before we'd barely left the house.'

Jim laughed. 'Aye, that's for sure. But a few months of army training on assault courses has got me fit.' He hitched the bag to a more comfortable spot so Daisy's head rested on his shoulder. 'Mind you, this one weighs enough to slow me down. I can't believe how much she's grown in such a few months.'

They started walking again, but at a slower, more accommodating pace. 'She'll have grown even more by the time you're home again,' muttered Ron.

'She will that,' Jim said sadly, 'and she probably won't even know who I am.' He came to a halt as they reached the flat top of the hill. 'That's what worries me, Da,' he confessed. 'I hadn't seen Cissy for months until this leave, and then only fleetingly because of her responsibilities with the WAAF. As for my boys, and Anne and wee Rose Margaret . . .' He gave a deep sigh. 'Telephone calls and letters are all very well, but there are times when I just want to see them and hold them and get to be an intrinsic part of their lives again. They're all growing up without me, Da, and 'tis a terrible, painful thing to be a stranger to your children.'

Ron gripped his son's shoulder in sympathy. 'To be sure 'tis a sacrifice we must all bear until this war is won,' he replied. 'Try and take comfort from the fact that you're not alone in this.'

'I know my Peg feels the burden of it all,' Jim continued. 'She doesn't say much and never complains, but I've seen her face after she's talked to everyone down in Somerset, and it's clear she's suffering.' He ruffled his short black hair in frustration. 'If only she'd take Daisy down there. At least then they'd both be safer and could be with the others again. But she won't hear of it.'

'She'll not abandon Cordelia and the girls to my dubious care,' Ron replied as he pulled his pipe and tobacco from his coat pocket. 'Our Peg has a deep sense of duty, and as long as she knows the others are safe in Somerset, she'll keep the home fires burning here.'

'I still can't believe she went through the bomb blast and the operation without saying a word to me,' said Jim as they started walking again. 'It came as a shock, I can tell you. But she's a tough little body, is my Peg,' he added with affectionate pride, 'and if she can weather that, she can weather pretty much anything.'

Ron knew how adept Peggy was at hiding her true feelings, for he'd witnessed the struggle she'd had to keep the tears at bay when everything had got too much for her, and she'd felt the absence of her family most keenly. And he'd overheard her muffled sobs late into the night when the rest of the house was sleeping. But he made no comment. Peggy wouldn't thank him for telling Jim how things really were at Beach View, and he knew she wanted his enforced departure to go smoothly and without any worries for her or the rest of the family he was leaving behind.

'At least Cissy seems to have forgotten her daft ideas about going on the stage, and is turning into a sensible young woman,' said Jim as they strode through the wiry grass and skirted round clumps of gorse and rabbit scrapings. 'I like her young American, too. He seems a sensible, down-to-earth sort – which is just what she needs.'

'Aye, he's a fine chap so he is,' agreed Ron, 'and Martin speaks very highly of him. We can only pray he doesn't suffer the same fate as so many of his fellow flyers. The RAF has suffered too many losses, and with every influx of new recruits they seem to be getting younger and younger, their odds of survival shortened by their lack of proper training and experience.'

'To be sure, these are dangerous times, and it doesn't bear thinking too deeply about any of it.' Jim nudged Daisy's bottom to a more comfortable position on his arm as she slept against his shoulder. 'But I am thinking young Rita is in the same boat as Cissy with her boy Matthew. At least, if things do go wrong, the girls will have each other to lean on. After all,' he continued, 'they've known each other since they were babies.'

'We can only pray it never comes to that,' said Ron.

They walked on for a while in companionable silence. Daisy was still asleep and a seemingly tireless Harvey continued to hare about chasing intriguing scents. Ron lit his pipe and puffed on it contentedly, enjoying these precious moments with his son even though the dark clouds of an uncertain future overshadowed them.

'I am going to miss all this,' sighed Jim as he stopped to look around him at the glittering sea, the soft folds of the hills and the sprawling farmland down in the valley beyond the Cliffe estate. 'It's a perfect English autumn day, with the sun and the crisp wind that makes a man feel alive.'

Ron felt a pang of sorrow at the thought that this boy of his would soon be far from these familiar and beloved hills of home. 'Aye, 'tis that,' he said softly. 'Take a good deep breath of that air, son. There's nothing like it anywhere else in the world.'

They stood there for a moment, enjoying the quiet beauty as gulls hovered above the clifftops, their white wings gilded by the sun, and the wind ruffled the grass. Then they went on walking, each with their own thoughts, but comfortable in their close companionship.

They were soon approaching the shattered remains of a hillside farmhouse which the army had used for target practice and then abandoned. They crunched over the broken bricks and charred beams and headed for the far wall which would shelter them from the wind.

'I know you've made light of army life in front of Peggy and the rest,' Ron said as he sat down on a fallen roof beam and rested his back against the crumbling wall. 'But how are you really finding it?'

Jim carefully eased the straps of the bag from over his shoulders and gently placed the sleeping Daisy, still in the bag, on a sheltered tuft of grass. He adjusted the knitted hat over her ears, tucked her mittened hands inside the cocooning shawl, and covered her wool-clad legs with his thick scarf. Once he'd settled her to his satisfaction, he sat down next to his father on the rotting beam and dug out a packet of cigarettes from his coat pocket.

'The army hasn't changed much since the last time I had the misfortune to be in it,' he replied once he'd lit his cigarette. 'We might have more modern machinery and better uniforms, but sergeants still shout, officers still strut about with their swagger sticks and their toffee-nosed voices. Reveille is still before dawn, and there's the same amount of tedious marching and rifle drill. The accommodation at the barracks is basic, but the food's all right, and the other men enjoy a good craic, so it's not all bad.'

Ron regarded his son, knowing that although his words were lightly spoken, there remained much that was unsaid. 'It will be different in India,' he said round his pipe stem, as a panting Harvey flopped at their feet.

'Aye, it will that.' Jim smoked his cigarette, his gaze settling on the fields and hamlets far down in the valley as he idly stroked Harvey's head. 'We've had the lectures about the heat and humidity and the thousand and one stinging, biting things that can either kill you or give you something nasty.' He grimaced. 'We've also had the lecture about not fraternising with the local women, and taking precautions against the clap – but then that's the same no matter where you're being sent.'

Ron knew his son liked women, but he was fairly certain that, since his marriage to Peggy, he'd never gone any further than mild flirtation – however, this posting would take him to exotic ports and he'd be away for months, if not years, and a man could only stay celibate for so long. 'Keep it in your trousers, son. That's my advice.'

Jim grinned as he looked at his father. 'I've had it on good authority that the army puts some heavy-duty stuff in the tea on all foreign postings, so even if I wanted to, I doubt I'd be able to manage it.'

Ron grinned back. 'Aye, I remember that in the first shout. Powerful stuff, to be sure, and it stayed in the system long enough to put a damper on home leave and upset the wife.'

Jim rolled his eyes, and then his expression became serious. 'I've been tempted, Da,' he confessed. 'Women like a man in uniform, and I'm not beyond enjoying a bit of flattery. But that's as far as it goes. I love and respect Peggy too much to cheat on her.'

'I'm glad to hear it,' rumbled Ron. 'You've got a good woman there, and she loves the bones of you. If you hurt her, you'll have me to contend with.'

Jim chuckled as his gaze flickered over his father's broad chest and large hands. 'To be sure, Da, I'll not want to be tangling with you – or Peggy. I don't know which of you scares the bejesus out of me more.'

Ron smiled. He was flattered that his son still saw him as a force to be reckoned with – even though he'd rarely raised a hand against him or his brother Frank when they were growing up.

Jim finished his smoke and ground it out beneath his boot heel. 'But what about you, Da? Mam's been gone for years now, and you must get lonely down in that basement with just Harvey and the ferrets for company. I'd have thought that by now you'd have moved into the comfort of the Anchor with Rosie. How come you two haven't tied the knot?'

Ron puffed on his pipe as he wondered if he should reveal Rosie's closely guarded secret. Then he decided it wouldn't hurt, for Jim was leaving in a few hours, and within two days he'd be sailing from

Liverpool to the Far East. 'There are reasons, son,' he began. 'But what I'm about to tell you is known only by a very few, and I'd like it to stay that way.'

Jim raised his eyebrows. 'You're being very mysterious, Da.' He smiled. 'Let me guess; the lovely Rosie has a shady and rather wicked past.'

Ron shook his head. 'She has a past, certainly, but it's far from something to be ashamed of. In fact it's all rather tragic.'

As Jim's smile faded, he told him about Rosie's husband, and how his family had shunned her since she'd moved down to Cliffehaven and made a new life for herself.

Jim gave a low whistle. 'Well, she certainly kept that quiet. I'd never have guessed,' he murmured. 'She's always so bright and cheerful.'

'Aye, she hides it well, I'll give her that,' agreed Ron. 'But her greatest sadness is that she never had children. She'd have made a wonderful mother,' he added wistfully.

'It's probably why she spoils Monty, and lets him sleep on her bed,' said Jim. 'To be sure that pup rules the roost.'

Harvey's ears pricked at the sound of his offspring's name and he wagged his tail.

'Aye,' Ron replied, 'she said only the other day that she thinks of him as her substitute baby, and can't help but spoil him.' He grinned. 'She's in for a nasty shock when he reaches his full size. He's already galloping about like an unbroken colt, and is proving as wilful and disobedient as this old rogue.'

He ruffled Harvey's ears and then shivered as the cold finally made itself felt in his bones. 'We'd better be getting back. Peggy will never forgive either of us if we spend too much of your last day away from her.'

Daisy was beginning to grizzle, so Jim strapped her back against his chest and then softly kissed her cheek. 'She's getting cold too, despite being wrapped up like an Eskimo,' he said as he dug into his pocket and fished out a rusk to keep her occupied.

Ron's joints creaked stiffly as he got to his feet, and he felt the twinge of pain in his lower back as the fragment of shrapnel caught him out. Everyone might find his affliction funny and enjoy his tall stories about how he'd been wounded – some even doubted the metal was there at all – but the reality of it was no laughing matter, especially when the cold and damp got to it.

'Are you all right, Da?' Jim's concern showed in his face.

'Aye, I'm fine,' he replied gruffly.

'You can't fool me with your blarney, Da,' Jim said solemnly. 'You're obviously in some pain.'

Ron glared at him from beneath his brows. 'I said I'm all right,' he growled.

Jim continued as if he hadn't spoken. 'Why the divil don't you go to the doctor and see if they can get that shrapnel out? Things have changed radically since 1918, and I'm sure . . .'

'I'll not be having some quack digging about down there and possibly turning me into a bloody cripple,' Ron retorted. 'It's fine where it is, so I'll thank you to stop going on about it.'

Jim heaved a sigh. 'If you say so, Da.'

'Aye, I do, so let that be an end to it.' Ron checked the ferrets were snug and asleep in his coat pocket and stomped out of the lee of the ruins and into the brisk wind that came up from the sea. Heading for home, he kept up a steady, fast pace, determined to ignore the pain in his back and show his son that he had nothing at all to worry about.

They didn't speak much as they walked, and as they reached the path which eventually led down to the twitten that ran between the terraced houses, Harvey galloped off, no doubt in eager anticipation of the biscuit and saucer of tea Peggy always gave him after his morning exercise.

Ron grinned. 'He's a man after me own heart,' he said fondly. 'To be sure I'm looking forward to a nice cup of tea meself.' He was about to follow Harvey when Jim grasped his arm.

'Da. Da, wait a minute. There's something I need to say before we get home.'

Ron regarded him with sharp concern. 'What is it, son?'

'Da, I know I've put a brave face on things for Peggy's sake,' Jim said hurriedly, 'but the fact is . . .' He swallowed and couldn't meet his father's eyes. 'The fact is . . .'

'The fact is you're frightened,' said Ron with infinite tenderness. 'We all are, my boy. And if you weren't, I'd be more worried about you than ever. Lack of fear makes men careless.'

'It's not for meself – not really.' Jim stumbled over the words. 'Of course I'm scared about being so far from home in a strange place, but it's Peg and the wains I'm really frightened for.' He gripped Ron's sturdy shoulder, his dark eyes pleading. 'You will look after them for me, won't you, Da?'

Ron blinked away the prick of tears and grasped Jim's hands. 'I will guard them with my life,' he promised gruffly. He reached up and placed his horny hand against the soft, freshly shaved skin of his beloved son's face. 'God go with you, Jim, my precious boy.'

'And with you, Da,' Jim replied brokenly.

Ron took his son in his arms, Daisy between them, and they stood in that awkward embrace for countless minutes as they strengthened the bonds of love that bound them, and found comfort.

Peggy had taken advantage of the men's absence by scrubbing out the kitchen, cleaning the tiles on the hall floor and changing the linen on the beds. She had also plastered on a smile along with her lipstick, determined to confront the day as cheerfully as possible and not ruin Jim's last few hours at home with a long face and tears.

She'd bathed and put on her best blue woollen

dress – a cast-off from her sister Doris, so therefore of fine quality – and had taken time over her hair. With a knitted cardigan over her dress for added warmth, she'd changed out of her old slippers into a pair of smart navy heeled pumps. Turning quickly away from the sight of Jim's freshly pressed uniform hanging from the wardrobe handle, the polished boots and neatly repacked kitbag on the floor beneath it, she went back into the kitchen.

Glancing at the clock, she realised Jim and Ron had been out for over two hours, and put the kettle on the hob. They'd be back soon and in need of a cuppa. It felt strange to have the house to herself, for all the girls were at work and Cordelia was out with Bertram Double-Barrel, as he'd come to be known by them all, at a morning whist drive. Unable to sit still or tolerate the silence, Peggy turned on the wireless for company, and started on the pile of ironing.

She listened to the news as she ironed the sheets and pillowcases, and was relieved that, for once, it wasn't all gloom and doom. British commandos had raided the occupied island of Sark in the Channel Islands, and the Americans had defeated a huge fleet of Japanese ships off Cape Esperance, sinking a cruiser and several destroyers. The American battle for Guadalcanal had been going on for a while now, and the loss of life had been truly awful, but this single victory had meant the Japs were thwarted in their attempts to bring even more troops on to the island.

The fighting in North Africa continued, but with Montgomery in charge, it looked as if the Germans were getting more than a taste of their own medicine. The battle for Stalingrad was still being fiercely fought, however, and although the Red Army seemed to be holding back the German Panzers, the isolated victories were minor and all too fleeting.

Peggy continued with her ironing as the news came to an end and was replaced by lively music. She hummed along to 'A String of Pearls', remembering how she and Jim had gone dancing the other night at the Grand Hotel. It had been a magical evening, quite like old times, and they'd come home slightly tipsy and laughing like fools, to tumble into bed and make tender, sweet love and talk throughout the remains of the night.

She hastily blinked back her tears as she finished the ironing and carried it upstairs to the airing cupboard. She and Jim had forged wonderful memories during these past few days, and she wouldn't mar them with tears and regret, but count herself lucky they'd had this precious time together to reinforce the ties that bound them.

Having stowed the clean laundry away, she drifted into the bathroom to check that she hadn't smudged her mascara, then went along the landing to the empty bedroom to make sure Jim's repair to the window had stopped the rain getting in. It seemed to be holding, for there were no puddles on the windowsill now, so she turned from the window and tugged fussily at the bedspread.

Kitty Pargeter had slept in here while she recovered from the horrific plane crash that had resulted in her leg amputation. She was married now and back in her beloved planes with the ATS, ferrying them to all corners of Britain, while her husband, Roger, continued to fly his Spitfires under Martin's command.

Peggy sat down on the bed and stared unseeing out of the window that looked over the garden and the twitten between the houses. Once Suzy and Anthony were married in December they would move into their tiny cottage, and Fran would move out of the double room she and Suzy shared into Cissy's single. There was little point in jealously keeping it unoccupied for Cissy rarely came home now – and then only for a fleeting visit, as she'd done last night.

Peggy gave a deep sigh. She should have notified the billeting office of this empty room, but had held off until Jim's leave was over and she could think straight again. She'd been rather selfish, really, she thought, what with so many people needing a roof over their head, but somehow she couldn't find the energy to deal with anyone new and the problems they would no doubt bring with them.

She continued to stare out of the window to the roofs of the terraces that climbed the hill behind the house as her thoughts drifted. There were so many brave youngsters fighting this war – just as there had been in the first conflict. Yet she knew the battles weren't just being fought on the land, the sea, or in the skies, but also here on the home front by the women left behind.

Cissy drove for the WAAF, and young Rita, whose father hadn't made it home on leave since he'd joined the army, had become an intrinsic part of the local firefighting service. Both girls were in love with pilots, and although they never voiced their fears, Peggy had seen it in their eyes every time the planes took off from Cliffe.

Anne's fear for Martin's safety had been eased somewhat now he'd been ordered not to fly any more and was mainly behind a desk, but airfields weren't the safest places to be at the moment and their enforced parting was beginning to wear her down – especially as she was expecting her second baby any day now.

As for Jane and Sarah, they were both doing their bit, but they were very far from their home in Malaya, and still had to cope with the fact they'd heard no news of their father, or Sarah's fiancé, since the fall of Singapore. Fran and Suzy were kept busy at the hospital, and although Suzy was happily organising her wedding, and Fran put on a show of cheerful cheekiness, Peggy knew both girls were homesick at times and missing their families – especially Fran, for journeys to Ireland were now forbidden, and she wouldn't be able to get home until this blasted war was over.

Peggy sighed and thought about her own struggles to feed everyone now money was so tight and the shelves in the shops were almost bare. The long queues waiting outside every shop were exhausting, the lack of even the most basic things was frustrating, and the constant air-raid warnings and hours spent in the horrid Anderson shelter had taken their toll. And then there was the overwhelming yearning for her children and her husband that would catch her unawares and bring her low.

'Now I have to go through the agony of seeing him off again,' she murmured into the silence. She could already picture the scene at the station, and knew exactly how she would feel when his train became a speck on the horizon and she would have to return home to an empty bed and the debilitating uncertainty of when they might be together again.

Peggy got off the bed, straightened the cover and went over to the window. She would *not* give in to such thoughts. They made her cry and she had to keep calm, remember how difficult it was to get mascara these days, and try to look her best so that Jim never guessed how hard this latest parting was for her.

Yet, as she looked down to the twitten, she really had to battle to keep her tears at bay. Jim and his father were embracing, not ashamed of their tears or their love for one another as they stood in full sight of the back windows of the two terraces.

Peggy watched as they slowly drew apart, their

hands clasped as they talked. Then Ron's large, rough hand was softly patting Jim's cheek and ruffling his hair, just as he'd done when he was a boy.

Peggy turned from the window, not wanting to be seen intruding on such a private and deeply personal moment. She pulled her frail emotions together as she went downstairs to the kitchen to boil the kettle again, and was composed and dry-eyed by the time Jim and Ron followed Harvey into the room.

'Well,' she said brightly, 'it's about time. I thought you'd both got lost up there.' She lifted a gurgling Daisy out of the satchel and, giving her a hug and kiss, began to divest her of the thick woollen cardigans, hat and mittens.

'I've never been lost up there in me life,' grumbled Ron as he dug about in the pockets of his long, heavy coat and dumped the four dead rabbits on the draining board.

Peggy finished with Daisy and after giving her another kiss, put her on the floor so she could crawl about and play with her toys. She was beginning to be sick of the sight of rabbit, but at least it meant they would have a proper meal tonight before Jim left.

Jim set the bag aside and shed his coat and scarf before turning to Peggy with a broad grin. 'To be sure, Peggy girl, you're looking beautiful today,' he said as he wrapped his arms round her, lifted her off her feet and smudged her lipstick with a smacking kiss.

Peggy giggled. 'It's amazing what a bit of make-up will do. Now, put me down, and I'll find some biscuits to go with the tea. You must both be parched.'

Harvey nudged her with his nose to remind her that he usually had tea and biscuits after a walk, and Peggy patted his head. 'Did you enjoy the walk?' she asked Jim.

'Aye, it's a pretty day up there,' he replied as he eased off his boots. 'The auld man had a bit of a struggle to keep up with me, mind,' he added, shooting Ron an impish wink.

Ron tried to glower, but failed. 'Aye, well, at my great age I've found it better to take things at a steady, dignified pace,' he said airily. He began to gut the rabbits. 'I was hoping to bring back some birds today, but with that new gamekeeper on the Cliffe estate and all that fencing the Land Army has put up, there wasn't a chance to get anywhere near them.'

'Ron, take those boots off and put the ferrets in their cage before you do that,' said Peggy with more than a hint of asperity. 'I washed that floor only a while ago, and if the ferrets escape your pockets, I'm in no mood to go chasing after them all over the house.'

Ron heaved a great sigh and, leaving a mess of entrails, blood and fur on the drainer, went muttering to himself down the cellar steps.

Peggy shuddered at the gruesome sight, and opened the biscuit tin only to discover it was all but empty. 'Have you two been at this?' she asked Jim.

Jim's eyes widened in innocence. 'Now, would we do such a thing, Peg?'

Peggy chuckled. 'You know damned well you would, you scallywag,' she said fondly as she gave Harvey the last few morsels. 'If you want any more,' she told Jim, 'then you'll have to go and queue for them.'

'Ach, I'll not be wasting me last day at home in a queue of gossiping housewives,' he retorted as he pulled her on to his lap. 'I've got a much better idea of how to pass the time.'

She saw the gleam in his eyes and, as always, her body responded to it. 'Perhaps a bit later,' she murmured as she heard Ron clumping along the cellar floor towards the steps.

'I'll hold you to that,' he whispered against her ear.

She hastily kissed his cheek, and was standing by the sink when Ron stomped back up the steps in his disreputable socks.

The day seemed to fly past, and although they'd managed to go to bed for an hour while Daisy had her afternoon nap, it wasn't long before everyone had come home and filled the house with noise and laughter.

The evening meal was over, the dishes being

washed and put away by the girls while Ron fed Harvey the scraps and Cordelia settled down to untangle her knitting by the fire. Peggy had left them to it and was now back in their bedroom, Daisy chirruping and trying to pull herself up on the rails of her cot as Jim reluctantly got dressed in his uniform.

'It feels stiff and awkward after a week in civvies,' he said, his smile not quite as broad as usual. 'But at least the boots are well worn in and very comfortable.'

Peggy sat on the bed watching him trying to put on a brave face and not show the emotions she knew were in turmoil just beneath the surface. 'That's good considering all that marching you have to do,' she managed.

Jim fastened the button at his waist and adjusted his shirt collar and tie. 'There won't be much marching where I'm headed,' he replied as he reached for his hairbrush.

Peggy saw how his hand trembled and quickly reached to take it in her own. 'Remember it's the adventure you've always wanted, Jim,' she said softly. 'And before you know it, you'll be home again.'

He turned from the dressing table and drew her into his arms. 'I love you, Peg,' he murmured against her lips. 'Promise me you'll take care of yourself and not leave out the important things in your letters.'

'Of course I will,' she replied. 'But it'll be difficult

to write much on those silly little airgraphs, and I still don't really understand why I can't send you a proper letter.'

He reached for the stack of slips he'd piled on the top of the chest of drawers. 'It's to save room and weight on the aircraft,' he told her. 'You write this, it's photographed on a huge roll of film along with thousands of others and sent abroad. When it arrives at the other end, people will develop the film and send each message to where it has to be.'

'That's all very clever,' said Peggy with a sigh, 'but it means that even more people can read every word we write to each other.'

Jim smiled and gave her a hug. 'I doubt they'll bother. There are millions of these things going round the world and there simply wouldn't be time to snoop.'

Peggy still wasn't really convinced, but she didn't want to waste these precious moments arguing about something she had no hope of changing. 'You will write regularly, won't you?' she asked as he pulled on his khaki jacket and fastened the Sam Browne belt.

'Aye, I'll write every day, and tell you about all the wonders I'll be seeing. 'Tis a long sea journey to India, and we'll probably stop off in some exotic ports on the way.'

'Never mind wonders and exotic ports,' she teased. 'It's the exotic women I'm more worried about.'

He hugged her tightly and kissed her so hard she

became breathless. 'You're the only woman for me, Peggy Reilly, and don't you ever forget it.' He drew back and looked down at her, his eyes suspiciously bright. 'We'll say our goodbyes here, darlin',' he said. 'It's too hard on a station platform with you standing there looking so forlorn.'

'But I want to come with you,' she gasped. 'I want to be with you for every last second.'

'No, it's better we do it here.' He held her close, his chin resting on the top of her dark curls. 'I want to remember you in our home, with our baby – not standing on a cold draughty platform amongst strangers. Please, Peg.'

She couldn't speak so she nodded against his chest, the smell and feel of the khaki material already distancing him from her.

'That's my girl,' he soothed as he kissed away her tears. 'We'll all be together again soon, and this moment will be as swiftly forgotten as a bad dream. I promise.'

She kissed him fervently, wanting him to feel the love she had for him and to gain strength and courage from the knowledge that she would be here waiting for him.

Jim eventually drew reluctantly from her embrace and turned to Daisy. He picked her up and kissed her face, held her for a few moments and then tenderly set her back beneath the covers. Grabbing his kitbag and cap, he walked out of the bedroom and into the kitchen.

'Well, I'll be off then,' he said with enforced brightness. 'You stay here in the warm and look after my Peggy, and I'll see you all when I next come home.'

Ignoring the general protest, he kissed and hugged Cordelia and the girls and then turned to his father. 'Would you walk with me some of the way, Da?'

'Aye, I'll do that,' Ron replied gruffly.

Peggy caught Jim's eye as his father pulled on his boots and coat. 'I love you,' she mouthed over the chatter of the others.

He winked back at her as he settled his cap on his head and hoisted up his kitbag. And then he was turning away and running down the cellar steps to the back door, his father and Harvey hard on his heels.

Peggy followed them as the others remained, hushed, in the kitchen. Her shadow fell across the moonlit garden as she went down the path and into the twitten, her gaze fixed on Jim's back as he and his father walked towards the main street.

'I love you, Peggy Reilly,' he called through the darkness, his voice echoing against the walls of the surrounding houses before he disappeared round the corner.

'I love you too, James Michael Reilly,' she called back, her voice breaking as the tears began to stream hotly down her face. When she could no longer hear his footsteps, she turned away and closed the gate behind her. 'I love you too,' she whispered.

Chapter Nine

Peggy had managed to get through the past seven days surprisingly well, for the others had been endlessly supportive and she'd made sure she'd kept very busy. Yet there was no escaping the nights, and the restless dreams that left her with a dull headache and the sense that she'd slept for only a few minutes at the most.

Her mood wasn't improved by the awful weather or Daisy's temper tantrum as she refused to sit in the sink and be washed that morning. Peggy sympathised with Harvey as he slumped in despondency by the fire, his eyebrows twitching each time Daisy's high-pitched screams tore through the room and right through their heads, but there was nothing for it but to struggle on.

Daisy planted her feet firmly against the side of the large stone sink and stiffly resisted all of Peggy's efforts to sit her down as she bawled with fury and waved her fists about.

Peggy's skirt and sweater were soon soaked, which meant she would have to change before she went to do her stint at the Town Hall for the WVS. Feeling tired and very out of sorts, she gave up.

After a hasty sponge-down, she lifted Daisy out and plonked her on her lap to dry her and get her dressed.

Daisy was having none of it and she arched her back, stiff as a rod, then squirmed and kicked as she yelled at the top of her voice.

'To be sure 'tis enough to wake the dead,' grumbled Ron as he came into the kitchen and put the kettle on the range. 'What the divil's got into her today?'

'She's most likely teething again,' Peggy replied wearily as she finally managed to get the nappy pinned.

Ron scooped Daisy off Peggy's damp lap and bounced her in his arms, whereupon her tears immediately turned to gurgling laughter and she joyfully clapped her hands.

'I don't know how you do that,' said Peggy, who was more than a little put out at Daisy's sudden change from virago to angel. 'She's been nothing but a misery ever since she woke up.'

Ron grinned and managed to detach the tiny gripping fist that was tugging on his eyebrow. 'Ach, well, she knows her grandda loves her, don't you, *Acushla*?'

Daisy giggled as he tickled her tummy.

'You're as bad as each other,' Peggy complained as she warmed the teapot and hunted out a packet of aspirin. Her head was splitting and if she didn't take something for it now, she'd be in pain for the rest of the day.

Ron finished dressing Daisy, who was now as good as gold and burbling happily in his lap. 'There we are,' he said triumphantly as he placed her in the high chair and handed her a wooden spoon. 'Nothing to it if you've got the knack.'

Peggy swallowed two pills down with a slurp of tea and glared at him. 'Very clever, I'm sure.' She took the pot of left-over potato from the large corner larder and heated up a pan with some of the horrid, fishy margarine they were forced to use now. 'I hope the hens are laying well,' she muttered. 'I've only got three eggs to go with this, and I don't want to use that powdered stuff unless I absolutely have to.'

Ron lumbered off down the cellar steps, leaving Daisy to bash the wooden spoon against the tray of her high chair. Peggy was tempted to take it away from her, for every bang seemed to ring in her poor head, but Daisy would only start bawling again, so it was the lesser of two evils.

She concentrated on cooking the potato until it was golden and crisp at the edges, and put one of her precious eggs into boiling water for Daisy. A boiled egg and soldiers always had a soothing effect on her, and as she was entitled to two eggs a week, Peggy didn't see why she shouldn't have them.

Ron returned with a china bowl and placed it carefully on the draining board. 'It's a good thing Suzy and Fran are on night shift and will have their breakfast at the hospital,' he said. 'The hens appear to have gone on strike after that raid last night.'

Peggy regarded the two brown eggs in the bottom of the bowl. 'I don't feel like egg this morning anyway,' she muttered, 'so there are enough to go round as Jane's already at the dairy.'

'You'll be eating your egg, Peggy,' Ron said, his bushy brows lowering over his blue eyes. 'To be sure you do the work of ten men, and I can always get a snack at Rosie's to tide me over until lunchtime.'

'How is Rosie?' she asked as she spooned the egg from the water to Daisy's egg cup and smeared some margarine on the browned toast.

Ron began to slice the toast into fingers. 'To be sure she's not her usual sunny self,' he admitted as he chopped the top off Daisy's egg. 'She tells me she always feels depressed around this time of year, but I think it's more than just the weather and the early dark of every afternoon.'

Peggy drank her tea and said nothing as her father-in-law began to feed Daisy. She knew all about Rosie's sadness, and the reason behind it, but she was distressed to hear that her friend was still suffering after all this time. It just went to show, she thought, how very deep that initial betrayal had gone. 'I'll pop in and try to cheer her up when I've finished at the Town Hall,' she said.

'Aye, she'd enjoy that.' He looked at her quizzically as Daisy smeared egg and toast over her face.

'You wouldn't know what's wrong with her, would you? Is it just a woman thing, or is there something that really bothers her this time every year?'

'It's a woman thing,' she said truthfully, 'so it would probably be best if you made yourself scarce for the afternoon.'

Ron gave a deep sigh as he fed Daisy more egg and toast. 'Aye, I'll do that. I hate seeing her brought so low, and she's refused point-blank to talk to me about it.'

Breakfast was its usual hurried, noisy affair, and once the girls had left for their day at work and Cordelia was settled by the fire with the newspapers, Peggy decided her clothes had dried enough not to have to change.

Having made the bed and whipped round with a broom and duster, sorted out with Cordelia what she could have for lunch and washed down the kitchen lino, she was ready to leave for the Town Hall. With Daisy firmly strapped into the pram and well insulated from the weather in layers of wool, she fastened the rain-cover and pulled up the hood. Slipping into comfortable shoes, she pulled on her raincoat and headscarf and waited for Ron to get the pram down the cellar steps. At least it's stopped raining, she thought as she wheeled the pram down Camden Road, but that wind is like a knife.

By the time she'd reached the High Street her face was frozen and her eyes were streaming, so it was something of a relief to pass into the shelter of the stacked sandbags that guarded the Town Hall's marble steps. There wasn't a Home Guard member on duty today to help her, so she dragged the pram up step by step, and was soon in the warm, fusty fug of the hall. She was looking forward to a cuppa and a fag before she started her morning's work.

Having parked the large coach-built pram in a corner, she checked on Daisy who was now, thankfully, asleep, took off the pram's rain-cover and put down the hood. Hanging her coat over the handlebar, she pulled her wrap-round pinny out of her bag and tied it tightly around her slender frame. With the scarf tied into a knot over her hair and the apron covering her from shoulder to knee, she was ready to tackle whatever was needed – but first that cuppa.

She weaved round the laden trestle tables which were heaped with donated clothes, shoes, cooking utensils, toys and books, and returned the greetings from the other women who were busy filling comfort boxes for the troops. The WVS did a marvellous job, and Peggy was proud to be a small part of it all, even though she usually only sorted clothes or made sandwiches and tea to give the troops a bit of refreshment when they stopped at the station on their way to God knew where. The really good news was they'd been selected to have one of the proper motorised wagons that the Queen had so generously funded, so at least they didn't have to lug the old one up and down the hill, and could drive the new vehicle anywhere it might be needed during an emergency.

Peggy walked through the chaos into the café which had been set up to provide tea and snacks, and bring in some much-needed money. The WVS didn't only cater for the troops, or provide tea and sympathy after a bombing raid; they did sterling work for the homeless, which was why the main hall was filled with mattresses every night. Thankfully the numbers had dwindled over the past few months as the raids had decreased, but there were always new arrivals now the factories were going day and night, so there was always someone in need of a bed.

Peggy paid for her tea and biscuit and sat down to enjoy a cigarette before she got stuck in. She rather hoped she wouldn't be put in charge of sorting out the donated clothing, for people didn't seem to think it necessary to wash anything before they gave it away, and at the end of the morning her hands would be filthy and she'd smell of old, unwashed cloth.

'Margaret.'

Peggy started at the sound of her sister's voice. That was all she needed today. She looked over her shoulder to find Doris was looming and clearly in one of her bossier moods. 'Hello, Doris,' she said as she took in her immaculate appearance. 'You're not usually here at this time of day.'

Doris sat down, tugged down her tailored green uniform jacket and smoothed the skirt over her knees.

Her hair looked freshly set, her make-up was flawless and her polished shoes and handbag were made of the best brown leather. 'I have been asked to run the café this morning,' she announced as she looked scathingly at the woman standing behind the urn. 'But unfortunately I have a prior engagement, so I would appreciate it if you would stand in for me.'

Peggy wasn't at all surprised her sister was wriggling out of her morning's duty. Doris didn't like getting her manicured hands dirty. 'What's the prior engagement?' she asked.

'Margaret, I really don't feel I have to explain anything. Will you do it or not?'

'Not if you're skiving,' said Peggy as she stubbed out her cigarette and folded her arms.

Doris's expression was pained. 'I do wish you wouldn't use such vulgarities, Margaret. It's so common.' She edged forward in her seat. 'I have to meet the billeting people, not that it's any of your business. I caught one of those ghastly factory girls trying to sneak a man in last night, and I will not tolerate such behaviour.'

'Quite rightly,' murmured Peggy. 'But you can't just throw her out, not unless she has somewhere else to go.'

'I already have,' said Doris flatly. 'I put her, bag and baggage, on the doorstep last night.'

'That's a bit harsh, but I can't say I blame you.'

Doris arched a finely plucked brow. 'I'm glad we've finally managed to agree on something, Margaret.'

'I do wish you'd call me Peggy like everyone else,' she sighed.

Both eyebrows shot up. 'Why on earth should I do that? Margaret is a perfectly respectable name, and being called Peggy by everyone makes the wrong sort of people overfamiliar.'

Peggy snorted in disgust at her snobbery. 'I'll do the café, but you owe me, Doris, and I won't let you get away with it again.' She held her sister's gaze. 'By the way, I haven't heard from Jim since he left for the Far East; Daisy's well but teething, and the rest of the household is bumbling along just fine – thanks for asking,' she said with deep sarcasm.

Doris's cheeks went pink and she looked away. 'What with the wedding to organise and those awful lodgers to keep an eye on, I really have far too many things to think about to worry about your disreputable household,' she replied. 'And I'm quite sure that if anything was amiss, I'd be the last person you'd confide in.'

'You've got that right,' snapped Peggy as she pushed back from the table. She turned her back on her sister and walked quickly towards the counter and the tea urn. Doris could wind her up like a clock, and there were times when she was sorely tempted to give her snooty face a resounding slap.

Peggy's feet were aching by the time her shift was over. She'd made what felt like hundreds of cups of tea and thousands of sandwiches during the past four hours, and was now sick of the sight of dirty crockery. No wonder Doris had weaselled out of doing it.

Having managed to feed Daisy earlier, she took off her apron and pulled on her coat, determined to escape before someone found her something else to do. Ron had probably told Rosie she was going to pop in after the pub's lunchtime session, and she didn't want to be late.

The sky was black over the sea, and the wind had lost none of its brutal cold, but at least it wasn't raining, and Daisy was happily sitting up in the pram watching everything go on around her. Peggy took a deep lungful of the fresh air as she strode down the hill towards Camden Road, glad to be away from the tea urn and the pervading fustiness of too many people in one place.

Turning into Camden Road, her thoughts were on Rosie and how best to cajole her out of this annual gloom, when Eileen Harris stepped out of her doorway and straight into the pram.

'Oh, I'm sorry. But you appeared out of nowhere. Are you hurt?' Peggy asked.

'You should look where you're going,' said Eileen crossly as she checked her rather splendid silk stockings for any damage. 'Luckily for you these haven't been torn, or you'd've owed me a new pair.'

'And it's lucky for you there's no damage to my pram, either,' retorted a bristling Peggy, who was in no mood to be spoken to like that by Eileen Harris, of all people. 'Knowing your front door opens out on to the pavement, you should watch what you're doing.'

Eileen folded her arms as she blocked Peggy's way and glared.

Peggy glared back, daring her to start a good row. Eileen was the older sister of a young midwife who'd lodged with Peggy for a few months back in 1941, and although she'd found Julie to be a delightful girl, her sister was quite another kettle of fish. There were things she'd been wanting to say to Eileen for years, but because of Rosie, she'd held her tongue. But one wrong word from this cow and she'd let her have it.

Eileen must have noticed the light of battle in Peggy's eyes, for she suddenly moved out of the way. 'Well, no harm done,' she said with an uncertain smile.

'Don't you talk to me about harm done,' hissed Peggy. 'I know what you are, Eileen Harris, and you should be ashamed to walk these streets.' Before she really lost her temper, Peggy gripped the pram handle and was about to walk away when Eileen stepped in front of her again.

'What exactly do you mean by that remark?' she snapped.

'Get out of my way before I ram this pram into your fancy stockings.'

'No, I want an explanation,' persisted a furious Eileen, her brown eyes narrowed and venomous in her carefully made-up face.

'Rosie Braithwaite is my friend, and you don't need me to say anything further,' retorted Peggy.

Eileen's face paled and the brown eyes widened. 'You know? About that?'

Peggy tightened her grip on the pram, uncaring that the women in the queue outside the butchers were finding their spat hugely entertaining. 'I certainly do,' she replied. 'Want to make something of it, Eileen – or are you going to let me pass?'

Eileen shook her head and was unsteady on her high heels as she moved back into her doorway.

Peggy marched away, head high, a broad smile on her face. That had put the uppity piece in her place and no mistake, and she couldn't wait to tell Rosie so they could have a proper good laugh about it.

She wheeled the pram down the narrow alley which led to the side entrance of the Anchor and pushed it through the door into the square hallway. To her right was the entrance to the large cellar which Ron had turned into a bomb shelter, ahead of her was the entrance to the bar, and to her left were the wooden stairs which led up to Rosie's private apartment. 'Rosie?' she called. 'Are you up there?'

Rosie appeared on the landing and hurried down the stairs. 'Oh, it's so good to see you, Peg. Thanks so much for coming.'

As they hugged, Peggy could feel the tension in her, and was mortified that she hadn't made the time to visit before this. 'I've got something to tell you that will cheer you up no end,' she said as they drew apart and Rosie turned to make a huge fuss of Daisy and lift her out of the pram.

Rosie held Daisy close, her cheek resting on her downy head. 'I know,' she replied with a rather wan smile. 'I saw you and Eileen from my sitting-room window. It looked quite a humdinger.'

'Oh.' Peggy's mood for gossip was immediately deflated.

Rosie must have seen this, for she reached out a hand and squeezed Peggy's arm. 'Come on upstairs and tell me all about it. We can talk in peace now that Ron's taken Monty out with Harvey – and I've got a special treat for us.'

Peggy liked treats, for they were in short supply at Beach View. 'What sort of treat?' she asked eagerly.

Rosie began to climb the worn stairs with Daisy in her arms. 'One of my Yankee customers has given me a carton of cigarettes and a box of chocolates,' she said as she reached the landing. 'I thought we could have a glass of sherry, kick off our shoes, and really spoil ourselves.'

'That sounds heavenly,' sighed Peggy. 'My feet are killing me after standing behind that tea urn for four hours.'

She wasn't at all fooled by Rosie's bright chatter, for her sapphire eyes were dull and shadowed by recent tears. But Peggy made no mention of this as she entered the cosy sitting room that overlooked the street and sat down in the chintz-covered armchair. It was the same every year, and Peggy had willingly taken her troubles on board knowing she was the only person that Rosie trusted to talk to about her very private sorrow.

It was the end of October now, and Mary had managed to resist opening the diaries even though they'd been temptingly piled on top of her bedroom chest of drawers for five days. Yet her curiosity had finally won over her reluctance to pry, and with trembling hands she'd opened up the earliest one two days before, and was soon swept away into another time and another world by her father's lyrical and descriptive prose.

'I'm glad Gideon had something interesting stowed away in that trunk,' said Barbara as they sat in the warm kitchen that wintry evening. They were alone, for the girls had gone down to the pub and Joseph was on fire watch at the school. 'Those diaries have certainly kept you occupied these past two evenings.'

Mary closed the little book and ran her hands over the tooled leather. 'Yes, Daddy wrote so well that I feel I'm walking beside him as I read.' She smiled. 'Did you know that Mother was the daughter of a Presbyterian minister? He was very strict, by all accounts, and of course disapproved fiercely of her association with a Protestant vicar, which was why they left it so late to marry.'

'No, I never knew that,' murmured Barbara as she turned the collar on one of Joseph's shirts with neat stitches.

'Daddy writes so eloquently about the loss of their first two babies,' sighed Mary, 'that I can feel his pain in every word. And yet that anguish was not just for himself, but for Mother, and he shielded her from it, pouring it all out in his diaries in an attempt to find some kind of solace.'

Barbara dipped her chin, putting her sewing aside. 'I remember how devastated I was when I lost mine,' she said softly. 'It's the cruellest thing to bear, and I count myself fortunate that I had Joseph to lean on.'

'I didn't realise,' Mary gasped. 'Oh, Auntie Barbara, I'm so sorry if I've upset you by talking about all this.'

Barbara shook her head and gave her a wan smile. 'It was a very long time ago, Mary love, and the miscarriages were quite early on in each pregnancy. Joseph and I began to wonder if I'd ever carry a baby full term, and so when I gave birth to Jack, it seemed like a miracle.' Her smile warmed and broadened. 'We were in danger of smothering him in love and spoiling him, but I think he's turned out all right.'

'Yes, he has,' Mary replied softly. She looked down at the diary on her lap. 'I just wish Mother had felt the same way about me,' she said unsteadily.

Barbara reached across the table and squeezed

her hand. 'I've always been puzzled by that,' she said. 'Emmaline could be kindness itself, and obviously adored your father, but when it came to you . . .' She bit her lip. 'It was almost as if she resented you coming between her and Gideon – which of course was ridiculous,' she added hastily. 'How could one resent such a sweet, pretty little thing like you after all the sadness of losing the others?'

'I don't know,' said Mary. 'But I've realised over these past days that there's no point in dwelling on things I can't change.'

Barbara patted her hand in empathy, then picked up her sewing again. 'At least you know your father loved you,' she said comfortably, 'and you have his diaries to keep his memory alive.'

'Yes, but the years he spent in Flanders don't make for easy reading,' Mary admitted. 'He describes too well the horror of the rat-infested trenches, the mud and the shelling. The conditions were obviously intolerable, even far behind our lines in the hospital tents, and he had nothing but praise for the overworked doctors and nurses.'

'I was still a young girl back then and living with my parents on our farm near Lewes. I remember the bands and the cheering as my father and brothers paraded down the streets, eager to join in a war that everyone said would be won by Christmas.' Barbara gave a deep sigh as her eyes glistened with tears. 'I lost two brothers, an uncle and a cousin, and my father was a broken man by the time it was all over.

He'd been gassed, you see, and he spent his final months as an invalid.'

'Oh, Auntie Barbara, how awful.'

'Yes, it was at the time, and my poor mother was inconsolable. Yet here we are again, fighting another war. We never learn, do we?'

Mary shook her head and set the diary aside. 'My father wasn't injured, so he was lucky in that respect. But he had a crisis of faith during that time, unable to reconcile his beliefs in a loving and forgiving God with the sheer carnage he was witnessing.'

'That's understandable,' said Barbara as she neatly stitched the collar. 'And yet one would never have guessed it from his wonderful sermons.'

'They were marvellous, weren't they?' Mary sighed. 'But that conviction in his faith was hard-won. I can tell from his diaries that he returned home a very different man to the one that had left in 1914, and although Mother welcomed him with open arms, he found it very difficult to fit back into normal life again after all he'd been through.'

'It was the same for so many of those poor men,' said Barbara. 'It can't have been easy for Gideon to return to a quiet seaside parish after the noise and horrors of war.'

'I think they both struggled to adapt to married life again after four years apart. When Mother lost another two babies in quick succession, Daddy accepted that God didn't wish them to have children, and so he threw himself into his parochial duties and battled to renew his shattered faith.'

Barbara looked up from her sewing. 'It all sounds terribly sad. Are you sure that reading about their early life together is helping to ease your grief?'

'Strangely enough, it is,' Mary replied. 'I feel I know them both a bit better now, especially Mother.' She paused to find the right words. 'From the way he writes about her it's obvious that he absolutely adored her, and tried very hard to make up for the loss of their babies by encouraging her to help in the parish and be his constant companion and guide. I do believe that she loved him, but I also think she was very aware of how important her place was in the village community, and how easily she could use the loss of their children as a means to tighten her hold on him and manipulate him to her will.' She gave a tremulous sigh. 'That sounds awful, doesn't it?'

Barbara shook her head. 'Not at all. And actually, I agree. Emmaline was like Gideon's shadow; she followed him about, clung to his arm when they were walking, and looked up at him as if he was the font of all knowledge.' She gave a rueful smile. 'Now I'm being rather catty, aren't I? But I always got the impression Emmaline knew exactly how to flatter and coerce to get her own way and that Gideon was far too soft with her.'

'You didn't like her, did you?'

'Not much,' admitted Barbara. 'Which isn't to say I didn't admire the good works she was involved in,' she added hurriedly. 'But her treatment of you was so odd that I just couldn't warm to her.' She smiled. 'I'm not ashamed to confess that I was only too delighted to look after you when you were tiny, and at one point, Joseph and I even discussed the possibility of adopting you.'

Mary's eyes widened in shock. 'Adopting me? But Daddy would never have agreed to that.'

Barbara nodded. 'We both realised that, which is why we never broached the subject outside these four walls.' She gave a deep sigh. 'To all intents and purposes Emmaline gave an outward show of caring for you, but I very quickly realised it was all a sham and my silly old heart went out to you. I probably shouldn't have, but I tried to make up for her lack of affection with lots of hugs and kisses.'

'Oh, Auntie Barbara.' Mary reached for her hand across the table. 'I always knew you loved me, and I do appreciate everything you and Joseph have done for me over the years. This lovely home, and the warmth and love you've shown me, have given me more than you could ever know.'

Barbara cleared her throat. 'It's no more than you deserve, and as far as I'm concerned, you'll always be my little girl,' she said gruffly. She blinked rapidly and bent her head to her sewing. 'Tell me how you see your father now you've read some of his diaries.'

Warmed by her heartfelt words, Mary found it difficult to speak for a few moments. 'I think he was always a quiet, thoughtful sort of man,' she said eventually. 'But his experiences during the First World War, and the subsequent struggle to adapt to married life again and restore his faith, made him more solitary. I can understand now why he spent so many hours alone in his study, or reading through the night in the spare room.'

Mary paused as she remembered the last night when he'd been so tired, and yet had found the time to thank and bless her for her help with Gladys. 'But he always had time for me,' she murmured, 'and I never doubted for a minute that he loved me deeply.'

Barbara finished her sewing and pushed back from the table. 'I think we've earned a cup of cocoa,' she said as she reached for a saucepan and poured in some milk. 'We're getting far too gloomy, and there are other more exciting things to discuss.'

Mary's mood lightened immediately. 'Is Jack coming home on leave? He didn't say anything in his last letter.'

'Not as far as I know,' replied Barbara as she waited for the milk to warm through. Taking it off the heat, she stirred in the cocoa powder, added a spoonful of sugar and gave it a good stir. 'Did he tell you about his volunteering to try out for the Commandos?'

Mary nodded. 'I was rather hoping he'd come home for some leave before he went off to try and pass the course.'

Barbara placed the two steaming mugs of cocoa on the table and sat down. Lighting a cigarette, she stared into the glowing embers of the fire. 'I don't know that I want him doing dangerous things like that,' she said, 'but from what I hear it's the toughest course the army has, and very few make it into the Commandos at the end of it. I'm rather hoping he isn't successful.'

Mary grinned. 'So am I,' she confessed, 'though Jack would be horrified at our lack of support.'

Barbara smiled back. 'It's a good thing Joseph's on fire watch tonight and can't hear us,' she said. 'He's cock-a-hoop at the thought of his son being one of an elite fighting force, and is already crowing about it down at the pub.' She puffed on her cigarette. 'Anyway, that wasn't what I wanted to talk about,' she went on, briskly dismissing her fears for her son. 'Joseph has managed to sort out those insurance policies of yours, and there should be a cheque in the post quite soon for just under a hundred pounds.'

Mary was lost for words. A hundred pounds was an enormous sum of money.

'I thought you'd be surprised,' said a smiling Barbara. 'But that's a lot of money for a young girl, and I want you to promise to put it straight in the bank.'

'I'd rather give some to you for my keep and put the rest towards going back to college to get my teaching certificate,' Mary replied breathlessly.

'Yes, well, that's the other thing I wanted to talk to you about,' said Barbara. 'Joseph and I have discussed it fully, and agree that we don't want any of your money, and that you should keep it for when you might really need it. A sum like that is a healthy backup if things should go wrong.'

'But—'

'No buts.' Barbara spoke firmly. 'That money was left to you by your father so you would have something behind you. As for your teaching certificate, Joseph and I have some savings, and as Jack showed no signs of wanting to further his education, we've decided to use them to help you.'

Overwhelmed and tearful at her generosity, Mary pushed back from the table and flung her arms around Barbara. 'Thank you, thank you,' she breathed, 'but I can't take it, Auntie Barbara, really I can't. I have my own money now, and—'

'And you'll do as you're told and let me and Barbara support you through college,' declared Joseph as he strode into the room in his Home Guard uniform. 'Your money will come in useful when you and our Jack set up home together, and if you refuse to let us help you, then we'll both be very hurt.'

'We will,' Barbara confirmed sternly.

Faced with such determination from both of them, Mary knew she was defeated. 'I'll pay you back every penny,' she promised after hugging them both.

'You'll do no such blooming thing,' said a highly embarrassed Joseph, 'and that's an end to it.' He turned to Barbara as he dug in his bag and pulled out two Thermos flasks. 'It's brass monkeys out there and we've emptied both of these. Could you top them up, love?'

As Barbara warmed more milk and filled the flasks with cocoa, Mary sat in a daze of happiness at the kitchen table. She had never dared dream she could go back to college, or that Barbara and Joseph would willingly use their savings to fund it – and with the legacy of a hundred pounds to put away for the future, she was doubly blessed.

She looked down at Gideon's diary and ran her fingers across it, silently thanking him for his fore-thought. He'd known that because of their age, the time would soon come when Mary would be alone in the world, and he'd ensured that she had some financial security so she wouldn't be dependent on others.

Joseph's voice broke into her thoughts. 'I'll say goodnight to you both, and see you in the morning.'

He kissed Barbara on the cheek and gave Mary a bashful hug. 'Don't stay up too late plotting and planning,' he gently teased. 'These things take time to organise, especially when there's a war on and hard-working farmers have to stay up all blooming night staring up at an empty blooming sky.' As he opened the back door a gust of cold air rushed into the warm kitchen before he slammed it behind him and tramped out into the blackness.

Barbara settled back at the table and sipped her cocoa. 'I know he wants to do his bit, but these nights on fire watch leave him very tired, and I worry about him getting careless when he has to use all that heavy farm machinery.'

'I'm sure he's experienced enough not to be careless,' soothed Mary as she drank her own cocoa. She looked across the table, unable to hide the excitement that was bubbling up inside her. 'Tomorrow, first thing, I'll telephone the college in Lewes and see if they've got any places. I know it's a bit late in the term, but—'

'I've already rung them,' said Barbara, 'and all the places have gone. In fact there's a waiting list.'

The sharp disappointment dispelled Mary's excitement. 'I suppose it's because the other college was bombed and Lewes was the nearest one they could relocate to.' She stared into the mug of cocoa, her thoughts whirling. 'There are other colleges, of course, but it's probably a bit late to try and get in now.'

'The administrator at Lewes suggested two other colleges which still have places,' said Barbara. 'But one's in Sheffield and the other's in Wales.'

Mary shook her head. 'I don't want to be that far from home. It would be much more sensible to apply for next year at Lewes, and find something else to do in the meantime.'

Barbara nodded. 'I think that would be best in the circumstances. You can telephone them in the morning and ask them to send the application forms, then we can sit down and discuss the sort of job you might like to do while you wait.'

Mary finished her cocoa and took the empty mugs to the sink. 'I'm feeling very positive about things now,' she said as she washed the mugs. 'And as it'll only be for a year, I might see if there are still jobs going at the rope factory. Pat tells me the wages are very good, and it'll be a way of supporting myself and even perhaps putting a bit by for when I start the course next year.' She dried the mugs and put them away before turning to Barbara with a broad smile.

Barbara smiled back. 'Let's just take one thing at a time for now,' she said gently. 'I know you're excited, but it's late and well past both our bedtimes. Come on, you can conquer the world tomorrow.'

Mary threw her arms about her and kissed her cheek, revelling in the soft warmth of her and the love she radiated. 'I'll make you so proud of me, Auntie Barbara,' she breathed.

'I know you will, love.' Barbara kissed her and patted her cheek before she shooed her out of the kitchen. 'And don't stay up all night reading,' she called up as Mary took the stairs two at a time. 'We've got a busy day tomorrow.'

Mary was almost skipping along the landing as she headed for the bathroom. She hummed to herself as she washed and prepared for bed, and then drifted in a haze of euphoria back to her room. 'I'm going to be a teacher,' she breathed in awe as she closed the door behind her. 'And I'll be the very best teacher I can possibly be.'

Her excitement made her careless as she felt her

way across the room to pull the blackout curtains, and she stubbed her little toe on the base of the chest of drawers. With a gasp of pain she hopped on one foot, shot out a hand to steady herself, and knocked everything off the top of the chest.

Breathing deeply to try and ease the pain in her toe, she limped to the window, closed the curtains and then turned on the bedside light. A quick examination of the injury proved there was no bleeding, and although it was throbbing a bit, there didn't appear to be anything much wrong with it. This was more than could be said for the appalling mess she'd made when she'd knocked everything to the floor.

She changed into the winceyette nightdress as she waited for the throbbing to ease, and then went to clear up. There were four diaries sprawled about the floor along with the tortoiseshell hair clip, her emergency clothing coupons and a tin of talcum powder which had burst open to dust everything in white.

With a cluck of annoyance, she picked up the tin and secured the lid before she shook the talc off the coupons and cleaned the hair clip with the hem of her nightdress. The powder had gone everywhere, but she could already hear Barbara moving about in the next room and it was far too late to go back downstairs for the brush and dustpan.

With a groan of distress, she carefully retrieved the diaries and sat on the bed to try and clean them off. Having given the first three a good rub with her nightdress hem, and a careful shake to get the powder from between the pages, she turned to the last. As she held on to the spine and cautiously wafted it back and forth, something drifted to the floor.

Horrified that she might have loosened one of the precious pages, she scooped it up. But it wasn't a page from the diary. It was a piece of paper that had been folded several times.

Mary set the diary aside and came to the conclusion that her father must have used the paper as a bookmark, and forgotten about it. But then she realised it had been formally sealed with wax. Whatever it was, it had to be very important, and she was suddenly afraid to open it. She stared at it, her curiosity battling with a deep uneasiness as she turned it over and over in her hands. But she knew that having discovered it, she had no option but to see what it said, and her fingers were clumsy as she broke the seal and tentatively flattened out the folds.

She had to read the document twice before she could fully absorb the awful words. But once she had, time stood still and she felt her world slowly and inexorably crumble to dust.

Chapter Ten

Mary stared and stared at that piece of paper, unwilling to comprehend fully that it had anything to do with her. And yet, deep down, she knew it did, and there was no escape from it. The hurt was so deep and all-encompassing that she was numb, unable even to cry.

As the bedside clock ticked away the minutes she finally came out of her stupor and set the formal letter to one side. She reached for the diary it had fallen from and, after a shuddering breath for courage, began to read the entries for 1924.

Gideon was in turmoil, for although Emmaline had put on a brave face and appeared to have come to terms with the terrible loss of their babies, he knew how much she was suffering. She never said a word to him about the pain she carried so bravely, but he could sense it in her quietness, and in the way she looked at him and sighed so sadly, clinging to his arm as they walked, as if she needed his strength to help her put one foot in front of the other.

He became possessed by a terrible guilt, certain he had been the cause of her deep unhappiness, and it was at that point he'd decided to move out of their bedroom, not only to spare her from his all-too-human desires, but to suppress and control them in solitary prayer.

As the weeks went on and there was no improvement in Emmaline's silent anguish, he decided that a change of scenery might be good for them both. He'd written to the bishop explaining his deep concern for his wife's health, and asked to be sent to another parish where the memories of their lost children would not be so poignant. By the middle of October they were preparing to leave Carmine Bay for Harebridge Green, and to Gideon's delight and huge relief, Emmaline seemed to have found some of her old spirit.

Mary came to the end of the page and found she was shivering, not only from the cold, but from the fear of what she might find in those following pages, for they would describe events around the time of her birth. However, she'd gone so far and knew she had to carry on no matter how painful it became, for it was vital to discover what had led to that signed and sealed document. She fearfully turned the page and began to read.

October 29th 1924

I have had the most extraordinary day, and it all began with a very difficult conversation with an infrequent member of my congregation. As I sit here, surrounded by packing cases waiting for Emmaline to come home from her women's Bible group, I am overwhelmed by the power of God, and how He can miraculously provide the answers I have so earnestly been seeking these past years.

Cyril Fielding is not from this parish, but as a successful travelling salesman who likes to keep up his faith, he attends my services when he can, for he most kindly told me he loves listening to my sermons. On the occasions over the past months when I have met and talked to him, he seems to be a very pleasant, rather earnest young man who is as generous in spirit as in his donations to the church.

I have to confess I was extremely shocked by Fielding's story, but to err is human, and at least he was doing his best to atone for his sin in trying to put things right for everyone concerned. The poor man was quite beside himself as he told me about the brief affair he'd had with a girl he'd met in Cliffehaven on his sales round. He'd brought the affair to an end when he realised how much hurt it would cause his beloved wife and children if they found out. But a few months later he was back in Cliffehaven, and was confronted by the girl who was about to give birth to their child.

He admitted to me in shame that at first he'd denied being the father, but his innate sense of justice wouldn't allow him to deny patrimony once the baby was born. Although he couldn't offer her marriage, he was willing to set the girl up comfortably in a small flat in Cliffehaven and pay a regular sum of money to ensure that she and the baby didn't go without. But within days of settling in, she left him minding their daughter so she could go shopping, and never returned.

He was wild with anxiety and desperate to find her, but there was absolutely no trace of her anywhere. The poor man was in such torment as he told me his tragic tale that he broke down in tears, and it was quite some time before I could calm him. My heart ached as he told me of his own nightmare childhood experiences in an orphanage, and I could fully understand why he was so desperate not to abandon his precious baby to the same fate. I admired him for his courage in facing his wife with his sorry tale, and was saddened but not really surprised that she'd refused to contemplate raising his illegitimate child – and had in fact threatened to divorce him and take away his other children should he keep the baby.

He was a wreck of a man, totally bewildered and unable to decide which way to turn. He understood that he'd committed a terrible sin by being unfaithful, and was tortured by the thought that his innocent baby would be the one to suffer. As he wept and prayed for an answer to his dilemma, I became aware of God's presence in my heart and knew what I must do. The babe could not be abandoned, and Emmaline and I have so much love to give, of course we would take her in.

Cyril was embarrassingly grateful. He fell to his

knees and kissed my hands as he cried in relief, and I hardly knew how to deal with him, for I have never witnessed a man in such a wild state before. But once he'd calmed down enough to talk properly, he came to see that he couldn't just hand the child over to me and Emmaline – there had to be some sort of binding, written agreement between us so that the child was secure in our care.

So, with the sweet little baby asleep in her blanket on my study sofa, we worked out a document between us. We both signed it, and I sealed it, promising him I would not open it again or show it to the child until she had reached twenty-one. He left shortly afterwards, and now I sit with the baby in my arms, waiting for Emmaline to come home.

I have decided she will be called Mary – Flora isn't suitable, and it would always be a reminder of her unfortunate beginnings. This child will be the greatest gift I can bestow on my darling Emmaline, for I am convinced that in His wise and mysterious way, she has come into our home and our hearts from God.

Mary blinked back the tears. 'Oh, Daddy,' she whispered. 'What a wonderful, kind-hearted, loving man you were. I was blessed when you rescued me, truly I was.'

She sat in the pool of light from the bedside lamp as the old farmhouse creaked and groaned and the room slowly took on the chill of the night. She clambered into bed and pulled the eiderdown up to her chin as her thoughts and emotions whirled.

Her father had truly believed she'd been a gift from God – a precious gift that would bring joy to his sad, bereaved wife. But how had Emmaline reacted? And what of the man who'd given her away – and the mother who'd abandoned her? Were they still alive – and if so, did they regret giving her away – or even think about her?

Most of the questions seemed to be unanswerable, and Mary took a deep breath as she picked up the diary again. At least now she could begin to under-stand the reason for Emmaline's lack of affection and the cruelty of her scathing tongue, for she'd been forced – through Gideon's misguided devotion and faith – to take on a child that was not her own, and one with a far from respectable background. To a proud woman like Emmaline, it must have been the ultimate shame.

October 30th 1924

My darling Emmaline couldn't hide her shock and dismay when she returned home last evening to discover me trying to change Mary's nappy. She quickly recovered and took over my rather ham-fisted efforts with an ease and efficiency that gladdened my heart. She is a natural mother, and my joy is over-whelming, for at last, at last we are a proper family.

As she warmed a bottle and fed our little one, she

of course bombarded me with many questions. I have to confess that she has serious doubts as to the wisdom of taking in an unwanted, illegitimate child, and was worried that Mary's unfortunate parentage would show itself in later life and bring only shame and disgrace to our door. I was surprised, and rather hurt by this, for I've always thought my Emmaline to be the most gentle, charitable woman – but I suppose she was still reeling from the shock.

As this day dawned and we adjusted to having Mary in our family, it seems Emmaline is at last content, and as she sits by the fire in my study on this last night in Carmine Bay, with the baby asleep in a cradle beside her, I see a little mother finally fulfilled. I give thanks to God, and pray that He will continue to watch over us as we begin our new life in Harebridge Green.

Mary went on reading through the night. It was patently clear that Gideon adored her, and as the little family settled here in Harebridge Green and became an intrinsic part of the community, he was blind to the fact that Emmaline simply wasn't able to feel the same way.

And yet the signs were there, for as time went on he'd begun to worry about Emmaline's willingness to leave Mary with the Boniface family for longer and longer periods – and her strange lack of interest in her school reports and minor childhood triumphs. He wrote that he couldn't understand why she preferred him to read the bedtime stories, or kiss and cuddle their sweet girl. And as Mary had grown into a beautiful young woman, he'd even had a sneaking, rather guilty suspicion that Emmaline had been jealous of her.

His doubts had increased over the years, making him wonder if his act of kindness and love had been rash and misguided – and if he should have consulted Emmaline before he'd taken Mary in. And yet he still saw Mary as a gift from God, and refused to believe that his darling wife was incapable of loving her. He'd finally accepted her maternal shortcomings, seeing them as only natural for a woman with a large house to run and a busy life, and gladly took over the fatherly duties of guidance, love and interest.

Mary continued to read in the hope there would be another mention of Cyril Fielding, for he must have known through his conversation with Gideon that they were moving to Harebridge Green – and having proclaimed his love for his daughter, surely he'd have been anxious to know that she was well and happy.

But his name never cropped up again, and there was no sudden appearance of anyone claiming to be her mother either. And, as her eighteenth birthday approached, her father wrote that he was dreading the time when she turned twenty-one and he would have to tell Mary the truth. He'd even contemplated burning the letter, but had realised it wasn't really his to destroy, for it was her only link to her true parentage, and one day she might decide to try and find them.

Mary was so deeply immersed in the diary that when the door creaked open she gave a start of fright.

'What on earth are you doing reading at this hour?' asked a bewildered and sleepy-eyed Barbara. 'It's four in the morning.'

Mary hastily smeared the tears from her face. 'Oh, Auntie Barbara,' she gasped. 'I'm so sorry. I didn't wake you, did I?'

Barbara shook her head. 'I needed the bathroom and saw the light under your door.' She came into the room, her expression concerned. 'Whatever's the matter, Mary? Why are you crying?'

As Barbara perched on the side of the bed and took her hand, Mary had to fight to hold back more tears. 'It's Daddy's diaries,' she managed. 'They've shaken me up a bit.'

'You look rather more than just shaken up,' said Barbara as she smoothed Mary's long hair away from her tear-stained face. 'I've always worried that they would upset you. And it seems I'm right.'

Mary stilled her hand as she tried to collect the diaries to put them away. 'I found out that Daddy did something a long time ago – and although it explains a good deal about Mother's strange behaviour towards me, it's rocked the very foundations of everything I knew and believed in.'

Barbara frowned as Mary's tears streamed down her face. 'Goodness me,' she said anxiously as she found her a handkerchief. 'But your father was such a good man – how could he have done anything so wrong to upset you like this?'

Mary struggled to control her emotions and, once she had stopped crying, handed her the letter. 'You'd better read this, and then I'll explain the rest,' she told her.

Barbara regarded the letter and the seal, her troubled expression deepening as she read the contents. 'Oh, Mary,' she said brokenly. 'This can't be right – not right at all.'

'It's probably not legal, and there's no sign of any formal adoption papers or even my birth certificate. Neither is there any mention of my mother's name. I don't know who I am, Auntie Barbara,' Mary said calmly. The time for tears was over and she needed to think clearly.

Barbara's eyes widened as Mary told her all she'd learnt from the diaries, and when she'd finished they sat holding hands, each stunned by the revelation and unable to absorb the enormity of its consequences.

Barbara was the first to break the silence. 'It's an awful thing to discover,' she said, 'but it certainly explains why Emmaline was the way she was with you.'

Mary nodded. 'Poor Daddy, he'd thought I was the answer to his prayers, but he should have talked to Mother first.' She sighed deeply. 'I actually feel very sorry for her,' she admitted softly. 'She must have been shocked to the core to come home and find me there, and to be forced to take me – an illegitimate baby with a dubious background – into her care.' She gave Barbara a wry smile. 'I got the feeling from Daddy's diaries that Emmaline had played the part of a bereaved, helpless, childless woman to the hilt – and because of that she was completely undermined by his act of love.'

'In other words,' said Barbara flatly, 'she got her comeuppance.'

Mary nodded. 'It's no wonder she resented me, and of course it fully explains why she was always calling me sinful and no better than I should be.'

Barbara's lips tweaked in disgust. 'She should have been honest about how she felt right from the start, and arranged for you to be adopted or fostered with another family. Joseph and I would have taken you in like a shot. No question.'

'And that would have been wonderful,' sighed Mary. 'But we can't change what happened, and at least I had Daddy. I'll always feel blessed because of that.'

Barbara was silent with her thoughts for a moment. 'This has come as a shock to me, and I can barely imagine how deeply it must have affected you,' she said finally. 'I'm sure your head is spinning with it all – I know mine is – but you mustn't do anything hasty, Mary.'

'There isn't much I can do about anything,' she replied wistfully. 'But I think I might try and get hold of my birth certificate.'

'Oh, love,' sighed Barbara. 'Don't hold out much hope of doing that. Your mother would have been registered under her maiden name, and in the circumstances I doubt very much if she'd put Fielding down as your father. And then there's the question over your actual date of birth – there's nothing in that document to prove it. In fact it doesn't help at all really.'

Mary knew she was right, yet was unable just to turn her back on everything and get on with her life as if she'd never found that beastly document. 'But I have to try, don't you think?'

Barbara didn't reply immediately, for she was deep in thought. 'I suppose you do,' she said eventually, 'but even if you're successful, what would you gain from it? There's very little chance of tracing either of your parents after all this time. People move away, get married, change their names – and with the war on, who knows where they might be – or even if they're still alive?'

'If I can't get hold of my birth certificate, then I think I'd like to go to Cliffehaven and see if I can find anyone who knew Cyril,' replied Mary thoughtfully. 'I know it seems a silly sort of thing to do, but I feel as if my life has become a sort of jigsaw puzzle, with lots of missing pieces. And I need to find those missing bits, Auntie Barbara. Really I do.'

'I can understand that,' said Barbara as she put her arm round her and held her close. 'But even if you find one or another of them, it might not be a pleasant experience. After all – and I'm sorry to have to say this – they more or less abandoned you and haven't made the slightest effort to stay in touch these past eighteen years. You could be badly hurt, Mary – and I don't want that.'

'That's a risk I'll have to take if I'm to find out who I really am,' Mary replied with a stoic determination that belied the fear fluttering in the pit of her stomach.

'I know you must be impatient to discover the truth, but I think it would be better if you didn't rush into anything you might come to deeply regret,' advised Barbara. She kissed the top of Mary's head. 'You've had a nasty shock, love, and you need to come to terms with it and think carefully about what the consequences might be, should you decide to take it further.'

Mary nestled into her embrace. 'I'll still apply for Lewes,' she promised. 'But I'll also write off and see if there's the slightest chance of getting hold of my birth certificate.'

'And if that proves impossible?'

'Then I'll go to Cliffehaven.'

'Oh, Mary,' sighed Barbara. 'I do wish you wouldn't.'

Mary drew back from the embrace and held Barbara's hands. 'If my application to Lewes is successful, then I'll have a year to find them. But I promise to do things properly and plan it all carefully.'

'But you've hardly left this village, let alone travelled so far on your own,' fretted Barbara.

'Then it's time I did,' Mary replied firmly. 'I'll see if I can find out what sort of jobs are going in Cliffehaven before I travel all that way, and also get in touch with the billeting people. It might be a bit scary, and I'm sure there will be times when I'll wish I was back here with you. But I have to do this, Auntie Barbara, really I do.'

Barbara sat back and regarded Mary with deep concern. 'You've already made up your mind about this, haven't you?'

Mary nodded. 'I've had all night to think about it, and I'm sorry if it's upsetting you, but I won't be able to rest until I've done all I can to find at least one of them and get some answers.'

'How long do you think you might stay in Cliffehaven, Mary? And what if neither of them can be traced?'

'If they can't be traced, then I'll come home. But someone in Cliffehaven must remember Cyril, or at least have heard of him. And an unmarried girl with a new baby would have caused a certain amount of gossip – especially if Cyril had set her up in a flat and then she'd run off leaving him literally holding the baby.'

'Oh, Mary, you've opened a Pandora's box by

looking in that trunk. I wish Joseph had never found it.'

'I'm glad he did,' said Mary decidedly. 'Those diaries have explained a lot of things, and once I can fill in the gaps I'll feel whole again and ready to face the future.'

'You're being very brave,' murmured Barbara, 'but I still don't like the thought of you being on your own so far from home. Christmas is only eight weeks off, and that's no time to be away from people who love you. I think we should discuss this with Joseph.'

Mary gave Barbara a hug. 'I'd like that, but it won't change my mind, Auntie Barbara.'

'No, I can see that.' She gave a deep sigh and reached for Mary's dressing gown. 'Let's go down and make a start on breakfast. Joseph will be home soon, and I can already hear the girls out in the yard.'

Peggy had been on tenterhooks for the past few days, rushing to answer the telephone every time it rang in the hope there was news of Anne's safe delivery of her new baby. She was beginning to worry as the due date came and went, and tried to find comfort in the fact that babies arrived when they were ready, and some could be much more reluctant to be born than others.

'I do wish that baby would hurry up,' she said to Cordelia as she ironed the pillowcases. 'Poor

Anne is almost two weeks overdue now, and I'm beginning to worry that something isn't right.'

'What's that, dear?' Cordelia fiddled with her hearing aid. 'I do wish you wouldn't mutter.'

Peggy repeated what she had said loudly and clearly and then gave a deep sigh. 'And I wish you wouldn't keep turning that thing off, Cordelia.'

'I like a bit of peace and quiet,' she replied with a sniff. 'What with all the shenanigans of those girls racketing about in the other room, it's hard to hear oneself think at times.'

Peggy smiled and carried on with her ironing. Rita and Jane were in the dining room playing their new records and practising their dance steps for the evening's party at the old drill hall. It had been organised by the RAF to celebrate Cliffehaven's purchase of a Spitfire, which would fly over this afternoon to show off the town's name on its side.

'It's all thanks to Rita that the town has its own Spitfire,' said Peggy. 'If it hadn't been for all those motorcycle races she's been holding, it wouldn't have been possible. I think she's earned a couple of hours of noise, don't you?'

'I suppose so,' Cordelia admitted grudgingly, 'but I don't see why it has to be so loud.'

Peggy had to grin at this, for Cordelia would turn the volume right up on the wireless when her favourite tunes were being played, and she was amazed the neighbours hadn't complained. 'Come on, Cordelia,' she coaxed. 'It's not like you to be grumpy.'

Cordelia sighed. 'I know, but it's so cold and damp and my arthritis is playing up, and to be honest, I'm feeling a bit sorry for myself this morning.'

Peggy put down the iron and gave her soft cheek a kiss. 'I'm sorry you aren't feeling quite the ticket. Let me reheat that hot-water bottle and make us both a nice cup of tea.'

'That would be lovely, dear. You are kind.'

Peggy checked that Daisy was still happy with her toys in the playpen and had just refilled the stone bottle and made the tea when someone knocked on the front door. Thinking one of the girls might go and answer it, she waited for a moment, then heard the knock again.

Clucking with amusement, she went out into the hall and opened the door to find her friend Betty Fuller on the doorstep, dressed in her Post Office uniform and laden with an enormous box. 'Goodness me, Betty. That looks heavy.'

'It is,' said Betty, who was red-faced with the effort of carrying it. 'I'll put it on there, if that's all right.' She didn't wait for Peggy's reply and deposited the box on the hall chair. 'You've got to sign for it, Peg.'

'Gosh, whatever can it be?' Peggy hastily signed the chit and took a closer look at the parcel. 'Oh, how lovely. She'll be thrilled.'

Betty grinned. 'It's one of the best things about this job, delivering nice surprise parcels, and I've got several airgraphs for you too.'

'Goodness, that was quick,' Peggy said as she eagerly took the brown envelopes. 'Jim's only been gone for a few weeks.'

'Well the new Kodak processing place is open for business on the factory estate now, so I suppose they can be developed a lot quicker. I hear there are other places opening up all over the country, so it's quite an operation.'

'It's the Post Office in charge then?'

'Sort of. They've joined forces with the Royal Engineers Postal Services.' Betty looked at her watch. 'I'd better get on, or I'll get it in the neck from my supervisor.' She grinned as she cocked her head at the music. 'It sounds like someone's having fun. Are you going to the dance tonight?'

'I certainly am,' said Peggy, who was now impatient to see what was in the parcel and to read her letters. 'Ta ta for now,' she called as Betty ran down the steps to her Post Office van.

She slipped the airgraphs into her apron pocket. With some difficulty, she carried the box into the kitchen, relieved to put it down on the table. 'Look what came for you just now,' she said excitedly to Cordelia.

'For me?' Cordelia's eyes widened as she stared at the large box. 'But I never get anything in the post.'

'Well you have now, and it has come all the way from Canada. Will you please hurry up and open it? I'm dying to see what's inside.'

'Canada?' Cordelia's little face became quite pink with pleasure. Her sons and their families lived there, and weren't at all good at keeping in touch.

Peggy helped her to struggle out of her chair and then rushed to find a knife to cut through the string. Carefully harvesting the brown paper and string, she slit through the heavy tape that held the box flaps together and waited breathlessly for Cordelia to delve inside.

'There's a letter,' she said eagerly, 'and, oh dear, my clumsy old fingers make it so hard to open anything.'

Peggy slit open the thick envelope and discovered it contained three letters, a number of photographs and some childishly drawn greetings cards. 'Oh, Cordelia,' she sighed happily. 'It looks as if your family have all sent you something.'

'Goodness me,' said a tearful Cordelia as she examined the children's cards and looked at the small black and white photographs. 'Look, those are my sons – and they must be their wives – and children – and grandchildren. Don't they all look well? And isn't that a fine house? Canada has certainly done them proud.'

Peggy regarded the happy family gathering with some distaste, for poor Cordelia had rarely had any letters from them and this was the first time in many years that they'd bothered to send photographs, let alone presents. 'Yes, they all look very prosperous and pleased with themselves,' she said drily.

Cordelia's soft hand rested on Peggy's arm. 'Don't be angry with them on my behalf, Peggy. I know they have their own busy lives to lead, and I'm glad they took the opportunity to make a better future for themselves by going so far from home. I write regularly and keep them up-to-date with my news, so they know they don't have to worry about me.'

'It all seems a bit . . .'

'I know,' Cordelia soothed, 'but not every family is as close as yours, and I accepted long ago that it's just the way things are.' She smiled impishly. 'Now, let's see what they've sent. It's a bit like an early Christmas, isn't it?'

Peggy helped her dive into the box, and they gasped in awe and delight as they pulled out a large tin of ham, another of strawberry jam, one of marmalade and three of tuna in oil. There was a tin of biscuits, two tins of tea and coffee and another of evaporated milk, which was an absolute luxury. Beneath the sturdy bags of dried fruit and nuts was a tin of chocolates and some lovely pale blue writing paper and envelopes.

In the bottom of the box were several skeins of beautifully soft new wool, steel knitting needles, a packet of pins, another of sewing needles and a length of tweed fabric the colour of lavender heather. A pair of suede fur-lined gloves and matching hat completed the bounty, and Peggy and Cordelia sat at the kitchen table in stunned silence as they regarded everything.

'Well,' said Cordelia, 'I shall look terrifically smart in my new hat and gloves, and that tweed will make you a lovely skirt.'

'It will do no such thing,' protested Peggy. 'That tweed is for you, and there's probably enough there for a skirt and a little jacket. If Sally has time, I'll ask her to make them so you'll have something new and smart to wear to Suzy's wedding.'

'I expect she'll be too busy with that new baby of hers,' said Cordelia. 'Dear little thing, I'm so very glad she's settled down and is so happy with John Hicks. When I think of how she was when she and Ernie were evacuated down here . . .' She pulled her thoughts together. 'I'd advise you to hide that food before Ron gets back. You know what he's like, and that ham will come to good use at the wedding reception.'

'Cordelia, that's very generous of you,' said Peggy as she began to gather everything up. 'But these are your gifts, and *you* should enjoy them, not give them all away.'

Cordelia stared at her. 'Good heavens, Peggy, just what do you expect me to do? Sit and eat ham and chocolate biscuits while you have rabbit stew or dried egg?' She gave a grunt. 'Really, you are a silly girl sometimes. Now hide all that before everyone comes home and descends on it like a plague of locusts. But keep the chocolate biscuits out. We can have a couple with our tea, and the girls deserve a bit of a treat.'

'I'll keep it all in my wardrobe,' Peggy said.

As she left the kitchen the music came to an abrupt halt, and Rita and Jane came flying out of the dining room to dash upstairs and sort through what they would wear for the evening. Peggy's smile was wistful. It was lovely to have the girls about, but it reminded her of the kerfuffle that Cissy and Anne had always made before an evening out, when they'd been younger and carefree.

When she returned to the kitchen she found Cordelia happily immersed in her letters, so she put a blanket over a sleeping Daisy, sat down and drew the airgraphs from her apron pocket. They were so small, barely two inches wide and three inches long, and what with Jim's writing being so cramped, and the censor blacking out most of it, they were almost impossible to read.

Peggy managed to glean the fact he'd left Liverpool as scheduled to join the vast convoy which would soon set out for the Far East. It had been a terrific thrill to be on board a large ship and to watch all the tugs hauling other ships into Belfast harbour to join them. The food had turned out to be not too bad, but the tea was served without milk, which he hadn't liked at all.

He'd spent that first evening playing nap, and had won nine shillings, but the wind and rain had churned up the sea making the ship roll quite alarmingly, which soon made him and several of the other men feel very sick. It was hot and stuffy below decks, and he'd found it impossible to sleep in the hammock that was one of hundreds slung side by side, with their kit on a rack above their heads. He was already missing her.

The second airgraph made her smile. Jim had been elected Mess Orderly, but had got out of this onerous job by persuading a Major and a Lieutenant Colonel to take him on as their Batman. The Marines on board had got drunk on their rum ration and started a fight which ended up with one man being put in irons.

The rules were stiff and several men had been put on charge for smoking between decks. He'd been paid ten shillings wages, and had won another eight at cards, so was feeling very pleased with himself, and having turned his hammock to another position, had managed to get a good night's sleep in which he'd dreamed about Peggy.

The third communication told her they'd finally set sail. He'd been sleeping in his clothes ever since he'd embarked, the soap wouldn't lather in the salt-water showers, and he had a nasty cold. Apart from that he'd discovered two old mates from Cliffehaven were on board, and although he was delighted to be with them, the talk of home had made him think about her all day.

The final airgraph described mountainous seas and high winds. One look at Jim's breakfast of liver had sent him rushing on deck to be sick, and he'd found sailors, marines, soldiers and airmen lying about on the decks feeling just as bad. He reckoned he'd never spent a worse day in his life, and was beginning to yearn for good solid land as well as the comforts of home and family.

'So, how is that rogue of yours doing?' asked Cordelia.

'He's managed to wheedle his way into being a Batman for a couple of senior officers so he's been excused all other duties, and I think that apart from being horribly seasick, and winning at cards, he's getting a bit bored.'

'It strikes me that young Jim will always wangle an easy ride. He has only himself to blame if he's bored.' Cordelia sniffed and tried to look disapproving, but the twinkle in her eyes betrayed her.

Peggy chuckled. 'You know him too well,' she replied. 'So, what's your news?'

'Both my sons should have retired by now, but they've kept running the family construction business while their boys are fighting in Africa, and their wives are occupied with various war-effort charities. Their three girls have all gone into nursing, and two of them are actually working overseas, one in a hospital ship, the other at the combined forces hospital in Cairo. The family photograph was taken just before war started. Two of my granddaughters are working in an aeroplane factory, and the third is at home looking after two young babies while her husband is flying with the RCAF.'

Peggy was about to question her further when

the telephone rang. Leaping to her feet, she raced into the hallway. 'Hello,' she said breathlessly.

'Hello, Peggy, Vi here. Anne's had a beautiful baby girl.'

Peggy did a little dance. 'Oh, Vi, how lovely. Did everything go all right?'

Violet's voice sounded as clear as a bell, despite the fact she was living miles away on a farm in Somerset. 'Anne's perfectly fine, if a bit tired, and the birth was quite normal. Emily Jane was born at seven this morning, and weighed in at seven pounds two ounces.'

'Good grief,' muttered Peggy. 'Poor Anne. No wonder she's tired.' She sat down on the hall chair, suddenly feeling most put out that another woman had been with her daughter through the entire thing, and even knew the baby's name before she did.

Then she reminded herself how very kind Sally's Aunt Vi had been to take on Anne and Peggy's own two boys as well as Ernie and Rose Margaret for the duration – and felt utterly ashamed at her momentary jealousy. 'Emily Jane, what a lovely name. When did she decide on that?'

'She and Martin had long talks about names, and they'd got it down to two or three. Then the moment she saw her baby she decided she was a perfect Emily Jane.'

Peggy couldn't help but be relieved that Vi hadn't known after all. 'Who does she take after?' she asked wistfully.

'It's hard to tell at the moment,' said Vi with a chuckle. 'All babies look like Churchill to me for the first few days. But she's got dark hair and a snub nose and a pair of lungs on her that would drown out any air-raid siren. I took Rose Margaret in to see her for a few minutes this morning, and she's quite thrilled about the whole thing. I think she regards Emily as her new and rather exciting dolly.'

'Tell Anne I'll write tonight, and give her my love, won't you?' Peggy swallowed the tearful lump in her throat. 'And give Emily and Rose a kiss for me.' She sniffed back the tears, determined not to let it all get on top of her. 'How are my boys? Have they grown much?'

'I should say,' said Vi cheerfully. 'Bob is as tall as me now and has joined the Scouts to learn first aid and map reading. Charlie's growing like a weed and is in the Cubs with Ernie, who is doing extremely well without the calipers and hardly ever uses his walking stick. It seems he's beaten the polio, and is as rambunctious as any boy of his age. The pair of them decided to build a fort down by the duck pond so they can play at being soldiers. I've had to confiscate the slingshots, I'm afraid. They killed two ducks and a moorhen.'

Peggy was having the most awful time trying not to cry. 'Oh, dear,' she managed hoarsely. 'They are a pair of scallywags, aren't they?'

If Vi had heard the quaver in her voice, she didn't remark upon it. 'They certainly are. Your Charlie is still fascinated by machinery, and he took it into his head to strip one of our tractors down to see how it worked.' She added drily, 'Luckily for me, Fred, our local mechanic, knew how to put it back together.'

'Oh, Vi, I'm so sorry.'

'There's no need to apologise,' laughed Vi. 'Curiosity is a marvellous thing, and he's learnt a lot from that little adventure. Fred made him help put each piece back, so he now knows more about tractors than I ever will.'

'Are they there? Can I speak to them?'

'I'm sorry, Peg, but they're both at school, and tonight is their Cub and Scout meetings. I'll try and get through again at the weekend, but you know what communications are like, so I can't promise.'

The pips went and Peggy gripped the receiver. 'Tell them I love and miss them and—' The line went dead, and she replaced the receiver and burst into tears. God, she hated this bloody, bloody war.

Chapter Eleven

Things had advanced at a remarkable pace once Mary had set her plans in motion. She had telephoned the college in Lewes, and was surprised and delighted to be given an interview the following day. The principal looked as if she would be stern and no-nonsense, but she'd heard about the tragedy that had befallen Mary's family and was kindness itself.

The outcome of the interview was that Mary would start the teaching course the following September, and move into the college accommodation block for the first year. Delighted at her success with this first and most important part of her future plans, Mary had travelled back to Hillney on the train and ridden her bike to Black Briar Farm in a haze of happiness.

As for her plans to go to Cliffehaven, they had moved on swiftly too, but not without some trouble along the way. Mary had gone to the labour exchange in Hillney and at first the woman behind the counter had been most unhelpful, for she simply wouldn't accept that Mary wanted to find work so far away. Mary had been forced to tell her about the bombed rectory and the loss of her parents, and had insisted that she needed a new start far from home. The real reason was none of this woman's business and Mary wasn't about to enlighten her.

The woman had relented finally, and after a great many telephone calls managed to get her a job with the Post Office at the Kodak factory, which she would start on Monday next. Accommodation would be with a Mrs Williams, and she was assured that it was a perfectly respectable home in a good area of the town. There were some other girls billeted there, and as they also worked on the factory estate, this would ease her into things quite quickly.

The birth certificate proved far more difficult, for in answer to her enquiry she'd received a very nice letter from someone called J. Collins who was frightfully apologetic, but who couldn't possibly be expected to track it down with so few salient details. J. Collins did suggest she might try and find her father's birth certificate if she had any idea of when he might have been born, but that wouldn't really help as he almost certainly wouldn't still be living at the same childhood address.

Mary had to accept that that was as far as she could go with this line of search, and although the lack of a birth certificate might prove to be a stumbling block later on, at least she had her official identity card to see her through any awkwardness now.

It was the end of the first week in November, and Mary would be leaving early the following morning on the train which would take her to Cliffehaven. The lady at the billeting office had advised her to spend a couple of days with Mrs Williams before she started at the factory so she could get to know the other girls in the house, find her way round the town, and not feel quite so alone and new to everything.

'I do wish you weren't going,' said Barbara as they finished washing the supper dishes. 'I hate to think of you all alone in a strange place. And what with Christmas only round the corner . . .' She gave a deep sigh. 'You will write, won't you, and let us know how things are going?'

'Of course I will. Please don't worry about me, Auntie Barbara. I've managed to sort out everything so far, and I'm sure I'll be quite comfortable and safe with this Mrs Williams.' Mary put her arm round Barbara's plump shoulders. 'And if I can, I might even try to get back for Christmas.'

'Have you told Jack about your plans?'

'I've written nearly every day, telling him about my progress, and giving him my new address. He's a bit dubious about it all, I think, but he understands why I have to go.' She gave a shaky little laugh. 'After all, we're both on a sort of quest, aren't we, what with him signing up to see if he can make the grade in the Commandos, and me off to try and find out who I really am and where I came from.'

Barbara gave another sigh. 'I worry about the pair of you, really I do. I just want you both home and safe, and if it wasn't for all my commitments here, I'd be on that train with you tomorrow morning.'

Mary rather wished she could be, for nerves were knotting her stomach and she was beginning to realise the enormity of what she was setting out to do. 'I know you would,' she soothed, 'but I'm eighteen now, and it's time I grew up and learnt to do things on my own.' She gave Barbara a brave little smile. 'And I haven't done too badly so far, have I?'

'No, you've managed very well,' agreed Barbara. She poured the tea and lit a cigarette as she leant against the rail of the large black cooking range. 'Did you and Pat have fun in Hillney this afternoon?'

Mary was glad of the change of subject, for the arrangements and plans had taken up her every thought over the past week. She nodded and smiled. 'We walked round the shops for a bit and then went to the flicks and saw *Gert and Daisy's Weekend*, which was so funny we were both in tears. After that we treated ourselves to coffee and scones in the High Street tearooms.'

'That was nice,' said Barbara.

'Yes, it was. We had a really good gossip, and we were both sad when we had to go our separate ways. But she's promised to write, so I won't miss out on everything she gets up to.'

Barbara raised her eyes to the ceiling. 'Pat Logan is in danger of getting herself a bad reputation,' she remarked. 'I do wish her mother would take more interest in what she gets up to and put a stop to it.'

'She's not really up to anything more than a lot of the other girls,' said Mary loyally.

Barbara's lips twisted in disbelief, but she didn't pursue her condemnation. 'Did you tell Pat the real reason you're leaving?'

Mary could feel herself reddening as she shook her head. 'I'm ashamed to tell anyone outside these walls that I'm illegitimate,' she confessed. 'I just repeated what I'd said to the woman at the labour exchange – that I needed to get away and make a fresh start.'

'That was probably wise.'

Mary chewed on her bottom lip in distress. 'I hate keeping things from her. Pat's been a good friend, and we've always shared our secrets before. That revelation has changed so many things, Auntie Barbara. It's like a stone dropping into a pool and the ripples spread and spread and spread.'

'You did the right thing, keeping it to yourself,' Barbara replied as she patted Mary's hand. 'There are those who, unfortunately and unfairly, see such things as shameful and make judgements they have no right to make. I'm not saying Pat would be like that,' she added hastily, 'but gossip spreads so quickly, and you have quite enough to contend with already.'

Mary fully understood how the stain of her

illegitimacy could so easily ruin her life, for it was considered a most heinous crime. Even though the sin had been of the parents' making, it was their innocent child who became the scapegoat. It was all terribly unfair, and Mary was finding it extremely hard to accept this shadow hovering over her.

They sat in the warm kitchen as the rain pelted against the windows, and Mary turned her thoughts to tomorrow. The journey itself didn't really worry her, for she only had to change lines once and then it was a clear two-hour run straight to Cliffehaven. But she did worry about her billet and Mrs Williams, and the fact that she'd never worked before, let alone in a factory. It was certainly going to be a huge upheaval, for she would be amongst strangers in an unfamiliar town, and she would have to keep her wits about her, especially when she started asking about Cyril.

'If you're having second thoughts, then stay here. It won't take more than a telephone call to cancel everything,' said Barbara.

'It's not that,' Mary replied. 'I was just thinking about Cyril, and what sort of man he is. I've read that bit in Daddy's diary about their meeting over and over again, and there's something about it that doesn't feel quite right.'

Barbara's eyes widened in surprise. 'What do you mean?'

Mary chose her words carefully. 'I know how tender-hearted Daddy was, and I'm afraid to say he was also rather gullible. Cyril's story certainly pulled the heartstrings, but there was something about the whole thing which makes me wonder if he was all he seemed to be.'

'He seemed to me to be a man at the end of his tether,' said Barbara. 'And although he certainly laid it on a bit thick, he had no reason to lie about any of it.' She smiled comfortingly at Mary. 'I think you should trust Gideon's judgement, and accept that Cyril was a rather weak, emotional man who simply couldn't cope.'

'I suppose so,' she murmured, still not totally convinced. The knot of tension tightened in her stomach and she pushed back from the table. 'I think I'll just go and check on Daddy's car before I go to bed,' she said.

Barbara grasped her hand as she walked past. 'Don't make judgements too quickly, love,' she advised softly. 'We're all weak at times, and at least Cyril did all he could to ensure you were safe.'

Mary kissed her cheek and went to retrieve a thick raincoat and wellingtons from the boot room. She didn't want to think about Cyril or the rest of it any more tonight. Her head was aching with it and her stomach was churning so, it made her feel quite sick. She grabbed the torch, checked the batteries were working and then went outside into the dark, wet night.

Splashing through the puddles and into the barn, she closed the doors behind her and switched on the torch. The Austin 7 had been covered in a large tarpaulin, and its tyreless wheels were now supported on bricks, the springs, coils and engine heavily greased to protect it from the damp and cold. It would stay in the barn for the duration of the war, and it could be many months before she saw it again.

Mary drew back the tarpaulin and ran her fingers lightly over the lovely coachwork which was already dulled by a layer of dust. It would be a terrible wrench to leave it behind, but she had no choice.

Opening the door, she carefully climbed inside and sat behind the steering wheel. The leather seat was cool and still redolent of beeswax, and Jacob had promised to look after it while she was away. It was the memories this car evoked that finally brought her peace, and she knew that no matter what happened after tomorrow, she could always be certain that Gideon had loved her.

The rain of the previous night had petered out and as the train pulled in to Hillney station, a weak sun pierced the clouds above the South Downs to reveal a patch of hopeful blue. Mary and Barbara were tearful, each trying very hard not to show how difficult this parting was, but dearest Joseph couldn't disguise his doubts.

'I don't know why you have to go all that blooming way,' he muttered. 'It won't do you no blooming good, you know, girl.'

Mary gave him a hug. 'I'll be back before you know it, Uncle Joseph.'

'You shouldn't be blooming well going at all,' he grumbled as he released her, his dark brows lowering. 'You watch out for them strangers, you hear?'

Mary nodded but didn't have time to reply, for Barbara had swept her into a tight embrace. 'Any kind of trouble and you come straight home,' she said gruffly. 'Take care, Mary love, and try to ring me as soon as you get settled.'

The stationmaster cleared his throat. 'The young lady has to board now,' he announced. 'Can't have me schedule mucked up.'

Mary hugged and kissed both of them, picked up her suitcase, shouldered the straps of her handbag and gas mask and climbed on to the train. Walking swiftly to a seat by the window, she pulled the leather strap and leant out.

Joseph and Barbara looked horribly forlorn standing there, and Mary was momentarily tempted to get off the train and rush back to them. But she stayed by the window, and as the stationmaster blew his whistle, she reached down for Barbara's hand. 'I love you both,' she called above the hiss of steam and the clank of the great iron wheels that were starting to turn.

'We love you too,' shouted Barbara as she reached the end of the platform. 'Come home soon.'

Mary leant out as far as she dared until the train

eased round a bend and she could no longer see them. She closed the window and sat down with a thump. Reaching into her pocket for her handkerchief, she caught the eye of the young woman sitting opposite her. 'I hate goodbyes,' she said as she dried her eyes.

'You're not alone,' the woman agreed. 'But with a war on, it's all about saying goodbye to those we love. Ghastly, isn't it?'

Mary realised she was right, for there had been so many partings these last few weeks, and she suspected there would be a lot more before this awful war was over. She determinedly blocked out these dark thoughts and pulled herself together. She was starting a new life in a new place, and she would need to be strong and calm and completely focused on her search.

Chatting to her new companion, the journey seemed to fly past. When they had wished each other luck, Mary got off the train at the mainline station and quickly made her way down the long platform to the ticket barrier.

It was a large, bustling station, with servicemen and women rushing to catch trains or gathering in groups with their kitbags to drink tea and smoke cigarettes while they waited. Housewives carried laden baskets, office workers strode about looking frightfully important and porters trundled huge trolleys across the concourse. It was all very confusing and she had a moment of panic before she found the platform she needed. Her train to Cliffehaven was on time.

Hurrying across the vast concourse, she showed her ticket and found a seat. With her suitcase on the overhead rack, she shed her coat, scarf, beret and gloves and placed them on top. As the journey was expected to take a couple of hours, it was best to be comfortable.

As she settled by the window, she glanced around the open carriage which had seats forming two ranks on both sides with a narrow aisle in the middle. Most of the other passengers seemed to be middle-aged civilians, apart from a group of Australian soldiers who were playing a rowdy game of cards. She went bright scarlet and quickly looked away as one of them caught her watching them and gave her a wink.

As the train pulled away from the station she took a book out of her handbag and settled down to read. But the sorrow of leaving Black Briar Farm and the Bonifaces, and the realisation that she really was leaving everything she'd ever known, proved too much and she simply couldn't concentrate. She stared out of the window as the train took her through towns and villages and eventually out to marshlands and open countryside.

She'd never gone much further than ten or so miles from Harebridge, and as she looked at the farmlands and cottages, at the country lanes and hamlets, she felt a glimmer of excitement. This was what she'd wanted – an adventure – a chance to try new things and meet new people. She had to stay positive and believe she was doing the right thing – and if it proved to be anything else, then it would be a valuable experience and a lesson learned.

Peggy's sad mood following that telephone call from Vi had been lifted later that day by the glorious sight of the Cliffehaven Spitfire flying low over the beach. This had been shortly followed by the dance in the old drill hall, which had been so well attended that a good many people had ended up drinking and dancing outside, much to the warden's fury. Peggy had come home tired but happy, having been danced off her feet by numerous young men who didn't seem to mind at all that she was old enough – almost – to be their mother.

It was back to reality today, and as she finished cleaning the outside lav she eyed the newspaper squares that had been skewered on to a hook embedded in one of the upright struts. Proper lavatory paper was as rare as hens' teeth now; newspapers were collected to be pulped and made into clean paper again, and notepads and decent writing paper were things of the past. Which reminded her, she had to go to the Post Office this afternoon and get some more airgraphs. At least they only cost thruppence and weren't rationed.

She hurried back indoors to check that Daisy was still happy with her toys in her playpen. Daisy put out her arms and beamed up at her. 'Mumumumumum,' she gurgled.

'Oh, darling, you're trying to talk.' Peggy scooped her up and gave her a big kiss. 'Who's a clever, clever girl then?'

Daisy gave a shriek of laughter and jiggled about in Peggy's arms as she was danced around the room in time to the music on the wireless.

'It looks as if someone's in a good mood,' said Suzy as she came into the kitchen. 'I wish to goodness that I was.'

Peggy quickly turned down the volume on the wireless. 'Why? What's the matter, love?'

'Doris.' Suzy's pretty face was suffused with pent-up anger.

'Oh, lawks, what's she done now?' Peggy sighed.

'She's only gone and invited the Mayor and half the town council to our wedding,' Suzy snapped. 'Anthony and I have told her a hundred times that we don't want anyone we haven't personally invited, but will she listen? No, she goes her own sweet way and now we'll have to put up with those pompous . . .' Suzy ran out of steam.

'Oh dear, you are cross, aren't you?' Peggy put Daisy on the floor and gave Suzy a cuddle. 'I'm so sorry my sister is such a pain in the neck, but if the invitations have already gone out, I don't see how we can do anything about it.'

Suzy's blue eyes were bright with tears of frustration. 'We can't. They've already accepted,' she said stonily. 'Anthony is furious with her, but you know what she's like, she puts on her hurt-mother face, summons up the tears, and he backs down. Urrgh. I could throttle her, really I could.'

'Yes, I've had that urge many a time,' muttered Peggy as she poured the girl a cup of very weak stewed tea. She glanced at the clock on the mantelpiece. 'I've got time to go round there and see if I can't find a way to sort this out.' She glanced across at Suzy. 'That's if you want me to?'

'Would you, Auntie Peg? Only I'm at my wits' end. It's supposed to be *our* wedding and Doris is bulldozing her way through all the arrangements and simply taking over everything.' The tears slid down Suzy's face and she angrily dashed them away. 'She's ruining what should be the happiest time for both of us, just because she wants to show off.'

'Right, that's it. I've heard enough.' Peggy took off her wrap-round apron and knotted headscarf. 'Would you look after Daisy while I'm out? I should be back by lunchtime, but if not, there's enough bread and spam to do sandwiches, and you only have to heat up the vegetable soup.'

'Are you sure about this, Auntie Peg? Only I don't want to cause any more trouble, and I can't really see what you can do about it anyway.'

'I don't either,' Peggy admitted, 'so I'll have to wing it, as the pilots say. But I'll do my very best.' She reached for her coat which hung on the back of the kitchen door and slipped it on. After digging in the pockets for her gloves, she gave Daisy a cuddle and a kiss and then put a comforting arm around Suzy. 'I'll see you later.'

Peggy walked swiftly away from the house and down Camden Road. She had absolutely no idea how she would tackle her sister and put things right for Suzy and Anthony, but Doris had to be forced to realise this was not her wedding – and that through her interfering, she was turning the whole thing into a circus.

She was so deep in thought that she barely acknowledged the greetings from those in the long queues outside the shops, and as she passed the fire station, she didn't stop as she usually did to chat to Rita, who was washing down a fire engine.

As she waited to cross the High Street which ran up the hill from the seafront, she saw the cause of all the trouble between Doris and her husband, Ted. Ted's former floozy was strolling down the hill in a skirt that was too tight and too short for a woman of her girth and age. With high-heeled shoes, bleached hair, dangling earrings and a cleavage deep enough to sink a battleship, she was the epitome of everything Doris hated. And that gave Peggy an idea.

Crossing over the High Street, she hurried down Havelock Road, past the small park and the two bombed-out houses until she reached Doris's. Set back from the tree-lined road behind a high brick wall and sheltering foliage, the fine detached house stood grandly at the end of a gravel drive.

As Peggy walked to the front door, she noted that the grass had been cut, the flower borders weeded and the earth turned, and the windows had been cleaned. Doris was very big on keeping up appearances, and Peggy didn't mind betting she'd made her unwanted lodgers do the bulk of the work. She rapped the brass knocker with some vigour and stood there, rather breathless from her quick and angry walk.

The door opened and Doris regarded her with little pleasure. 'I can guess why you're here,' she said coolly.

Peggy pushed past her and walked into the hallway. 'Good. So you won't be surprised if I give you an earful.' She pulled off her gloves and unbuttoned her coat. 'What *do* you think you're doing, Doris?'

'I am organising the best possible wedding for my son,' Doris replied. 'Not that it is any business of yours.'

'It is when you upset my little Suzy,' Peggy retorted. 'She and Anthony wanted a quiet wedding with just family and friends. You inviting the Mayor and the rest of them without asking their permission is completely out of order.'

'Susan's family are extremely well connected, and I wanted them to see that at least one side of this family has friends in high places,' Doris said loftily. 'I'm sure they wouldn't feel at all comfortable being surrounded by the likes of Rita and Fran, and that utterly disgusting old father-in-law of yours.'

Peggy's hackles rose and she itched to slap that snooty face. 'Ron is worth ten times more than any one of those councillors,' she snapped. 'How dare you think you're above everyone?'

'It's not my fault that my social circle is regarded as upper class,' sniffed Doris.

'Your social circle fell apart the minute they all found out about Ted's affair,' retorted Peggy. 'So don't come the high and mighty with me, Doris. It won't wash.'

'If you're going to be so aggressive, then I'd like you to leave.' Doris reached for the doorknob.

'I'll leave when I'm good and ready and not before.'

Doris gave a dramatic sigh. 'You'd better have your say then. But make it short. I have a committee meeting to go to.'

'This interference has got to stop,' Peggy insisted. 'It's causing great upset to both Anthony and Suzy, and ruining all their plans for a happy day.' She took a breath. 'You'll have to write back to the council members and tell them the invitation is for the church only – and not the reception,' she said with dangerous calm.

'I will do no such thing,' Doris declared.

'Yes you will, Doris,' replied Peggy softly, 'or I shall send my own invitation out to Ted's floozy and her latest man.'

Doris paled beneath the careful make-up. 'You wouldn't dare,' she breathed.

'Try me.' Peggy folded her arms and held her sister's gaze.

Doris was the first to look away. 'I don't believe that even you would stoop that low,' she muttered.

'I would if I had to.'

'But that would cause no end of trouble,' Doris said furiously, 'and I will not have my Anthony confronted by his father's disgrace on his special day.'

'Then write those letters, Doris. This has got to stop – now.'

'But it will be so embarrassing,' whined Doris. 'It will show an appalling lack of etiquette on my part to have to withdraw part of an invitation. I'll never be able to look them in the eye again.'

'You survived the scandal over Ted's affair, so you can survive this.' Peggy wasn't usually so heartless, but her sister was the absolute limit and she'd had enough.

Doris was wavering, and her hand wasn't very steady as she lit a cigarette. 'How do I word such a letter?' she muttered. 'You've put me in the most ghastly situation, Margaret.'

'Actually, Doris, this "situation", as you call it, is all your fault. You've gone steaming in with no regard for what Suzy and Anthony want for their day, and now you'll have to find some way of wriggling out of it. You shouldn't find that too hard after all the wriggling out you've done over the years.'

Doris looked at Peggy with blank dislike. 'You're enjoying this, aren't you?' she hissed.

'Not really,' Peggy replied truthfully. She relented slightly. 'Come on, let's go and sit in your lounge and sort out what to write, then I can deliver the letters to the council chambers on my way home.'

'It's not a lounge,' said Doris through gritted teeth. 'It's a drawing room.'

Peggy shrugged. 'Whatever it is, it will be more comfortable than standing about in the hall. And while we're at it, a cup of tea wouldn't go amiss either.'

'You'll have to make it then. I have one of my migraines coming on.' Doris drifted into the sitting room, collapsed dramatically on the couch and closed her eyes.

Peggy rolled her eyes to the ceiling and went into the pristine kitchen to make the tea. She hunted in the cupboards and found a tin of rather splendid shortbread. Putting four pieces on a plate, she ate one while she waited for the kettle to boil. Of course she'd had no real intention of inviting that awful woman or her latest, highly dubious boyfriend, but the threat had been enough to make Doris see sense, and that was all that really mattered.

Doris certainly knew how to live well, she thought as she carried the tea tray in and put it carefully on the low table in front of the settee. The sitting room had huge bay windows that overlooked the broad back garden to the sparkling sea, and Peggy was drawn to that view every time she came.

The room itself was large enough to accommodate two richly upholstered couches on either side of the elegant marble fireplace, three armchairs, and even a piano. Doris had bought it many years ago in the forlorn hope that Anthony might learn to play it. Now it stood in the corner, tuned and polished to a gleam, to be admired as an expensive piece of furniture that no one knew how to use.

'It's lovely and quiet. I suppose all your girls are at work,' Peggy commented as she left the magnificent view to pour the tea.

'Two of them took umbrage and left after I threw out their friend, so there's only the ghastly Ivy, and she'll be back at six.' Doris opened her eyes, made a show of struggling to sit up, and took the cup of tea from Peggy. 'There's another one arriving sometime today. She's probably as awful as all the others – another factory girl.'

'Just because she works in a factory doesn't mean she has to be horrid,' said Peggy firmly. 'Now, drink your tea and take an aspirin, then we can decide how best to word these letters.'

Chapter Twelve

As the guard came along the train calling out, 'Cliffehaven. Next stop Cliffehaven,' Mary took her case down and slipped on her coat and beret. Gathering up her handbag and gas-mask box, she felt a flutter of anticipation and fear in her stomach. This was it.

The train slowed, and with a great clanking of wheels and screeching of brakes it came to a stop with a billow of smoke and steam. Mary followed two other women down the step to the platform, and as the thick smoke cleared, she looked around her. For a seaside station, it had clearly once been quite large, but there was bomb damage to the siding wall, and where she guessed there had once been a waiting room and ticket office there was now only a pile of rubble.

She noticed a woman in dungarees and the ubiquitous knotted headscarf sitting on a bench holding a cup of tea while she puffed on a cigarette, and a younger one busy pulling weeds out from between the row of cabbages that grew in an earth-filled cattle trough beside the signal box. They must be the stationmaster's wife and daughter, she thought as she breathed in the salty air and listened to the mournful cries of the gulls.

Hitching the straps of her bag and gas-mask box over her shoulder, she gripped her suitcase. The elderly stationmaster had just finished talking animatedly to the two women passengers and was now looking at her with undisguised curiosity. He was probably in his sixties, wide of girth and quite tall, with a ruddy face, kind eyes and rather wayward eyebrows.

'Hello, dear,' he said as he examined her ticket. 'My goodness, you've come quite a way today. Got family here, have you?'

Mary smiled, recognising a cheerful, nosy gossip. 'I'm starting a job on Monday,' she replied.

'Ah, so you've come early to get settled in.' He grinned at her as he stuck his thumbs into his waistcoat pockets and rocked on his heels. 'Very wise,' he said. 'Always best to get your bearings in a new place. So, where are you staying?'

'Havelock Road.'

'Blimey, there's posh,' remarked the woman who'd been drinking tea. 'You'll be set up nice there.' She got up from the bench, grinned at Mary and stuck out her hand. 'I'm Ethel, by the way, and this 'ere's me daughter Ruby.' The girl looked up from her weeding and smiled pleasantly.

Mary shook her hand and introduced herself, rather overwhelmed by this friendly greeting.

Ethel dug the stationmaster in the stomach with

her elbow. 'And this 'ere's Stan. Anyfink you wanna know about this place, you come and ask 'im.'

Mary decided to take the bull by the horns. 'There are two things, actually,' she said rather nervously. 'One, how do I get to Havelock Road – and, and . . . Do you happen to know a Cyril Fielding?' she finished in a rush.

Stan rubbed his chin with a meaty hand. 'I know several Cyrils, but the name Fielding doesn't ring a bell.'

'He would have been here about eighteen years ago,' Mary told him.

He shook his head and then his frown cleared and he smiled. 'I'll have a think on that one. Eighteen years is a long time past. But I can help you with Havelock Road.'

'Who are you billeted with?' asked Ethel, the cigarette bobbing up and down as she spoke. 'A lot of them posh houses have been rented out to families now the owners have gorn orf to somewhere safer.'

'I'm staying with a Mrs Williams,' Mary replied. 'Do you know her?' She didn't miss the look of dismay that went between Ethel and Stan, and felt a stab of alarm.

'She ain't too bad,' said Ethel hurriedly. 'But she's got ideas above her bleedin' station, if you asks me.' She took the cigarette from her mouth, tapped off the ash with some deliberation, and stuck it back in.

'I do think we shouldn't judge too harshly, Ethel my dear,' reproached Stan. 'This young lady seems to be very respectable, and I'm sure they'll get along just fine.'

Ethel narrowed her eyes against the cigarette smoke as she folded her arms. 'If you say so, Stan, but I reckon she'd be better off with Peggy Reilly, and no mistake.'

Mary looked puzzled. 'Who's Peggy Reilly?'

'She's Mrs Williams's sister and ever so nice. A proper diamond is Peg,' declared Ethel, who was settling in for a good gossip. 'Looked after my Ruby, she did, when she first come down from London.'

Stan must have realised this could go on for a while, and intervened. 'Come on, love,' he said to Mary as he picked up her case. 'Let me point out how to get to Havelock Road. I'm sure you and Doris will get on fine as long as you can put up with her airs and graces. After all, she's Peggy's sister, so she can't be all bad.'

Mary decided he was probably right, and having said goodbye to Ruby and Ethel, followed Stan out into the street.

'This is the High Street and you follow it all the way down the hill until you get to the last turning on your right,' he told her. 'That's Havelock Road. Walk past Havelock Gardens, and Mrs Williams's house is the last but two. You can't go any further, cos it's a dead end.'

'Thank you for being so helpful, Stan.'

'Not at all,' he said expansively. 'Now you're not to fret over what Ethel said. She's never seen eye to eye with Doris and is very protective of Peggy. I'm sure you'll settle in nicely, but if you do have any problems, you come and see me. If I'm not at the station, then I'll be on my allotment.' He waved in a general northerly direction.

'That's really nice of you, Stan, but I'm sure I'll be just fine.' Mary shook his hand, retrieved her case from him and set off down the hill.

Taking her time to look in the shop windows, she meandered down the High Street past several bomb sites, the Town Hall, billeting and recruitment offices and the labour exchange. Cliffehaven was busy, with women pushing prams along the pavement, standing in queues outside the grocers and bakers, or hurrying along with laden shopping baskets. From the number of servicemen strolling about or passing at speed in their open trucks, it was clear there had to be several Allied bases nearby – including an airfield.

She tried to ignore the admiring glances and the occasional wolf whistles, and was disconcerted by how easily they made her blush. Yet it was rather flattering, and she could now understand why her friend Pat was having such a jolly time of it after being stuck in a tiny country village for most of her life. Mary also rather liked the look of Cliffehaven. It wasn't as old or sprawling as Lewes, and there were no cobbled streets or rows of ancient houses, but it seemed to be quietly respectable, and it had the bonus of being by the sea.

Mary stood and gazed down at the sea, sparkling in the early afternoon sun, for a trip to the seaside had been a rare childhood treat. This was an attractive sight, despite the gun emplacements and the coils of barbed wire and she was looking forward to exploring the promenade once she'd settled in.

Then her stomach rumbled, reminding her she hadn't eaten since her six o'clock breakfast, and as she walked on, she came to Camden Road and saw the sign for the Lilac Tearooms. It wouldn't matter if she was a bit late getting to Havelock Road, for she hadn't mentioned a specific time of arrival, and she really did need to eat something before she had to face the undoubtedly tricky Mrs Williams.

The Lilac Tearooms were opposite a large hospital. The room itself was small and intimate beneath a heavily beamed ceiling, and it seemed it was very popular, for chattering women filled nearly every seat. It was all very reminiscent of the tearooms in Hillney, with gingham cloths on the tables and pictures of kittens and rose-clad cottages on the walls, and Mary felt quite at home as she found a spare place at a table and sat down.

She realised that a new face was an immediate target, and before she knew it, she'd told the other women on her table where she'd come from, what work she was starting and who she was billeted with. The general consensus seemed to be that she was lucky to get such a comfortable billet, but that Doris would need careful handling.

Having finished her lunch, she paid the bill, bid the other women goodbye and set off again. She had asked them about Cyril, and even though the rest of the customers in the tearoom had joined in the discussion, none of them had heard of him. She hadn't wanted to mention the young woman who'd run off leaving her baby behind – that sort of thing was far too personal for a general debate in a tearoom full of gossips.

Mary passed the remains of what looked like a church and vicarage, and the sight made her falter as all the memories came flooding back. Determined not to allow the past to overshadow the present, she gripped the handle on her case, took a long, appreciative look at the sweeping promenade, then walked on down the tree-lined road.

The park must have once looked quite lovely, with a weeping willow drooping over the pond and arched rose bowers sheltering the wooden benches. Now there were no metal railings, and most of the flower beds and lawns had been turned into vegetable patches.

She carried on down Havelock Road, past the remains of two bombed-out houses, her shoes scuffing the rustling leaves that lay across the pavement and in the gutter. She could see now what Ethel meant by being posh, for the houses were large and detached, with generous gardens and high walls, and being so close to the promenade, they would have had the most magnificent views of the sea from their back windows.

Mary found the right number and crunched across the gravel drive to knock on the door. It looked very nice, with clean windows, fresh paint, and a neat front garden. There were pristine white net curtains, the brass knocker gleamed, and no fallen leaves were lying about. Mrs Williams obviously ran a tight ship, as her father would have said.

Receiving no reply to her knock, she tried again, rather more firmly. Minutes later she had to accept that Mrs Williams had gone out, but as she'd left no note on the door Mary had no idea how long she might be.

'What to do?' she murmured as she dithered on the doorstep. 'I can't lug this case round the town, or spend any more money in a tearoom.'

After a fruitless search for a key beneath the doormat and the nearby flower pots, she gave a sigh of frustration. She shouldn't have spent so much time on her lunch. It was an inauspicious start to her new life, and as there didn't seem to be anyone in the street or the neighbouring houses, there was only one thing left for her to do. She put down her case, sat on the doorstep and waited for Mrs Williams – or someone – to come home.

Harvey and Monty were stretched out in front of the fire, slumbering happily now the pub had closed for the afternoon. Ron had finished changing the beer barrels, and now carried up the crates of bottles from the cellar and dumped them on the floor behind the counter. He was distracted for a moment by the undulation of Rosie's generous bosom beneath her frilled blouse as she energetically polished the broad sweep of oak that formed the bar – and he couldn't help but stop and watch in admiration.

She caught him looking and gave a cluck of annoyance. 'If you can bear to concentrate on something other than my chest, those bottles need putting on the shelves before we open again.'

Ron was startled by her unusually brisk tone, and he regarded her with a frown. 'What's eating you today, Rosie? You've been short with me since this morning.'

Rosie gave the bar a final sweep with the duster and sighed. 'I'm sorry, Ron. I didn't mean to snap at you, but I've got things on my mind.'

So had Ron, but Rosie was certainly in no mood for a bit of slap and tickle, so he knew better than to mention it. 'And what things might they be?' he asked casually as he began to stack the bottles neatly on the shelves beneath the bar.

'Just things,' she hedged as she turned away and began to polish the battered upright piano with unnecessary vigour.

Ron continued to deal with the bottles. Rosie was clearly furious about something and it was bubbling away inside her, fit to bust. He'd let her stew for a bit, he decided. She couldn't keep it to herself for much longer.

He finished doing the bottles and stacked the crates neatly out of the way. Rosie had stopped trying to rub the veneer off the piano and was now dusting down the horse brasses which hung either side of the inglenook fireplace. Her whole body seemed to be involved in this exercise and he watched the wiggle of her hips in silent longing. To be sure she's a fine-looking woman, he thought with a smile.

'What are you grinning at?' she snapped, still with her back to him.

Ron's smile disappeared. 'How the divil do you do that?' he asked in genuine amazement.

'I know you,' she said. 'If you're not on the move, then you're standing grinning and leering at me like a loon.' She threw down the duster and turned to face him, her arms tightly folded round her waist, her expression stormy.

Ron noticed Harvey slink away from his customary position in front of the fire, swiftly followed by Monty. They'd obviously decided to make themselves scarce before Rosie really got going. 'Well, if you don't appreciate being admired, I'd better be off,' he replied. 'To be sure this is no place for man nor beast while you're in this mood.'

'Oh, Ron.' Her shoulders slumped and she dipped her chin so her platinum hair fell round her face. 'I'm sorry for being so horrid to you all day – and now I've even upset poor Monty and Harvey. Please don't go.'

He heard the tremor in her voice and knew she was close to tears, so he swiftly crossed the room and gently drew her into his arms. 'What is it, *Acushla*?' he crooned. 'Come on, you can tell me.'

She relaxed into his embrace, her head resting on his shoulder as she wrapped her arms round him. 'It's all suddenly got too much,' she gulped as she sniffed back her tears. 'And I don't know if I can stand it for much longer.'

He drew back and lovingly eased her hair from her face so he could look deeply into her sapphire eyes. 'You'll always have me to rely on, Rosie,' he soothed. 'Whatever it is that ails you, you won't have to deal with it on your own.'

She nodded and drew a handkerchief from the sleeve of her blouse. 'I know, but it seems so unfair that I have to burden you with all my endless troubles.'

Ron drew her down to sit beside him on the cushions of the old settle. 'A trouble shared is a trouble halved,' he soothed. 'And you know I'd rather share them than have you worrying alone.' He paused, reluctant to broach the subject, but knowing he must. 'Is this to do with whatever you and Peg talked about the other week?'

She lifted her head from his shoulder, her eyes startled. 'What did she tell you about that?' she asked sharply.

'Absolutely nothing. Told me to mind my own business,' he replied gruffly.

Her relief was almost tangible as she sat there in silence and mangled her handkerchief. 'That's only a part of it,' she said eventually. 'I had a letter from my husband's sister this morning, and it wasn't pleasant. She accused me of being heartless and unchristian – of abandoning him by living so far from the asylum.' She dabbed the handkerchief over the last of her tears. 'She even called me a Jezebel,' she went on with a shaky laugh, 'because she thinks you and I have broken my marriage vows.'

'I'd like five minutes with that witch,' he growled. 'She'd soon be put right and no mistake.'

'I don't doubt it.' She gave him a watery smile.

'You've had those sorts of letters before,' he said, 'so I'm surprised you've let her get under your skin like this. You usually tear them up, put them in the bin, have a gin and forget about them. What's so different today?'

'That wasn't the only letter that came this morning.' Rosie's voice wobbled. She looked up at him, her eyes swimming with fresh tears. 'And you're not going to like what I'm about to tell you, because it will change things for both of us.'

Ron experienced a sharp pang of alarm. 'I don't understand,' he managed.

Rosie took his great rough hands in hers and looked at him squarely. 'My brother's been given parole, and he'll be moving in here until he can find somewhere else to live.'

Ron stared at her, unable to believe what he'd

261

heard. Her brother had another two or three years to serve, and Ron had thought he'd finally managed to get rid of him. 'But men like Tommy are sent into the army the minute they're released.'

Rosie shook her head. 'Not in this case unfortunately. He has asthma and has been declared medically unfit for service. As part of his parole agreement, he has to have a permanent address for six months and must work full-time on warden and fire-watch duties.'

'He has a wife,' Ron rumbled crossly. 'Why can't he go there?'

'She wants nothing more to do with him now they're divorced.' Rosie's tone was bleak. 'And neither do his children.' She gave a deep sigh. 'I can't say I blame any of them. He might be my brother, but I'm not proud of him – and the last thing I want is for him to move in here.'

It was the last thing Ron wanted, too. On the previous occasion when Rosie had left her brother in charge, he'd not only managed to damage the pub's reputation by bringing in a rowdy and unruly crowd, but had used the cellars to hide his black-market goods. Ron had discovered them and had had a quiet word with his policeman friend – and Tommy had been arrested. Not that Rosie knew of the part he'd played in getting rid of her brother. And he hoped she never would.

'Then don't let him,' he said gruffly.

Rosie gave a tremulous sigh as she gripped his hands. 'But I have no choice, Ron. If I don't agree to take him in, he'll have to serve out the rest of his sentence in that awful prison.'

'If he can't do the time, then he shouldn't have done the crime,' Ron stated flatly. 'He's more trouble than he's worth, Rosie girl. Leave him to stew where he is.'

She shook her head. 'I can't do that. He's been very ill apparently, and feeling terribly low after he received the divorce papers. I'm worried he might do something silly.'

Ron knew it wouldn't do his own cause any good at all if he voiced his thoughts on Tommy. The man was a shark, a womanising spiv and double-dealing all-round bastard, and if he slit his wrists, he'd be doing the world a favour.

'You've gone very quiet, Ron,' Rosie said. 'I know you don't like him, but please try to keep the peace with him, for my sake.'

'You're too soft, Rosie,' he replied sadly. 'But I'll not be the one to cause trouble, as long as he behaves himself and doesn't upset you. When is he due to be released?'

'Monday.'

'But that's only three days away,' he gasped.

Rosie stood and tugged at his hand. 'Let's go upstairs where we can be more comfortable, and I'll make us some lunch. We only have this weekend to ourselves, and I don't want to spoil it by talking about my brother.'

*

Despite her thick overcoat, scarf, gloves and beret, Mary was feeling cold and miserable as she huddled on the doorstep and tried to shelter from the rising, bitter wind. She'd attempted to pass the time by reading, but found she couldn't concentrate. In an effort to keep warm she's wandered back and forth across the front garden, and even over the road to the park to watch the swans regally swimming on the pond.

The hours dragged slowly by, and it would soon be dark, the thick clouds gathering overhead and threatening rain. She'd tried the garage door, but it was firmly padlocked, so there would be no shelter there – and the porch offered little respite from the elements either. If there was an air raid she didn't know what she'd do, for she had no idea where the nearest public shelter was, and she hadn't spotted an Anderson shelter in any of the other gardens.

She wrapped her arms about her, closed her eyes and leaned her head back against the front door. If she stayed here much longer she would freeze to death. Perhaps she should go back to the station and ask Stan's advice – but she didn't like to do that, for it would be admitting she needed help, and she didn't want to appear feeble. But where could Mrs Williams have gone? Surely she hadn't forgotten she was coming?

'Hello. What on earth are you doing there?'

Mary's eyes flew open and she stumbled to her feet as a girl approached. 'I was waiting for someone to come home,' she stammered. 'I was supposed to be moving in today, but Mrs Williams seems to have gone out and—'

'Yeah, she 'as an 'abit of going out, does Old Mother Snooty Drawers,' the girl replied with a grimace. 'I'm Ivy, by the way,' she said and grinned. 'You must be Mary.'

Mary's face was so cold she could barely smile back as she shook the rather grubby little hand. Ivy was about Mary's age, but small and thin, with a mop of brown curly hair, an urchin face, dimples, and dark brown eyes. Dressed in overalls, jacket, boots and headscarf, her face smeared with grease, she'd clearly just come home from work.

'Yeah, I look a proper mess, don't I?' Ivy said without rancour as she fished a key out of her gas-mask box. 'I work with oily machinery every day up at the factory estate, so it can't be 'elped.' She opened the front door. 'Let's get you inside. You look 'alf frozen.'

She led the way into a square hall that had an expensive Turkish rug covering part of the highly polished parquet floor, an oak table with a telephone on it and a mirror above it. There was a coat stand and several ornately framed seascapes and land-scapes on the white walls, and carried on the rela-tively warm air inside the house was the overall scent of beeswax.

'Better get them shoes off. She don't like us getting her posh floors mucky.'

Mary slipped off her shoes as Ivy stood on the doormat to unlace her boots and toe them off. 'Is she very fussy, then?'

'I'll say, but at least the billet's comfortable and warm, and the food ain't bad either. Her old man is the manager or something of the Home and Colonial, so there's always tins of stuff from under the counter.' Ivy picked up her boots and the dimples reappeared as she grinned. 'It's a bleedin' long way from 'ackney, I can tell yer, so I keeps me 'ead down and gets on wiv it.'

Mary didn't know how to reply to this, so she clutched her shoes and case and awkwardly smiled back.

'I expect you need the lav and a cuppa after sitting out there in the cold,' said Ivy. 'The lav's in there.' She pointed to a door. 'Make sure you clean the basin when you've finished and try not to use too much soap or get 'er towel dirty. I'll be in the kitchen which is just at the end of the hallway.'

Mary put down her case and shoes, slipped the straps of her handbag and gas-mask box off her shoulder and tentatively opened the door to what turned out to be a very smart, spotlessly clean cloak-room. She was almost afraid to use the lav, and when she'd finished she polished the handle with the pristine towel, washed her hands with the merest smear from the luxurious bar of sweetly scented soap, and dried the basin before putting the towel back exactly how she'd found it.

'I'm in here,' shouted Ivy from the other end of the hall.

Mary left her belongings neatly at the bottom of the carpeted stairs and found Ivy in the well-equipped kitchen, busy making a pot of tea. She'd clearly washed her face and hands in the kitchen sink, for there was a tidemark of dirt around it, and her coat had been thrown over the back of a kitchen chair.

'I'll show yer round when I done this,' she said. 'There's only you and me billeted here now. The other girls went off in a huff after their mate got thrown out over some Yank shinning up the drainpipe to her bedroom.'

'Goodness,' breathed Mary. 'That must have caused trouble.'

Ivy giggled. 'Not 'alf. Old Mother Snooty went off on one like I don't know what. I ain't seen nothing like it.'

Mary smiled, for it seemed to be expected. 'So does Mrs Williams have any family?'

'Her old man lives in a flat above his shop. I heard tell he went off with another woman and she ain't quite forgiven 'im yet. There's a son, Anthony. He's ever so nice, works for the MOD, and only comes home now and again. He's getting married soon, and her ladyship's in a right flap over all the arrangements.'

'You really don't like her, do you?' Mary took the cup of tea Ivy offered her and gratefully cradled it in her cold hands.

'Not much,' Ivy shrugged, 'but then I'm out most of the time so I don't 'ave to put up wiv 'er.' The dimples showed again. 'I 'opes you can cook and clean, Mary, cos I'm sick of doing it all on me tod now the others 'ave gorn. That one's far too posh to get 'er hands dirty, and would probably burn water if she tried.'

Mary stared at her in shock. 'But we shouldn't have to do that,' she protested. 'The terms of agreement with the billeting people state quite clearly—'

'Yeah, but that don't apply to 'er ladyship,' said Ivy dismissively. 'If yer wanna eat in this house, yer cook. Same wiv the laundry and such – so I'm glad you're 'ere to lend an 'and.'

Mary decided she didn't like the sound of Mrs Williams at all, but Ivy seemed to be very nice and as she didn't want to cause trouble on her first night here, she made no comment. But she would go to the billeting people on Monday and find out exactly what was expected of her. She hadn't come all this way to be Mrs Williams's skivvy.

'She keeps 'er food and stuff in the larder, and we gotta keep ours there.' Ivy opened the larder door and pointed to the top shelf. 'Milk and that goes on the bottom shelf of the fridge,' she added. 'There's a washing machine and dryer in a lean-to out the back, but she don't like us using them unless we're doin' 'er stuff.'

'She sounds as if she's a real dragon,' said Mary,

by now a bit befuddled by all the rules and regula-
tions of this house.

'Yer right there,' Ivy agreed.

They leant against the warm range and drank
their tea. 'So what's a girl from Hackney doing down
here?' asked Mary as she took off her overcoat.

'We got bombed out and me mum and nan went
to live wiv me aunt in Shoreditch. I didn't fancy it,
so when I heard about the jobs going 'ere, I jumped
at the chance to be by the seaside.' The brown eyes
were curious as Ivy looked Mary up and down.
'What about you?'

'I was bombed out too,' said Mary, 'and thought
it was a good chance to start afresh. I start at the
Kodak place on Monday.'

The dimples reappeared in the urchin face. 'You
worked in a factory before?' As Mary shook her
head, she grinned. 'I didn't think so. You sound
quite posh. But you'll be all right,' she added hastily.
'I knows a lot of them girls, and they're a good
bunch. We can walk up there together on Monday
cos I'm on early shift.'

'That would be nice,' said Mary with some relief,
for she'd been dreading going on her own and trying
to find her way around.

Ivy drained the last of her tea. 'Right, come on,
let me show you round while we've got the place
to ourselves.'

Mary quickly finished her cup of tea, and followed
the chatty little Ivy in a slight daze.

The dining room was full of dark, heavy furniture that had been polished to a gleam, and above the ornate marble fireplace was a gilt-framed portrait of a young woman in a blue silk dress and pearls. 'She 'ad that done when she got engaged,' said Ivy with a contemptuous curl of her lip.

Mary would have stayed to admire the painting, but Ivy was already halfway out of the door and heading across the hallway.

'This 'ere's what she calls 'er drawing room.' Ivy crossed the floor to pull the blackout curtains and switch on the standard lamp. 'It's a smashing view, right to the sea, but you'll get a better idea tomorrow when it's light.' She gazed round the room. 'It's ever so lovely, ain't it? Like a palace, really. Me mum would think she'd died and gorn to 'eaven if she could live 'ere.'

Mary had eyes only for the beautiful baby grand that stood in the corner. She crossed the room and almost reverently lifted the lid. Pressing her finger gently on middle C, she heard the rich tone of a well-tuned instrument.

'No one can play it,' said Ivy. 'I reckon she just likes to 'ave it there so people can admire it.'

Mary glanced over her shoulder nervously. 'Do you think she'd mind if I tried it out? It's got a lovely tone.'

Ivy's eyes widened. 'Cor, can you really play that thing – proper like?' At Mary's nod, she grinned impishly. 'You're full of surprises, ain't yer?' She shot a glance at the clock. 'Go on then, but be quick. She's bound to be back any minute.'

Mary pulled out the padded piano stool and sat down. Rubbing her stiff hands, she thought for a moment and then executed a series of scales to get her fingers supple. The tone was exquisite, and she forgot about Ivy and Mrs Williams and was soon lost in the sublime sound of one of Beethoven's piano sonatas.

Neither of them heard the front door, or the footsteps coming down the hall, and were completely unaware of the woman who was now standing watching from the doorway.

As Mary came to the final, haunting notes of the first movement, she bent her head and slowly took her fingers off the keys. The worry and weariness of the day had been dispelled, and she knew she could put up with any discomfort while she had access to this wonderful instrument.

'Bloody hell,' breathed Ivy. 'That were lovely – and you didn't have no music, or nothing. You're brilliant, Mary. You should be on the stage.' She was grinning with delight. 'What were it called?'

Mary was blushing at the praise. 'Beethoven called it *Quasi Una Fantasia*, which roughly translated means "Almost a Fantasy". But it became better known as the Moonlight Sonata after a music critic said that the first movement reminded him of how the moonlight fell over Lake Lucerne.'

'That is all very commendable,' said Doris as she

strode into the room. 'But I would have preferred it if you'd sought my permission before touching my piano.'

Mary leapt off the stool as Ivy quickly put herself behind the piano. Mary saw a carefully groomed woman in her early fifties who was wearing an expensive-looking wool dress, with real pearls in her ears and in a string round her neck. Her demeanour was not encouraging.

'I'm so sorry, Mrs Williams,' she stammered. 'But I haven't been able to play for such ages, and I simply couldn't resist such a lovely instrument.'

Doris dipped her chin in regal acceptance of her praise and apology. 'You must be Mary,' she said grandly. 'Where did you learn to play like that?'

'My father taught me at first, and then I was lucky enough to have more formal lessons at school.'

The gaze sharpened. 'Your father is a music teacher?'

'No, he was a vicar.' Mary eased from one foot to the other. This was like being interrogated by a headmistress, and she didn't feel at all comfortable.

The plucked eyebrows rose. 'A vicar? Well, well, you do surprise me.' Doris suddenly seemed to notice Ivy, and glared at her. 'What are *you* still doing in here? You should be starting on supper.'

'Sorry,' Ivy muttered and shot out of the room.

Mary carefully closed the piano lid and started edging towards the door. 'I'd better go and help her,' she murmured, as desperate to escape as Ivy was.

Doris waved her hand. 'Ivy is perfectly capable of cooking supper on her own,' she said dismissively. 'Sit down and tell me all about yourself. I'm intrigued that a vicar's daughter should want to work in a factory.'

Mary perched on the very edge of the silken upholstery, aware that she was under close scrutiny, and that her sweater and skirt were second-hand. She took a deep breath, determined not to be cowed by this imperious woman whose accent betrayed her social-climbing ambitions, and gave her a potted history of her background and how she'd come to be in Cliffehaven.

'I felt I needed to do something for the war effort until I start my teaching course next year,' she finished.

Doris lit a cigarette with a gold lighter and regarded her with something approaching excitement. 'Well, I have to say it's a pleasure to meet a respectable gel for a change. You have no idea how ghastly it has been to lodge East End guttersnipes in my home.'

Mary was about to protest when she blithely carried on. 'I do a great deal of charity work, fund-raising for the many causes that are so desperate these days. I'm sure you wouldn't object to playing at a concert here or there, or perhaps even at my son's wedding.'

Mary was horrified. 'Oh, I'm not really good enough for things like that,' she said hastily.

'Well, of course you are,' insisted Doris. 'We can't allow a talent like yours to go to waste, now can we? After all, there is a war on, and you said you wanted to do your bit.'

'Of course,' stammered Mary most reluctantly. 'But it will all depend on my shifts at the factory, so I really can't promise anything.'

'You leave that to me,' said Doris firmly. 'I have a great many very important friends, and once they've heard you play, I can assure you, the manager of the factory will certainly allow you to take time off.'

'But I have to earn a living,' protested Mary. 'And if I keep taking time off the other girls will start to resent me.'

'Nonsense,' said Doris. 'And what do you care whether such girls resent you or not? They are uneducated and not at all suitable colleagues for a girl of your class.'

She stubbed out her cigarette and didn't seem to notice that Mary was silently fuming at her appalling snobbery. 'I shall arrange for Lady Chumley and some of my other friends to call round on Sunday afternoon for a little recital,' she announced with a gleam in her eyes. 'But we don't want anything too heavy. Perhaps a little of the Beethoven, followed by some Rachmaninov – then you could follow up with something from the stage or screen? That always goes down well.'

Mary gritted her teeth. 'I have plans for Sunday,'

she said, desperately trying to think what they could be.

'Then you'll have to change them,' Doris told her imperiously. 'Now run along and get settled in while I telephone Lady Chumley to make the arrangements. I think it would be better if you take the second bedroom. You won't want to be sharing with the likes of Ivy.'

'Actually, I'd prefer to share,' said Mary coldly.

The eyebrows shot up and she looked down her nose. 'Really?'

'Yes.' Mary was firm. 'Really.'

'Well, I don't have time to discuss this now,' said Doris irritably. 'Not with so many other things to organise.'

Mary followed her into the hall and slipped into the kitchen while she was busy dialling her friend's number. 'She's the worst kind of snob,' she hissed at Ivy, who was peeling potatoes. 'How on earth do you put up with her being so rude?'

Ivy giggled. 'I ignore her,' she whispered back. 'It's all hot air, really, ain't it? That Lady Chumley woman and her snooty cronies don't like her at all, I can tell, and they only puts up with 'er cos she's a whizz at fundraising and flattery.'

Mary rolled up her sleeves and found another knife to help with the potatoes. 'Well, it looks as if I'm stuck with the lot of them on Sunday,' she said crossly.

'We'll probably both be stuck, cos she'll want me

handing out the tea and sandwiches,' Ivy replied gloomily. Then she grinned. 'But at least you and me can share a room and 'ave a bit of a laugh. Thanks for that, Mary.'

Mary smiled back. 'I'm glad you don't mind, but she was so awful, I couldn't possibly let her try and divide us up.' Her smile broadened. 'At least I'll get the chance to play on that piano and practise some-times – even if it does mean performing for her and her horrid friends.'

'Good on yer, Mary. That's the spirit. I'm going to enjoy having you about and no mistake.'

Chapter Thirteen

Rita was on duty at the fire station, and Anthony and Suzy had already left to go to the pictures, and perhaps have a fish supper afterwards. Peggy bundled Daisy up in her knitted clothes and tucked her into the pram while Harvey excitedly skittered about the hall getting under everyone's feet. Jane, Sarah and Fran were already in their overcoats, and Cordelia was searching in her handbag for a handkerchief.

'I do so enjoy a good evening out,' Cordelia twittered as she found the handkerchief and popped it in her coat pocket. 'And it's lovely that you and Daisy can come too for a change. You don't get out enough, if you ask me.'

'I'm lucky Rosie has agreed to have her upstairs,' said Peggy, who still wasn't too sure about the wisdom of taking her baby to a pub. She poked her head round the kitchen door. 'Are you ready, Ron? Only I said we'd meet them at seven and it's nearly that now.'

Ron stomped up the cellar steps looking quite respectable for once in a tweed jacket, clean shirt and freshly pressed grey trousers and polished shoes. 'Keep your hair on, woman,' he grumbled. 'To be sure 'tis only a five-minute walk.'

Cordelia regarded his finery. 'Well,' she said, 'it's good to see you've made an effort for once. Now, give me your arm and help me down the steps. And I hope you've remembered to bring your wallet. Those poor moths must be gasping for air.'

Ron's brows lowered, but he said nothing, for he was used to Cordelia ragging him.

The girls helped Peggy get the pram down the front steps, and once the front door was slammed behind them, they set off. It was a cold, still night, with a clear sky and a sickle moon that was reflected on the sea, and although no one said anything, they all knew it was a perfect scenario for an enemy raid.

The Anchor was already bustling, so Peggy left the others to go in through the front and wheeled the pram down the alley to the side door where she didn't have to push it through the crowd. She took off the blankets and started divesting Daisy of her hat, mittens and top cardigan. The combined heat from the fire and the press of humanity was quite overpowering after the cold outside.

Rosie came hurrying into the hall, swiftly followed by Ron. 'I can't stop and chat,' she said. 'It's madness in there tonight. But Ron will help you up with the pram, and there will be a gin and tonic waiting for you when you come back down.' She gave Peggy a swift hug, kissed Daisy's cheek and hurried off.

Ron carried the pram up the narrow stairs, which

was no mean feat, for it was large and unwieldy, and must have weighed quite a lot with plump little Daisy sitting in it.

'Thanks, Ron. I'll just get her settled and then I'll be down. Are the others here yet?'

'They got here early enough to grab the big table by the back window. I'd better get back down and help behind the bar. Poor Rosie and the girls are rushed off their feet.'

Peggy smiled at this, for the 'girls' were well past middle-age – as was Rosie. She heated up a few ounces of milk in Daisy's bottle and sat on the couch to feed her.

It was a lovely room, she thought, as she looked round at the chintz upholstery and curtains, and the rose-pink rug by the gas fire. Rosie certainly knew how to make a place homely, and it was a terrible shame that Tommy was about to spoil it all by moving in again. She'd been shocked when Ron had told her of his imminent arrival, and fervently hoped he wouldn't cause any further trouble. Poor Rosie had enough on her plate at the moment without him stirring things up.

Daisy's eyelids drooped and she didn't stir even when a great shout of laughter came from the bar downstairs. Peggy carefully settled her back into the pram and pulled the sheet over her to keep her snug. After watching her for a moment, still rather reluctant to leave her, she went downstairs and having nodded to Ron and Rosie who were busy at the bar, pushed her way through the crowd to the table by the back window.

'Ruby, how lovely, and you've brought Mike as well.' She smiled at them both.

The young Canadian stood and shook her hand. 'I hope you don't mind, Ma'am, but the hospital discharged me today, and I've got a twenty-four-hour pass.'

Peggy carefully avoided looking at the patch which covered his blind eye, for she knew how sensitive he was about the injury he'd sustained in the Dieppe raid. 'It's lovely to see you out and about again,' she said truthfully. 'And I take it you're staying on in the army over here?'

'Yes, Ma'am. They agreed I could work in administration.' He reached for Ruby's hand. 'So Ruby will have to put up with me for the duration.'

Peggy laughed as she sat down and glanced at a radiant Ruby. 'I don't hear our Ruby complaining about that.' She picked up her glass. 'Cheers.'

'Happy days,' said Ethel, who was squashed up next to Stan on the settle.

They all drank and then started talking, their voices rising to match the surrounding laughter and chatter. Peggy was delighted that Mike had been given permission to stay in England until this blasted war was over. It was clear that he and Ruby were in love and the poor girl had been fretting that he'd be discharged and sent home to Canada, which would have been the end of things really, for Ruby would not have been able to go with him – and who could tell how long this war would last?

Fran, Jane and Sarah had gone to chat with a group of Americans who were standing by the piano, and Peggy sharply regarded each of them, wondering if Captain Hammond was amongst them. He'd taken to giving Sarah rather a lot of lifts home just lately, and Peggy was deeply suspicious of his motives – and of the fact that Sarah had yet to invite him in to meet her. Quite what Sarah thought she was up to, Peggy didn't know. It was less than a year since the girl had left her fiancé Philip in Singapore to face the horror of the Japanese invasion. Surely she wasn't so fickle to have set her cap at someone else already?

Making a mental note to have a quiet word with Sarah, she made sure Cordelia was happily sipping her sherry and enjoying a chat with Stan before she turned to Ethel, who was eager to tell her the latest gossip.

Ethel related several stories about the goings-on at the tool factory, and how she'd kneed the overseer in his privates when he'd tried to get fresh. Then she went on to talk about Stan's allotment, and the vegetable garden she and Ruby had at the back of the bungalow they rented from Cordelia.

'I swear to God the old bugger next door keeps nicking stuff when Rubes and I are at work,' she confided. 'I counted them carrots yesterday, and this morning there was two missing. I wouldn't mind if he'd only ask – but 'e's taking bleedin' liberties, that's what.'

Peggy nodded and smiled, but her thoughts were on Daisy, and she wondered if she ought to go up and check on her now the noise was louder than ever.

'Your sister's got a new lodger,' Ethel said as she drained her glass of beer and sent Stan off to get another round of drinks.

Peggy just nodded, for having seen Doris this morning it was old news.

'She arrived this afternoon and seems ever so nice. I warned her that Doris could be a bit on the tricky side, but I don't reckon she'll have much trouble. She's the sort Doris would approve of.'

'Why? Is she a bit stuck-up then?'

Ethel lit a fag, had a couple of puffs then stuck it in the corner of her mouth. 'Nah, she's just a nice young girl wot speaks a bit posh and 'as lovely manners. She's not the usual type to work in a factory, but these are strange times, and girls from all walks of life are taking on all sorts now.' She grinned. 'But as she's sharing the billet with Ivy Perkins, she'll soon get to know the ropes.'

Peggy had met Ivy on several occasions and rather liked her, but she did wish the girl would stand up for herself and refuse to act as Doris's unpaid cleaner and cook. 'Let's hope she and Ivy get on then,' she said, still distracted by thoughts of Daisy. 'Perhaps this new girl will give Ivy the courage to say no when Doris demands things of her.'

Ethel shrugged. 'Who knows.'

Stan returned with a laden tray of drinks and handed them out. He sat down, took an appreciative sip of his beer and gave a sigh of satisfaction. 'So, what are you girls nattering about?' he asked cheerfully.

'That new girl Mary, wot's going to live with Doris,' replied Ethel. She took the fag out of her mouth, drank some beer and put it back again without spilling ash.

'Ah, yes, that reminds me,' said Stan. 'I've been meaning to ask you, Peggy. Have you ever heard of a Cyril Fielding?'

Peggy gave it some thought and then shook her head. 'Can't say I have, Stan. Who is he?'

'I've no idea. It's just that Doris's new girl, Mary, was asking about him, and I've been racking me brains ever since. The name sounds vaguely familiar, but I just can't place it, and it's driving me mad.'

'Did the girl say why she was looking for him?'
Stan shook his head.

Peggy drank her gin. 'Well, I wouldn't worry about it, Stan. I expect it was just someone her family knew, and she was hoping to find a familiar face in a new town.'

'I don't like mysteries, Peg,' Stan said after taking a long drink of his beer. 'And it's annoying not to be able to put a face to a name. I'll think on it for a while more and ask round.'

'Best of luck with that,' she said lightly. 'You and I have lived in this town all our lives, and if we don't recognise the name, then no one will.' She glanced up at the large clock on the wall above the inglenook fireplace, and stood up. 'I really must go and check on Daisy.'

She hurried away from the table and tiptoed up the stairs to the relative quiet of Rosie's sitting room. She needn't have worried, for Daisy was fast asleep, her thumb plugged into her mouth.

With a sigh of relief, Peggy sank on to the couch, reluctant to return to the noisy crowd downstairs just yet. Lighting a cigarette, she remembered the times when she and Jim had spent long evenings in the pub, or out dancing, and she missed him so much that it was a physical ache round her heart.

She closed her eyes and leant back into the soft cushions, her thoughts drifting back to when they'd all thought there could never be another war, and life had been comparatively easy, the future less uncertain.

Rosie had made her home here in the Anchor for two years when the trouble had flared up, and during the following months she and Peggy had forged a deep and unwavering friendship. Only Peggy knew the lasting damage that had been inflicted on her friend during that awful period, and she was glad that Rosie now had Ron at her side. She would need him too, with that brother of hers turning up again like a bad penny.

*

Mary had helped Ivy prepare the supper of shepherd's pie, which had only a small amount of minced meat in it, but was hot and filling. The meal had been awkward as they'd sat in the formal dining room, for Mrs Williams had blatantly ignored Ivy while she bombarded Mary with questions.

'I'll take coffee in the drawing room,' Doris told Ivy once the meal was over. 'There's a recital on the wireless that I would like Mary to hear.'

Mary glanced at Ivy in panic and horror. 'It's been a long day, Mrs Williams,' she said hurriedly. 'If you don't mind, I'd rather go to my room and unpack.'

'Are you sure you don't want to have the comfort and privacy of your own room, Mary?'

'Quite sure,' she replied firmly. 'But thank you for the offer.' Mary edged out of the dining room and went to fetch her things which were still languishing at the bottom of the stairs. She hadn't been given time to see her room, let alone unpack and settle in.

'I'll show her up,' said Ivy.

'Don't forget my coffee,' Doris instructed as she went into the drawing room.

Ivy stuck out her tongue at Doris's back, grabbed Mary's bag and gas-mask box and took the carpeted stairs two at a time. 'We're in 'ere,' she said, pushing open the door at the end of the square landing. She dumped the things on the second bed and hurried to pull the blackout curtains before switching on the very dim central light.

Mary saw a comfortable room with twin beds, a large wardrobe, chest of drawers and dressing table. The beds were covered with chintz spreads that matched the curtains hanging over the blackouts, and the bedside lampshade was of pink pleated silk. There was a seascape on one wall, and a small collection of framed sepia photographs on another. 'It's very nice,' she murmured.

'I'll say,' Ivy agreed as she flopped on to her bed. 'I ain't never 'ad a place like this before, cos we lived in two rooms in Hackney, and I 'ad to share with me brothers and me sister.' She giggled. 'It were quite a laugh most of the time, but me brothers used to snore and fart all night, which weren't too nice.'

'I envy you having a large family,' said Mary as she hung her overcoat in the wardrobe and opened her case. 'I was an only child.'

Ivy sat up abruptly and began to strip off her dungarees and shirt to reveal rather tatty underwear. 'There ain't much to envy when yer living on top of one another in a place that stinks of damp, old boiled cabbage and mouse droppings,' she said without rancour. 'But then we 'ad each other, and I suppose that were enough to get us through most things.'

'Where are your brothers and sister now?' asked Mary as she stowed away her underwear and sweaters in one of the empty drawers.

'They're all in the navy,' Ivy replied as she stepped

into a grey skirt and fastened the side buttons. 'Me sister works as an assistant to some Admiral, cos she can type and do shorthand. The boys are on the Atlantic convoys.'

Mary heard the slight tremor in her voice and made no comment, for platitudes couldn't ease the worry of knowing that the convoys were suffering huge losses as they battled to bring in supplies. She finished unpacking and placed her hairbrush and washbag on the dressing table. 'Is there a bathroom upstairs?'

'Yeah, it's right next door.' Ivy grinned. 'Ever so posh, ain't it? I don't know meself after all the years of sitting in a tin tub by the kitchen fire.'

'Are you going out?' Mary asked as Ivy put on a clean blouse.

'Yes, and you're coming with me,' she replied firmly.

'Oh, I don't know, Ivy. I think I'd rather read for a bit and then go to bed.'

Ivy stilled and put her hands on her hips, her expression stern. 'How old are you?'

'Eighteen.'

'Well then,' said Ivy, 'you should be out and about having a bit of fun – not sitting in 'ere on yer tod reading a flamin' book. If 'er ladyship has 'er way, you'll be down there with 'er listening to the flamin' wireless.' She finished buttoning her blouse and pulled on a knitted cardigan. 'So you gotta choice. Out with me, or in with 'er.'

The thought of being trapped with Doris was too awful, and although she was tired, Mary was quite tempted by the idea of going out with Ivy. 'Where were you thinking of going?' she asked hesitantly.

'The Anchor.'

'But that's a pub,' gasped a shocked Mary. She'd never actually been in one, but knew from her parents that they were disreputable places that respectable girls should never be seen in.

Ivy laughed as she borrowed Mary's brush to get the tangles out of her hair. 'Ten out of ten for observation,' she chuckled. 'So what's wrong with that? Me and the girls often go there for a bit of a singsong and that.'

'But isn't it a bit . . . a bit . . .'

The dimples appeared. 'Bless you, gel, you ain't never been in a pub before, 'ave ya?'

Mary shook her head and could feel her face reddening.

'Well, there ain't no time like the present,' said Ivy as she finished brushing out her hair, smeared on lipstick and dabbed her nose with a bit of powder. Clipping on a pair of very sparkly earrings, she checked her reflection in the mirror. 'Come on, get yer coat.'

Mary couldn't resist this force of energy and did as she was told, but although she was excited by the thought of doing something so outrageous, the years of her strict upbringing meant she still harboured grave doubts as to the wisdom of it. 'Will we be meeting other girls there?' she asked nervously as she picked up her bag and gas-mask box.

Ivy nodded and then opened the bedroom door. 'Now, you gotta be quiet going down the stairs and out the front door. With any luck the old bat won't hear us over 'er wireless.'

'But what about making her coffee?' hissed Mary.

'She can stuff it up 'er jumper,' Ivy hissed back.

Mary had to stifle a giggle as they silently went down the stairs, which thankfully didn't creak. They tiptoed into the hall, opened the door and stepped out into the night as the sound of the music recital drifted from the drawing room. Ivy turned the key so the latch didn't make any noise when she shut the door behind her.

The gravel sounded very loud as it crunched beneath their shoes and they ran across it hand in hand, giggling like schoolgirls. They slowed down once they'd reached the corner and linked arms. Mary's pulse was racing, and the cold night air was stinging her face, but for the first time in ages she felt young and carefree. She was ready to enjoy her first proper evening out.

They walked arm in arm down Camden Road, past the fire station, the tearooms and hospital and the shuttered shops. As they drew near to the Anchor, Mary could see the battered sign hanging over the heavy oak door, and the way the old walls sort of leaned out towards the pavement beneath the low, uneven roof. Not a chink of light penetrated the blackout curtains behind the lead-paned windows, but the sound of voices and laughter could clearly be heard from inside.

Ivy opened the door and they were met by a wall of noise, the smell of beer, and a thick cloud of cigarette smoke.

Mary hesitated, suddenly feeling horribly shy and out of place. The pub seemed to be full of men – of all ages, and in the uniforms of every allied service.

Ivy had no such inhibitions and grabbed her hand. 'Come on. I can see me mates over by the bar.'

Mary found herself being pulled through the press of people, and blushed furiously as she was greeted and winked at by every man she was forced to squeeze past.

'This 'ere's Dot, Mabel, Glad and Freda,' shouted Ivy above the racket. 'This is Mary,' she continued to yell.

Mary greeted the other girls shyly, noting that they'd dressed up for the occasion, with shining hair and full make-up – and that they were surrounded by young RAF officers.

Ivy turned to one of them and grinned. 'Wotcha, Charlie. Gunna buy me and me mate a drink then, or what?'

'I'd be delighted, my sweet Ivy,' he replied as he smoothed his flowing moustache. His amused hazel eyes rested on Mary. 'And what can I get you, young lady?'

'I'll just have lemonade,' stammered Mary.

Ivy's brows rose. 'Blimey, you ain't 'alf gotta lot to learn, Mary,' she muttered. 'I'll have me usual beer,' she said to the young and rather dashing Charlie.

Mary stood in an agony of shyness as everyone plied her with questions, and reassured her that working on the factory estate wasn't too bad because the wages were good, the girls were a jolly bunch, and the food in the canteen wasn't half bad either.

Armed with her beer, Ivy handed Mary the glass of lemonade. 'Mary can play the piano,' she told everyone with pride.

There was a chorus of surprise and delight, and before Mary could protest she was being enthusiastically bustled through the mass of people to the other side of the room. 'Make way,' boomed Charlie. 'This lady's about to play us a song or two.'

Mary gripped Ivy's hand as the crowd parted and she caught her first sight of the battered upright piano.

'It's a bit old,' shouted Ivy. 'But the landlady keeps it in good nick, so you shouldn't have no problems.'

'I can't,' protested Mary in terror. 'Not in front of all these people.'

'Course you can,' said Ivy as she peeled Mary's coat from her shoulders. 'We ain't had no one decent playing the thing for ages, and we've been missing our sing-songs, ain't we, boys?' She dimpled up at the circling men.

Mary could feel the perspiration trickling down her back, and her hands were clammy and not at all steady as she looked round at the others. 'I can't, really I can't,' she stammered, desperate to escape all the attention – to push her way through this stifling mass of people and escape to the cold and the calm beyond these walls.

'Come on, honey, give us a tune. Don't be frightened. We won't eat you.'

Mary looked up into the smiling face of an American soldier, saw she was surrounded with not the slightest chance of escape, and gave in. Gathering her courage, she put her bag and gas-mask box on top of the piano, sat down and opened the lid.

The ivory keys were yellow with age and the pedals were stiff, so it was probably out of tune and perhaps a bit tinny. But Ivy had put her in this very awkward position, so she had no option but to make the best of things.

Her mind raced, for although she knew most of the popular songs and had practised them in secret on the school piano, she was so nervous that she doubted she'd be able to play anything properly.

'Take a deep breath, mate,' said an Australian soldier in her ear. 'You'll be right. No worries.' He turned to the others. 'Give the lady a bit of air, you blokes,' he drawled. 'She can't play with you lot breathing down her neck like a bunch of galahs.'

Mary smiled up at him, placed her fingers on the keys and executed a quick practice run of scales which told her that the tone was a little tinny, but not as bad as she'd expected. A profound silence fell, and she could almost feel the anticipation as she took the deep breath the Australian had advised, relaxed her shoulders and began to play 'I'm Dreaming of a White Christmas'.

As the Australian's rich baritone was joined by the rest of the crowd, she relaxed further, forgot she was the centre of attention, and actually began to enjoy herself.

Peggy had finished her cigarette and was stubbing it out in the ashtray when her hand stilled. There was a hush downstairs, and then someone started to play the piano quite beautifully. She recognised the tune immediately, for Bing Crosby's Christmas song was one of the most popular at the moment, and the girls had been playing the record endlessly at home.

'Goodness me,' she muttered. 'They've found someone at last who can actually play the thing.'

She left the couch and quietly went down the stairs as the customers sang along, their voices soft and dreamy at the thought of Christmas, snow and their families at home.

Easing through the gathering, Peggy came to stand beside Rosie. Slipping her arm round her waist, she found she was too short to see over all the heads, so swayed in time with her as they sang along.

When the last chord faded there was an explosion of cheers and clapping, and shouts for more. 'I'd better get the girl a drink,' said Rosie as even more people began to cram through the front door and into the bar. 'She's certainly earned it.'

There was an immediate response from the men standing nearby who insisted upon paying for Mary's drink, and Rosie charged them each a couple of bob and put the money in an empty jar under the bar.

'I doubt she'll drink that much,' she confided quietly to Peggy as the girl started to play 'Little Brown Jug'. 'She's actually only on lemonade, but I'm sure she'll appreciate the money.'

'Who is it?' asked Peggy as Rosie poured lemonade into a clean glass.

'I've never seen her before,' said Rosie. 'But she came in with Ivy, so I'm guessing she's your sister's new lodger.'

Her eyes were thoughtful as she regarded her latest influx of customers, who'd been drawn in by the music and were clamouring to be served. The Anchor was the only pub in Cliffehaven which had a piano, and there was nothing the boys liked more than to have a good sing-song. 'I wonder if she'd come in at the weekends and play. I'd pay her of course and she'd have tips and such – but once word gets round, this place will get busier than ever.'

'Then ask her,' said Peggy. 'She can only say no.'

She reached for the glass. 'I'll take this over as you're so busy.'

She weaved her way through the massed gathering to the piano, where a girl with long dark hair and nimble fingers was leading the singers through the popular song. Peggy watched as she came to the end and rather shyly acknowledged the shouts of encouragement. She was a young, pretty girl, with lovely cornflower blue eyes and a sweet smile, and was clearly thoroughly enjoying herself.

'This is on the house,' said Peggy as she handed her the lemonade.

'Oh, that is kind,' the girl replied and took a long, grateful drink.

'You've certainly earned it,' said Peggy. 'I've never heard that old thing being played so well before.'

The girl blushed. 'It's a bit out of tune, but it's lovely to be appreciated.' She smiled. 'I'm Mary Jones, by the way.'

'And I'm Peggy Reilly.'

The blue eyes widened. 'Goodness. Stan and Ethel told me about you earlier today,' she said. 'It's nice to meet you.'

'It's nice to meet you too.' Peggy found she had to shout to be heard above the noise of everyone yelling for another tune.

Mary looked rather flustered by all the noise. 'Oh dear, I didn't realise what I'd started – or rather what Ivy started when she told everyone I could play the piano.'

'Don't let them bully you, or you'll be at it all night,' shouted Peggy. 'I'm sitting over there if you want to come and join us later.'

Mary nodded, and then silenced the crowd momentarily by playing a couple of rippling scales before she embarked upon 'Don't Sit Under the Apple Tree'.

Peggy went back to her table and sat down. Mary Jones seemed to be rather a sweet, unassuming girl, and she could only hope that she would be happy living with Doris – for if her sister discovered how well she could play the piano, she would no doubt have her doing fundraising concerts quicker than you could blink.

She took a long drink and lit a cigarette, tapping her feet in time to the music as Cordelia trilled away in blissful ignorance of how out of tune she was. It was lovely to hear the old piano being played properly again, and Rosie couldn't go wrong by asking the girl to play here on a regular basis. It certainly livened up a Friday night and no mistake.

Chapter Fourteen

Mary had been playing for most of the evening, with only a couple of stops to drink her lemonade and catch her breath, so she hadn't had time to go to Mrs Reilly's table, or even get to know Ivy's friends. And yet she was enjoying herself, for this was a night of new experiences, and it was very flattering to be guarded by the large Australian who'd remained at her side all evening and become quite proprietorial as he'd kept the other men from crowding her.

She finished her third glass of lemonade, wishing she could have had water or even tea, for it was very sweet and didn't really quench her thirst. The shouts for another tune made her smile, and because the loudest request had come from an American, she began to play 'Deep in the Heart of Texas'.

This had them stamping their feet and clapping to the chorus, and she could feel the old piano shudder from the vibrations, which made her grin. It was lovely to be an intrinsic part of a happy evening – even though she'd probably get it in the neck from Mrs Williams when she returned to the billet.

The wail of a siren penetrated the noise and there was an instant hush, and a frozen pause before everyone began to gather their things and make an orderly escape through the front door.

Mary quickly grabbed her belongings and looked for Ivy, as one of the dogs she'd seen earlier began to howl piteously.

'No worries, love,' said the Australian. 'Rosie's got a shelter in the cellar. Your mates are regulars so they'll be down there.' Before she could protest, he'd taken her arm and was determinedly steering her across the room against the flow of people who were hurrying outside.

Mary saw that Mrs Reilly was running up the wooden stairs as the press of people slowly made their way through the entrance to the cellar and down the stone steps. But where was Ivy? She looked round frantically as the whine of the sirens reached screaming pitch, the dog howled even louder, and everyone moved that bit quicker as a sturdy older man took charge of the two dogs and chivvied the mass along.

Mary saw the dogs cowering in a corner as she was led across the cellar towards a collection of couches and chairs. The poor things were obviously terrified, but at least they hadn't been left alone upstairs. Ivy's friends were chattering away to their pilots, but there was still no sign of Ivy.

'The name's Bob Ashton,' said the Australian soldier as he plumped down on to a sagging couch next to her. 'But me mates call me Smoky.'

Mary smiled at him distractedly as she continued her search for Ivy. 'Why's that then?'

'Ashton – ash – no smoke without fire,' he drawled. 'You're Mary, aren't you?'

She nodded, and then felt a huge surge of relief as she saw Ivy running down the steps, swiftly followed by the dashing Charlie. 'Ivy,' she called. 'I'm over here.'

Ivy came over and threw herself down next to Mary. 'Whew, I thought we'd never make it in time.' She grinned. 'Me and Charlie decided to go for a bit of a walk on the seafront for some fresh air, if yer get me drift,' she said with a nudge and a wink. 'And we 'ad to run like the blazes when the warden yelled at us.' Her impish brown eyes regarded the Australian. 'Who's this then?'

Mary introduced them, and Ivy was soon chattering away to him as if she'd known him for years. Mary admired her confidence, for she'd felt awkward and rather tongue-tied in his company. He seemed to be very nice, but he wasn't Jack, and she didn't want him getting any ideas.

She sat and tried to ignore the piteous howls that came from the large shaggy dog that was now trying to get under one of the low tables. She watched as the final trickle of people came down the steps to settle in the chairs or stand about talking in the dim light from two naked bulbs.

The cellar was huge, with a low, beamed ceiling and dark doorways that no doubt led to smugglers' tunnels, but with so many people crammed down here it would get hot and stuffy once the door was closed. Yet the old, sagging furniture made it welcoming, and with a makeshift bar, a gramophone, and even a small primus stove and kettle, it was quite cosy. The thought of a cup of tea was enticing, for she was very thirsty after drinking all that sweet lemonade, and she wondered if she dared go and ask for one. The barmaids seemed to be very busy serving bottles of beer from the stacks of crates piled in the corner.

'Well, this is a rotten ending to a lovely evening, I must say.'

Mary realised that Mrs Reilly had plumped down into a nearby chair and was now holding a sleeping baby while she tried to soothe the poor howling dog. She smiled in welcome. 'It's not too bad at all,' she replied. 'In fact it's far nicer than an Anderson shelter.'

'You're right there. Ron's done a good job of fixing the place up, and the party usually carries on until the all-clear sounds.' Mrs Reilly pointed to the older man who was now closing the door on the shrieking sirens. 'That's my father-in-law, Ron, and that's the Anchor's landlady, Rosie Braithwaite.' She leant a bit closer. 'They're walking out together, but it's supposed to be a secret,' she said in a stage whisper.

Mary regarded them and thought it was rather sweet that people of that age were courting. Yet Ron looked sturdy and fit, and Mrs Braithwaite was certainly no shrinking violet. She looked down at the shivering dog which mercifully had stopped howling now the sirens had fallen silent, and was trying to climb into Mrs Reilly's lap. 'Is he yours?'

'This is Harvey,' Peggy said as she eased his great paws from her lap and ordered him to lie down. 'He's Ron's, and that other one is his pup, Monty, who now lives here with Rosie.' She smiled and looked down at her sleeping baby. 'And this is Daisy, my youngest,' she said proudly.

Mary admired the baby who had long dark lashes, plump cheeks, and a mass of curly hair. 'She's lovely, Mrs Reilly, and very good not to be worried by all the noise.'

'You must call me Peggy, dear,' she replied firmly. 'Everybody does, and I prefer not to be too formal.' She tucked the blanket more firmly round Daisy and smiled. 'I don't usually bring her out at night, but I've got fed up with being stuck indoors now Jim's away with the army.'

She turned to introduce an elderly lady called Cordelia, who was sitting on another couch squashed between Stan and Ethel. Ruby and a young Canadian officer with an eyepatch were standing talking nearby.

As the muted sound of several squadrons of Spitfires and other fighter planes roared overhead on their way to tackle the incoming enemy, Peggy told Mary all about Beach View Boarding House, her family and the history of her lodgers. She related the story behind Ruby's arrival in Cliffehaven, and how her young Canadian fellow had been injured. Barely pausing for breath, she went on to explain that Ethel and Stan had seemed to come to some sort of understanding, and then embarked on the stories of the girls who lodged with her, introducing them as they came over to see if she and Daisy were comfortable.

Mary warmed to Peggy and was delighted to learn so much in such a short time. It was clear that Fran, Sarah and Jane adored her, and that she was a warm-hearted, sweet woman, who tackled even the darkest trials with stoic determination never to be beaten. She was very different to her sister.

As if Peggy had read her thoughts, she smiled. 'Me and my sister Doris are chalk and cheese,' she said lightly. 'But as long as you take her airs and graces with a pinch of salt, you'll be fine. It's a comfortable house – much grander than mine, but I'd be careful not to let her know about your piano-playing, or she'll be on your back to do concerts and things for her charities.'

Mary smiled ruefully. 'It's too late for that,' she admitted, before going on to explain about the forthcoming recital.

'Oh dear,' sighed Peggy. 'Well don't let her force you into anything you don't want to do. And try to get Ivy out of the habit of being used as a skivvy. Give my sister an inch and she'll take a mile, no mistake.' She licked her lips. 'I don't suppose you'd fetch me a cup of tea, would you dear? Only I'm parched, and I can see that Rosie's finally put the kettle on.'

Mary struggled out of the sagging couch, rather amused that she seemed to have been forgotten by Smoky now he had the lively Ivy to chat to. She noted that Charlie didn't seem at all bothered by this, for he had his arm draped round Gladys while they flirted.

She was suddenly struck by the awful thought that Jack could very well be doing the same sort of thing in some pub down in the West Country, and she had to stifle a pang of anxiety. Boys in uniform attracted girls, it was a fact of life, and if Jack could have seen her earlier, he too might have jumped to the wrong conclusion. She had to keep faith in him, and not let her imagination run riot.

The deep thunder of many heavy bombers made the old walls shudder and brought a sprinkling of plaster dust and ancient cobwebs sifting down. No one else seemed to notice, so Mary swallowed her momentary fear, eased her way through the crush and went over to get the tea. She couldn't allow herself to think about that terrible night when she'd lost everything, for if she did, every raid would be torture.

'It's all right, dear.' Rosie greeted her with a cheerful smile. 'This old place has been standing for a couple of centuries and it's not about to fall down now. I expect you'd like a cup of tea after all your hard work tonight – and one for Peggy and the others, if I'm not much mistaken. I know how Peg, Ethel and Cordelia like their cuppas.'

Mary nodded and waited while the kettle boiled, the bombers continued to thunder overhead and the dust silently sifted down. 'I hope you didn't mind me playing, Mrs Braithwaite, but I didn't really have much choice,' she said.

'Goodness me, of course I didn't mind,' she replied. 'And please, call me Rosie. It's a bit daft to be so formal under the circumstances.' She smiled as she casually brushed the dust from her blouse and stirred the tea in the pot.

Mary felt rather awkward about calling women of that age by their Christian names, for she'd always been taught to respect her elders. Yet Rosie and Peggy seemed very relaxed about things, so she supposed it didn't really matter.

'You did very well tonight, Mary, and I'm rather hoping you'll come and play every Friday and Saturday evening. I'll pay you, of course,' Rosie added hurriedly, 'and the boys are very generous, so there'll be lots more of this.' She reached under the table and held out a jar of coins.

Mary stared at the jar. 'Goodness,' she breathed. 'Where did all that come from?'

'The boys wanted to buy you a drink, so I took their money and put it aside. Take it, love. You've earned it.'

Mary felt the weight of the jar and guessed there

had to be almost a week's wages in there. 'Gosh,' she breathed. 'I didn't expect this.'

'So, will you come and play tomorrow night?' Rosie placed the thick china cups on a tray.

'I'd love to,' she replied. 'But it will depend on my shifts at the factory, so I can't promise I'll do it every weekend.'

Rosie grinned. 'Then come when you can. You're good for business, Mary, and while you're enjoying it and earning a bit of pin money, I'll be pleased to see you any night.'

Their conversation was brought to an abrupt halt by an enormous explosion that shook the very foundations of the old pub. Everyone stilled as they looked up, and after a moment of stunned silence, carried on talking as someone put a record on the gramophone. 'That sounded as if it's hit the promenade,' said Rosie with a sigh. 'Those poor old hotels have taken a terrible battering. I do hope no one was hurt.'

Mary balanced the money jar alongside the cups on the tray and weaved her way through the couples who were now dancing to 'Begin the Beguine'. She set the tray on the floor and handed out the tea which was gratefully received by Peggy and her friends, and having stowed the jar in her large handbag, sat down to enjoy her own.

It was wonderfully refreshing, and she sighed with pleasure. If she was to play here again tomorrow, she'd ask Rosie to give her water or tea.

She couldn't be doing with all that sickly-sweet lemonade.

Harvey inched towards her and put his muzzle on her lap, his great hazel eyes looking at her beseechingly. She patted his head and stroked his ears, apologising for not having a biscuit to give him. It felt quite homely down in the pub cellar, with a dog at her knee and friendly people surrounding her. Perhaps life in Cliffehaven would prove to be rather pleasant, for it was clear that few, if any, of its inhabitants were as fearsome as Mrs Williams.

The all-clear sounded just before midnight, and everyone seemed most reluctant to leave, for the party was in full swing.

'Come on you lot,' shouted Rosie as she turned off the gramophone. 'It's way past drinking-up time. Haven't you got homes to go to?'

The trickle became a flood as people gathered up their things and traipsed up the concrete steps to where Ron was chivvying them out of the side door. Mary, Ivy and the other girls followed the general exodus, shivering as they stepped out into Camden Road and were met by a bitterly cold wind and the stench of burning.

'Someone's copped it,' said Ivy after they'd cheerfully said goodbye to Smoky, Charlie and the other boys, who had to return to their various barracks. 'And it looks as if it was on the seafront, going by that glow.'

Mary and the others looked to where a haze of orange and black smoke eddied in the wind above the rooftops. They could already hear the clanging fire-engine and ambulance bells, and knew they'd only get in the way if they went to see what had been hit. Besides, they'd all seen enough damage caused by the Luftwaffe to understand all too well the tragedy that could be unfolding down on the seafront. It wasn't something to stand and gawp at.

'That were a bit too close for comfort,' muttered Gladys with a shiver. 'Come on, girls, let's get home. I'm freezing.'

They walked quickly down Camden Road and had to wait while a fire engine raced off the fire-station forecourt. The girl driving it didn't look old enough to be in charge of such a beast, but they all gave her a cheer of encouragement before they hurried on.

When they reached the High Street, Mabel, Gladys, Dot and Freda said goodnight and hurried up the hill to their billet in what had once been a youth hostel. They were all on night shift tomorrow and Sunday, but would meet again at the factory estate on Monday to show Mary around and help her settle in.

Ivy put her arm through Mary's. 'That were fun, weren't it?' she said as they tucked their chins into their coat collars against the cold night air. 'You played a blinder there, Mary. I 'ope you didn't mind me dropping you in it like that, but we was all getting fed up with no one to play the thing properly.'

'Yes, well don't volunteer me for anything else until you ask me first,' Mary replied. 'It's not that I didn't enjoy it,' she said hurriedly, 'but I could have done with some sort of warning.'

'Yeah, sorry about that, but I knew that if I said anything you'd refuse to do it.' They reached the house and paused for a moment to steel themselves against any sudden appearance of Mrs Williams. 'You didn't really mind, did you?' Ivy asked with a frown of concern.

Mary chuckled. 'Not once I'd got going. And, actually, I'll be playing there again tomorrow night.' She dug the jar out of her handbag and shook it. 'I even managed to earn a few bob as well, so all in all you've done me a favour.'

'Cor.' Ivy's eyes widened as she felt the weight of the jar. 'How much d'ya reckon you got in there?'

'I don't know.' Mary shoved it back in her bag. 'Let's get in before we freeze to death, and we can count it.'

They tiptoed across the gravel drive so as not to wake Mrs Williams who slept in the front bedroom, and Ivy slotted the key in the door. Entering the warm, silent house, they began to creep up the stairs.

'And what time do you call this?'

They looked up to find Mrs Williams at the top of the stairs, resplendent in a silken negligee and thick, shining white face cream, her head prickling with curlers covered in a bilious green hairnet.

Mary stifled the urge to giggle and continued up the stairs. 'I know it's very late, but there was a raid and we couldn't get here any earlier,' she said, her voice not quite as steady as she would have liked. 'I'm sorry if we've disturbed you.'

'I have been at my wits' end wondering where you'd got to,' Mrs Williams replied crossly. 'You told me you were going to spend the evening in your room, but when I went up to see if you'd changed your mind about listening to the recital, you weren't there.'

'Yes, I'm sorry about that.' Mary edged towards their bedroom door. 'We had a sudden change of plan.'

'I suppose this is your doing?' The beady gaze settled on Ivy, who was fighting a losing battle against her giggles.

'Not at all,' said Mary hastily. 'I simply decided to go to the Anchor with Ivy, and it turned out to be great fun.'

'The Anchor?'

She sounded like Lady Bracknell at her most imperious, and Mary had to bite her lip as Ivy spluttered behind her hand.

'I am terribly disappointed in you, Mary. I thought that as the respectable daughter of a vicar, you would have had higher aspirations than a night in a common public house.' She looked down her nose at them. 'I don't know what my friend Lady Chumley would say if she heard about your questionable behaviour. It's really most upsetting.'

Mary didn't reply, for she couldn't have cared less what she thought.

'Go to bed, the pair of you. We will discuss this further in the morning.'

They didn't need to be told twice and moments later they were collapsed on their beds in fits of giggles – which they had to smother in their pillows in case she heard them, and came in to berate them further.

'Lawks almighty, Mary,' spluttered Ivy some time later, 'I ain't seen nothing like that since *The Monster from the Deep*, at the pictures.'

Mary buried her face in her pillow as a fresh bout of giggling overtook her. She was so glad she had Ivy to share with.

Ron had stayed at the Anchor to help Rosie and the two barmaids clear the wreckage of the party in the basement and tidy up the bar. It had been a very busy night and he was feeling his age suddenly, for he was an early riser and it had been a long day.

'I do like little Mary,' said Rosie after she'd locked the front door and they finally had the place to themselves. 'She did very well tonight, considering how young she is, and it hasn't done my takings any harm either.'

'To be sure it was great to hear them all singing,'

Ron replied. ''Tis a good thing to forget your troubles in these difficult times, if only for an hour or two.' He eyed her quizzically. 'I suppose you'll be wanting her to come again?'

'She's already agreed to that,' she said as she slipped off her high heels and wriggled her toes. 'So I might need you to help behind the bar again tomorrow.'

'Aye, well, I'll be glad to lend a hand, Rosie, but for now I must take meself off to bed.' He put his arms round her and held her close, then softly kissed her. 'Sleep well, *Acushla*, and try to dream of me and not all that money dropping into your till,' he teased gently.

'Get away with you, Ron Reilly,' she giggled. She kissed his lips and led him out towards the side door. 'I'll see you tomorrow.'

He went out with Harvey at his heels, waited to hear her shoot the bolt in place on the other side of the door, and then sauntered down the street. It was a cold night, the stench of burning polluting the air, the accompanying smoke veiling the bright stars. The silence was disrupted by the urgent clang of bells, and he realised the emergency services must still be dealing with whatever had been hit down on the seafront.

Harvey seemed to have made it his aim to water every lamp post and downpipe along the way, and as he'd been cooped up all night, Ron thought his dog might appreciate a bit of a stroll down to the seafront before they went home. If they were still fighting the fire, they might need some help – although he doubted he could do much tonight after being on his feet all day.

After the smoky fug of the crowded bar he found that the cold night air had revived him somewhat, so he dug out his pipe from his pocket and paused for a moment to light it before heading down the hill. The sea rolled like molten lava beneath the glow of the moon, the surf splashing on the shingle as regularly as a heartbeat. The sound soothed him, for he'd spent his younger years at sea, and he felt at one with it.

But as he reached the bottom of the road he came to an abrupt halt. His contented mood fled, to be replaced by one of horror.

The four-storey Grand Hotel and the two boarding houses beside it had been reduced to nothing more than an obscene pile of smoking, blackened rubble. It was like a scene from Dante's *Inferno*, for dark figures were moving about within the swirling grey and ebony smoke and orange flames, their shapes distorted by their protective clothing, giving them the look of twisted demons.

Five fire engines had arrived, as well as the usual rescue wardens and the engineers from the electricity and gas boards. Even the doughty ladies from the WVS were there in their new motorised wagon to hand out tea, biscuits and sandwiches.

As Ron stood frozen in shock, an ambulance

pulled away with a screech of tyres and a stridently clanging bell. He knew that the boarding houses had been closed down for the duration, but had recently been requisitioned to house some of the homeless who had been camping out at the Town Hall.

As for the hotel – it would have been packed on a Friday night, with people having dinner or drinks and dancing in the magnificent ballroom. And although they had a shelter in the basement, it would have offered no security at all against a direct hit – and there was very little doubt that this was what had happened.

He peered through the choking, acrid smoke still coming from the remains, and spotted young Rita, who was working furiously alongside her colleagues to put out the last of the flames so that the emergency heavy-lifting crews and rescue services could go in to try and find any survivors.

'Holy Mother of God,' he breathed as he quickly put out his pipe. 'Come on, Harvey. They'll need all the help they can get.'

But Harvey was nowhere in sight, and as Ron hurried towards the fire chief, John Hicks, he finally spotted him nosing about in the rubble of the second boarding house. Knowing he would bark if he found anything, Ron left him to it. 'What can I do, John?'

'It's a bad one, Ron,' he replied, his handsome young face drawn with anxiety and streaked with soot and sweat. 'We've managed to get everyone out of the boarding houses, and accounted for those that were missing, but we have no idea how many are trapped down there in the hotel basement.'

Ron eyed the smoking devastation, certain that no one could possibly have survived. 'Has *anyone* got out?'

'More than we could have hoped for, but we still had twenty casualties and ten fatalities.' John gave a deep sigh. 'God alone knows what we'll find in there.' He looked round at his hard-working colleagues and watched them for a moment. 'I shall need you and Harvey's nose to help the rescue crew once the heavy-lifting team have made that cellar ceiling safe.'

Ron nodded and looked around for the dog. He was still rummaging in the rubble of the boarding houses. 'Harvey,' he shouted. 'Stop messing about and come here.'

Harvey ignored him, his nose to the ground as he anxiously circled a particular spot. His ears were pricked and his hackles were high. He was on the trail of something.

'Blasted dog,' muttered Ron. 'Leave it, I said,' he roared. 'Come here.'

Harvey whined and started to scrabble into the heart of the rubble, and before Ron could stop him, managed to wriggle beneath a precarious pile of charred timber and shattered bricks and then disappeared.

Ron was furious, for John had said everyone from

the boarding houses had been accounted for, and if Harvey was busy chasing vermin instead of concentrating on his job properly, he'd stop his biscuits for a week.

He stomped over the debris, his boots sliding over sharp-edged bricks and broken masonry as he approached the place where Harvey had disappeared. There was a narrow tunnel burrowing beneath the wreckage. 'Harvey, get your hairy arse out of there this minute,' he yelled down it.

There was a muffled bark from deep beneath the shifting, treacherous rubble, and Ron became really afraid that his dog might get buried. 'Ach, you heathen beast,' he muttered. 'Will you come outta there before this lot falls on top of you?' he shouted down.

There was no answering bark this time, but as Ron lay carefully on the debris and put his ear to the tunnel entrance, he could hear the dog whining and the scrabble of paws. It sounded as if Harvey was stuck and couldn't get out.

Ron began to dig furiously, praying that the whole mess didn't cave in and bury them both, for it was slippery with water and sliding and collapsing beneath him every time he moved. Careless for his own safety, he began chucking bricks, mortar, window frames, lead piping and masonry aside. Scrabbling with his bare hands, he tried desperately to make the hole bigger so that Harvey could climb out. He could still hear the dog whining piteously, and he was almost blinded by tears of frustration as the tunnel never seemed to get any bigger and the debris shifted and swayed beneath him.

'I need help over here,' he shouted. 'Harvey's stuck and this lot is about to collapse.'

Rita and three others came rushing over. But before they could even reach him, Harvey's head appeared and after a momentary scramble, he emerged with something firmly clasped in his mouth. He gently placed the bundle in Ron's open arms, stood and wagged his tail, gave a bark and shot straight back down the hole again before anyone could stop him.

Ron looked in stunned disbelief from the bundle in his arms to the hole where his beloved dog had disappeared.

'Oh my God,' breathed Rita. 'It's a baby. Is it alive?'

Ron pulled back the filthy blanket, stroked the tiny cold, dirty face and felt a pulse in the delicate neck. 'Yes,' he said softly as he hastily wrapped the infant back in the blanket and handed it over to her. 'Get her to the ambulance, quickly,' he ordered. 'She's very cold and her pulse is weak.'

He watched Rita stumbling over the rubble with the bundle clasped tightly to her chest, and once she'd handed it over to the ambulance crew he turned his attention back to Harvey, who was barking determinedly deep underground. 'There must be someone else down there,' he said anxiously. 'Quick, get more help to shift this lot.'

As more willing hands came to remove the piles of broken masonry, bricks, mortar and wood, Harvey continued to bark. 'We're coming,' shouted Ron as he threw aside a length of lead drainpipe.

The sad remnants of clothes and toys lay charred and twisted amid the chaos. As they dug and cleared, they found ruined photographs and letters, a delicate dancing shoe – and a baby's rattle.

'Dear God,' breathed Rita, who was working frantically beside Ron. 'I hope she's still alive down there.'

'I thought you'd accounted for everyone?' he rasped as the dust and smoke filled his mouth and nose and made his lungs ache.

'We thought we had, but a chap's just turned up from the billeting office to verify things, and it seems a young woman and her baby were due to move into the basement room tonight. She must have gone in without anyone seeing her. But why, why didn't she get out when the sirens went?'

Ron didn't reply, for he could barely breathe, let alone talk – and people had grown careless over the past months once the raids had tailed off. He continued to clear the tunnel, urged on by Harvey's anxious barking. Once it was big enough to get a man through it, Ron took off his coat and grabbed the rope. 'He's my dog. I'll do it,' he said in tones that brooked no argument.

The rope was tied in a noose round his waist, the slack taken up by two burly firemen who would bear the strain should the debris collapse beneath him. After several deep breaths, he took a torch from John Hicks, knelt down and began to crawl along the steeply sloping tunnel that was as black as sin and claustrophobically narrow.

It reminded him of the tunnels they'd dug in the first war so they could lay mines beneath enemy territory, and those nightmare memories made him stop for a moment. His pulse was racing, and all the old terrors had returned, for he'd once been buried in a tunnel like this, and it had taken many hours before they'd managed to dig him out. Now, he had no idea of how deep he would have to go, or what he might find there. But Harvey needed him. He had to overcome his fears and get on with it.

His hand was slippery with sweat and shaking as he switched on the torch. The powerful beam swept unsteadily over the unstable surface of the surrounding tunnel that sloped alarmingly down towards what looked like the remains of a cellar. And there was Harvey, his eyes shining in the reflected light as he stood protectively over the prone figure of a woman.

'Good boy,' Ron soothed as the dog whined and nudged the woman with his paw. 'I can see them,' he shouted back to the others. 'Another few feet and I'm there.'

More torches shone down the tunnel as Ron scrambled towards the pair, but the wavering beams simply made the scene even more macabre. He pulled off the rope and ruffled Harvey's head. 'Good lad,' he praised, before kneeling next to the young girl whose clothes had been ripped from her in the blast.

She was lying too still beneath the shattered concrete and brick, and her face was ghostly white in the torchlight. Covered in blood, her leg was clearly broken and there was a deep gash on her forehead.

Harvey sat and panted as Ron touched her neck to see if he could find a pulse. It was there, but very faint and irregular. 'Send the stretcher down,' he yelled. 'She's alive, but only just.'

The stretcher slithered down the tunnel, hauled by Rita, who'd shed her heavy protective clothing and wore little more than trousers and a vest.

'Why have they sent you?' asked a horrified Ron.

'I'm the only one left that's small enough to fit through that, and someone had to bring the stretcher,' she said calmly. She knelt by the girl, felt the thready pulse and nodded. 'We'd better move quickly before we lose her,' she muttered.

They lifted away the debris that had almost buried her and put her gently on the stretcher. Placing a blanket over the girl's almost naked body, Rita buckled the straps firmly and then tied the end of the rope that had been round her waist to the end of the stretcher. 'Pull her up,' she shouted. 'But carefully. The whole tunnel is deteriorating.'

Ron stroked Harvey's head as they watched Rita slowly crawl up the tunnel behind the stretcher, her guiding hand keeping it from hitting the crumbling sides. Once they'd got to the many willing hands who reached out to help, Ron gave a deep sigh of relief.

'Come on, auld feller,' he said affectionately. 'It's our turn now.'

Harvey whined and flinched as slates and dust and debris came sliding down to shatter on the stone floor. The tunnel was slowly but surely beginning to disintegrate.

Ron took Harvey's head in his hands and looked into his eyes. 'You got down here twice, so you can go back up. And to be sure there'll be a biscuit in it for you if you'd just do as I say for once.'

Harvey's eyebrows twitched, and at Ron's nudge, he gave him a lick on the nose and started to scramble up the tunnel.

Ron dodged the bits of brick and mortar that came flying down from beneath the dog's paws. If he stayed here any longer he'd never get out, and his old terrors of small dark places deep underground would have won.

He began to crawl, feeling each handhold sink and shift, and every scrape of his ruined shoes dislodge something. He could hear the crash of heavy debris hitting the concrete floor behind him. Could hear the sigh of things moving all around him. And then hands were reaching down – pulling him out into the cold, smoke-filled night where

Harvey joyously welcomed him. Ron's legs felt weak and trembling, but he hugged him hard and led him back off the rubble to the firm pavement.

Harvey shook himself, spraying everyone with filthy water and sooty dog hair before he sat grinning like a fool as he was patted and praised by one and all. There was a bowl of water put down for him and one of the ladies from the WVS even brought him a couple of biscuits.

John Hicks ordered his crew to get back to the hotel bomb site now that Ron and Harvey were safe, and Ron had just taken a mug of tea from the WVS woman when the tunnel collapsed. It went with a mighty crash that sent a great plume of dust and soot into the air, and Ron's legs finally gave out.

He sank on to the kerb, his arms around his beloved dog as he fought off the waves of giddiness that made him feel as if he was caught in a storm at sea. 'You're a brave, brave boy,' he managed gruffly as the tears ran down his face. 'Thank God you turned your usual deaf ear and ignored me shouting at you, or those two would have died down there.' Harvey whined and licked away Ron's tears before turning and rushing off to see what everyone else was up to.

Ron suspected Harvey was thoroughly enjoying himself, for he was now nosing about in search of something else. He scrubbed at his face and struggled to his feet. His body might be aching from weariness, and his head spinning from shock, but his spirits had been reinforced by Harvey's bravery, and the miracle of finding the mother and baby alive. There would be no rest until everyone had been accounted for, and now the heavy-lifting crew had finished securing the cellar ceiling, all hands would be needed on deck.

Ron and Harvey worked tirelessly alongside the others throughout the night. It seemed that God, or whoever was in charge of such things, had been keeping watch, for there was only one fatality amongst fifty people trapped in the hotel cellar, and that had been an elderly woman who'd suffered a heart attack.

The sky had lightened by the time the last ambulance left. The walking wounded had long since gone, and the fire crews and rescue workers were now on their weary way back to their headquarters where they would attempt to wash off the dirt, sweat and horror of a harrowing night's work.

And yet there was a lightness in their hearts, for the baby was unharmed and thriving in her hospital crib. Her young mother's injuries had been treated, and now she was slowly recovering from her ordeal in a nearby ward. It had indeed been a night of miracles.

Ron stood for a moment and said a silent prayer for the souls of those who'd been lost tonight, and then stroked Harvey's head. 'Come on, you auld heathen,' he said through a vast yawn. 'Let's go and raid Peggy's larder for a slap-up breakfast.'

Chapter Fifteen

Peggy had been woken early by a fractious Daisy, and not wanting the whole house disturbed, she'd quickly pulled on her dressing gown and slippers, bundled her up and carried her into the kitchen.

What she saw there brought her to a stunned halt. With rising fury she regarded the table littered with dirty plates, breadcrumbs and raided jam and pickle jars – and the greasy frying pan on the top of the range as well as the numerous smeary bowls lined up on the floor. Jane was always the first one up, but she never left the kitchen in such a mess, so there was no doubt who the real culprits were.

A quick check on her larder showed there were no eggs, only the crust of the hated wheatmeal loaf, one onion, and a heel of cheese. The potatoes she'd been saving to fry for everyone's breakfast had also gone, along with the last of the margarine and lard ration and most of the sugar.

Fairly vibrating with rage, she put Daisy in the playpen and was about to go down and give Ron a right royal ear-wigging when a bedraggled and clearly exhausted Rita traipsed in.

'I can't promise you breakfast,' Peggy said, barely

able to contain her temper. 'Ron and Harvey have been through my larder like a plague of locusts. But don't you worry, Rita. I'm about to go down and tear them off such a strip their ears will be ringing for a bloody week.'

Rita looked rather shocked by Peggy's language, for she rarely swore. 'You must be really cross,' she said as she took in the mess, 'and I understand, really I do. But please don't tell them off, Auntie Peg. They've been up all night helping us rescue people from the bomb site on the seafront.'

'That's no excuse for raiding my larder,' stormed Peggy.

'Auntie Peg,' the girl pleaded. 'Please listen, and then you'll understand why they both deserve more than just a good breakfast.'

Peggy tightened the belt on her dressing gown and folded her arms. 'Well it better be good, Rita,' she snapped. 'Because I've just about had enough.'

'They're both heroes,' said Rita, 'especially Harvey, because he saved the life of a young mother and her baby tonight.'

Peggy's temper dissolved immediately and she sat down at the table with a bump, as Rita described in detail everything that had happened.

'We missed them entirely,' Rita finished. 'And if it hadn't been for Harvey they could have died down there, because the whole thing was on the point of collapse.'

Peggy was chastened and she found that her hand

was shaking as she lit a cigarette. 'I had no idea,' she murmured. 'Oh God, and to think I was about to go down there and give the pair of them an earful.'

Rita squeezed her hand in sympathy. 'You weren't to know.'

Peggy regarded her more closely and felt worse than ever. 'You look so tired,' she said. 'It must have been a terrible night for everyone, and here I am moaning about a mess in my kitchen. At least they've left me tea, and if the hens have laid more eggs I could do you one with the last of the bread.'

'Don't worry about anything for me, Auntie Peg, I've drunk enough tea tonight to sink a battleship, and I had breakfast at the fire station.' Rita pushed back from the table and began to collect the dirty dishes. 'Come on, it won't take long if we clear up together.'

Peggy took the dishes from her. 'No,' she said firmly, 'you're as exhausted as they are. Go and have a bath, then get to bed. I can do this.' She patted the wan, grubby little face, and gave her a hug before nudging her towards the door.

'I'll probably sleep straight through,' said Rita as she yawned. 'Could you wake me up at five? I have to be back on duty again at seven.' At Peggy's nod, she trudged out and headed for the stairs in her soot-stained clothes, every movement of her small slender body making it clear she was completely drained.

Peggy stacked the dirty dishes on the wooden draining board, wiped down the table and replaced the lids on her raided pots of home-made jams and pickles. She looked down at Daisy who'd fallen back to sleep with her teddy bear in the playpen, and decided the washing-up could wait for a while.

She slumped back into the chair and gazed at Jim's photograph on the mantelpiece. The Grand Hotel had been their favourite place to go for an evening when they were feeling flush and wanted to splash out, and she had many fond memories of the elegant dining room, the comfortable lounge bar, and the marvellous dance floor in the very grand ballroom. Now it was all gone – smashed to smithereens.

There had been so many changes to Cliffehaven since this awful war had begun that soon she wouldn't be able to recognise the place – and if it went on for much longer, neither would Jim. There were the remains of a German fighter plane rusting amid the skeleton of the once-lovely pier; hotels, guest houses, the cinema and half the station buildings were gone, and the entire area behind the station had been firebombed flat. Not that it was too much of a loss, for it had been no more than a slum that should have been cleared years ago. And yet it had been home to Rita and a hundred other families, who'd been forced to find alternative accommodation.

The factories had flourished in the north of the town and new people were arriving every day, and what with the parks being turned into vegetable plots, their fine railings melted down for the war effort, and the majority of the town's children sent away to live with strangers, it just didn't feel the same any more.

And yet, Peggy realised, the nature of the people hadn't changed. In fact they were more close-knit than ever, united in their determination to battle on against a common enemy. Churchill had talked about the need for blood, sweat, toil and tears, and the people of Cliffehaven had taken his message to their hearts, willingly giving everything they could to bring an end to this war.

She looked around her shabby, untidy kitchen and felt strengthened by its warmth and familiarity. She would get through today and tomorrow and every day until Jim and her children came home again, but for now she must pull herself together and get on with writing a shopping list and cleaning this kitchen.

Leaving her chair, she hunted out a piece of scrap paper and began to make a list of all the things she would need to restock her larder. Then she quickly washed up the dishes, scrubbed out the frying pan and cleaned the splattered grease from the top of the range. Once the floor had been swept of sugar and crumbs, she poked some life into the fire and used the last of the oats to make a thin but warming porridge.

Daisy was still asleep, and the others wouldn't be down for at least another hour, so she fetched a bowl and went down the cellar steps intending to search the henhouse for any fresh eggs. But as she reached the scullery, she could hear the resonant snores coming from Ron's bedroom. Tiptoeing down the narrow corridor she peeked in, and couldn't help but smile.

Ron was lying on the unmade bed, flat on his back, still fully dressed and snoring for England. His good trousers and shoes were ruined, his shirt, hair and face were black with soot and grime, and his tweed jacket had a tear in the sleeve.

As for Harvey, he was stretched alongside Ron and also snoring. His brindled coat was matted and filthy, and his two front paws had been bandaged in what looked suspiciously like strips from one of Ron's old shirts.

Peggy watched them sleeping, the tears blinding her. They were heroes – her heroes – and she couldn't have loved them more than she did right at this moment.

Mary was woken by the sound of someone moving round the room. Startled and disorientated, she sat up and peered into the gloom. 'Who's that?'

'It's only me,' said Ivy. 'Who did you think it was? Your Australian?'

Mary realised where she was and sank back into the pillows. 'He's not *my* Australian at all,' she replied as she yawned and snuggled back beneath the covers. 'What on earth are you doing up at this time of the morning, anyway?'

'I'm going to work. And it's not that early, it's nearly six.'

Mary groaned as Ivy pulled back the thick blackout curtains and the room was filled with a grey light. 'Did you have to do that?' she asked as she pulled the sheet over her head.

'And here's me thinking you was a country girl, up and out milking cows and such before it were even light,' Ivy teased as she finished lacing her sturdy boots.

'I lived in a rectory, and don't know one end of a cow from another. Go away and let me sleep.'

Ivy bounced on the end of the bed. 'You'll have to get used to early mornings once you start at the factory, Mary. Late nights an' all, cos like the good old Windmill Theatre, they never close.'

Mary was now fully awake, so she sat up and gently swatted Ivy with a pillow. 'Are you always this annoying in the morning?'

'Yeah,' she replied blithely as she dodged the pillow, grabbed her gas-mask box and coat, and headed for the bedroom door. 'I'll see yer tonight.' With that she closed the door and was gone.

Mary sighed deeply and reached for her dressing gown. It would have been nice to have had a bit of a lie-in after the late night, but she was now fully awake, so she might as well follow Ivy's example and get on with the day.

She dug her feet into her slippers and, picking up her washbag, hurried quietly along the landing to the bathroom. It was quite cold, with gleaming white tiles, and the claw-footed tub was deep. Pristine towels were folded neatly on a shelf, and a quick glance into the wall cabinet revealed a sparse collection of toothpaste, talcum powder, shampoo and bath salts. As these were all clearly recognisable as having come from Woolworths, Mary realised they must belong to Ivy. No doubt Mrs Williams kept her expensive toiletries in her bedroom so they wouldn't get used by her lodgers.

Having washed and cleaned her teeth, Mary went back to the bedroom and got dressed. She chose her warm skirt, a white blouse and the blue sweater. Ankle socks and her sturdiest pair of lace-up shoes completed the outfit, for she was planning to explore the town today, and perhaps spend some time on the seafront.

She heard Mrs Williams moving about, and wondered what the routine of this house was in the mornings. Would she be expected to cook breakfast for them both – or just for herself? Or did Mrs Williams actually do it? It was all a bit awkward, and she didn't feel she could go down and start poking about in cupboards or making tea without asking permission first. If only she'd asked Ivy what the form was before she went rushing off. But it was too late now, so she decided she would wait until she heard the woman go downstairs.

Feeling restless and rather hungry, she made the bed and tidied up the clothes Ivy had left strewn all over the floor, then brushed her hair. Going over to the window, she drew back the thin sprigged curtains, lifted the white nets, and gasped in delight.

The view was quite magnificent, for the sun was rising above the sea and she had an uninterrupted panorama of the whole of the promenade right to the white cliffs that towered at the very end. And although the rusting ribs of the enemy plane looked forlorn amid the crumbling remains of the pier, and the coils of barbed wire and gun emplacements were ugly additions to the promenade, they couldn't detract from the beauty of the sun-gilded sea, which rolled like silk on to the pebble beach.

Mary watched the waves, almost mesmerised by their symmetry and rhythm, and then she slowly drank in the majesty of the towering cliffs with their brows of green, the long, gentle arc of the beach, and the tall houses lining the street which followed this curve.

She opened the window and leaned out to breathe in the clean, crisp, salty air, admire the clear blue sky and listen to the cries of the wheeling gulls. As her gaze drifted over the numerous rooftops to the lines of terraces that climbed the hill in the distance, she realised that Cliffehaven must have been an elegant town before the war. She could imagine the holidaymakers walking along the promenade, or sitting in deckchairs on the beach with their picnics while children paddled in the shallows. The pier would have been lit up, and offering music, dancing and variety shows – and in the hotels there would have been waiters in white coats serving cocktails to women dressed in silks and furs.

The sound of footsteps passing the door and going down the stairs brought her out of her daydream and she shut the window. Checking that she looked presentable, she took a deep breath to prepare herself, and then left the bedroom.

'There you are,' said Mrs Williams, who was making a pot of tea in the kitchen. Her hair was immaculately groomed, and she was wearing full make-up and a beautifully cut tweed skirt and jacket over a white blouse. There were pearls in her ears and around her neck, so she was probably planning on going somewhere important today.

'Good morning,' said Mary as she hovered in the doorway.

The gimlet gaze scrutinised her. 'I hope you are not suffering any ill effects from your less than salubrious night out – but if you are, it is entirely your own fault, so don't expect any sympathy.'

'I'm feeling very well, thank you, Mrs Williams, and had an excellent night's sleep. May I help with anything?'

'No thank you,' she replied rather sharply. 'I prefer to prepare my own breakfast. When I have done so, you may prepare yours.'

'I brought down my food stamps,' said Mary as she placed them on the table. 'I was wondering,' she went on hesitantly, 'may I use the telephone to call my friend Mrs Boniface to let her know I've arrived safely?'

'Certainly not. I cannot allow my instrument to be used by all and sundry, and I have to keep a close eye on the bills which are high enough already. There is a public telephone box in the High Street which is perfectly adequate.'

Well, thought Mary, that tells me. 'Then may I ask where the nearest air-raid shelter is, and what the usual daily routine is?'

Doris poured out two cups of tea and placed them on the kitchen table. 'There is an Anderson shelter in the back garden. I simply couldn't abide being enclosed with so many ghastly people in the public one behind the park. One never knows what one might catch,' she said with a sniff.

Mary made no comment.

'Your breakfast is to be eaten in here, and you must ensure that you leave everything clean and tidy. I am not always here for luncheon as I am terribly busy with my various committees, so you may make yourself a sandwich or something. Ivy usually cooks the evening meal if she's not working, because I have a frightfully packed schedule and cannot possibly be expected to cater for everyone.' She gave a dramatic sigh. 'I am trying to teach her the refinements of good housekeeping and cooking, but sadly she's still very slapdash.'

Mary realised she was expected to make some sort of placatory comment. 'It must be very difficult for you with your lodgers coming in at such odd hours.'

'It is a trial, certainly, but one does what one can in these troubled times.' She broke an egg into the pan of swirling water, placed two slices of bread in the smart-looking electric toaster and carefully drew up the sides until they clipped at the top. 'I used to have a girl who came in to cook and clean, but she decided to leave for the dubious delights of the factory production line, so I must soldier on alone.'

Mary sipped her tea, thinking how much she disliked this woman.

'My son has a very important post with the MOD and he occasionally stays overnight, and as I have warned Ivy, I expect you girls to conduct yourself with utter decorum – especially when using the bathroom in the mornings. My Anthony is to be married soon, and his work is stressful enough without having to see you girls in your nightclothes or listen to your silly chatter.'

Mary wondered if he was as priggish as his mother, and felt very sorry for Suzy who was marrying him. To have this woman as a mother-in-law would be a complete nightmare. 'I met your sister Peggy last night, and three of the girls who lodge with her. She seems very nice,' she said carefully.

Doris tutted with disapproval. 'My sister has very few refinements, and her habitual use of that ghastly public house is not something I wish to discuss.' She scooped out the egg and placed it on the golden toast. 'My future daughter-in-law is thankfully from a most respectable and well-connected family, and although she's far too well-mannered to say anything, I'm sure she must have found it a trial to have to live at Beach View.'

From what Peggy had told her last night, Suzy was a lovely girl who had few airs and graces and worked extremely hard as a theatre nurse at the large hospital. Mary just hoped she was of strong enough character to withstand this woman's constant and undermining snobbery.

'You may now cook your breakfast, and then I suggest you go and practise the pieces you'll be playing tomorrow afternoon.'

'I'm not at all sure I really know that music well enough to play for an audience,' Mary replied, as she regarded the toaster with some trepidation.

'There is sheet music in the piano stool.' Doris loaded her breakfast on to a tray. 'I have made all the arrangements now, so you'll just have to manage.' She picked up the tray. 'I am expecting you to do me proud,' she said and left the kitchen.

Mrs Williams was clearly the sort of woman who could steamroller her way through life and didn't care one iota if it was awkward or inconvenient for other people.

Mary gave a sigh, eyed the toaster and decided she'd just have bread and marge with her egg. She'd never come across a contraption like it before, and was terrified of breaking it. Once her egg was cooked, she hunted out cutlery and china, poured a second cup of tea, and sat down.

As she ate, she planned her day. She would practise for an hour on the piano, and then go and explore until teatime. She should probably tell Mrs Williams about the arrangement she'd come to with Rosie, but had a nasty feeling that wouldn't go down terribly well, so decided to leave it for another day. No good would come from rocking the boat so early on, and she suspected that the seas would always be choppy with Mrs Williams at the helm.

Ron woke to discover the day was half gone, and that Harvey had deserted him. He rolled off the unmade bed and groaned as he stretched. He ached all over, his hands were stiff and sore, and all that clambering down tunnels had done no favours to the pain in his back, which was particularly sharp this morning. No doubt the shrapnel was on the move again.

He discarded his ruined shoes and the rest of his filthy clothes, then pulled on his old warm dressing gown. He would have a bath and then eat something, and because Rosie wouldn't need him until tonight, he'd go and see Stan up at his allotment to ask if he had any more seedlings going spare. A walk might ease his back, and after the unpleasant fug of his bedroom, it would be good to get some fresh air into his lungs.

He stomped up the cellar steps to find Peggy and Cordelia busy in the kitchen as Daisy crawled about on the floor. Harvey was stretched out in front of the range, and he raised his head to look at Ron, his eyes soulful as his ears drooped.

'What's the matter, boy?' Ron asked. 'To be sure you're looking very sorry for yourself this fine day.'

'I've given him a bath,' said Peggy. 'He stank to high heaven and it took me ages to brush all the clumps of muck out of his fur. I've also put cream and clean bandages on his poor old paws. He's scratched and torn them quite badly after digging in all that rubble.'

'No wonder he's looking so down in the mouth,' Ron muttered as he stroked the silky head. 'He hates having baths.'

'Much like his master,' said Peggy. She threw her arms round him and gave him a kiss on the cheek.

'What the divil's that for?' he blustered as he went pink with embarrassment.

'It's for being a hero,' she replied fondly.

'I'm no such thing,' he protested.

'Oh, but you are,' trilled Cordelia, who was industriously chopping cabbage. 'We've had the man from the local paper knocking on the door asking to interview you, and there have even been calls from the national papers – and just about everyone in Cliffehaven has been round today wanting to see and congratulate you.'

Ron frowned and tightened the belt on his dressing gown. 'Well it's all stuff and nonsense,' he rumbled. 'I'm going to have a bath, and if anyone else calls, tell them I've gone to Timbuctoo.'

'The girl you saved rang earlier,' said Peggy. 'She sounds terribly young, but she's on the mend and is anxious to see you and Harvey so she can thank you for saving her baby's life. She said that Matron has agreed you can go in at any time.'

He glowered at her from beneath his bushy brows, still uneasy at all the unwarranted fuss. 'She's all right then?'

Peggy smiled. 'She and little Louise will probably be discharged tomorrow. Her mother is coming down from the Midlands, and she and the baby will go back with her to live.'

'Well, I'm glad everything turned out all right in the end,' Ron said. 'Now I'll be having me bath.'

'Try having a shave as well,' advised Cordelia with a hint of asperity. 'You never know, you might get your picture in the papers, so you should try to look at least half respectable.'

'Over my dead body,' he muttered as he stomped into the hall and clumped up the stairs.

An hour later Ron was walking up the High Street. His natural abhorrence for doing what people expected of him meant that he'd decided not to shave, and was wearing his favourite old corduroy trousers which were held up at the waist by a length

338

of garden twine, a warm shirt, a thick but rather ragged sweater and his poacher's coat.

Harvey was trotting along beside him and didn't smell quite as sweet as he had when he'd left Beach View, for he'd rushed off at the first opportunity to roll in some fox droppings.

Ron was strolling along, minding his own business, and enjoying the fresh air and sunshine. But it seemed the story of last night's events had spread throughout the town, and as he tried to make his way up the street he kept being stopped by people who wanted to talk about them and congratulate him on his bravery. It was all very embarrassing, and by the time he'd reached the Town Hall he was feeling decidedly grumpy.

Harvey, of course, was delighted by all the fuss, but people soon recoiled when they smelled him, and Ron began to wish that he too was redolent of fox droppings. It was certainly a deterrent to being pestered.

He pulled down the peak of his battered cap and shoved up the collar of his coat in an effort to avoid being recognised, but as he stomped past the Home and Colonial he was almost blinded by a flash of light. He blinked and glared at the man with the camera. It was the reporter from the local paper. 'I never gave you permission to do that,' he barked as he strode menacingly towards him.

The man edged away. 'Would you like to say a few words for our readers?'

Ron bunched his fists. 'To be sure I'll have a few words for you,' he growled, 'but they'll not be suitable for your rag.'

'Now, Ron, don't get het up,' the man said as he backed hurriedly away. 'You're a hero, and the public want to hear your story.'

'Well the public can mind their own damned business,' he roared.

The man shrugged – he was an old hand at dealing with reluctant interviewees – but clearly he realised it wouldn't be wise to hang about any longer. With a cheerful grin, he turned and hurried down the street towards the newspaper offices.

'Ach, to be sure, Harvey, there'll be no peace for us today,' Ron muttered. He carried on walking up the hill. If this was what happened when a man and his dog did something that anyone else might do, then he'd had enough of it. Hero indeed. He was nothing of the sort. The real heroes were the lads doing their bit on the battlefields and in the air and seas.

He checked that Stan wasn't at the station and hurried over the humpbacked bridge and up the hill, through the wasteland that had once been home to little Rita and hundreds of others, until he came to the allotments. But even here he was called to and congratulated and made a general fuss of, so he was glad when he reached Stan's quiet corner and could hide in comfort behind his shed.

'I'll just say it once.' Stan got up from his deckchair

to make a pot of tea on the primus stove. 'Well done. You did a marvellous thing last night.'

'It was Harvey, not me,' Ron replied grumpily as he plumped down into the other deckchair. 'It's a lot of fuss about nothing. I've even had that blasted reporter flashing his blasted camera at me. To be sure the only consolation I have is that by tomorrow night it will all be forgotten and the newspaper will be wrapped round someone's fish and chips.'

Stan made the tea while Ron hosed Harvey down from the standpipe and made him smell better. Once that was done they sat enjoying the sunshine as they talked about seedlings and cabbages, and then went on to discuss Jim's posting abroad, Ruby and her young, injured Canadian, and Ethel's masterly cooking.

Ron began to relax finally and removed his heavy coat as Harvey went off to explore the possibility of cadging sandwiches or biscuits from the other allotment holders. It was very pleasant in the sun, and no one bothered him with their talk of heroes and such, so he could enjoy some peace with his friend before he took the back roads home.

'Rosie keeps a good pint,' said Stan. 'It's always a pleasure to drink in the Anchor.'

'Aye, she does that.' Ron puffed on his pipe. 'But it's only because I look after the barrels and keep the pipes clean.' He shifted in the deckchair. 'It was a good night, wasn't it? That little Mary certainly knows how to entertain a crowd.'

'Yes, Ethel and Ruby thoroughly enjoyed themselves, and it was lovely to see all the young people having such fun.'

Ron chuckled. 'To be sure I can see the pound signs in Rosie's eyes now the girl has agreed to play every weekend.'

'She'll certainly bring the customers in,' agreed Stan. 'But I pity her having to live with Doris.'

Ron grimaced. 'Aye, 'tis not something I'd wish to be doing after she dumped herself on us when Peggy was laid up.'

Stan dunked a biscuit in his tea. 'By the way, there's something I meant to ask you, but never got the chance last night. Do you know a Cyril Fielding?'

Ron froze with his pipe halfway to his lips. Hearing that name after so many years had come as a shock, and he could feel the hairs prickling on his nape. 'Why do you ask?'

'Mary asked if I knew him, and I've been trying to place the name ever since. I'm positive I've heard it before, but I'm damned if I can remember how or when.'

Ron's thoughts were churning. He wasn't really surprised that Stan couldn't place Cyril, for it hadn't been him who'd had the run-in with him all those years ago. He pressed the tobacco down in the bowl of his pipe and took his time to relight it so he could think how to respond. 'Why was Mary asking after him?' he asked quietly.

'I have no idea.' Stan eyed him sharply. 'You know

who it is, don't you? So come on then, put me out of my misery.'

Ron told him and Stan stared back in disbelief. 'Good grief,' he managed. 'But why would a young girl like Mary want to find him, of all people?'

'That's what you're going to have to find out, Stan.'

'Why me?' he spluttered.

'Because she knows you a bit better than she knows me,' Ron replied firmly. 'And I can't get involved with this. You know I can't.'

Stan thought about this as he lit a cigarette. 'We've only exchanged a few words,' he said eventually. 'But she seems to get on all right with Ethel. Perhaps she should be the one to talk to her?' he suggested hopefully.

Ron shook his head. 'The fewer people who know about this, the better,' he declared. 'I know Ethel means well, but she's got a loose tongue, Stan, and you know how gossip can spread.'

'Aye, you could be right,' Stan muttered regretfully. 'But how on earth do you expect me to get her to confide in me?'

'Just be your usual self. You managed it with little Ruby well enough, and she didn't know you from Adam when she arrived.' Ron puffed on his pipe, his thoughts in a whirl as he tried to figure out the best way of going about things.

He finally came to a decision. 'The next time you see Mary, tell her you've forgotten the name and ask her to remind you. Then you can ask why she's looking for him.' He gripped Stan's arm. 'Do not under any circumstances let on that you know who it is. I'm deadly serious about that, Stan.'

'All right, keep your hair on,' Stan replied grumpily. 'I am blessed with some common sense, you know.'

Ron did, but he'd had to make certain Stan understood how important it was to shield the girl from any unpleasantness. She was, after all, very young and still innocent enough to need protection.

'When you've found out her story, come to me and we'll work out what to do next. It might not be anything at all serious and we can just fob her off by saying we don't know him. But there's always the danger that she'll ask others about him, and sooner or later he'll get to hear about it, and that could cause a whole heap of trouble.'

'God, what a mess,' sighed Stan. 'I do wish you hadn't dumped all this on me. I was having a lovely peaceful couple of hours off, and now you've ruined it.'

'I'm sorry. But it's more than my hide is worth to be seen getting involved in this one.'

'I realise that. But you'll owe me, Ron.'

'To be sure we've been owing each other favours for over fifty years, my friend. Now, pour me another cup of that fine tea. A man gets thirsty from all this talking, and I've yet to ask you about your spare seedlings.'

Stan grinned. 'I might have known you'd only come up here to cadge something,' he said without rancour. 'And I suppose you'd like one of my cheese sandwiches to go with the tea?'

Ron grinned back. 'To be sure you know me too well, Stan, and a cheese sandwich would go down a treat. I was wondering when you'd get round to offering me one.'

Chapter Sixteen

It was a cold, brisk but sunny Sunday afternoon and Peggy was pushing the pram along the seafront. Ron was spending some time with Rosie at the Anchor, the girls were all out, and Cordelia had been collected by her elderly admirer to be taken to the golf club for afternoon tea, so she had the rest of the day to herself.

She hadn't lingered at the tragic sight of the great piles of rubble that had once been the Grand Hotel and two boarding houses, but had determinedly pressed on until she reached the end of the promenade. Too many people had lost their lives already, and each bomb site and every coil of barbed wire were terrible reminders of the sacrifices they were all having to make.

Havelock Road was quiet, but several people she knew were tending the vegetable patches in the park and she returned their waves as she passed. Glancing at her watch, she saw it was just after four, so she wasn't too late. Wheeling the pram over the gravel drive, she rapped the knocker, and was delighted when Ivy opened the door.

'Hello, dear. I hope I haven't missed anything?' Peggy enquired.

Ivy grinned and helped her get the pram over the doorstep and into the hall. 'Nah, Mary ain't started playing yet, but she'll be ever so glad to see you,' she confided in a stage whisper. 'All the old trouts are circling, and I think she's feeling a bit trapped.'

'That's why I decided to come,' Peggy replied. She checked on Daisy who was peacefully sleeping, hung her coat on the rack and went into the sitting room. 'Hello, Doris,' she said blithely. 'I hope you don't mind me gatecrashing your tea party.'

Doris didn't look at all pleased, but surrounded by her snooty cronies, she didn't dare make a scene. 'Of course not, Margaret,' she said stiffly. 'Do sit down. Mary is about to play for us.'

Peggy shot Mary a smile of encouragement. 'How lovely of her to give up her Sunday afternoon to entertain us all,' she remarked with more than a touch of irony – for she knew Mary had had no real choice in the matter.

She crossed the room and gave the girl a hug. 'I am looking forward to this, dear,' she said quietly. 'And don't mind them, just play for yourself.'

'Thanks, Peggy. I'm so glad you're here,' she whispered back.

'Then I'm very glad I came.' Peggy ignored her sister's glare and sat down with only the barest acknowledgement to the other women. She poured herself a cup of tea, took a sandwich and settled back into the cushions, knowing she was behaving badly, but not caring a hoot. Lady C and her clique of smug, overdressed rich women wouldn't have given her the time of day usually, and as she disliked every last one of them, she didn't see why she should pretend she did.

'Now that everyone is *quite* settled,' said Doris with a furious glare at Peggy, 'I would like to introduce Mary Jones, who has very kindly offered to perform for us this afternoon. Her repertoire is quite outstanding, and I am hoping you will agree that she would be an excellent choice to help with our fundraising.'

As Doris waffled on, Peggy noticed that Ivy was standing in a corner looking very uncomfortable in the presence of so many daunting women, so beckoned her over to share her large chair. As they were both skinny, it wouldn't be too much of a squash. She poured the girl a cup of tea and, with a conspiratorial wink, offered her a piece of shortbread.

'Mary will begin with a sonata by Beethoven,' Doris announced grandly before sitting down and giving the girl a nod.

Peggy was swept away in the exquisite sounds of the Moonlight Sonata, and when the final note faded and was met with overly polite, muted applause, she shot to her feet and clapped enthusiastically. 'Well done, oh very well done, Mary. That was wonderful.'

There was a stony silence as the other women looked at her in cold disapproval.

Mary must have sensed the atmosphere, for she

immediately began to play the first movement of Rachmaninov's Second Piano Concerto. This was followed by a selection of tunes from the most popular musicals of stage and screen, which had everyone discreetly tapping their well-shod feet.

Peggy was entranced, for she hadn't realised just how talented the girl was, and this private little recital was a far cry from the sing-song at the Anchor. As she stood once again to cheer and clap alongside Ivy, she wondered if Doris knew about Mary's successful evenings at the pub. She very much doubted it, for if she did, she probably wouldn't have even considered asking the girl to play for her horrid friends.

'That was wonderful, dear,' said Peggy enthusiastically. 'Now, let me go and make a fresh pot of tea while you have something to eat. I'm sure you must be thirsty after all that playing.'

'Ivy will make the tea,' said Doris.

'I'm perfectly capable of making a pot of tea,' retorted Peggy. 'Ivy is not your servant.'

She picked up the pot and went into the kitchen, noting that the other women were now rather patronisingly praising Mary and badgering her with questions. Putting the kettle on the hob, she decided to go back in while it boiled. The girl would need support, and Ivy was too overawed by everyone to be of much help.

The ghastly afternoon dragged on, and Peggy stuck it out until all the women had left. Thankfully,

Daisy had slept through it all, but now she was beginning to whinge and whine, and doubtless needed her nappy changing before they went home.

Peggy returned from the cloakroom with a clean and gurgling Daisy to find Ivy busy clearing away the china and napkins and Mary looking distinctly uncomfortable as Doris bossily talked at her. 'What's the matter, Mary?' she asked.

'Mrs Williams has organised another recital for next Saturday, but I have already made other arrangements.'

Peggy caught the desperate look in the girl's eyes and realised at once that she didn't want to make any mention of the Anchor. 'Then you'll have to cancel it, Doris,' she stated firmly. 'You can't expect the girl to fall in with your plans if you don't have the courtesy to ask her first if she wants to do it – or indeed is available to do it.'

'Mary has agreed to perform a series of recitals to raise funds for the homeless,' said Doris.

'Actually, Mrs Williams, I said I would do one.' Mary was blushing furiously and clearly trying to remain calm and polite.

'It simply isn't good enough,' snapped Doris. 'You'll have to change your plans.'

Peggy had heard enough. 'Why should she? Mary has her own life to lead, and it's not up to you to tell her what she can and can't do.'

'This is none of your business, Margaret, and I

would appreciate it if you kept your opinions to yourself.'

'I'm sure you would,' retorted Peggy, 'but Mary isn't doing your concert next Saturday, and that's an end to it.'

The steely gaze settled on Mary. 'What is it that's so important you have to let everyone down, after all the trouble I've taken to introduce you to the cream of Cliffehaven society?'

'If my shift at the factory allows, I've promised to play for a friend,' Mary replied. She glanced at Peggy, licked her lips and took a deep breath. 'I play at the Anchor at the weekends,' she said in a rush.

Doris went quite white and had to sit down. 'The Anchor? But it's a ghastly dive, full of drunks and girls who are no better than they should be. As for the landlady . . .' She gave a sniff. 'Well, the least said about her the better. A girl from your background has no business consorting with such people.'

Mary refused to be cowed. 'Rosie Braithwaite is an extremely nice person, and we have become friends,' she said stoutly.

'Good grief,' gasped Doris. 'This is worse than I could have imagined.'

'I agree that my parents might not have approved,' Mary admitted, 'but it's fun, and I feel I'm doing my bit by entertaining the servicemen and women who go there. Not only do they enjoy a good sing-song round the piano, but Rosie is paying me. I earned nearly eight pounds in wages and tips this weekend,' she finished in a rush.

'Blimey, you earned that much?' breathed Ivy. 'Bloody hell, I wish I'd learnt to play the old joanna – I'd jack in me factory job and be down there every night.'

'Don't be so vulgar,' snapped Doris. 'Go and do the washing-up.'

Ivy must have felt emboldened by Peggy's presence, for she folded her arms and glared at Doris. 'I ain't your skivvy, and you're paid to 'ave me and Mary 'ere, so I reckon you can do yer own washing-up.'

Doris went puce. 'How *dare* you speak to me like that?' she rasped.

'You asked for it,' said Peggy mildly.

'I might have known you'd side with her. But then I should have expected it, as you share your home with riff-raff.'

Peggy could have slapped her for that, but she wasn't about to get into a row with Doris. It was late, she had a long walk home, and the sniping was nothing new. 'Come on girls, get your coats. I think we could all do with a bit of fresh air, and I'd appreciate your company for part of the way on my walk home.'

'Sorry, Peggy, but I've made arrangements to meet someone, and I'm already in danger of being late,' said a flustered Ivy.

'It wouldn't be a certain Australian, would it?'

Mary was grinning as they turned away from a fuming Doris and headed into the hall.

Ivy giggled. 'Well you did say he weren't yours, and he's ever so nice. We're going to the flicks and then 'aving chips and spam fritters after.'

Peggy strapped Daisy into her pram and gave her the bottle of orange juice from her bag to see her through until they got home. 'Come on then, girls, it's dark out there, and my lot will be waiting for their tea. Would you like to join us for tea, Mary?'

'I'd love to,' she replied. 'I'll just tell—'

'No need,' said Doris stiffly from the doorway. 'I would prefer to dine alone this evening anyway. I can feel one of my heads coming on.'

'Take an aspirin,' advised Peggy. 'And while you're at it, try a good dose of humility. It might cure what really ails you.'

Ivy and Mary smothered their giggles and hurried to help Peggy with the pram. Once it was over the threshold and the door shut behind them, Ivy said goodbye and rushed off to keep her date with Smoky Ashton.

'I'm sorry you got caught up in that,' said Peggy as she and Mary strolled along the drive. 'I'm not usually so catty, but my sister is impossible at times and needs to be firmly squashed.'

'I think you're very brave to stand up to her like that,' replied Mary.

'It took years of practice, believe me,' muttered Peggy as she paused by the gateway to pull up her coat collar and tug on her gloves. 'You need to stay firm, Mary, because if you let her, she'll have you doing concerts every weekend. And you won't earn a penny, let alone any gratitude from that bunch of snobs.'

'I don't mind doing the occasional one,' said Mary, 'after all, it would be for a good cause. But I really enjoy playing at the pub, and I do like Rosie, she's not only funny, but has a sweet nature.' She wrapped her scarf a little more firmly round her neck and dug her hands in her coat pockets as they left the shelter of Doris's front garden and were met by the blustery wind. 'I bumped into her yesterday, and she asked me upstairs for a cup of tea. We got on like a house on fire, and it was as if we'd known each other for years.'

'Good, I'm glad. Rosie's one of the loveliest people I know, but because she runs a pub she finds it difficult to make women friends, and she can get a bit lonely up there during closing time when Ron can't be with her.'

'Yes, she did say that, and told me I could always pop in if I was passing.'

The buffeting wind made it difficult to walk very fast, but Peggy was glad to have the opportunity of really getting to know this sweet girl. 'So,' she said, 'how have you spent the weekend?'

'I practised for the recital Saturday morning and then spent the rest of the day exploring Cliffehaven, and finding my way around. Rosie gave me a rough map, so it was quite easy to locate the factory estate, and I even spotted Ron and Stan sitting outside a shed in the large allotment up by the dairy.'

'They're up there most days, especially Stan. He's made his shed into quite a little home from home, and there's always a cup of tea going should you want one. He's a nice man, is Stan – the sort you can confide in and who gives good advice.'

'They were deep in conversation and didn't see me,' said Mary. 'So I just carried on walking and found myself up on the hills. You get a lovely view of Cliffehaven up there, don't you?'

Peggy smiled as they strolled along Havelock Road. 'You certainly do – not that I get much chance of going up there any more now I've got Daisy. But getting back to Stan and Ron: they were probably plotting some sort of mischief,' she chuckled. 'They've been friends since they were barely out of short trousers, and they haven't got any better behaved over the years.'

Mary smiled back. 'That's nice, isn't it – to have a loyal friend of many years who knows you inside out and who you can trust with just about anything. I've got a friend like that called Pat Logan. She and I have known each other since our mothers left us with Mrs Boniface to mind while they were working.'

'You must miss her,' murmured Peggy.

'Yes, I do rather,' she replied with a sigh. 'And what with my friend Jack enlisting in the army, it's quite hard to get used to how things are.'

Peggy heard the wistfulness and understood how homesick the girl must be so far from home, friends, family and Jack, who was clearly important to her. 'What about your parents? It must have been very hard for all of you to have to part.'

Mary tucked her chin into her scarf. 'They were killed in a tip-and-run. The rectory and church took a direct hit, so I only have Mr and Mrs Boniface and Jack, who's their son, now.'

Peggy's heart went out to her, and she stopped walking to take her hand and give it a squeeze. 'Oh, my dear, how awful for you. I'm so sorry.'

Mary's smile was a little wan. 'Yes, it was awful, but I'm trying very hard to come to terms with their loss. Being here helps of course, because there are no memories at every corner, but now and again it hits me that I'll never see them again, and that's when I miss Auntie Barbara and Uncle Joseph, the Bonifaces. They were very good to me.'

Peggy glanced across at her. 'And Jack?'

'I miss him quite dreadfully,' she replied with a fetching blush.

'Why don't you tell me about Jack and your parents and where you lived?' coaxed Peggy as she began to walk on towards the end of Havelock Road. 'It often helps to talk about these things rather than bottle them up, you know.'

Mary described the Sussex village, the rectory and church, and the warmth of the Boniface family, whose son she hoped to marry one day. Peggy wasn't at all sure she liked the sound of Mary's mother, for she came across as rather a cold fish, but she could hear the undoubted love in Mary's voice as she spoke of her gentle father, so her home life hadn't been all bad.

They reached the end of the road and hurried across the High Street into the relative shelter of the buildings in Camden Road. 'So what brought you all the way here to Cliffehaven?' Peggy asked as they slowly walked past the shuttered shops.

'It's a bit complicated,' Mary replied hesitantly, 'and not really a very nice story.'

Peggy liked a story, nice or not, and she was deeply intrigued by this quiet, unassuming young girl who clearly had far more to her than she'd first thought. 'I'm sure it's no worse than many others I've heard over the years,' she said comfortingly. 'And I can assure you it will go no further if you decide to trust me with it.' As Mary hesitated, she prompted her. 'I'm guessing that Cyril Fielding has an important part to play in this story of yours.'

Mary stopped and stared at her. 'Yes, but how did you know?'

Peggy smiled. 'Stan told me you were asking after him and thought I might know him. I don't, I'm sorry, Mary,' she said hastily. 'The name doesn't ring a bell at all.'

'Oh.' Mary bent her head.

They began walking again, even slower now they were out of the wind. 'Why were you looking for him, dear? Is he a family friend, or a relative of some kind?'

Mary took a deep breath, and as she told Peggy about her father's diaries and the document she'd found between the pages, Peggy realised what a terrible burden she'd been carrying. It was indeed an appalling set of circumstances for any girl to find herself involved in, especially one who seemed to have such a sweet, trusting nature.

'I came to Cliffehaven because my mother was living here when I was born eighteen years ago,' said Mary as they finally reached the end of Camden Road. 'I have no idea who she was, but she left here shortly afterwards, leaving me behind with my father.'

Peggy tightened her lips at the thought of any woman doing that to her newborn baby. What a cow. But the father wasn't much better by the sound of it, and if she ever got to meet either of them, she'd give them what for and no mistake. 'And your father was . . . ?'

'Cyril Fielding.'

Peggy thought about this as they crossed the road and were virtually pushed by the wind up the hill towards the twitten that ran behind the backs of the terraced houses. Hurrying into the shelter of the tall buildings, they stopped to get their breath. 'Do you know anything about him which might help to track him down?'

'He was a travelling salesman who had a large

area to cover, and was successful enough to put generous amounts into the church collection box. He attended Daddy's services fairly regularly for a while, and enjoyed his sermons, so he must have been Church of England, and according to Daddy's diary he was married, with young children.'

Peggy thought he sounded a complete and utter rotter. She sighed as they reached the back gate to Beach View. 'It doesn't help very much, does it? If only Stan could remember where he'd heard that name before, it would make things so much easier.'

'He's heard the name?' asked Mary sharply.

'Please don't get your hopes up, Mary,' she said quickly. 'He said he *thought* he'd heard the name before, but he could have been mistaken. Especially since all this happened so many years ago. And this Cyril had only been passing through when he'd had the affair, so he could have been based anywhere on the south coast.'

'It's all a bit hopeless, isn't it?' Mary fastened the gate behind them.

'Not necessarily,' Peggy hedged. She enjoyed a good mystery as much as anyone, but Mary clearly hadn't thought things through. She came to a halt by the back door and turned to face her. 'Mary, dear, have you fully considered the consequences of all this if you do manage to track down this Cyril?'

'I've thought of little else ever since I discovered that document.' Mary bit her lip and hunched her shoulders. 'Daddy was a trusting man, who took people at face value, and I just got the feeling from the diary that Cyril wasn't all he appeared to be.'

Having heard the bare bones of the story, Peggy was fairly certain Mary was right, but as she hadn't read either the diary or the document, it wasn't her place to comment.

'I know there's a danger that I won't like him,' Mary said with a sigh. 'But there's this need in me to find him – because until I do, there will always be a part of me that's missing.'

Peggy nodded. She'd heard of other adopted children needing to know who they were and where they'd come from – but their search for the truth rarely had a happy ending. 'Well, if you're absolutely certain about pursuing this, I want you to know you'll always have me to turn to if the going gets rough.'

'Oh, Peggy, that is kind. But—'

'There are no buts about it,' she replied firmly. 'You're in need of a friend, of someone who can help and advise you as a mother would. I might not be your mother, or even your Aunt Barbara, but my heart is warm and there is always room there for one more stray chick.' She saw the tears glitter on the girl's eyelashes and swiftly embraced her. 'There's no need for that,' she murmured. 'You've got me now.'

She drew back and waited for Mary to compose herself. 'That's better. Now, if you've got no objections, I think I should ask Ron about Cyril. He knows more people than you and I can shake a stick at, and if he can't pin him down, then no one can.'

'Won't he be shocked that I'm, I'm . . . Well, you know,' Mary stammered.

'Good grief,' Peggy gasped in amazement. 'Ron's the last person to be shocked by anything, least of all something like that. It's not your fault, and you mustn't ever think it is. Besides, I'm not about to tell him your personal business. I just want to ask if he knows Cyril.'

Mary smiled. 'Thanks, Peggy. And what if he does know who he is? What then?'

'I'll ask him to tell me all he knows about him, and then you and I can come to a decision as to whether or not we take it any further.'

Mary suddenly looked anxious. 'I don't want to cause any trouble.'

'Trouble? Who for?'

'Well, Cyril, I suppose – or rather his family.'

Peggy was of the opinion that Cyril Fielding deserved all the trouble he got and more besides. 'Let's deal with one thing at a time and not get ahead of ourselves,' she said briskly as she pushed the pram into the scullery. 'I don't know about you, but I'm ready for another cuppa, and a good dollop of that Irish stew I've left simmering in the slow oven all afternoon.'

Chapter Seventeen

Mary had spent a lovely relaxed and homely evening at Beach View. Rita and Fran were on duty, but Cordelia, Jane, Suzy and Sarah had been warm and welcoming, and the stew had been delicious. They had commiserated with her over having to lodge with Doris, and chattered away nineteen to the dozen about Suzy's wedding plans as they lingered over the meal and several cups of tea.

Unlike the routine in Doris's fancy house, everyone mucked in willingly without a word from Peggy, and they'd set to on the washing-up while she'd settled Daisy in her cot. The house might have been shabby, but the atmosphere was friendly and it was clear that the girls all adored Peggy, as well as the elderly Cordelia, and they gently teased Cordelia about her gentleman friend Bertram, which made her blush and twitter.

Once the kitchen was tidy again, they'd settled down by the fire. The other girls got out their knitting or mending, and Mary helped to roll Cordelia's beautiful new wool into balls as they regaled her with Ron and Harvey's heroic efforts of Friday night.

As the clock struck ten and Mary reluctantly prepared to leave, Peggy had been rather put out that there was still no sight of Ron, for she'd been hoping he would walk Mary back to her billet. Mary had assured her she would be fine, and had left the boarding house armed not only with a torch but with the certain knowledge that she'd been amongst true friends tonight, and that Peggy Reilly would keep her promise and be there for her should things go wrong.

The house was in darkness and utterly silent as she'd tiptoed up the stairs to find that the blackout curtains in the bedroom had not been pulled, and Ivy had yet to come home. Tired after the long day, she'd quickly used the bathroom, set the alarm on her clock, and climbed into bed with a contented sigh. She was asleep within minutes and didn't even hear Ivy coming in very much later.

The alarm shrilled at six o'clock and Ivy groaned as she pulled the pillow over her head. Mary shot out of bed, eager not to be late on her first day at work. 'Come on, sleepyhead,' she urged as she tugged at the pillow. 'It's time to get up.'

Ivy clutched at the pillow. 'Go away,' she moaned.

Mary grinned as she bounced on the end of the bed. The boot was on the other foot today. 'I'm not going anywhere until I'm sure you're properly awake,' she said. She gave Ivy a nudge and then went to open the curtains.

'Gawd 'elp us,' groaned Ivy as she struggled to sit up. 'Yer worse than me mum.'

Mary ruffled her already tousled head. 'That's what you get for being a dirty stop-out,' she teased. 'Good night, was it?'

Ivy's gamine face lit up with a naughty grin. 'I ain't telling you nuffing,' she said. 'Now clear off and sort yerself out while I try and wake up properly.'

Returning from the bathroom, Mary dressed in slacks and sweater, and her comfortable lace-up shoes. Unlike Ivy, she wasn't expected to wear heavy boots and dungarees, and would be given a coverall to protect her clothes. She found her scarf and had to spend some minutes tying up her hair and getting the thing knotted above her forehead. Eyeing her reflection in the mirror, she couldn't help but smile. She looked like a real worker now.

There was thankfully no sign of Doris while they cooked and ate their very early breakfast of dried scrambled egg on toast, and drank cups of strong tea. Grabbing their overcoats and gas-mask boxes, they hurried down Havelock Road and began the long trawl up the hill to the factory estate.

Surrounded by high wire fencing, overshadowed by many barrage balloons, and guarded at the gate by a soldier armed with a rifle, the estate was an imposing and rather forbidding place. They joined the long queue of other girls and older men, and had to show their identification papers and Mary's letter from the labour exchange confirming her job at the Kodak factory.

Once they were through the gate, Mary followed Ivy as she weaved her way through the bustling crowds of people entering and leaving the great corrugated-iron buildings that had been painted a uniform grey.

'They fill flak jackets with kapok in that building there, make camouflage netting in there and barrage balloons over there,' said Ivy. 'That's the tool factory where Ruby and her mum work, and behind that there's the really big factory wot makes parts for planes.'

They came to a long, single-storey building where the sound of a wireless programme blared out above the cacophony of loud chatter. Ivy continued, 'That's the canteen, and beside it are the washrooms and lavs. We have two ten-minute breaks for tea during each shift, and an hour for a main meal. You'll know when it's time cos a bloody great 'ooter blasts off and it's a stampede fer the door.'

'Too blooming right,' said Mabel as Ivy's friends joined them outside the canteen. 'It's a relief to get out in the fresh air to have a fag after being cooped up with a load of flaming explosives and cordite, I can tell you.'

'That's where the ammunition factory is.' Freda pointed towards the roof of a distant building. 'They keep us well away from everyone in case we blow up.'

They all giggled and linked arms. 'Best of luck, Mary,' said Gladys. 'See you at lunch as we're all on the same shift.'

'We'd better get a move on or we'll both be late,' muttered Ivy. 'You're over there,' she told Mary as she pointed to a large corrugated shed with heavy doors that were tightly closed. 'You go in that small door at the side, see? They 'ave to keep the place clean cos of all the expensive machinery they've got in there, which is why the big doors are always shut except during an emergency.'

Mary's mouth went dry and there was a flutter of panic in her stomach. 'Do I just walk in? Who do I tell that I've arrived? How do I find my way around?'

Ivy put her arm about her waist and gave her a grin. 'Lawks, yer really are green, ain't yer, gel? Come on, I'll go with yer and make sure yer don't get lost.'

Mary was very grateful, but it didn't make her any less nervous as Ivy opened the door and they stepped inside to find their way barred by a second door and an officious-looking woman in army uniform.

'This is as far as I can go, gel,' said Ivy as she squeezed Mary's hand. 'Good luck.'

'Identification,' boomed the woman as she held out her hand.

Mary fumbled her identification card and letter from her coat pocket and dropped both on to the concrete floor. She heard the woman tut and sigh and she scrabbled about in embarrassment until, red-faced, she finally handed the paperwork over.

Her papers were closely scrutinised and given back. 'I am Sergeant Norris,' the woman said briskly. 'You will always address me as Sergeant. Follow me.' She turned on her heel as if on a parade ground, marched to the second door and opened it.

Mary gazed at the grey paint on the iron walls and concrete floor and the strings of lamps that hung from the raftered ceiling. It was a huge, cool, clean space that hummed with the sound of machinery. A wireless was playing softly in the background as line upon line of silent women sat at long trestle tables sorting through stacks of rustling paper slips. On the far side of this vast place stood several very large machines.

'Pay attention, Jones. I don't have time to say everything twice.'

'Yes, Sergeant.' Mary almost stood to attention as she listened carefully and learned how to clock in at the beginning of every shift, and then clock out again at the end. Then she followed the doughty figure of her guide as each process was explained.

'We deal only with the outgoing airgraphs here,' the sergeant said as she reached the first table, where women in white coats were handling what seemed to be endless slips of paper. 'Incoming mail goes straight to Kodak's factory in Wealdstone. These women are sorting the airgraphs according to the service or theatre of war of the recipient.'

She went to stand by the table, her gimlet eyes watching every movement, and Mary noticed that none of the women dared look up or falter in their work. She was clearly very much in charge and ran the place with frightening efficiency.

'The airgraphs from naturalised British citizens, or nationals from enemy countries, have to be marked accordingly by the sender. These are also sorted here and put to one side so they can be thoroughly scrutinised by the censors.'

The sergeant marched on deeper into the factory. 'Everything has to go through the censors for each of the services. When they are passed, they will then be numbered and stamped.' She looked proudly at yet another long table where around twenty women of all ages were stamping the airgraphs, their speed so fast it made Mary blink with admiration.

'Yes, there's no machine to compare with the swift right arm and the deft left finger and thumb of a woman worker,' declared the sergeant with a satisfied nod. She turned away and Mary meekly followed.

They came to an enormous piece of machinery where a girl in a white coat sat at what looked like a flat desk with a slit in the top. 'You will see that each airgraph is held inside the slot for a matter of only seconds. This activates the camera beneath the desk, and the image is photographed in miniature on the 16-millimetre film which is 100 feet long. When it arrives at its destination, it will be enlarged to approximately a third of its original size and printed on to sensitised paper. Then it is placed in a brown window envelope and delivered to the recipient.'

She moved to where the endless strip of film was slowly being wound into a tin canister. 'A film such as this will carry the reduced images of 1,700 airgraphs and weigh five and a half ounces. That number of letters would weigh 50 lb. This is vital to the war effort, for it takes up less space in our aircraft and ships, and the lighter weight means more vital, heavier equipment can be transported in its stead.'

'That all sounds marvellous,' said Mary. 'But what happens if the films get lost because of enemy attack?'

The woman stiffened as if she'd been insulted. 'That has happened only once, and the delay in getting the mail to our boys was minimal because we always make two copies of each airgraph. When the flying boat *Clare* was sunk back in September '41, it was carrying mail from India, East and South Africa. Upon confirmation of that loss, the countries of origin were quickly contacted by telegraph and the duplicates of the lost films were received in London on the 15th of October. They were processed and delivered to the recipients within three days.'

'Goodness,' breathed Mary in admiration.

'Indeed,' she replied smugly. 'Now we've wasted enough time with chit-chat. You will begin at the sorting tables under the supervision of Cartwright. There is to be no talking, no eating or drinking – and absolutely no smoking. Is that understood?'

'Yes, Sergeant.'

Mary was handed a long brown duster coat that buttoned down the front before being led back to the first line of tables. 'Wear that at all times when you are on duty,' she was told. 'This is Cartwright, and that is your seat. You are not to leave it unless there is a raid or an emergency – or it's time for your break.'

'Whew,' breathed Mary as she sat down next to a tall willowy girl with grey eyes and wisps of fair hair drifting from beneath her headscarf. 'Is she always like that?'

'Yes, unfortunately,' the girl said without moving her lips as she continued to sort through the airgraphs. 'The name's Jenny, by the way.'

'I'm Mary.'

'Get stuck in and work as quickly as you can. The old girl has eyes everywhere.'

Mary looked at the piles of airgraphs in front of her, worked out what went where and made a start. It was easy, monotonous work, but the thought of all those men receiving letters from their loved ones kept her going until the hooter went at ten.

The factory erupted with noise as chairs were pushed back and the chattering began to coincide with the tramp of feet hurrying towards the door.

Mary rose from her chair, eased her stiff neck and shoulders and followed Jenny out of the building. The time had flown past, and, thirsty from the dry atmosphere, she was looking forward to a cup of refreshing tea.

Having left Stan at the allotment the previous afternoon, Ron had rather reluctantly gone to the hospital to see the girl he'd rescued and her baby, to satisfy himself that neither of them had suffered any permanent injuries. Her mother had been sitting by the bed, and she'd flung her arms round him and sobbed wetly against his neck, which had been horribly embarrassing. To make things worse the girl, who was feeding the baby, had burst into tears too, and the other women on the ward started making a fuss of him and Harvey.

Harvey had got carried away by all this attention, and had tried to climb on the bed so he could inspect the baby. Matron's sudden appearance had them beating a hasty retreat to the Anchor where Rosie had cooked him a lovely tea of sausage, onions and mashed potato, which he'd washed down with a couple of pints of nice warm bitter.

Harvey had done all right too, for he'd also had sausage mixed with special biscuit, which he ate from a bowl next to Monty's. Both he and Ron had stayed late after the pub was shut, so that they could all enjoy their last private evening together before Tommy turned up the following day.

Now it was morning, and Ron had gone out early to walk the two dogs up in the hills and try to get some rabbits for the pot. He'd returned Monty to the Anchor and had sat down to a delicious filling breakfast before he helped to change the barrels and bring up the crates from the cellar. There were a couple of repair jobs to do, and after he'd boarded over parts of the cellar ceiling to stop any more plaster falling off, he'd dithered about upstairs, reluctant to go home.

'You're getting under my feet,' said Rosie rather crossly as she tried to hoover the carpet and get the spare bedroom ready for her brother.

'Well, that's nice,' he rumbled. 'I walk your dog and mend your ceiling, and now I'm being a nuisance.'

Rosie sighed and gave him a hug. 'Sorry, Ron. I didn't mean to be sharp with you, but I'm feeling a bit anxious.'

'When's Tommy due to arrive?'

She shrugged. 'He didn't say in his letter, just that he was being released today.'

Ron gathered her into his arms and gave her a kiss. 'To be sure, I love the bones of you, Rosie, and I hate the thought of him here.'

She nodded against his shoulder. 'I'm not over-joyed by it either, but he's all the family I have and I can't leave him in that prison.'

Ron thought it was the best place for him, but knew better than to say so, for love him or loathe him, Rosie was protective of her younger brother. 'Ach, I'd better be leaving you to it,' he said after kissing her again. 'Peggy's got a list as long as her arm of things for me to do, and I can't avoid it any longer.'

'You'll come in tonight?'

'Aye, you can be sure of that.'

He whistled to Harvey who was lying on the couch next to Monty, and they went downstairs and out into the street. Now Tommy was expected, Ron would make it his business to keep an eye on Rosie, for he knew how easily the man could manipulate her – and before too long he'd be behind the bar, helping himself to free drinks, and acting the friendly host.

Harvey raced on ahead as they climbed the hill towards Beach View, and was lying on the back step panting as Ron came through the gate.

'It's about time you showed up,' Peggy greeted him, as she worked the wringer over the stone sink in the scullery. 'There are a dozen and one things that need doing round the house, and I'm too busy with the weekly wash to get to the shops.'

Ron gave a deep sigh and looked with longing at his shed. He had hoped to while away a couple of hours in there to read his newspaper and smoke his pipe, but Peggy would evidently not be happy about that. He turned on the outside tap to fill Harvey's tin bowl and then went to fetch the heavy basket of wet washing from the scullery, which he carried into the garden and placed beneath the clothes line.

Peggy nodded her thanks. 'The window in my bedroom is still rattling, and the shelf under the kitchen sink is so bowed with damp and rot it's become useless. I'd like you to mend the kitchen chair, clean out the fire in the range and bring me in more logs, and when you've done that, the front-door hinges need oiling.'

'Ach, to be sure, you're not wanting much, are ye?'

'If you did each thing as I asked, they wouldn't mount up,' said Peggy as she briskly hung out the washing.

'Aye, well, I'll just have a smoke first, then I'm all yours,' he replied as he opened his shed door and plonked down into the deckchair. He could see she wasn't at all happy, but that was a long list and a man could only do one thing at a time.

He lit his pipe and puffed contentedly as he contemplated his vegetable garden. The winter lettuces, beetroot, parsley and radishes were planted in wooden troughs and covered with glass to protect them from frost. The peas and broad beans were doing well and would be a good crop come December and January. There were lines of spinach, chard and kale in another wooden trough, and the carrots, leeks, onions, shallots and potatoes were flourishing. All in all, it was a most satisfactory sight. Now he had Stan's beetroot to plant, he would have to dig out some of the old cloches to cover them with.

'I went to Doris's for afternoon tea yesterday,' said Peggy. 'Young Mary is an accomplished pianist, and she played for us all quite beautifully. My sister was on her high horse as usual, but the girl did actually manage to stand up to her.' She grinned. 'As did Ivy, so there's hope yet for the pair of them.'

Ron nodded, for he knew she wasn't really expecting an answer.

'Mary came back with me and had tea with us all,' Peggy carried on. 'She fitted in so well with everyone, I was quite tempted to ask her to stay. After all, I've got that spare bedroom.'

Ron lowered his brows and clenched his teeth round his pipe stem. 'That could cause trouble between you and Doris.'

'Hmmph, it wouldn't be anything new, would it?' She snapped the creases out of a blouse before she pegged it on to the line. 'But I do realise it would make it very awkward for her – and I couldn't ask Mary and not Ivy. And if I did that, the billeting people would be on Doris's back to take in others.'

Peggy paused for a moment, deep in thought, before selecting another blouse. 'Doris might be difficult, but her home is comfortable and the girls are well fed. Perhaps I shouldn't meddle.'

'That'd be a first,' he rumbled.

'There's no need to be grumpy, Ron,' she retorted. 'I was just saying, that's all. And if the girls really aren't happy there, then I wouldn't mind taking them in. Mary's a lovely girl, you know.'

Ron thought about the long and troubling conversation he'd had with Stan the previous day. If he could get Mary's story from Peggy, it would save his friend from having to question the girl. 'Oh aye?' he said casually. 'And I suppose you've managed to learn everything about her within a couple of hours, have you?'

Peggy abandoned the empty laundry basket and dug her hands into her wrap-round apron for her packet of Park Drive cigarettes. 'Yes,' she replied softly, 'and it isn't a pretty story. The poor girl has certainly been through the mill these past few weeks.'

Ron was immediately alert, but he covered it by closely inspecting the bowl of his pipe. 'How's that then?'

'Well I promised to keep most of it to myself,' said Peggy, 'but the gist of it is, she's all alone in the world since her adoptive parents were killed by a bomb, and now she seems set on trying to find this Cyril Fielding.' She lit a cigarette and blew out a wreath of smoke. 'You don't happen to know who that is, do you?'

He avoided the question and continued to tamp down the tobacco in his pipe. 'Why's she looking for him? Can you tell me that?'

'Not without breaking my promise.' Peggy eyed him thoughtfully. 'You've lived in this town nearly all your life and know just about everyone.' Her gaze never wavered. 'It's very important, Ron, and if you know who he is, then you must tell me.'

Ron knew when he was cornered. 'If you tell me why it's so important, then I'll tell you about Cyril Fielding,' he said. 'And be assured, Peggy girl, nothing you tell me will go any further.'

Peggy closed the back door and sat down on the step. 'So you do know who he is, then?'

'Aye. But I'm waiting to hear why young Mary is looking for him.'

Ron listened as Peggy related what the girl had told her, and as the full implications of it began to register, he felt a cold shiver trickle down his torso and settle into the pit of his stomach. This was far worse than he ever could have imagined, and he couldn't begin to think of how much trouble it would cause Mary if her story reached the wrong ears.

Peggy stubbed out her cigarette and threw the butt into the nearby rubbish bin. 'Now you know it all,' she said as she looked at him squarely. 'Who is Cyril Fielding, Ron – and why are you so reluctant to talk about him?'

He couldn't avoid it any longer. 'I'm reluctant because Cyril Fielding was the false name used by a man who was selling fake insurances, making off with the proceeds, and leaving people who could ill afford it out of pocket and holding bits of paper that weren't worth a light.' He took a deep breath.

'He's been out of town for a while now, but he's due to come back today. Cyril Fielding was only one of his many aliases. You'd know him better as Tommy Findlay.'

Peggy stared at him in shock, her mind whirling with everything she'd learnt about Tommy over the years. The very real possibility that he could be Mary's father was unthinkable.

'You can't tell her, Peggy,' said Ron earnestly. 'It will only bring her more heartache.'

'I know,' she breathed, 'but what if she keeps asking people about him and he gets to hear of it?'

'We'll have to stop her from asking by telling her we'd heard he'd died some years ago. It's the only way, Peggy.'

She thought about it and then gave a sigh. 'I hate lying to her, Ron, and lies have an awful way of coming back to haunt you when the truth is uncovered. What if she discovered somehow that he's still alive and living at the Anchor?' Her eyes widened in horror. 'Oh God. The Anchor. Mary has made friends with Rosie and will be in and out of there to see her and play the piano in the bar – and Tommy will be there too.' She scrubbed her face with her hands. 'What a mess, Ron. What a terrible, terrible mess.'

There was a long silence before Ron spoke again. 'I suppose you could have a quiet word with her, and without naming names, tell her the bald truth about her father's character. From what you've told me, she's a nice girl who's been carefully brought up, and is already a bit suspicious that Cyril wasn't quite what he seemed when he handed her over to the vicar and his wife and then disappeared. Faced with the fact that he's a sleazy out-and-out crook, and has spent time in gaol for fraud, embezzlement and black-marketeering, it might put her off trying to find him.'

Peggy thought about this. There were so many things that Ron didn't know – secrets that she'd held for years – which were now in danger of being brought out into the open if something wasn't done quickly. She felt as if she was trapped on a runaway train, with no way off and no one to turn to for help.

'Peggy?'

She returned to the present and got to her feet. 'I'll do as you suggest, Ron,' she said wearily. 'The girl trusts me, and knows I only want what's best for her. It will be all too easy to put Tommy in a very black light – and I'll make sure she takes my advice and stops her search.'

'I can see you don't like having to do this, Peg, but to be sure 'tis the only answer.'

'But I still worry about her meeting him at the Anchor, Ron. You know what that man's like when it comes to women – especially the young pretty ones.' She gave a little shiver of revulsion. 'He's a lounge lizard and thinks his vulpine charm is irresistible.'

'I'll keep an eye on her, don't you fret. If he makes

one move on her, or says something I don't think is appropriate, I'll soon put him in his place,' he growled.

'Don't go getting into a fight with him, Ron,' said Peggy hastily. 'It will only make things worse and raise questions you have no way of answering if we're to keep Mary's secret to ourselves.'

Ron got out of the deckchair and stretched. 'D'ye think Rosie ever had an inkling that he might have fathered a child outside his marriage? If Mary was born here, she could easily have got to hear about it.'

'Who's to say what Rosie knows,' she replied almost dismissively as she picked up the laundry basket and headed back into the scullery. She watched as he fetched some tools and the oil can from his shed, and waited until he'd gone up the steps into the kitchen before she slumped against the stone sink, her thoughts in chaos.

There were parts of Mary's story that didn't fit the picture as she knew it – but then Tommy always had had a glib tongue, and no doubt lied through his teeth to that poor naïve vicar. Yet Mary was not the only one who had to be protected from all this, and although she hated having to be economic with the truth to the girl, it was necessary if Rosie was to remain unaware of the dangerously unfolding drama that surrounded her. She'd been hurt too badly and had suffered because of it over the years – and it was vital not to reopen those old wounds.

Peggy stood there for a long while, her thoughts

churning. There was one other person inextricably involved in all this – and as she had no reason to doubt the validity of the vicar's diary entry, she began to wonder how big a part they had played in the cruel deceit. It was a tangled, deadly web of lies and betrayal, and she would have to be very careful not to disturb the spider of truth that lurked at its heart waiting to ensnare them all.

Chapter Eighteen

Mary's shoulders and neck ached, and her bottom felt quite numb from the hours of sitting on a hard chair as she bent over the table. Yet, as the hooter went for the end of her shift, she was feeling very positive about things. The job was easy, if a little tedious; she was doing her bit for the boys fighting abroad, the money wasn't at all bad, and the girls she was working with seemed a nice bunch.

Having collected her coat and gas-mask box from the locker, she followed the others and almost forgot to clock out in her eagerness to get into the fresh air.

'You'll soon get used to the routine and the stiff neck,' said Jenny as they walked out of the factory into the dark of a winter's late afternoon. 'If you roll your shoulders and ease out the muscles regularly, you won't feel half as sore.'

Mary smiled. 'I suppose it must get easier as time goes on. How long have you been doing it?'

Jenny pulled off her headscarf and ran her fingers through her tangled fair hair. 'For almost a year,' she replied. 'The factory only opened here back in August, and I was seconded down from Surrey to take charge of the initial sorting. It's nice being by the sea again,' she said, smiling. 'I remember coming here on holiday before the war with my parents. What about you?'

'I only arrived on Friday, and this is the first real job I've ever had, so everything is all still very new to me.'

'It won't take long to settle in.' Jenny hitched the strap of her gas-mask box over her shoulder. 'Which way are you heading now?'

'Down there. I'm billeted in Havelock Road.'

The other girl gave a wry grin. 'Lucky you. I'm stuck right over there in a requisitioned house with three families, all of which have at least one screaming baby. It's murder trying to sleep, because one seems to be on the go whatever the hour.' She glanced over Mary's shoulder. 'There's your friend. I'll see you tomorrow.'

As Jenny headed for the gate, Ivy came thudding up in her heavy boots. 'I'm sorry, gel, but I've been offered two hours' overtime at extra money, so you'll have to go back on yer own.'

'That's all right. I'll make sure there's something hot for you when you get in.'

'Thanks – and don't let 'er ladyship boss yer about. After what Peggy said yesterday, I reckon it's time she done 'er own cooking and cleaning. Neither of us should 'ave to do it after an 'ard day's work.' She chuckled. 'How did you get on today then?'

'Just fine. I'll tell you all about it later.'

Ivy went running off back to the armament factory, and Mary walked through the gate and down the hill. It was very dark, with no moon or street lights to show her the way, but as her eyes adjusted, she found it was quite easy to follow the pavement down the hill towards the darker shadows of the town's rooftops.

She heard the train whistle blowing and the chuff of the engine as she approached the hump-backed bridge, and because she'd always liked trains, she leaned over to watch it slowly pull into the station. A great plume of smoke and steam threatened to engulf her and she stepped back hurriedly. Once it had cleared she looked down again and, in the strong beams of the engine's lights, watched the guard offload several large bags of mail while the passengers stepped down to the platform where Stan was waiting.

There weren't many getting off at Cliffehaven, just a few women and young girls, and an old man who hobbled on a walking stick, his equally aged dog limping alongside him. Then a middle-aged man in a suit jumped down, carrying a suitcase. He handed his ticket to a glaring Stan and strode off, whistling cheerfully.

Mary frowned and wondered who the man was, for Stan seemed to be friends with everyone, yet he'd made his dislike obvious. Shrugging off this thought, she watched as the mail van arrived to collect the sacks before she continued her walk down the hill, only to discover that the man in question was a few yards in front of her.

He looked as if he hadn't a care in the world as he sauntered along and doffed his hat to every woman he passed, but their expressions of shock and disapproval told quite another story, and Mary became even more intrigued. Whoever he was, he seemed impervious to their glowers, for he continued to stroll casually along, whistling quite happily.

She regarded his suit which, on closer inspection, was a bit flashy, and the fedora set at a jaunty angle over his light brown hair, and wondered if he was what people called a spiv. He certainly looked pleased with himself, and his manner was that of a man who was very comfortable in his surroundings, for there was a definite swagger to his shoulders and in his step.

As the man stopped outside the large department store to admire his reflection in the heavily taped window, Mary saw him adjust his tie and straighten his hat. She carried on walking towards him, hoping he was too occupied to notice her.

Yet, as she drew level, he turned from the window and raised his hat. 'Good evening, young lady,' he said with a bright smile.

Not wanting to get into conversation with him, she bent her head and hurried on.

'I say, you're new here, aren't you?' he said as he caught up with her. 'Do you live nearby? I can escort you home, if you like? It's really not safe for a lovely young girl like you to be out on her own in the dark.'

Mary realised he wouldn't be shaken off, so she abruptly stopped walking and regarded him stonily. He had once been handsome, she could see, but his pallor was sickly, his hair was cut brutally short, and his eyes and smile held a feral quality that made her skin prickle with distrust. 'I would appreciate it if you didn't bother me,' she replied flatly.

He simply smiled at this, and adjusted the brim of his hat again so it tipped over one very blue eye. 'I didn't mean to be a bother,' he said smoothly. 'And perhaps next time we meet you'll see that I am a perfect gentleman. Good evening.' He gave a rather unpleasant snicker of laughter and strolled away.

Mary waited by a shop window until he reached Camden Road where he turned off, and with a sigh of relief, she slowly continued down the hill. He was decidedly creepy, and she sincerely hoped she never would see him again.

There was no sign of him in Camden Road and she hurried past, breaking into a run as she reached Havelock Road. She fumbled to put the key in the lock and then slammed the door behind her and leant against it to get her breath.

'Good heavens,' exclaimed Doris as she came out of the drawing room. 'I would prefer it if you didn't slam my door like that.' She looked at Mary more closely. 'What's the matter? Has something happened?'

Mary pushed away from the door and gave her a shaky smile. 'I'm all right, really,' she said quickly. 'Some man tried to talk to me, that's all, and because I didn't like the look of him, I ran all the way back.'

Doris frowned. 'Well, as long as you're all right, but perhaps tomorrow you should walk home with Ivy. It isn't safe in the blackout – especially with so many Americans and Free French lurking about.'

'He was an Englishman who was old enough to know better,' said Mary, who was still cross with herself for being so easily frightened.

'Well he can't have been a local,' said Doris dismissively. 'The men in Cliffehaven are well known for being gentlemen.' Her frown deepened. 'Where is Ivy? She should be home by now.'

'She's been given some overtime and will be back in a couple of hours.' Mary took off her coat and hung it on the hall stand alongside her gas-mask box. 'I told her we'd keep her food warm. Now, I would like a bath before supper, if that's all right.'

Doris looked rather disgruntled. 'Just remember not to use more than two inches of water,' she said. 'Supper will be in half an hour as I have to go out this evening. If you're not down in time, I shall leave the remainder of the fish pie keeping warm in the slow oven.'

The thought of fish pie drying out was not enticing, but Mary needed a bath rather more urgently than food right at this moment, so she thanked her and ran up the stairs.

There was no sign of Doris when she went back down to the kitchen, so she carefully rescued the fish pie from the oven and doled out two portions, one of which she put under a plate to stop it drying out any further.

It was surprisingly delicious, and when she'd finished she mopped up the remains with a chunk of the wheatmeal bread. Having washed her plate and left the baking dish to soak in the sink, she decided to go and play the piano. With Mrs Williams out of the house, it was an ideal opportunity to practise some of the popular songs for Friday night.

It was late afternoon and very dark by the time Ron had completed the long list of tasks Peggy had set him, so he hurried off with Harvey to go and find Stan. He was at the station, waiting for the next train, and Ron quickly told him not to worry about questioning Mary, for Peggy was going to deal with her.

'That's a relief,' said Stan as they shared a mug of tea in the Nissen hut that now served as ticket office and left-luggage store. 'Peggy is far better at that sort of thing, and I really wasn't looking forward to doing it.'

'To be sure it's something best left to women,' agreed Ron as he sat back and filled his pipe. He regarded his friend from beneath his brows. 'Peggy has already befriended the girl, and, in her usual way, managed to find out more than either of us could ever have hoped for.' He struck a match and lit the tobacco, puffing away at it until it was burning satisfactorily.

'So why is the girl looking for Tommy?' asked Stan as he fed part of his jam sandwich to Harvey.

'I'm sorry I can't tell you that, Stan, me old friend. I promised Peggy not to repeat what she told me. Suffice it to say we must look out for the girl, and try to keep her well away from that toerag.'

'That will be difficult,' muttered Stan. 'He arrived on the mail train less than an hour ago, and she'll be playing the piano in the Anchor at the weekend.'

'How did he look?'

'Full of himself, as usual,' Stan replied with a grimace. 'Flash suit, expensive leather case and smug grin. His hair was shorter than any army recruit, and he had the pallor of a man who's spent time in a prison cell, but he was his usual arrogant self for all that.'

Ron finished the mug of tea and stood up. 'I'd better get to the Anchor and make sure Rosie's all right. See you, Stan.'

He went out into the cold, black afternoon, pulled his cap over his ears and drew up his coat collar. As he and Harvey went down the hill and turned into Camden Road, Ron was deep in thought.

Like him, Peggy had naturally been concerned about Mary being in such close proximity to Tommy. Yet Ron had the feeling that his daughter-in-law knew far more than she was letting on. He'd caught a glimpse of her as she'd stood in the scullery that morning, and her expression was that of someone who was far too deeply worried – which was odd, because she'd only known the girl for such a short time.

His thoughts meandered as he went over their conversation, and as he remembered her almost casual dismissal at his mention of Rosie, he stopped dead. Did his Rosie have anything to do with this? Was that why Peggy had clammed up? Or was his overworked imagination playing tricks with him?

He looked down the street to the Anchor, and a shiver of apprehension ran down his spine. Whatever the truth was, he knew without any doubt that if it didn't remain buried, it would bring trouble to them all.

It was now Thursday night and Peggy was deeply anxious. She'd left several messages with Doris over the past few days to get Mary to call her, but so far she'd had no response. Now it was a matter of urgency, for it was imperative that she talked to her before she went to the pub tomorrow night.

Peggy lit a cigarette and looked at the mantel clock. Luckily the girl had been working every day at the Kodak factory and hadn't yet called in to see Rosie. But it was only a matter of time before she did, and there was no guarantee that she wouldn't mention her search for Cyril – which would be a disaster if Tommy was listening to their chatter.

'Whatever is wrong with you, Peggy?' Cordelia looked at her over her half-moon glasses. 'You've been on edge all week.'

Peggy shot her what she hoped was a reassuring smile. 'Oh, you know me, Cordelia. I'm always fretting over something.'

'It's not Jim, is it?'

Peggy shook her head and glanced at the clock again. 'I just have to telephone Doris,' she said as she left the vegetables to simmer on the hob.

'You've been doing quite a bit of that lately,' Cordelia remarked drily. 'And as I doubt it's sisterly concern, it has to have something to do with young Mary.'

Cordelia was too sharp for her own good at times, thought Peggy. 'I just need to talk to her about something,' she hedged. 'Why don't you put the kettle on? I'll be back by the time you've made the tea.'

Without waiting for a reply, she hurried into the hall and picked up the receiver. Having given the number to the woman at the exchange, she waited impatiently for someone to pick up at the other end.

'Mrs Williams speaking.'

'Doris, did you give Mary my messages?'

'I do have rather more pressing things to deal with than acting as your message service,' replied Doris. 'The girl is out all day, and I rarely see her as I'm so busy every evening with my important charity committees.'

'You could have put a note under her door,' said Peggy through gritted teeth.

'My doors are fitted properly, unlike yours, and do not have gaps beneath them,' Doris replied snootily.

'Then why didn't you leave a note on the kitchen table? Surely that couldn't have been too taxing for you?' Peggy snapped.

'There's no need to take that tone with me,' huffed Doris. 'And if you wish to speak to Mary, then here's your opportunity. She has just arrived back from her work. Don't take too long about it, Margaret. Anthony has promised to telephone this evening to discuss the music for the wedding service.'

Peggy puffed on her cigarette as she heard Doris speaking to Mary, and the rustle of the receiver being passed from hand to hand at the other end.

'Hello, Peggy,' said Mary. 'It's lovely to hear from you, and I'm sorry I haven't been to see you, but I've been at work and the time just seems to have flown past.'

Peggy made a huge effort to calm down. 'Hello, Mary dear,' she replied. 'I have had a word with Ron about what we discussed,' she said carefully.

Mary was equally careful at the other end. 'I see,' she said. 'And having spoken to him, is there something we need to talk about?'

'Yes, there is. And if at all possible, I think it would be best if we spoke this evening.'

'I see.' There was a slight pause. 'Is it good news, Peggy?' Mary asked finally.

'Let me just say that there is news,' Peggy replied hesitantly. 'Whether it's good or bad, that will be up to you to decide.'

'Oh dear, that doesn't sound terribly promising,' Mary said on a sigh.

Reluctant to go into any further detail while Doris was no doubt earwigging close by, Peggy stubbed out her cigarette in the glass ashtray she kept by the telephone. 'From what Doris said earlier, she's not planning on going out this evening, and I wouldn't trust her not to listen at the door. Why don't you come here? We can talk in private in the dining room.'

'Yes,' said Mary. 'I think that would be best in the circumstances. I'll have my supper and come straight over.'

Peggy had a sudden thought. 'Why don't you bring your night things with you and stay here? It will probably be very late by the time we've finished talking and Ron isn't here to escort you home – and I don't want you wandering about on your own in the dark.'

'That's very kind of you, Peggy. Thank you. I'll see you in a little while.'

Peggy replaced the receiver and then went into the dining room to draw the blackout curtains before switching on the light. It was cold and not very welcoming, so she quickly set a match to the kindling and paper in the grate and waited until it was burning merrily before she added a couple of logs and a smattering of anthracite.

With the two armchairs placed invitingly on either side of the hearth, she plumped up the cushions and smoothed the creases out of the white antimacassars that protected the arms and backs. There wasn't much more she could do, she realised, as she used the hem of her wrap-round pinny to dust the tops of the furniture. But perhaps the standard lamp would cast a kindlier glow than the large central light. Having seen to this, she checked that the fire was burning satisfactorily and placed the guard in front of it before she went back to the kitchen.

'I'm expecting Mary over later,' she told Cordelia, who was sitting at the table with a freshly brewed pot of tea and the tin of Canadian biscuits in front of her. 'Would it be awfully cheeky to ask if we could have just a couple of those biscuits to go with our tea?'

Cordelia raised her eyebrows. 'You and she are welcome to as many biscuits as you want. Goodness me, Peggy. You should know better than to even ask.' She eyed her thoughtfully. 'You're up to something,' she said. 'I can always tell.'

Peggy kept her gaze averted as she poured out the tea. 'Mary and I just need to discuss something privately, so I've lit the fire in the other room.'

'Private, eh? It must be serious.' Cordelia's blue

eyes twinkled. 'I suppose you aren't going to let me in on the secret, are you?'

Cordelia couldn't keep a secret for more than a few minutes, and would have made a terrible poker player but Peggy didn't tell her so. 'I'm sorry, Cordelia, not this time,' she said gently. 'But I would appreciate it if you could keep the girls out of the dining room once she arrives.'

Cordelia nodded, kept her thoughts to herself and plucked a biscuit from the tin.

As Mary ate her supper, Doris's natural nosiness led to a barrage of questions which she managed to circumnavigate by being non-committal and vague. When the meal was over, she escaped to the kitchen to do the washing-up and make the coffee.

'I will be staying at Peggy's tonight,' she told Doris as she took the coffee in to her in the drawing room.

'You have a perfectly good bedroom here,' she replied frostily. 'I don't see why it should be necessary.'

'It's very dark and I shall be quite late, I suspect,' she replied. 'And after that man accosted me the other day, I don't feel safe walking home on my own.'

Doris seemed to accept this explanation and to Mary's great relief, made no more objections. By the time she'd packed her nightwear and washbag Doris was talking on the telephone, so she waved goodbye and hurried out of the door.

The trees on either side of the street creaked ominously as they swayed in the wind and hid the pale moon that appeared infrequently from behind scudding clouds. Feeling tense and all too aware of her solitary footsteps, Mary walked quickly towards Peggy's, her mind working on the short conversation they'd had on the telephone, and what it might mean.

She was walking along Camden Road when a movement across the street caught her eye, and she saw a man step out from the Anchor doorway. She hesitated and slowed to a stop. There was something about him that looked familiar – and as he struck a match to light his cigarette she felt a jolt of shock. It was the man from the station.

She looked wildly around, saw an alleyway and darted down it into the deep shadows cast by the buildings on either side. She pressed against the wall, her heart hammering so loudly she was certain he would hear it.

As she watched him smoke his cigarette, he turned towards the sound of light footsteps hurrying towards him and squared his shoulders as if preparing to face someone who posed a challenge.

'You're late, Eileen,' he said as the woman reached him. 'I thought you'd changed your mind and weren't coming.'

'I very nearly didn't,' she replied as she raised her chin and looked at him almost defiantly. 'But there's something very important that I have to tell you. Once I've done that, I don't want to see or speak to you again. Is that understood?'

He nodded and mashed out his cigarette beneath his shoe before they walked away from the Anchor towards the High Street.

Mary waited until she couldn't hear their footfalls, and then emerged from her hiding place and hurried on towards Beach View. Whoever she was, the woman certainly had the measure of that man, for he'd lost his swagger as they'd walked away.

Peggy opened the door. 'Hello, dear,' she said warmly. 'Come in quickly, so I can turn the light on. My goodness, it's cold and black out there, isn't it?'

As Mary stepped inside and put down her case, Peggy was distressed to see that she was shivering quite badly. 'Keep your coat on for a bit. I've lit the fire in the dining room, but it hasn't really warmed up properly yet.' She turned on the light and frowned. 'You look very pale, dear. Are you all right?'

'I'm fine, really. I've just had a bit of a fright, that's all.'

Peggy didn't like the sound of that at all, so she put her arm round Mary's trembling shoulders and drew her towards the dining room. 'Let's get you warmed up with a cup of tea, and then you can tell me all about it,' she soothed.

Peggy was pleased at how cosy the large room looked in the flickering light from the fire and the warm glow of the standard lamp in the corner. She pressed Mary down into one of the armchairs, and pulled the other one closer to it.

Mary held her trembling hands out to the fire. 'It's silly really to get frightened over nothing,' she said almost apologetically. 'I expect it was because it was dark, and I was on my own.'

Peggy poured tea from the large brown pot, handed Mary the cup and nudged the plate of Cordelia's chocolate biscuits nearer to her. 'I don't think it's silly at all,' she replied gently. 'The night changes things with all its shadows and strange noises. Why don't you tell me about it, then it won't seem so scary.'

As Mary sipped the tea, she told Peggy haltingly about the man from the station accosting her, and how she'd panicked and hidden in the alley when she'd seen him come out of the Anchor.

'He was met by some woman he called Eileen,' she continued, 'and by the sound of it, they didn't like each other at all.' She gave a tremulous smile. 'Her manner certainly wiped that sleazy grin off his face, and he'd lost his swagger as they walked off down the street.'

Peggy felt her blood run cold, and it took a great deal of effort to keep her expression bland. To hide her inner turmoil, she drank her tea and asked with studied casualness, 'What did this man look like?'

Mary grimaced. 'Middle-aged, with light brown hair and very blue eyes. He was flashily dressed and obviously regards himself as a bit of a ladykiller. Personally,' she added, 'I think he's a bit of a spiv.'

Her accurate description left absolutely no doubt, and Peggy had to clear the lump in her throat before she could speak. 'It sounds like Tommy Findlay,' she said. 'And you're right; he is all the things you said. Unfortunately, he's like a bad penny and keeps turning up here in Cliffehaven to stay with his sister.' She reached across and took the girl's hand. 'Now, I don't want you making more of this than is necessary, Mary, but Tommy is Rosie Braithwaite's younger brother, and he will be around for at least the next six months.'

Mary paled, and her blue eyes were huge in her little face as she stared in horror at Peggy. 'But that means he'll be in the Anchor,' she breathed, 'and I won't be able to visit Rosie or play the piano or . . .'

'Of course you will,' said Peggy firmly. 'Rosie knows full well what her brother is like, and will tell him in no uncertain terms to stay right away from you.'

'But—'

'There are no buts, Mary,' persisted Peggy. 'Tommy needs his sister more than she needs him right at this moment, and he'll be on his best behaviour, believe me. And, of course, Ron is there most nights – he'll be keeping a close eye out for you too. He and Tommy are old adversaries, and Tommy has learnt not to step out of line with him.'

Mary bent her head, her dark hair falling around

her face as she stared into the fire. 'You said he needed Rosie,' she said eventually. 'Why's that, Peggy?'

'Because his wife has divorced him and he has nowhere else to go at the moment,' replied Peggy. It was a half-truth, but the girl didn't need to know more. 'Rosie's not happy about it, but he's the only family she has, so you can see why she feels she has to have him there.'

Mary nodded and sat back in the chair as she tucked her hair behind her ears. 'I'd be silly to let him spoil everything, wouldn't I? I do like Rosie, and I love playing the piano for all those terrific sing-songs. It's such a happy atmosphere and I would miss it horribly if I couldn't be a part of it.'

'Yes, you would,' said Peggy, who was almost weak with relief that the girl was seeing sense and showing some admirable maturity. 'And you can count on me and Ron and the rest of the household who aren't on duty to turn out tomorrow night in support. You won't be alone, Mary, not now you've got us.'

'Thank you, Peggy. That means a great deal to me. Goodness, however would I manage without you?'

'You won't have to,' said Peggy as she patted her hand and smiled.

Mary smiled back. Slipping off her overcoat, she visibly relaxed, and settled down to finish the cup of tea and eat a chocolate biscuit. 'Now all that's cleared up, what news do you have about my father?'

Peggy took her time to draw a cigarette from the packet on the table beside her and light it. She blew smoke and then plucked a stray strand of tobacco from her bottom lip as she gathered the thoughts that had been troubling her for days. She would have to proceed with this very carefully now Mary had already had a run-in with Tommy.

'Before I tell you what I've learnt, Mary, there are a couple of questions I would like to ask. I hope you don't mind?'

Mary was hiding her impatience well. 'Of course I don't mind,' she said. 'What do you want to know?'

'Well, it might help to put things into clearer focus if I knew the date of your birth, and if there was any clue in your father's diaries as to whether you'd been given a name by either of your parents before they abandoned you.'

'I don't really see how it would help,' Mary replied hesitantly, 'but if you think it's necessary . . .' She thought for a moment. 'I was less than two weeks old when Cyril handed me over to Daddy in 1924. I have no *absolute* proof as to the actual date I was born, but I've always celebrated my birthday on the tenth of October. According to Daddy's diary, I was called Flora before he changed my name to Mary.' She smiled sadly. 'He thought it was more suitable for a vicar's daughter.'

Peggy knew with terrible certainty that she was

indeed Tommy Findlay's daughter. She cleared her throat. 'I see,' she said gruffly.

'So, are things clearer now?' Mary asked anxiously.

Peggy nodded, drank some tea to play for time, and then stubbed out her cigarette and reached across for Mary's hand. 'I spoke to Ron,' she began, 'and he remembers Cyril quite clearly – but for all the wrong reasons, I'm afraid.'

'Oh.'

Peggy heard the flat disappointment, and she wished with all her heart that she didn't have to destroy this poor little girl's dreams.

Mary sighed. 'I suppose I half expected it, so I don't know why I should feel so let down and disenchanted.' She gave Peggy a sad little smile. 'I'm sure everyone in my situation has a secret hope that their father will turn out to be a knight in shining armour – but that only happens in children's fairy tales, doesn't it?' She looked down at their interlocked fingers. 'Did Ron give you any details?'

Peggy tightened her grip on the girl's hand, knowing she had to face this challenge head-on. 'I'm very sorry, Mary, but Cyril was a con man. Eighteen years ago he was involved in a serious insurance fraud and served two years in prison.'

Peggy saw the colour drain from Mary's face, but she knew she had to continue this appalling catalogue of her father's sins if she was going to deter her from trying to continue her search for him.

'Five years later he was serving another sentence

for embezzlement and theft, and not long after he was released, he was caught selling stolen goods and had to serve an even longer sentence.' She squeezed Mary's hand. 'Ron heard that he has since lived off a succession of women who he's conned money from, and has been in and out of prison on a regular basis.'

Mary gave another deep sigh as she withdrew her hand from Peggy's grip and scrubbed her face. 'He sounds awful,' she said tremulously. 'I was lucky he at least had the decency to find me a good home.'

As she stared into the fire, Peggy wondered what she was thinking – and guessed that she was probably remembering the love and security that Gideon had provided over the years.

'Does Cyril ever come back to Cliffehaven?' asked Mary suddenly.

Peggy's heart missed a beat, and she had to think fast. 'I doubt it,' she replied with rather more vigour than she would have liked. 'After that insurance scam he pulled, he wouldn't dare show his face here again. Too many people were left in dire straits when it came to claiming on their useless policies.'

Mary nodded slowly. 'I can understand that,' she said.

Peggy reached once more for her hand. 'I think it's best if you put all thoughts of trying to find him to one side. He sounds a rotten sort – not to be trusted with anything – and asking questions about him could damage your reputation.'

Mary nodded and blinked back the tears. 'What about my mother? Does Ron know anything about her?'

Peggy heard the wistfulness in her voice and she hated herself for having to do this, but do it she must if Mary was to be protected. 'No, dear, he knows nothing at all,' she replied with the firmness of truth. 'And if there had been any gossip at the time, he would have heard it, believe me.'

'They must have been very secretive,' said Mary. 'I would have thought someone must have questioned what was going on when she went off, and then Cyril and I disappeared. It would have made for some juicy gossip.'

Peggy kept her expression carefully neutral. 'Well, it seems there was no hint of scandal or gossip at the time – and none since.' She hoped she'd be forgiven for that lie, and knew it would stay on her conscience for a long time after tonight. She gave Mary an encouraging smile. 'I think it would be best to try and forget all this, and look forward to the future,' she said softly. 'What is past must remain in the past, and you can't move on if you're always looking behind you.'

'But it's such an awful thing to realise that my father was no more than a cheap crook. Heaven only knows what sort of woman my mother was to get entangled with him.'

Peggy gave a shrug, unwilling to lie any more.

Mary's tears shone in the firelight. 'I've been so

certain about who I was and where I'd come from until now. But I've been guilty of lying and of deceit. What if I've inherited my father's dishonesty and slyness – or worse, my mother's morals? Emmaline was constantly telling me I was born with the mark of sin on my soul – and now I know why.'

Peggy couldn't stand it any longer, and she moved across to her and gathered her into her arms. 'My dear little Mary, please don't cry. Everyone fibs now and again, and it was horribly unkind and unjust of Emmaline to say such things.'

She felt Mary nestle against her and had to blink back her own tears. 'You're a sweet girl,' she continued as she stroked the long silky hair, 'and as honest as the day. Why, you even faced up to Doris about playing at the Anchor – and that took some courage, I know.'

Peggy drew back and gently cupped Mary's face as she looked into her eyes. 'You have been raised by a good and loving father who taught you right from wrong, and that is a lesson you will carry for the rest of your life, Mary. Don't let what you've heard tonight cast a shadow over all that Gideon taught you. You would be betraying his memory if you did that.'

'Yes,' Mary breathed through her tears, 'I would, wouldn't I?' She withdrew from the embrace and pulled a handkerchief from the sleeve of her sweater. Once her tears were dried, she seemed to be far more in control. 'I'm glad you've told me everything,

405

Peggy,' she said quietly, 'because knowing what I do now has made me see that I must put all this behind me and start afresh.'

Peggy kissed her cheek. 'I'm sure Barbara and Joseph will welcome you back with open arms,' she said warmly. 'After all, there's no place like home.'

Mary shook her head. 'No, you don't understand, Peggy. I'm not planning on leaving Cliffehaven.'

Peggy's pulse stuttered as she stared at her. 'But I thought you said you'd only come down here to look for Cyril – and if it proved impossible, you'd be returning home?'

Mary smiled. 'That was the initial plan,' she agreed, 'but going home now would be a very backward step, don't you think? I like it here. I'm enjoying my job and earning my own money, and I've started to make friends – lovely friends like you and Ivy and the girls I work with. And I really can't complain about my billet – not now I know how to deal with your sister.'

Peggy didn't know what to say.

'Don't look so shocked, Peggy,' Mary teased. 'Anyone would think you didn't want me to stay.'

'Of course I want you to stay,' Peggy told her hastily. 'You could even move in here, if you'd prefer. I have a spare room.'

Mary's smile widened. 'That's very kind of you, and it would have been lovely, but I'm settling in with Mrs Williams and Ivy quite nicely now. I will be a regular visitor to Beach View, though, so you won't be getting rid of me quite so easily.'

Peggy's emotions were all over the place, for on the one hand she was delighted – but on the other there was always the fear that her lies would be uncovered. 'How lovely,' she managed through a tight throat. 'So how long do you think you'll stay in Cliffehaven?'

'Until the end of next August,' Mary replied. 'I'll have to take up my place at teaching college in the September, but being here in Cliffehaven has already given me so many new experiences that I feel quite excited by the future possibilities.'

Peggy regarded the shining blue eyes and excited smile with deep affection before she gave the girl a hug. 'It will all be marvellous, I'm sure,' she said firmly as they finally drew apart. 'Now you run along and join the others in the kitchen while I dampen down the fire in here.'

She saw Mary hesitate, and shooed her out of the room with the assurance that she could easily tidy up on her own and would be with her soon.

Once the door had closed behind Mary, Peggy sank into her chair and stared unseeing into the glowing embers of the slowly dying fire. She wasn't proud of what she'd done tonight, but in essence she'd told the truth about the man who'd fathered Mary, and it seemed the girl was sensible enough to realise that she would gain nothing from finding him.

And yet Fate seemed determined to thwart her, tightening the threads of the tangled web of lies and secrets that held all of them prisoner. Unless something extraordinary happened, Peggy could see no way out of it.

Enter the world of Ellie Dean's
Beach View Boarding House series

HAVE YOU READ THEM ALL?